I0680191

They've experimented on us for 1,000 years.
They've manipulated our DNA and our destiny.
Now, the experiment's over.
Will any of us survive Evolution's End?

"What do we want?" Stevens finally responded, answering the question with the same question. "We want you, your ship, your planet—everything. In fact, the only reason we exist right now is for you. All of you will be N'Torr, servants of the Jek'Tan."

"Who the hell are the Jek'Tan?" Marshall asked, his gun never wavering.

With both hands, Stevens reached to the black circle burnt into his chest. He looked around and regarded everyone like a child regarding an anthill before stepping on it. "The Jek'Tan are the true gods, the masters of the heavens. They created us, and we serve their will. We are the hand and the fist of God!"

Kristin felt her gun coming up as well, like a knee-jerk reaction to that fear that sickened her. "Why?" she demanded.

Stevens laughed, as if she was a fool. "Because everyone deserves to eat," he said as the spiders began moving again.

Books by C.J. Daniels:

The DarkLight: Commando Inc. 1

The Karma Chronicles Trilogy The Coming
The Second Coming

Lost Planets and Rediscovered Science Fiction Manuscripts
(Anthology edited by Shirrel Rhoades)

Books from C.J. Daniels are available in ebook and print online from Amazon, Kobo, Barnes & Noble, Absolutely Amazing E-books (aa-ebooks.com), and published by Absolutely Amazing E-Books.com and the New Atlantian Library.

If you enjoy *Evolution's End* or any of C.J. Daniels' other books, please leave a review and tell everyone what you think.

EVOLUTIONS'S END

C.J. Daniels

Off the Beaten Path Press

Windham, New Hampshire

Evolution's End
by
C.J. Daniels

© 2016, Cary J. Daniels. All rights reserved.

Thank you for reading. In the event that you appreciate this book, please consider sharing the good word(s) by leaving a review, or connect with the author at www.thecjdaniels.com.

This book is a work of fiction; its contents are wholly imagined.

Aside from brief quotations for media coverage and reviews, no part of this book may be reproduced or distributed in any form without the author's permission. Thank you for supporting authors and a diverse, creative culture by purchasing this book and complying with copyright laws.

Copyright © 2016 by C.J. Daniels
Cover design by OCTAGONLAB
Copy editing by Autumn Conley
Interior Design; Pam Marin-Kingsley, Far-Angel Design
ISBN-13: 978-0692682340 (Off the Beaten Path Press)
ISBN-10: 0692682341

Acknowledgements

This is for Jan, the light of my life. The outfit is coming.

To my father, the man who introduced me to books, both with and without pictures. Thank you for providing me the reading material to make me the writer that I am today. I know you're smiling down at me from the pearly gates, and it gives me the strength to keep the words flowing.

Chapter 1

The party was a never-ending journey into tedium and self-indulgence, a boring, repetitive stroking of the host's ego to the point of farce. Of course, considering who the host was, this came as no surprise. Admiral Nicholas Dante reached a finger into the tight collar of his dress uniform and tugged on the fabric, a very noticeable attempt to get the blood and oxygen flowing back into his brain. The flute of expensive champagne contributed a bit to the numbness in his head; their host made sure there was a constant flow of bubbly for his roomful of VIPs and dignitaries. As a fleet admiral, he was no authority on wine, certainly no sommelier, but he knew enough about the vintage to realize that it had to be several centuries old, quite possibly a remnant from pre-Alliance Earth. He tasted it again before placing the fine crystal glass on a server's tray as it moved past him. Dante shook his head. *Sad that it has to be wasted on such a crowd,* he thought, but there was nothing their host wouldn't do for his flock of sycophantic admirers, and, if Dante's suspicions proved true, co-conspirators.

Their host was Ethan Striker, the CEO and president of Striker Industries. Striker was, perhaps, one of the wealthiest egotists in the Alliance; the massive penthouse at pinnacle of the Striker Industries corporate offices was a testament to that. It was designed in an old Earth motif. From the finely framed and lit Van Goghs and Monets that adorned the walls to the eighteenth-century piano that dominated the center of the huge hardwood dance floor, there seemed no end to the decadence that Striker had surrounded himself with.

He could certainly afford to live in that museum he'd built for himself. Striker Industries Consumer Division products occupied the homes of people throughout the system and the colonies from the sun to the outer rim, and his military contracts made him the chief supplier of ships and weapons to the Earth military and their Starfleet. In some respects, Dante owed his career to Striker and men like him—not bad for a third-rate manufacturer of consumer goods, who somehow found a way to rebuild the planet after a nuclear holocaust.

"God bless war," he said quietly to himself beneath the murmur of the noisy room. He glanced out the thick windows of the penthouse to the new New York City skyline. *Funny*, he thought. Up there, there really wasn't much of a difference from the old skyscrapers that made what was once the Big Apple, the Mecca of the world just centuries before. At least that was what they had strived for during the reconstruction. A few centuries prior, it was little more than a radioactive heap, and now it was the capital city of the Alliance. *Go figure.*

It was the third "war to end all wars," and, as most wars did, it had left destruction in its wake: billions dead and the planet in shambles. If anything good came from all those deaths, it was only that it had helped to bring the rest of the planet together. Countries and cultures that had been at odds with their neighbors for a millennium finally found common ground, as guns were traded for tools and killing for rebuilding. Like anything else that required the participation of human beings, the effort was wrought with glitches and did not go well at first, but ultimately, it happened. Science and medicine made substantial forward leaps as shareable knowledge became available. At that point, the long-awaited achievement of humankind's expansion out into the stars was simply a matter of time.

Spaceship drive systems improved over the years, and the moon was the first heavenly body to be colonized. Each advance in technology was another stepping stone that led farther out into the cosmos. The lunar landscape was divided by the corporations who funded those advances; no longer were nations involved in the endeavor, especially after it was discovered that the moon was a virtual goldmine of mineralogical riches there for the taking. Mining settlements were the first to stake their claims. Reminiscent of the California Gold Rush of the late nineteenth century, the brave and the wealthy mined the lunar dirt, on a quest for profit and power, that elusive fortune and glory. Those settlements soon grew in size, as more and more people journeyed there, spurred on by their high hopes. In time, and with plenty of support and funding from Striker Industries, Stratton Systems helped construct Lunar One. With a population of more than 500,000, it represented man's first off-world success.

With a functional model in place, the next step was Mars. Rather than a barren moon, it was actually a planet, one large and temperate enough that it had supported an atmosphere and liquid water in its past. Scientists theorized that Mars could be terraformed to a more hospitable environment over a period of forty to fifty years. With that as the goal, both colonization and terraforming began, and ships arrived with personnel and equipment to begin converting the atmosphere to something a bit more breathable. The long procedure of melting the Martian icecaps added moisture to the dry atmosphere, while huge atmospheric generators absorbed carbon dioxide and other gases, simultaneously giving off needed oxygen.

Similar to the situation with the moon, the colonization of Mars was a gradual process. Settlements for the researchers and scientists were constructed, housing the technical personnel necessary for construction and terraforming. Forty-three years after the switch was first thrown on the very first oxygen generator, the surface was proclaimed habitable, without the need for life support equipment. It was the dawn of a new age for a tired Earth. Immigration to Mars—or New Earth, as some referred to it—already had a waiting list years long, and special large transports were built to carry the colony builders to the new frontier. In cramped quarters and with few luxuries, they bravely made the thirteen-month journey, hoping for a new start in a brand new world. In less than fifty years, the red planet had become a paradise for those looking to flee the war-ravaged Earth of their origins. Oceans were now visible from orbit, refreshed from the rains brought by the seeded clouds. The first city, New Earth City, once enclosed in a protective dome, was now open to the environment most of the time.

The major difference between Earth and Mars was surface temperature. If Earth had an advantage over what many considered its planetary twin, it had to be that it orbited the sun more closely. Due to the distance of Mars from the sun, the planet was much colder, despite the cloud cover and atmosphere that tended to keep the daytime warmth from dissipating at night. At the equator, it was a balmy eighteen degrees Celsius, while the poles stood at a frigid minus eighty-seven.

There were other factors at play across the surface. The process of terraforming wasn't perfect. Violent storms periodically raged, as the ancient Martian ecosystem looked to reclaim its past. Heavy winds blew across the landscape, chasing the human population inside for a time. Still, even these occasional environmental imperfections did very little to halt the masses from immigrating. Eventually, the storms became nothing more than a distraction, though they did point out the necessity of maintaining the protective dome.

Eventually, research and exploration led to manned settlements on Venus and the moons of Jupiter and Saturn, continuing man's expansion into the void. Space was at a premium, quite literally. Space stations, floating cities of steel and precious life-preserving gases had risen outside the orbits of Earth and Mars, as well as beyond the asteroid belt. Initiated as research and communications relay stations, they soon morphed into waypoints for settlers, providing maintenance and recreation facilities on the way to the outer planets. Some thought they were turning into floating bordellos, one last shot for crewmembers to lose whatever money they had before moving deeper into space. Later, with advances in propulsion pushing vessels closer and closer to the speed of light, these stations became obsolete; too many were in need of repair, and they were eventually abandoned, left to remain as relics, symbols of time gone by.

Earth looked to her colonies for trade and resources, while the military needed their eyes and ears in space for intelligence-gathering and refueling bases for its growing fleet of FTL starships. One thing the Alliance realized early on was that there were distinct similarities between mankind's colonial expansion into space and the exploration of Earth oceans centuries earlier. For one thing, pirating could not be denied and had to be dealt with. The colonies had their own ships, but they were stretched thin with their own planetary duties, so Earth became the local cop and EMT. Pirates were not the most worrisome threat for the Alliance though; that was the unknown. Attacks on the Alliance by unidentified ships were on the rise. Either someone had created a new class of ship, or else there was a new player entering the game, an alien player at that.

Dante knew the Alliance had never suspected that the cost of doing business with the colonials would be closer to extortion. It reminded him of the caustic, uneasy relationship between a drug user and dealer. Energy was transmitted by Striker-owned transmitters orbiting Mercury, while most of the minerals that were used to build ships and cities of the overpopulated mother world came from mining equipment run by both Striker and Rosten. When Earth allowed the corporations to take the lead during the early years of expansion, they lost control of how those assets were managed. In a way, just as his kinfolk had before him, Ethan Striker held the deed to the sky and all the stars within it.

The charter of each colony was the same: They were all to be governed by democratic elections and responsible to the Alliance Council on the Earth. However, that charter proved to be more difficult to enforce than anyone had anticipated. In reality, they were governed by the same wealthy families to whom Striker had granted the initial contracts centuries before. The colonies on the moon and Mars put on a good show for Election Day, but when it was over, the results were always the same. There was no question as to who sat on the throne, nor did anyone wonder who the power was behind all those little kingdoms.

Dante stared across the crowded floor, casting his gaze on the emperor, who was toasting one of his few rivals; no one held that position very long, for taking any stand against Striker was somewhat of a death wish.

Dante—and many others—were well aware that crime was running rampant in the colonies. Drug use, prostitution, pirating, and smuggling were problems, but the crime only worsened in intensity, danger, and frequency the farther out in the system one went. He suspected that Striker was at the top of the pyramid when it came to illegal goings-on, but none of those accusations could be proven. Even if relatively solid evidence was available, the man and his company were legal Teflon; nothing would ever stick to them, and no one had the courage to make the attempt in the first place. Striker just walked the floor; a living god, just as generations of Strikers had done before him. Dante knew Striker would do whatever necessary to maintain his powerbase, even if it came down to murder. In the grand scheme of things, for Striker, the only life that really mattered was his own.

Dante pulled his eyes off of Striker and looked around at the other guests, all dressed in their Sunday finest. They were disguised as champions of industry and heroes of the downtrodden masses, but he knew better. Businessmen, politicians, and the rising stars of the military were all present, mingling with their counterparts as if their successes could be claimed by them at the touch of a handshake. It was strange to see so many naval officers in attendance. He knew most of the ships were built at Striker-owned shipyards, and there were rumors that Striker was even building his own private warships and looking to crew them with fresh recruits who would be well paid. Dante was sure that would not sit well with the admiralty, or at least he hoped so; from the looks of it, most of them were busy enjoying the party and had no problem schmoozing the devil himself.

The Alliance military tended to look the other way, as long as the weapons they purchased from Striker were supreme to the ones he sold to their enemies. Dante didn't care if the weapons were better or not; in his estimation, they all killed just the same. There were countless reports from the outer colonies of people suffering massive burn holes caused by the allegedly "inferior" weapons. *If it was only that simple...*

One simple glance at his fellow partygoers told Dante that Striker's powerbase was growing. The number of fleet admirals and Alliance politicians in the room was enough to scare the crap out of him. The influence and power Striker was able to buy offered him a sizable buffer between himself and any legal or military prosecution. There was no one he could take his suspicions to without word getting back to Striker, and Dante was sure that if Striker caught wind of that, it wouldn't be long before an accident would find him dead somewhere.

He knew there was something else going on, something even more sinister beyond the arms dealing and political payoffs. Fleet patrol routes were altered without reason. Attacks increased on both colonial planets and commercial shipping, totally unwarranted and with motives unknown, and with that onslaught came an increase in body counts. Some of the victims' wounds were inconsistent with weapons available to the Alliance, like those burn holes that even the most rookie forensics team wouldn't believe, and the energy signatures were completely unknown.

When Dante inquired about the attacks, his superior informed him that the information was classified and looked at him in disdain for even having the audacity to ask. After that came his transfer and the honor of endless piles of paperwork, a leaning tower of forms that would last until his retirement or death offered the tranquility of an escape. Time passed, but he still had contacts within Fleet Operations. Things seemed to be getting worse daily, especially toward the outer rim, but that was nothing compared to the insanity taking place back on Earth.

The mishaps began innocently enough: a car accident here or a malfunction in an airlock at the orbital station there, but it was obviously no coincidence that every victim was a person of influence, with ties to Striker. On Earth, Mars, and in the outer colonies, Striker's opponents were dropping like flies. The causes and the deaths themselves were so random that it was seemingly impossible to draw any connection between them. Basically, every case was closed or had to be put on ice. Whatever Striker was planning, it was clandestine and ugly. Dante desperately wanted to bring this to the attention of his superiors, but he had no way to know who was on Striker's payroll, nor did he have any desire to end up as the next casualty in that invisible, ugly war. He could only trust his family, but most of them had determined that he was nuts. It had already cost him his children and marriage, but he knew there was far more at stake than his personal problems.

Michael and Kristin were both commanders in the Alliance fleet; Michael served in naval intelligence, while his sister worked as an executive officer onboard the newest Alliance starship, the *Bonaventure*. Then there was Katherine. He had no idea where his eldest daughter had disappeared to. The most recent reports placed her on Mars, but he'd given up any hope of finding her or trying to keep track of his wayward offspring. Once, she had been the shining star of the intelligence community, even on the fast track to the admiralty herself, but that stellar path was cut short when Katherine was arrested and charged with smuggling weapons of mass destruction (WMDs) to a fringe colony. The case was dismissed due to lack of evidence, and she was dishonorably discharged and disappeared soon after. Dante had a feeling that the Rosten family on Mars had something to do with it, as it was well known that Kate was involved with Marcus Rosten, the son and heir to the current colonial governor for life, Clayton Rosten.

Dante surmised that the WMDs were probably Rosten's and that his daughter had attached herself to Marcus on purpose. Rosten certainly had enough pull with both Striker and the Alliance to get the charges reduced or dropped. According to the grapevine, the Striker and Rosten families were close and had been since the days before the last big war; it was impossible to put a value on that kind of loyalty. The court sentenced Katherine with five years in prison, but when all charges were mysteriously dropped, she simply fell off the radar. Dante felt it was a true shame they were no longer speaking, because he could have used her skill set, along with her connections with Rosten and his son. Mars was crucially important in the grand scheme of his plans.

Striker had a secret communications relay station on the red planet, and any sensitive communiqués would be stored on the data drives there. Dante was sure the relay connected Striker on Earth with Rosten on Mars and Stratton on the moon, in some sort of conspiracy-filled party line. If his suspicions were correct, there could also be a connection to whatever or whoever was attacking the Alliance ships out on the rim. *Maybe it would also throw some light on the mystery ships we observed outside the orbit of Neptune,* he conjectured. *Was it alien or just a hallucination brought on by deep space travel?* One thing was certain: The burn marks on the debris found out there was no hallucination; it was real enough to be a concern.

Dante looked at the antique watch he still wore on his wrist. He understood Striker's passion for antiques, as a love for the past was a weakness they shared. The timepiece had been in his family for generations, and he hoped Michael would wear it once he was gone.

"Sentimentality," he whispered softly to himself, shaking his head. "There's no place for it in this lie." In many ways, things were now far more complicated than they were when the watch was worn by its original owner so many decades before. Remarkably, it still kept perfect time, and at the moment, the hands were pointing to the hour when Michael's transport was scheduled to set down in New Earth City on Mars. It should have bothered Dante more that he was putting his own son in harm's way, but he had little choice. Something bad was about to happen, and there was little he could do to stop it.

Dante stared out the window and allowed himself a moment to enjoy the view. He felt a little guilty for enjoying it as much as he did, and he harbored a deep anger at Striker for taking such splendor for granted. Regardless of those feelings, though, he had to head back to his office to monitor his son and his mission. When he turned from the window, he found himself face to face with Ethan Striker, the man himself, and he realized by the angst in Striker's gaze that there was a very good chance he'd overstayed his welcome.

It was that sardonic smile that hit him first, framed in that blond, handsome package. Dante had to admit that the evil bastard could charm a thunderstorm into a sunny day. Striker played the role of the charismatic playboy exceptionally well, but Dante knew better. Inside that loveable shell lurked a demon from the pits of Hell.

"Admiral Dante," Striker said cheerfully, sticking his hand out. "How nice of you to make our little soiree."

Dante looked at the outstretched hand and decided it was in his best interest to shake it. He had to act as star struck as the rest of Striker's mindless, loyal minions. "I'm having a wonderful time, Mr. Striker. Your home is very impressive."

Striker look past him, toward the window. "Yes, it's a great view, Admiral. It gives me a perspective on the future…and what we need to do to get there."

Dante nodded and forced a smile. It was chilling to think about the future Striker had in mind, but he had to play along. "You and your family have done such amazing things to revitalize this planet since the war," he said, nauseating himself. "We all owe you a great debt. What can you possibly accomplish now, to surpass all this?" Dante asked, gesturing to the panoramic scene beyond the glass.

Striker turned back to him and nodded. "There's always more to do. One needs to create truth and beauty out of chaos, no matter the cost."

Dante could hear the conviction in Striker's voice, his main source of power over others. His tone was almost hypnotizing, almost mesmerizing, like the dreamy gaze of a cobra about to strike. He knew then that he had to get out of the snake's vicinity while he still could. Michael would be on mission shortly, and he needed time to review any intel he'd discovered. Not only that, but if he didn't get out of Striker's earshot, he was sure he'd say something they would both regret. "It's getting late, Mr. Striker," Dante finally said, nodding to the aged bauble on his wrist, "and I've got a long day ahead of me tomorrow. You've been very…enlightening."

Striker stared down at the watch and nodded. "Pre-Alliance?"

"Yes."

"Very nice. As you can see," he said with a gesture that encompassed his penthouse apartment, "I have a love of antiques from that time, no pun intended."

"Family heirloom." Dante stuck his hand out and grasped Striker's. "Again, sir, many thanks for the invitation. It's been a pleasure."

"The pleasure is all mine, Admiral. Do have a safe trip."

Something about Striker's last two words and the almost sarcastic way they rolled off his tongue stopped Dante in his tracks. "Thank you. An accident would certainly spoil what has been a wonderful evening," Dante said but regretted the proclamation almost as soon as the words waltzed off his lips. He made a mental note to himself: *For the love of God, skip the expensive champagne next time. The last thing your mouth needs in this guy's presence is stupidity disguised as liquid courage.*

"Keep in touch, Admiral," Striker added from behind him as the lift doors finally whooshed opened.

Dante walked in and turned to look back at his host. He wasn't at all surprised to see that Striker had disappeared. As soon as the door slid shut and the lift started its downward journey, he felt perspiration dripping down his back, saturating his uniform. For the first time, he realized that his legs felt a little weak, and he leaned against the lift wall for support. "Hold it together," he told himself, "at least till you get back to the damn office." One way or another, it was going to be a very long night.

Chapter 2

Commander Michael Dante watched as Mars grew larger outside the window of the passenger transport he'd booked passage on a few days earlier. Usually, he could count on a military ship of some sort to take him off-world, but his father, the almighty Admiral Dante, had insisted he go in undercover.

He suspected that paranoia was because of Kate and her connection to the Rosten family. Knowing his father and the relationship he shared with his eldest daughter, Michael wasn't really sure where his sister's loyalty lay. She had always been Daddy's little girl, but after the trouble she got herself into and the people she chose to associate with, the admiral had wisely kept his distance. The old man had trust issues to begin with, but he felt especially betrayed by Kate. Michael wholeheartedly believed that it was that perceived crack in her loyalty that had him approaching the mission under a false identity. Michael knew Kate, though, and he was sure his sister would never betray him.

The fact was that he and his two sisters shared a bond that went beyond whatever problems threatened to blow them apart. It was easy, really, as it was how their father raised them to be. He had taught them all that healthy paranoia wasn't a bad thing, and that when there was no one else, family could be trusted with one's life. Nicholas Dante never did anything without a reason, a well-thought motive. For this reason, Michael assumed there was a reason why he and his sisters were only two years apart; their parents left time between them so each of them could establish their own identity, yet they were close enough in age that they could enjoy a tight sibling bond.

The admiral's number-one rule was that he would give advice when asked, but he would never use his position to help any of them in their careers. Their failure or success was entirely dependent on their own efforts. With that in mind, they all entered the military. For Kristin, it was the space force, but Michael and Kate took the same military career path, Alliance Intelligence. Maybe it was all those years playing spy with his older sister, using the old man's scout ship as their headquarters, or maybe it just made him happy to follow in her footsteps on a path counter to their father's. There might have been an even simpler explanation, one their mother told them one day, the real reason they chose the world of cloak and dagger: They were the two most affected by the admiral's conspiracy theories and his lack of trust in the universe. Three days later, Michael discovered that his mother had filed for divorce, citing his obsession as part of the complaint. In all the twenty-nine years of his life, Michael couldn't find a single reason to argue her point. He loved her even more after the separation and continued to, even after cancer killed her. The admiral missed her, too, probably even more than his children did, and he mourned her passing in the same way he handled everything else in life: alone and in silence.

Michael followed Kate through the academy and graduated two years after his sister. After she graduated, he felt very much alone for the first time. Kate was reassigned, and while he followed her exploits as well as he could, their own personal contact was rare to say the least, and that only grew worse after his own graduation.

Kristin was the free spirit of the family, and she had no time for the crap that came out of their father. In fact, she looked forward to being out on her own and often said, "The farther out, the better." After her graduation, she entered flight training school and graduated at the top of her class. Immediately following that, she was assigned to the *USS Bonaventure*, a posting that Michael was sure the admiral had something to do with. The *Bonaventure* was the newest, most powerful ship in the Alliance, and she was assigned to it even before construction was finished. He found it funny that as much as Kristin claimed she couldn't stand the old man, she grew up to be just like him. He was proud of her, but he still played favorites with Kate. His disappointment in Kristin poisoned his relationships with all of them, to a certain extent. *Funny*, Michael thought, *because it sure didn't stop Dad from drafting me for this insane plan.* The *Bonaventure* was out of system, eliminating Kristin's participation, and his lack of trust in Kate, especially in light of her relationship to Marcus Rosten, made her a liability. It appeared that Michael had won the chore by default, but it certainly didn't feel like a victory or prize of any sort.

The transport shook as it was buffeted in the Martian atmosphere, and the turbulence drew Michael's attention back to the present. He turned to see the viewports, engulfed in flames from the friction of reentry. It was a big show for the passengers, who stared at the lightshow, practically clinging to their seats. It was easy to understand their excitement; the three-day trip from Earth was a bore for most of them, so from the time they had left Earth orbit till now, this was their only entertainment, other than the lackluster video entertainment centers furnished at each seat. The transport offered no cabins and very little privacy. The seats folded back into makeshift beds for an uncomfortable attempt at sleeping, and there was a small, cramped lounge that attempted to keep the thirty-five passengers and crew happy. Now, at least they could amuse themselves by ooh-ing and ah-ing at the pre-landing fireworks.

It took three minutes for the flames to dissipate into the air, and only then did the flight crew announce that they were making final descent into New Earth City. The ship buffeted once again, this time from the high winds that swept the planet. For the passengers who were on their first trip, the excitement of the fiery reentry was replaced with fear as they struggled in their seats, making sure their safety harnesses were all locked into position.

Michael knew they were on final approach when they passed over the directional markers leading to the city. He'd taken that same route more times than he could count, sometimes as a passenger and several times as a pilot. There had been a few high-altitude drops as well, but those were best left in the past.

The city came up quickly on the left side of the transport. Twelve miles wide and covered by a retractable pressure dome, it housed more than 100,000 men, women, and children. The transport passed over the city and dipped its starboard wing and then the port, to give the passengers a better look. Finally, it headed to one of the docking facilities located on the edge of the city, just outside the dome.

The pad was under them as the forward thrusters slowed the ship. Once the vessel's forward progress stopped, the landing thrusters activated, and the transport slowly settled to the pad. After powering down, the pad lowered the transport under the surface, into a spacious hangar bay. The journey continued as a conveyor system carried the transport to the terminal where they would disembark. When the transport came to a final halt, a boarding tube moved into position and locked against the outer airlock. The restraints automatically released and everyone exited the airlock, with luggage in hand, dispersing out into the terminal on the other side of the heavy door.

Michael traveled light and had only the small carryon bag he'd brought on the flight with him. The contents were not for the eyes of airport security and were specially shielded; he was confident that his military I.D. would allow him to avoid any prying eyes. From there, it would be easy to just blend in with the general population. His trip to the Striker Communications Center would be a little more difficult, but it was nothing he hadn't done before.

The admiral wanted him to tap the communications relay and record any relevant data he found bouncing around in the system. He was sure Striker, Rosten, and Stratton had something planned against the Alliance and that all those deaths surrounding Striker and the others were no accidents. The victims were politicians and military, all having held positions of power, and they were all working on things that were counterintuitive to the goals of Ethan Striker. While Michael didn't usually pay much attention to his father's conspiracy theories, that one made him stand up and take notice. He didn't report to the admiral, but he did have some leave time coming and decided this would be the best time to take it. His only competition would be Kate, his sister, and he sincerely hoped she'd steer clear of it entirely.

Michael made his way through the streets. The air smelled fresh, but there was a chill in it. When the weather permitted and the winds were weak, the dome was opened to the atmosphere to ventilate the accumulated gases. No matter how many times he'd been there, he was still taken aback by how well they were able to terraform that red ball of blowing, poisonous dust into another livable rock in the cosmos.

The city itself never ceased to amaze him. From ground level, it could have been New York, London, or any other major city on Earth. Even if the Rostens were on his father's hit list, he had to hand it to them: They and their ancestors had managed to create a slice of Heaven in the middle of Hell. He also agreed with the admiral's assessment about the interesting coincidence that they were the winners of every election, or at least supported the winning candidate. Regardless, they always managed to stay in control.

There was a disturbing similarity between the Mars cities and the cities on Earth, in that they managed to contain a fair amount of homeless and poor as well. This bothered Michael, but he wasn't on Mars now to crush poverty. If Admiral Dante was correct—and he usually was—lack of housing would ultimately prove to be the least of their problems.

He checked the time and noted that his father was likely still attending Striker's party. The old man couldn't afford to offend Striker at that point in his investigation. He knew a vehicle would be waiting for him outside the city, so he had time to stop for a bite to eat before the trip to the relay station. Michael expected five hours of travel time and another two inside the station to attach the taps and download whatever data was available. There was a military transport departing late that night and he intended to be on it. Before all that, though, he needed to refuel his body and mind with some form of sustenance.

Michael cleverly opted for a restaurant he had not frequented in the past. His identification and passport carried a different name, but there was not enough time to make any significant changes to his appearance, other than to change the color of his hair. He thought the blond locks suited him, but he still planned to change it back to its natural dark brown as soon as the mission was over.

The restaurant was a small, out-of-the-way eatery, and he really didn't stand out from any of the people on the street. The hat and glasses conspicuously hid enough of his features, and the old, dirty camouflage coat he wore was everyman's garb. He had learned many things from his wise father, not the last of which was that the secret in the intelligence field was to stay unpredictable. "The more you understand that fact," the admiral had told him more than once, "the longer you'll survive."

There wasn't much of a crowd at that time of day. The lighting was muted, an effort to conserve power from the grid. Michael was happy with the shadows that played across the tables and chairs, thankful for the additional cover. The sign on the door read "Utopia Planitia Pub," and from what he could see, the place was patterned after any Earth pub, complete with an ample supply of liquor occupying one whole wall, manned by the prerequisite bored bartender. He made a beeline to a corner table that would provide him with the necessary view of the entrance. As he slid into the seat, he found that it was some sort of immense comfort to have his back against the wall. His rumbling stomach called to attention that he hadn't eaten in more than a day, and, depending on the outcome of the mission, there was no guarantee when he'd have the opportunity to eat again. It was the perfect time to grab a meal, but first he had to grab the attention of a waitress.

Finally, a pretty girl with an apron tied around her thin waist walked over to his table. She laid out a knife, fork, and napkin, then handed him a surprisingly well-worn menu. She seemed to be in her late teens or early twenties and would have been pretty if her blonde hair wasn't in such a dire need of a brushing. She wore the same bored expression as the bartender, which amused Michael to no end. He nodded and, without saying a word, opened the menu and scanned the list of food choices. From what he could see, the menu was a pretty authentic representation of Earthside pub fare.

"Well? What can I get you?" the waitress asked, somewhat impatiently, in a demeanor that wasn't half as sweet as her face. She sighed, looking as if she would have preferred to be anywhere but there.

Michael looked up at her from behind the menu and smiled. "I just need a minute. Never been here before."

"Suit yourself," she said, then turned and headed to the bar to chat with the bartender.

Michael perused the menu again, and the beef burger caught his eye. His only issue was where the beef actually came from; the closest cow he knew of was more than thirty-four million miles away. He was a little pissed at the waitress for not taking his drink order or even offering him a glass of water, and he intended to mention that to her. A second later, he could feel her standing over him, so he muttered, "I'll take the burger and fries."

"How do you want it cooked?"

It surprised him that the voice didn't belong to the waitress. It sounded almost too familiar, ominously so, and he cautiously looked over the menu at the person standing over him.

"Hello, Michael."

"Kate?" he asked, aghast. There she was, his MIA sister, standing right in front of him, wearing the uniform of Mars Security Forces. The thing that worried him the most, though, was the imposing sidearm strapped to her hip. It was odd to see anyone armed in that city, as weapons were only distributed out on an as-needed basis. Her long, dark hair framed a beautiful face, but it did nothing to hide the anger she felt.

"Yes, Michael…Kate," she said, with a slow nod of her head. "What the hell are you doing here, and why are you dressed like that? Did the admiral send you?"

Michael smiled and gestured to the chair facing him. He knew he had to guard every word he spoke to her. Yes, she was family, but her loyalty to her bloodline was truly unknown. She also knew him too well for him to get away with lying to her. Kate was far superior to him when it came to reading people, something that gave her a distinct edge in the cat-and-mouse games she so expertly played. She paused for a quick second before pulling out the chair and settling into it. Her tight red and white uniform resisted the move at first, but the adaptable synthetic fibers of the fabric eventually gave in.

"How did you know you'd find me here?" he asked. His eyes met hers in the same game they'd been playing since they were kids. It was almost as if they both had some sort of built-in, genetically passed-down lie detector, and it was one of the reasons they were so close. Truly, it was almost impossible for either of them to lie to the other without getting caught in their fib. Now, there was an extra layer of danger, due to the training they'd received from Alliance Intelligence. Both were in the business of lying, and they did so with great expertise. In the past, a lie would catch one of them detention from the admiral; now, it could mean catching a bullet.

Without answering, Kate pulled the menu out of her brother's hand and held two fingers in the air.

Within seconds, the waitress hurried back to the table with two beers and a sudden, newfound enthusiasm for her job. "What can I get you, Captain Dante?" she asked excitedly.

Michael shook his head. *Really? All it took was a security officer's uniform to get decent customer service in here?*

Before answering, Kate turned to her stunned brother and smiled. "You really shouldn't have ordered that burger. The beef was either raised here, which isn't a good thing, or some artificial, generic meat substitute shipped here more than a year ago." Before the waitress or Michael could say anything in protest, Kate looked back up at the waitress and said, "We'll have two Number Fives, thanks."

"Yes, ma'am."

"And make sure the mucha is fresh this time," Kate called to the waitress as she scurried off.

Michael could see the sweat on the girl's face as she made the notation on her data-padd; she was happy to finally leave the table. "Mucha?" Michael asked. "What the hell is mucha?"

"It's what the locals call the livestock up here. It's more or less chicken, only with less gravity. They feed them special nutrients, and things grow as large as turkeys back home. Personally, it's the only thing I trust in these places, the closest thing you're going to get to Earth food. Trust me. This dive isn't like the places you've been to here before." She stopped talking to take a long swallow from her tall beer glass. She could see her brother was about to say something, so as she had done since childhood, she interrupted. "As for how I found you," she threw back at him, "I've got friends all over. I'm pretty sure you know that. I knew you took some time off from the service to visit the admiral. A couple days later, you hopped a transport for Mars. I've been tracking you ever since you landed."

"You have?" he asked, arching a curious brow at her.

"Don't misunderstand me, Michael. I've missed you, and I'm thrilled to see you, but I have to ask again, both as a sister and the chief of security of this city... *Why* are you here?"

Michael picked up the glass of amber liquid and took a long gulp from it. He was surprised to find that the local brew was quite tasty.

Before he could answer his sister's very official inquiry, the waitress returned with two plates and placed their meals gently in front of them: a tossed salad of local produce, topped with strips of white meat. To the side of each plate was a small cup, which Michael assumed to be dressing for the salad.

Michael watched as his sister stuffed a forkful in her mouth. He looked at the mucha for a moment before shoving a sample into his own mouth. Kate was right; it tasted like chicken back on Earth.

"This is really good," he finally said as he followed the next forkful with another drink. He knew his sister was hoping the alcohol would make him more talkative, but flapping his lips too much was not in his plans. When he looked back up at Kate, he could see she was back to her staring game, her eyes locked on his. "I'm contracting for the Martian Museum," he said, "but to be honest with you, I came because Dad is…worried about you."

The parental designation seemed to catch her off guard, as none of them ever referred to their father by anything other than his fleet rank, at least not since their mother left. Any reference to his paternal title was a term of endearment, and she hadn't heard anyone use the word "Dad" to refer to him. That alone made her uneasy about the direction the conversation was about to take. "I know what you're trying to do," she snapped. "I'm not going to fall for this damn Daddy dearest thing, Michael. He wasn't a dad then, and he goddamn sure isn't one now. What the hell is going on, and why did he really send you here?"

Michael downed the rest of the beer and put his military cred-card on the table. "Listen, Kate. The admiral is going through another one of his delusions, overcome by some conspiracy theory, convinced that we're on the precipice of the end of mankind as we know it. He sent me here to make sure you're okay. Really. That's all there is to it. Do you have to be so goddamn suspicious and paranoid all the freakin' time? I swear, you're worse than he is."

"If he wanted to check up on me, he could have just called and asked."

Michael could see his sister's attitude rising to the surface. She and the old man really weren't much alike, except in their paranoia and their ability to be so stubborn and pigheaded, and he was sure that was why they didn't get along. "He tried. He claims you never pick up when he calls."

"No," she said, her face softening a bit in introspective reflection, "I guess I don't. Maybe I would if he was more like a father and less like a friggin' admiral!"

Michael shook his head, clearly understanding the root of the issue. "Are you still pissed that he didn't throw his weight around for you at your hearing?"

"His weight?" she snapped, then smirked. Kate was well aware she was dealing with some major anger management problems, but her brother had picked the wrong time to dig up family history. A half-dozen military psych officers had tried to unravel her daddy issues, without much success. The fact that he had held his tongue while he sat on the tribunal that had kicked her out of the service only added to her anger. "His input was weightless. He sat in judgment of me and said nothing as they took my rank and commission and sent me on my merry way."

Michael shook his head again. He felt bad for letting the lie dredge up crap from the past. She was right about their father saying and doing nothing to get her out of hot water, but there was really nothing he could have done anyway. "He did what he had to. The evidence against you was too solid, and—"

"Solid? Pssh. It was circumstantial at best!" she interrupted, punctuating her statement with a kick to the chair next to her, sending it skidding across the pub floor.

"Calm down, Kate," Michael said slowly. "The last thing we need to do is cause a scene in here. The admiral is worried about your relationship with Marcus Reston, and he sent me here to make sure everything is okay. You may not believe me, but you're family, and we all still care about you."

Kate stood up from her seat and noted the cred-card on the table. "Aw. How nice that you still have that Alliance expense account to buy your meals for you. Put it back in your pocket though. This is my treat, little brother."

"Thanks," he said, withdrawing the card, "but what do you want me to tell him?" Michael cast a cursory glance around the pub, realizing he'd already spent more time than he could afford to with Kate. He needed to let her get the rest of all that drama out of her system, then get on with his mission.

"Tell the nosy old bastard that everything's fine here," she snapped. "You can also tell him that any relationship I may or may not have with Marcus—or anyone else, for that matter—is really none of his business. If that's really why you came to Mars, which I highly doubt it is in that ridiculous outfit of yours, you can hop on the next transport and haul ass back to Earth. Michael, please save the archeology research for someone who cares."

"Tell me, sis, is that suggestion for me to leave an official request from the Mars head of security or merely advice from a concerned relative?"

"Baby brother, you are an officer in the Alliance military, regardless of your paperwork. I would need a really good excuse to make you to leave this planet, so please take this as a friendly word of advice from your big sister. Go home, Michael. You don't want to be here. Trust me on that." With that, Kate turned to walk to the pub exit but stopped after a few steps and threw over her shoulder, "If I really wanted you off the planet, I could have officially arrested you before your first bite of mucha, your first slug of beer. Take care… and say hi to the admiral for me."

Michael watched as his sister turned and walked out of the pub. He was well aware by her tone and the untrusting look in her eyes that Kate knew he was up to something, but if the admiral was right, he needed to find out how bad things were. He had to elude his tail and make his way out of the city, but playing spy versus spy with his eyes-like-a-hawk's sister was no easy feat for anyone, not even him. *My odds aren't good,* he thought as he put his cred-card away. *Matter fact, I don't think I've ever won that game with her. I'm not sure anyone can.*

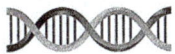

Kate walked out of the pub without even looking back at her brother. She felt horrible for playing the victim, the poor little girl-turned-bitch by her long-suffered daddy issues, but that role-playing was a necessary evil if she wanted to protect her family. She'd learned that lies were much easier when they were layered with a tinge of truth and lots of anger. Michael was a bit more transparent when he attempted to veil the truth in some ill-conceived fib. She knew he was on Mars for a reason far loftier than checking up on the wayward daughter, and she was certain the reason had something to do with their father. The admiral had sent his son there, and she wanted to know the motive behind it.

As far back as she could remember, their father had held tight to a particular theory of his, one regarding the colonization of the solar system and the exploration of the interstellar space beyond. After the war, the world was in chaos. Billions were dead, and civilization was in ruins. Rising from the ashes like a cosmic phoenix of legend, Striker Industries took the lead and rebuilt the infrastructure from the ground up. They brought Rosten Corporation and Stratton Systems in as major contractors to handle the rebuilding. Rosten offered immense pre-war construction and energy resources, while Stratton's specialty consisted of electronics, computers, and communications systems. Somehow, all three companies survived the battle and remained relatively intact, a trifecta that managed to reassemble a planet that was on the brink of crumbling, to put it all back together again like some enormous Humpty Dumpty. Other subcontractors were recruited, but it was always the big three, with Striker forever at the point, leading the way.

Eventually, when mankind made the leap to the stars, it was again Striker, Rosten, and Stratton leading the push. They financed, built, marketed, and eventually, several centuries and generations later, reaped the rewards. Now, they controlled Mars and the moon and had their hands in everything, from trade and military to deep space exploration. In the process, though, the attacks on shipments of resources from the outer colonies beyond Jupiter began to rise. The assailants were unknown, and the only evidence of the attacks was ship debris; while deaths were presumed, not a body was ever found. Not only that, but reports were also coming in of something else roaming the outer rim, though no evidence on any non-terrestrial thing was ever found.

Admiral Dante wasn't crazy. In spite of some personal opinions about him, it could not be denied that he was a strategist, historian, and architect of the Alliance space fleet, as well as a damn smart man. He spent years trying to draw criminal connections between Striker and what he called "the family dictatorships," on both the moon and Mars. There was just too much to attribute to coincidence, and if there was one thing the admiral refused to believe in, it was coincidence. There was just enough to create suspicion that Striker and the others had some kind of power play in progress, but he could never drum up enough solid evidence to involve the authorities. Kate knew her father had trust issues, and that explained why he'd chosen to recruit his own son for such a clandestine undertaking, as obvious as it was. *The question is, what orders did he give Michael?* she had to wonder. There was one thing she did know for sure: If Rosten's security caught her brother doing anything counter to their family business, he would return to Earth in a body bag, if he returned at all. She would do everything in her power to keep that from happening, but her ability to protect Michael depended deeply on Michael and his real plans on Mars.

She thought about following him, but that would only lead the agents following her right to Michael. It wasn't like Clayton Rosten didn't trust her; she'd bled for the family more than once. It was his son, Marcus, who decided to have her followed. The heir to the thrown was a jealous bastard who regarded everything that didn't belong to his father as his property, or at least an inheritable asset. That was the one and only reason she didn't leave with her brother; if Marcus knew she'd met with him, with anyone not listed on her schedule and especially someone with ties to the military, he would throw a fit. Kate wasn't ready for that, at least not yet.

The next stop on her daily rounds was back at the security shack. Kate had a feeling she was in for a long night, and she wanted to be where she would do the most good. It would also ensure that no one would be on her tail if she needed to bolt. She knew they were following her, and they knew she knew it. As if to make a point of it, she occasionally waved to them before moving on.

As if on cue, the comm in her ear buzzed to life, and Kate brought it online with a tap. "Dante," she said, then listened carefully as she walked to the listless voice of the dispatcher, informing her that there was a domestic dispute in one of the lower-rent districts. They wanted her there because it had disintegrated into a hostage situation, and for some reason she couldn't fathom, they thought her qualified to handle it.

Damn it. This isn't in my freakin' job description, she silently fumed. They had made her head of security, and though she retained her rank of captain, she seemed to be viewed as little more than a beat cop at best and a nuisance at worst. There was nothing wrong with law enforcement, in general, but they had lied to her, short-changed her with an old bait-and-switch tactic. That alone would have bothered her in the past, but now, even though it was occasionally irritating, it just brought was a smile to her pretty face. The truth was, she had lied to them long before the job offer. In fact, it was all a complete and total fabrication, everything single thing about her position and her post. She was quite the actress, and that worked to her benefit and had likely kept her alive thus far.

The charges, her dishonorable discharge from the military, and her alleged loyalty to Striker and Rosten were nothing but a well-written work of fiction, created so high in the black ops section of Intelligence that not even the Alliance president knew the truth. There were well-constructed lies, lies, and more lies, and only two people in the universe—Colonels Evers and Tobias—knew she wasn't the traitor and criminal everyone else thought her to be.

It took a long time to set the whole ruse up, and all the pieces of the jigsaw had to fit together perfectly. First, she had to find and attract Marcus Rosten, all while making it appear that her prey was actually her predator. Then she had to allow the sneaky, selfish bastard to manipulate her and let him think she was falling for him.

When this is all over, she thought, *I'm going to need a very long, very hot shower,* but she knew that getting his psychological stench off her would be almost impossible.

In the beginning, Marcus just used her for information. It was simple, with very little damage potential. Soon, though, the simple morphed into something a bit more complicated and more restricted. She provided Rosten with ship movements and timetables for transports, all while her cover pulled her deeper and deeper into the darkness. She took illegal payments and used her rank to move contraband all over the system, making sure cameras were running to record all of her illegal activities. She had to, for it was a test of her loyalty to Rosten, who managed to stay in the background, well away from the recording devices that helped turn an Alliance hero into a criminal.

Marcus had passed word to her that his father, Clayton Rosten, wanted her to smuggle two low-yield nuclear weapons into New Earth City. There was nothing like a nuke or two to quiet an angry populace. Kate could not bear to see nukes in the hands of a heartless monster like Rosten, even if refusing meant blowing her cover, so she implored her handlers to finally arrest her before she put weapons of mass destruction within the reach of a madman. Thankfully, they agreed, and she was taken into custody before he could blow the world to smithereens.

Kristin was already on the *Bonaventure,* and Kate's father was too angry with her to visit while she was awaiting trial, so only Michael came to see her. The cover story demanded that no one knew the truth, not even her family. It wasn't an easy time for any of them. The military trial lasted more than two weeks, and all the evidence that was introduced left little in the way of reasonable doubt about her guilt. The Board of Inquiry was comprised of three ranking admirals, one of whom was her father.

The ruling was unanimous: She was guilty. She would be immediately discharged from the service, and her ten years in a military prison would somehow be commuted to time served. The plan was for her superiors to step in to help her escape and find her way to Mars, but she seemed to have friends in even higher places. Both Ethan Striker and Clayton Rosten made a deal, defined as large pay-off, to have her removed to Mars. Her friends in Intelligence were thrilled they didn't need to stage something that might literally blow up in their faces.

Unfortunately, her father didn't speak a word to her, not during or after the trial. She wanted to bring him aboard, to reveal the true role she'd played in it all, but she was told that in order to make the illusion as solid as possible, no one could be told. Thus, she stood there alone, with a bad reputation her only payment for doing her job so damn well. In the eyes of her family, she was treasonous, and to the criminals on the moon and Mars, she was just like them: dirty, damaged, and dangerous. She was a traitor, a smuggler, and almost a mass murderer. They hated her on Earth and feared her on Mars, and the only people who knew the truth were two black ops officers. She was promised that when it was all over, they would come forward and clear her name. Kate just hoped she'd still be breathing to enjoy that day.

Now, there she was, playing cop on Planet Mars. *Who'da thunk it?* she thought, almost in amusement as she looked up at the Martian sky and increased her pace. The dome had been rolled back, since the wind outside the city was calm. She enjoyed the privilege of gazing up at the natural cloud cover that seemed to be present most of the time. At that distance from the sun, the natural light was about half of that on Earth, and the day remained overcast till the clouds broke to reveal the distant sun. The atmosphere machines had done their job well, almost too well, to bring about a breathable atmosphere. Sometimes, she preferred the dome to be shut, because it made the city more alien and less like the trash heap she called home.

Kate liked to take the extra time to walk the city streets, her only semblance of freedom as of late, even if she did have to constant-ly look over her shoulder. The hopelessness in the faces of the poor and indigent that peppered the dirty streets and alleys, begging for morsels of food, helped to keep her centered on her important mission. Most of those poor souls had made their original pilgrimages there in high hopes, mistakenly assuming it would be an opportunity to start over after the wars took so much from them. Those dreams died quickly as Rosten and his family sucked the life out of everyone and everything that dared to wander into their world.

Kate noted the time and realized she had wasted enough of it. As much as they wanted her to tend to some ridiculous domestic disturbance, she was sure there were enough of her trigger-happy comrades already on the scene to handle it. The whole stunt reeked of Marcus. She was the queen of the chessboard, but he preferred her to be a pawn and desired the freedom to move her wherever the hell he pleased. She hoped her tail would report her failure to report directly to him. For Kate, pleasure was a rare commodity, and she had to take what little she could get, whenever she could. Upsetting him always made her day.

When she finally located a transport tube, Michael crept back into her thoughts. The underground monorail system would carry her into the heart of the city and her office at Mars Security. Kate knew she needed to find out why her brother was really there, for her sake as well as his. If her brother died, the admiral would blame her. If Rosten, Striker, or anyone else got between her and her family, they would all pay. Many had questions about where her loyalties lay, but Kate would always protect her family.

Chapter 3

The *USS Bonaventure* was an enormous vessel by any standards. At a shade over 720 meters, she easily dwarfed any ship in the Alliance. The prototype cruiser, built at the Striker Orbital Shipyards high above the Earth, was created as the newest warship. With torpedo tubes fore and aft and state-of-the-art plasma cannons offering 360 degrees of coverage, the *Bonaventure* was certainly every inch the predator she was designed to be. Sleek and deadly, she was also the fastest ship in the fleet, as well as temporary home to more than 200 souls.

Out between the orbits of Neptune and Pluto the *Bonaventure* was on a search-and-rescue mission. She was also tasked with hunting down whatever had necessitated the mission in the first place. Like hunter-killer submarines of the past, she prowled space, her powerful sensors reaching out for any sign of a ship in distress or its yet-unknown attacker. In spite of all her bells and whistles, though, after hours of scanning they still had nothing to show for it.

Captain Henry Brady paced the spacious bridge, trying to hide the impatience and frustration that always overtook him in such scenarios. His comfortable command chair sat in the center of the bridge, offering views of every station and the large forward view screen, all accessible by the rotating chair. Its design was borrowed from an old, pre-war TV show; some had found that what worked well in fiction appeared to work equally well in reality. The men referred to the chair as his "La-Z-boy," and Brady truly hoped it was merely a reference to the history of that brand of furniture than it was to his command skills. He had to admit that they had a point, for all the chair was missing was the recliner and footrest.

After more than twenty years in space, commanding everything from transports to cruisers, the *Bonaventure* captured the skilled captain's attention like none before. She was equipped with every technological advancement the Alliance could throw into her, including the ridiculously exaggerated captain's chair. At the moment, the chair was empty, as he stared out the view screen and into space.

"Simpson," Captain Brady said as he walked over the tactical officer, "are you sure these are the coordinates of the distress call?"

Simpson studied the incoming sensor reading on the tactical console one last time before looking up at his captain. He hesitated before giving an answer. Not only was he new to the ship, but he'd only graduated from the academy a little more than a year ago, and it was definitely not a good time in his career to give anything but perfectly accurate information. "Sir, the transmission definitely came from this approximate position."

"You don't sound so sure about that, Simpson," Brady said, detecting a bit of nerves in the young man's voice. "Maybe they could have drifted into Neptune's gravity well."

Simpson straightened his white and blue military jumpsuit and punched a few more buttons on his control console. He was rewarded with a bell and a tweet and nothing more. When he dared a look back up at his superior, he saw that the captain was not at all pleased. Nevertheless, he mustered his courage and answered, "No, sir, I don't think so. There would have been residue from weapons fire or debris. We've got nothing here."

Brady nodded, proud of the boy, and turned back to the view screen.

"Maybe the message was faked," Kristin Dante suggested from her ops station.

Brady shook his head at the thought before responding to his second-in-command. "Why would anyone falsify a distress call out here?"

Kristin mirrored the head shake, then transferred the sensor display over to her ops console. She smiled at the fact that the newfangled ship gave her the ability to clone any other station on the bridge. She wanted to go over the readings herself. It wasn't that she didn't trust the young lieutenant, but she had to be sure he hadn't missed anything. "Wait," she finally said, without looking up. "Don't you see it, Simpson?"

Brady looked back at the tactical officer, who was staring in disbelief at the sensor display Kristin had transferred to his console.

"Uh, yes, Commander. I-I see it now," Simpson stuttered. "There's a signal, twenty-three degrees to port. It's the transport, sir."

"How far away is she?" Brady asked as he took his seat at the center of the bridge.

"She's about 62,000 kilometers out, sir."

"Helm, take us in, one-quarter, sub-light."

"Yes, sir," the helmsman responded, and the ship started to pick up speed.

"Tactical," Kristin added from ops, "keep an eye on those sensor scans."

"Yes, ma'am."

As the ship came into view, the black scarring on her hull was a sure sign of an attack. Considering the fresh carbon scoring, they knew the attacker might still be in the vicinity. Any ship capable of that type of blast damage was not something to be taken lightly, and they certainly didn't want it sneaking up on them.

"Anything from that ship?"

"No, sir," Kristin answered, already pulling up a schematic of the transport.

"Sensors are detecting minimal life support," reported Simpson. "Main power is out, but auxiliary is functioning at a low level."

Brady nodded and stared as the transport began to fill the view screen. He could see the breaches along the hull. The metal was twisted, blown inward in some sections and outward in others, due to explosive decompression. He knew it would have taken a miracle for any living thing to survive that, but he had to make sure.

"Kristin, take a shuttle over there with an engineering and medical team. See if there's anyone left to rescue."

"Yes, sir." Kristin waited for her relief to take her ops station before she headed for the bridge exit. She stopped just short of the door and turned back to the captain. "Sir, do you mind if I take Simpson with me?"

"What for?" Brady asked, a bit surprised by the odd request. When he glanced over at the young lieutenant, he saw that Simpson's face reflected his own surprise as well.

"I'm going to need him for tactical data analysis, if there's any worth recovering," she said with a smile, knowing that the lieutenant needed a break and that a quick shuttle trip would help take the training wheels off.

Brady turned back to Simpson and answered with a sigh and a nod of his head. "Go ahead. It's about time he learned something."

Simpson's smile went from ear to ear. "Thank you, sir!"

Brady smiled back before taking his seat in his fully equipped easy chair and turning to face the image of the transport that filled the screen in front of them. "Go now, before I change my mind. And Kristin…"

"Yes, sir?"

"Please bring Junior back alive."

Kristin flashed a full smile as she grabbed Simpson and hustled him to the double-doors to exit the bridge. "You heard the captain, Simpson. C'mon."

The lift ride to the hangar bay took only a few moments. They arrived outside the pressure doors and saw the engineering and medical teams loading their gear aboard the shuttle while it was being prepped for the short trip to the damaged transport.

"Hey, Commander. Our teams are ready to board. Johnson and I will run shotgun on security for you." Marshall was a big, fearsome sort of guy, but deep down and off duty, Kristin knew he had the disposition of a teddy bear. On duty though, she was sure there was very little Marshall and Johnson couldn't handle.

"Thanks, Marshall," she said with a smile. "You certainly do build one's confidence. Simpson, get whatever equipment you need and get onboard."

"Yes, sir…er, ma'am," Simpson said gleefully as he began pulling equipment from the supply room outside the hangar.

Kristin had other plans in regard to her equipment. Instead of electronics, she entered her code into the armory door control and went inside. She was only inside for a moment before she emerged with twin plasma pistols at her hip and a broad grin on her face.

The shuttle was ready to go, so she entered it, then reached behind her to shut the hatch. She took a seat right behind the flight crew, where she could keep an eye on things. She adjusted the seat and pulled the harness across her chest, then snapped the buckle into place. "Jakes, whenever you're ready," she said to the pilot.

"You got it, ma'am," Jakes said before activating the engines. "Flight Control, Falcon 129, ready for flight."

"Roger, Falcon 129," came the voice from Flight Control, who was overlooking the hangar deck.

Not another word was spoken before everyone onboard felt the atmosphere being sucked out of the bay and into space. When the process was completed, the twin doors opened, revealing wide open space. Jakes adjusted the helm, and the shuttle rose into flight position. Thrusters were used at the rear of the ship to move it away from the *Bonaventure*. After they cleared the bay, Jakes brought the engines online, and the thrust accelerated the shuttle toward the transport.

"Take us around it," Kristin ordered from over the pilot's shoulder. "I need to record the damage and compare any energy signatures to what's in our databanks."

"Yes, ma'am." Simpson pulled his sensor panel over from the wall to his right. "Recording now."

The shuttle banked around the transport so they could record the attack damage. It then settled over the airlock and docked with a heavy *thud*.

"Clamps are locked on, and pressure's in the green. Ready to move out, Commander Dante," Jakes added as he powered the engines down.

"Great. Good job, Jakes," Kristin said to the pilot as she removed her harness. "Alert the *Bonaventure* that we are entering the ship and will advise on status. Marshall," she said to the big security chief as he checked his weapon, "you and Johnson lead the way. Everyone else, the transport schematics are programmed into your padds. Medical, you come with me. We're heading to the bridge. Engineering teams, take a med tech with you and comb the ship on the way to the engine room. If you spot any survivors, I want to know about it immediately. Remember to stay clear of sections open to vacuum. We don't need any of you floating around out there like space debris."

Everyone nodded, and the two teams set out in opposite directions. Kristin and her team saw their first body on the way to the bridge, shortly after leaving the airlock where the shuttle was parked. The corpses they did come upon were bloody and torn to shreds. She shook her head and tried to imagine what could possibly have slashed and ripped a human body like that. Amazingly, most of the damage appeared to have happened from the inside out, and that made even less sense.

"What the...? Something about this just doesn't add up," Kristin said.

Marshall knelt by a body and turned it over; it was barely recognizable as human. "What could do this, ma'am?" he asked.

The flesh had been torn from the person's head, revealing a bloody skull. Interestingly enough, the lips were mostly in place, still frozen in the scream of what must have been the crewmember's last agonizing moments. One arm was missing, and the other was only holding on by stringy, bloody strands of muscle and flesh, but even that wasn't the most shocking thing about the body. Right in the center of the chest cavity was a hole, the size of a fist. It was perfectly circular, a contrast to the rest of the mutilated mess. Surrounding the large wound were eight smaller ones, about a half-inch or so outside the middle circle.

Kristin knelt by the bodies as one of the forensics personnel of the team took readings and skin samples. "I don't know. It couldn't be pirates, right? Tolliver?" The body looked like as if it had been dropped into spinning fan blades more than once. No matter who they represented, it wasn't the pirate *m.o.*, and none of them were that criminally insane. Something else had committed this heinous act; she was sure of it.

Lieutenant Tolliver graduated first in his class from Harvard Medical and had interned as a medical examiner in one of the more violent sections of Detroit, but he found it hard to think of a body being in worse shape. He knelt by the corpse and pulled a pair of latex gloves and metal forceps out of his bag. He examined the other damage before turning his attention to the circular hole in the dead man's chest. "It's hard to say which of these wounds actually killed him, but I can say for certain that it wasn't this round hole burned through his chest."

"Burned?"

"Yes, Commander," Tolliver replied as he poked the probe deeper into the cavity. "It's not a heat burn though. This was…like some sort of acid. The smaller wounds around it appear to be punctures of some sort."

Kristin watched him poke a little deeper, then noticed his expression change to one resembling surprise. "What is it?"

Tolliver shook his head. "I don't know, ma'am. Feels like small nodules. I'm going to remove a sample." He reached in with the forceps, grabbed hold of one of the round objects lodged deep in the body, and pulled it out. "Simpson, can you reach in my case and get one of those small specimen jars?"

Simpson nodded, happy to help in any capacity, then reached into the forensics case and pulled out the specimen bottle Tolliver had asked for. He unscrewed the top of the small cylindrical contain-er, about the size of a prescription bottle, and handed it to Tolliver. "This one?"

"Perfect. Thanks," Tolliver said. He placed the silvery nodule into it, then put the lid back on and twisted it shut.

"What is that?" Marshall asked, as curious as Kristin was.

"No idea." Tolliver answered coolly. "Shiny though."

"There are more down here!" one of the engineers called from farther down the corridor.

"Let's go," Kristin said quietly as she slowly ambled to her feet. "We've got a lot to do and not much time to do them. For starters, we need to get to that bridge."

Everyone nodded, with the exception of Simpson, who appeared to be about to lose his lunch. She knew things were beginning to get too real for the young lieutenant, and she worried that perhaps she'd made a mistake in bringing him along.

The complement of a transport of that size was twenty-four men and women. They found at least half of them, reduced to piles of dead flesh, before they reached the bridge. They were all like the first, torn to shreds, with holes burned in their chests.

Kristin led the way, but as they neared the bridge door, Marshall raised his plasma rifle and, with a nod and smile to his commander, took the lead. He pulled a small instrument from the belt at his waist and held it in front of the door. It beeped and chirped for a few seconds before he pulled it back and looked at the readout on the screen. "We've got some atmosphere on the other side of the door." He glanced down at the door control and noted that it was shorted out. "Moss, get your butt up here."

Ensign Moss, another of the young crewmembers of the *Bonaventure,* came forward with his engineering toolkit. "Excuse me, sir," he said timidly, trying to get around Marshall's muscular form. He knelt by the door and, without even looking, reached into his tool pouch and pulled out a probe. He moved it over the lock, corner to corner, before looking at the readings. The look on his face screamed confusion as he glanced from Marshall to Kristin and back again.

"Ensign, you got something to say?" Kristin finally said, in no mood for dramatic pauses.

"Yeah, what is it, Moss?" Marshall demanded.

Disproving the old adage that size doesn't matter, Moss turned to Marshall and held up the probe. "You might wanna take a look at this, sir. The door was shorted out from the bridge side, like they were trying to keep someone or something out."

"Can you open it?" Kristin asked, sensing the beginnings of an anxiety attack. *The admiral probably woulda pulled out his gun and shot the poor bastard by now,* she thought.

He turned to her and actually looked a little hurt by her lack of faith in him. "Yes, ma'am," he said with just a tinge of anger in his timid voice.

Kristin and the rest watched as he pulled off the panel and reached in with the probe. She could see the sweat glistening on his brow as he removed the probe and replaced it with his right hand. Moss pushed his hand deeper into the door circuitry, trying to reach the emergency bypass circuit that would allow them to open the door from the outside. They could blast it, but they all knew that might prove deadly to any survivors on the bridge side of the door.

A beeping from her headset alerted her to a call. "Yes?" Kristin said, expecting to hear from the engineering team at the aft end of the ship. "Understood," she said in response to their report that they'd found more bodies on the way to engineering but not a survivor among them. It really came as no surprise to her; after what she'd seen, she doubted they'd find anyone alive onboard.

"More of the same?" Marshall grimly asked, fearing they were in for more carnage when they finally got the bridge doors opened.

"Yep. The engines are damaged as well," replied Kristin. "Moss, any progress with that damn door?"

"Almost got it," the young ensign croaked. "There!"

With a *hiss* followed by a groaning, the door slid open, not all the way ajar, but it gave them more than enough room to gain entry to the command deck of the ship.

Marshall squeezed in first and realized immediately how wrong he was in his preliminary assessment of the bridge. The bridge crew wasn't butchered like the crewmembers they'd found strewn about the corridor. They had similar round holes in their chests, but they looked used up somehow, like ancient remains, almost mummified, as if they'd been dead for years rather than days or hours. They were all still seated at their stations, as if nothing had happened to them. "Geez..." he said, unable to mutter anything more.

"Simpson, pull the sensor tapes. There's got to be something on them about...all this," Kristin said.

Completely taken aback, Simpson seemed rooted in place like a tree, swaying a bit but not moving from his spot.

"Now!" Kristin snapped, hoping to knock him out of the shocked paralysis. "You too, Moss." Brady would be calling from the *Bonaventure* soon, and she needed some solid information for her captain.

They both seemed to snap out of it at the same time. Without a word, Simpson went to the tactical and sensor console, while Moss made his way to the science station.

"Commander?"

"Yes, Tolliver?" Kristin said, thankful that she'd at least have something to send back to the *Bonaventure*. "Report."

"They're all dead, but now I'll at least have a chance to examine a relatively whole body." Tolliver looked down at his scans before continuing, "My best guess is that something attached to them, sucked the life force out, and eventually found its way out through their chests."

"Sucked their life force?" Kristin asked, shaking his head. "Are you crazy, Tolliver, or did you just watch too much sci-fi as a kid? Are you telling me some kind of extraterrestrial lifeform killed the crew?"

"Much that used to be considered science fiction is now reality, Commander," he retorted.

"Touché," Kristin answered, thinking back to her captain's *Enterprise*-inspired chair.

"What I'm saying, Commander Dante, is that this is my best guess." He handed her the data-padd and pointed to the wounds around the hole. "Something grabbed these poor bastards and burned their way in. This is all I can surmise. Whether you believe it or not is entirely up to you."

"Yeah, great."

"What do you want to do, Boss?" Marshall asked.

"Contact *Bonaventure* for orders," Kristin decided. "I want to get the hell off this flying tomb."

"Ma'am!" came the call from one of Tolliver's team. "You need to see this…now!"

Kristin could see that they were standing in front of an open vent, pulling out someone, a woman in uniform. Based on her rank insignia, she appeared to be the second-in-command. She was obviously alive, because she had found a crawlspace to hide in. That was the good news. The bad news was that she seemed catatonic. "Doc, we need you!"

Tolliver came running with his medical bag and dropped down next to woman with a diagnostic scanner in hand. "Her nametag says, 'STACK,'" he said, peering up at Kristin.

"Marshall, have you reached the *Bonaventure* yet?"

"No, Commander. All I'm getting is static."

Kristin tapped her headset and listened. To her horror, she realized that it was more than just static. On the contrary, someone was jamming their signal. "Team Two, drop everything and head back to the shuttle…now!" She received her affirmative before turning back to address her own team. "Collect whatever you can. We're outta here."

Simpson seemed to be standing still, with his head cocked to the side, like a dog listening to an odd noise. "You hear that?" he asked no one in particular.

Kristin stopped and listened. Sure enough, there was a metallic tapping sound coming from the ventilation system above their heads. "Yes, I hear it. What the hell is it?"

Marshall pointed his gun at the sound, and his finger tensed on the trigger. "I don't know, but I've got a really bad feeling about this."

The sound had an interesting effect on Stack. Her eyes opened, and she started screaming. "They're back! They're back! Oh my God! I won't let them take me! Nooo!"

Tolliver attempted to restrain her, but it took three of them to hold her still while he administered a tranquillizer.

"Crap," Moss said weakly, pointing to the command chair.

Everyone looked to where Moss was pointing. The captain was moving, or at least something was moving him. Out of the hole in his chest crawled something horrible. It resembled a large black spider, about the size of a man's fist, but its legs were razor sharp. It was followed by another and another.

Marshall reacted with amazing speed for a man caught in a state of terror. Without hesitation, he fired bolts of plasma energy at the captain's body and into the things that seemed to be feeding off it. He only stopped when there was nothing left of either the captain or the arachnid-looking nightmares that were devouring him. "That should take care of them."

The clicking sound in the walls grew louder, but that was not the worst thing. Tolliver pointed to the other bodies. They were all disgorging the same creatures as the captain, and they looked hungry. Kristin pulled both her weapons out and began shooting at them, and Marshall followed suit. When the ceiling gave way, the bridge was suddenly filled with them.

"Everybody, back to the shuttle…now!"

They ran for the corridor, and Simpson and Moss even found strength in their terror.

"Jakes!" Kristin called into her headset. "Prep for emergency departure the second we're all onboard."

"Affirmative," came the reply from her headset.

She turned and managed to get a few shots off, even while running. The leggy creatures were closing the gap, but Kristin was relieved to look ahead and see that they were almost back at the air-lock. "Run!" she screamed. "Team Two, report!"

"Two, here," a breathless voice answered. "What the hell is going on, ma'am?"

Kristin was about to respond when she heard a scream coming from behind her. "Stevens?" she questioned, believing that was the name of the medical team member who was down on the floor, with a hungry space spider latched onto his chest. The other menaces stopped at the body as the thing on Stevens's changed into a circular black disk and began to eat into his chest. As furious as she was horrified, Kristin brought up her weapon to stop his suffering, but she didn't have to; his screaming suddenly stopped. At that moment, the spiders stopped pursuing the rest of them, and what appeared to be hundreds of them gathered near Stevens, as if protecting him. The remainder of her team, all farther down the corridor, slowed and finally stopped at the airlock hatch.

She turned and saw Marshall standing by her side.

Marshall's face was a blank mask as he pointed at Stevens. "No freaking way."

Stevens was busy pushing himself to his feet. The top of his uniform was burned away, revealing the black creature, with eight wiry legs anchoring it in place. When Stevens finally stood straight, he reached to his chest with both hands. Upon feeling the disk-like creature, he suddenly went rigid.

"Stevens?" Kristin asked, revolted by what she saw. Her weapon was in hand, pointed right at the head of what was once her shipmate.

"My... Oh my God! It's in my head!" he snapped out. "Get out of my head!" Then, without another word, Stevens stopped strug-gling and fell to the deck, as if an invisible puppeteer had cut his strings. After a moment, his eyes opened, and he stood again to face everyone, this time with a smile on his face as he stretched out his arms. "Yes and no, Commander Dante," he said calmly, the sickening grin never straying from his face, "less and more."

"Fuck you," Marshall snapped as he brought up his gun.

"Not yet." Kristin put her hand out to push the barrel of the energy weapon down. They needed to find out what was going on, why the spiders stopped. "Riddles all you got? What are you?"

"No, not riddles. It is simply the truth—or at least enough of it for your infantile minds to grasp." Stevens looked down at the spiders around him and closed his eyes. The creatures moved en masse, about a foot behind him. When he opened his eyes, he looked down at them again. "Better. *We* are the N'Torr, and I know everything this Stevens knows, Commander Dante."

"And what does Stevens get out of this...joining?"

"Bliss," Stevens replied with a smile, "at least for now."

Marshall shook his head. "Bliss? You killed everyone here, and I'm guessing Stevens will end up just like them," he said, inching his gun back up little by little.

"What do you want?" Kristin asked, trying to stifle the tremble in her voice. She was usually capable of pushing fear out of her mind. The admiral had taught his children that fear could make them weak, and that the weak often ended up as the losers. There were no prizes in the admiral's world for second place or weakness, but Kristin couldn't deny that she felt it now. An irrational fear began to creep into her psyche, like that of a child imagining a monster in the closet or under her bed. It was innate fear, the same terror that stretched back to the early days, when cavemen imagined dinosaurs lurking outside their cave. Within seconds, Kristin literally felt the hairs on the back of her neck stand up.

"What do we want?" Stevens finally responded, answering the question with the same question. "We want you, your ship, your planet—everything. In fact, the only reason we exist right now is for you. All of you will be N'Torr, servants of the Jek'Tan."

"Who the hell are the Jek'Tan?" Marshall asked, his gun never wavering.

With both hands, Stevens reached to the black circle burnt into his chest. He looked around and regarded everyone like a child regarding an anthill before stepping on it. "The Jek'Tan are the true gods, the masters of the heavens. They created us, and we serve their will. We are the hand and the fist of God!"

Kristin felt her gun coming up as well, like a knee-jerk reaction to that fear that sickened her. "Why?" she demanded.

Stevens laughed, as if she was a fool. "Because everyone deserves to eat," he said as the spiders began moving again.

"Now?" Marshall asked.

"Now!"

With that, they both began to fire. Marshall's first blast struck Stevens in the shoulder, spinning him into range of Kristin; her shot hit its mark and blasted off the top of his head. His half-decapitated body stumbled back but somehow manage to stand its ground. From what was left of the mouth came an unearthly, high-pitched scream.

Kristin and Marshall bristled at the ear-shattering echo, then fired again, finally blasting it to the ground in several chunks of smoldering flesh and bone. They were shocked to see the spider remove itself from the destroyed body and advance on them, with the arm of eight-legged nightmares in tow.

Marshall kept firing, blast after blast, to little avail. "There are just too damn many!" he yelled.

"Back to the shuttle!" Kristin snapped. The large security man seemed locked in a rage as he mindlessly continued fire.

Kristin punched him in the back of his head to get his attention. "Run! That's an order!"

Marshall blinked twice, as if he'd been awakened by a trance, and they both took off down the corridor, urged on by the clicking sounds that grew ever louder behind them. When they reached the airlock door, both Moss and Simpson popped out into the corridor, each holding a heavy MK-8 assault rifle. They opened fire on the spiders, covering Kristin and Marshall as they ran through the doors and into the shuttle. Noting that they were safe inside, Moss and Simpson followed suit and sealed the airlock behind them.

"Jakes, get us the hell outta here…now! Everyone strap in!" Kristin hurried to her seat and buckled in. She relaxed a bit when she heard the engines whirring to life, but they didn't seem to be building power fast enough. "Why aren't we moving?"

Jakes was working frantically over his flight controls and didn't bother to turn to respond. "The transport docking clamps are refusing to release."

"Commander…" Moss said, standing by the inner shuttle airlock door.

"Moss, you need to sit down," Kristin scolded. "We're about to take off."

"Commander, you need to see this."

"What now?" With a sigh, Kristin unbuckled and ran to the port to see what had sidetracked Moss enough to keep him out of his seat.

"Look at that," he said in awe, pointing.

The spiders had all joined together and now formed a large black mass. They worked in unison, trying to melt the airlock door with the same alien heat that had scalded through the chests of the crew.

Kristin was entranced by it but managed to pull Moss away from his vantage point and shove him toward his empty seat. She then ran to the pilot console and stuck her face right in Jakes's. "You need to break us free right now. I don't care how you do it."

"I know you usually give the orders around here, but you'd best sit down, Commander," Jakes said with a smile, pushing her back. "It's gonna get bumpy."

Kristin landed into her seat with a *thud* that jarred her teeth. She watched as Jakes moved like a man possessed, his hands flying over the controls like those of a mad concert pianist. The sound of the engines grew louder as Jakes applied more and more power from the maneuvering thrusters. The thrusters twisted the shuttle back and forth as it attempted to break the death grip the transport had on them.

"Commander!" Moss yelled from his seat at the rear of the shuttle. "The airlock port is...black."

Kristin looked out in horror and saw that he was right. The spiders had burned their way through the transport airlock and were now attempting to gain entry to the shuttle. She knew if that happened, they'd have nowhere left to run. "Jakes, you need to do it now!" she said. She'd already decided that she'd die before she'd let herself be turned into what Stevens had become, but she certainly preferred to get out of there in one piece.

"Hold on to your panties," Jakes said calmly. "Here we go!"

Kristin heard the sound of metal tearing and was relieved when she felt motion. She held on tightly to one of the cooling pipes as Jakes fought to regain maneuvering control. As the deck righted itself, she made her way back to the airlock port. The only blackness there was peppered with bright stars.

"Course?" Jakes asked when he finally got the ship under control.

Kristin looked at his hands as they brought the engines back under control, the hands of a hero. She couldn't believe it, but he'd somehow managed to save them all. The decision was pretty simple in her mind. "We need to get back to the *Bonaventure*."

"Aye-aye, ma'am. Setting course. ETA thirty-two minutes."

Kristin felt drained, almost like one of the bodies on the transport. She thought of her father and wondered how the admiral would have handled it. *He would have gone down to the last man, sacrificing even himself, to destroy the ship and the creatures onboard,* she finally surmised. She valued life and loyalty a great deal more than her father did, and their command preferences were at the heart of their differences. "Admiral," she said quietly to herself, "you certainly got your conspiracy. I hope you like it." Then, exhausted, she allowed her eyes to close.

Some indeterminable amount of time later, Simpson interrupted her catnap. "Commander..."

"What is it?" she asked in a daze, her sleeping eyes fluttering open. At that moment, she would have killed Simpson in his sleep for a good cup of coffee.

"I'm not getting any further jamming. I think we can reach the *Bonaventure*."

The thought of that pushed the need for coffee out of her mind and made her focus on the task at hand: giving the captain the information he needed about their visit to the transport. She went to the communications panel and switched it to the right frequency. "*Bonaventure*, this is Dante. Come in please."

The response was almost immediate: "This is Brady. What's your status?"

Kristin didn't know where to begin. "Sir, there were these... creatures on the transport. The crew is all dead. We need to go back there and destroy the transport before it's too late."

"There's plenty of time for that, Kristin. Just get back to the ship, and we can discuss it."

"Commander, get up here fast!" Marshall said in a panicked whisper from his place at the flight station.

"What's that I hear, Commander?" Brady inquired over the speaker.

"Hang on, sir." She moved to the pilot station and gave Marshall the most pissed-off look she could manage. "You do know I'm talking to the captain, right? What the hell is it?"

Marshall didn't say a word, but Jakes pointed out the window toward the *Bonaventure*.

Kristin took a look and instantly felt acid creeping from her stomach up her esophagus, carrying the remainder of her breakfast with it. "Sir, we have a bit of an emergency. I'll get right back to you." With that, she closed the connection with Brady and looked out into space at her ship. What should have been a welcome sight only intensified the horror she felt. The *Bonaventure* was docked by a large alien vessel of some kind. She was sure it had to be the same ship that had attacked the transport.

"What now, Commander?" Marshall asked.

"All stop! Hold position." Kristin stared, unblinking, at the two ships, joined in some perverted embrace. The alien ship was huge, at least four or five miles in length, and it dwarfed the ship she'd come from.

"We are so screwed," Jakes added as he throttled back on the engines.

Kristin dropped into the co-pilot seat and let out another huge sigh, this time more from defeat than relief or exasperation. She wasn't sure how the alien ship was able to dock with the *Bonaventure*, but she knew one thing: She did not plan to return to her ship anytime soon. She also had to admit that Jakes was right about them being screwed. Not only that, but she was the commander onboard, and if she didn't think of a way out, they'd soon have plenty of company.

Chapter 4

Mars

Michael made his way out of the city, covering his tracks every step of the way. The impromptu meeting with Kate had been quite a surprise, but he wasn't sure if bumping into his sister was a good or bad thing. She was the security chief on Mars, and her loyalties were in question. *Is she still a Dante, or is she now loyal to Rosten?* He knew she had no reason to be loyal to the Alliance; they'd turned their collective backs on her and tossed her out like day-old garbage. Even their father had abandoned her.

He and Kristin handled things differently. Kristin removed herself to the other side of the system, while he just ignored the admiral. Sometimes, Michael felt like a man in the middle. On one side was the admiral, who'd sent him to Mars to dig up evidence on Rosten's ties to Striker. On the other side was Kate, his sister but quite possibly an enemy. He couldn't help but wonder if it was just another rendition of the game they'd played as kids. As he recalled, those games never worked out in his favor. With so many unknowns afoot, the best he could do was watch his back and hope Kate stayed away.

Leaving the city wasn't difficult, at least not as difficult as getting back in. His papers portrayed him as a contractor and archeologist for the Museum of Martian Antiquities. If anyone bothered to really check his credentials, they'd all point to the museum, as would the old Martian rover reserved for his use. The official destination logged into the nav system was at the base of the Olympus Mons. In reality, he would be altering that course, by more than fifty kilometers south. *Forget artifacts,* he thought with a smirk. *The only digging I'll be doing will be at one of Striker's communication relay stations.*

Michael found the old-style rover parked exactly where he was told it would be. It was somewhat of a relic, left over from the days before the terraforming, but the treads were still deep enough to get him through anything, and the cockpit was still pressurized. Another benefit was that it lacked the electronic advances that would allow anyone to track him across the Martian surface. The only problem with it was that he'd never win a race with any of the newer models, nor would he be able to outgun anything. Stealth was the name of the game.

He climbed aboard and reached into the rear cargo pod to make sure the equipment he required was in place. Both the small plasma pistol and decryptor were contraband, illegal to transport through customs. Such smuggling carried stiff penalties, not to mention a stern talking-to by the security chief, Kate.

Michael climbed into the rover and was happy to see that the solar-powered batteries were already fully charged and ready to go. He hoped there was enough stored power for him to make the round trip, even if there were issues with the twin solar panels mounted to the upper rear of the vehicle.

Michael started the engine and waited for the centuries-old turbine to find its second wind. He would have preferred something a bit more modern, but to keep his cover, he needed a vehicle that his fictional employers could afford on a museum's budget. After a few seconds, the engine smoothed out, the turbines slowing to a steady whine. The beauty of the older rovers was in the ease of driving. There was a simple selector for forward and reverse and a joystick for steering, as easy to control as some 1980s Earth videogame. The only other thing to do was to switch off the transponder and switch on the decoy transmitter, which would give the trackers in the city a false GPS location on him. Kate had always underestimated him, and he hoped that would continue now; he'd learned some new tricks since the last time they'd played this game, but he didn't want her to know it.

Without any distractions, it would take about two hours to get to the relay station. Michael hoped they would be two very boring hours, just a lazy, uneventful jaunt to an empty relay station, with time enough to plan his exit strategy. Once inside, his decryptor would be able to download any and all transmissions stored in the relay and burst the transmission back to the admiral. Depending on the complexity of the download, though, the time inside could vary. With any luck, he'd be back on Earth in four days.

Kate sat in her office, feeling rather useless. Rosten had given her the job as a middle finger to the Earth Alliance forces and little more; it was a position with a title and not one lick of power. She knew she was just a trophy to the system, a turned traitor. The funny thing was that it was really the furthest thing from the truth, and if Rosten or anyone else suspected that she was really working undercover for the Alliance, he would make sure her body was never found again. Right now, there was no higher problem on her list.

Her brother showing up on Mars meant nothing but trouble for her, and the timing couldn't have been worse. It was another distraction, and she could not afford interruptions. Michael was another piece on the board, a pawn she had no desire to lose, and that made her somewhat vulnerable. *This damn cover of mine,* she fumed. *It hangs around my neck like a curse.* The veil of secrecy meant she couldn't tell anyone anything about her assignment, not even him.

To complicate things even further, Marcus always had her under surveillance. When cameras couldn't follow her, some low-level underling was more than happy to stay on the payroll by watching her every move. It wasn't that Clayton Rosten didn't trust her loyalty; rather, it was that jealousy made Marcus Rosten a lunatic of epic proportions.

Even though she was on a tight leash, with only the control Marcus would allow, Kate knew she still had full access to all security feeds, both in the city and in the areas controlled outside of it. From her terminal, she cycled through the cameras outside the city and at checkpoints leading out. Michael's request was sitting on her desk, with an approval by the Department of Antiquities, allowing him travel to the Olympus Mons dig site. All the paperwork came from the proper channels, and there was no reason for her to refuse the request. The only problem with it was that she knew her brother was not an archeologist, and she also knew the dig site was not his final destination. She regretted not sharing her thoughts as to the real reason for his visit with him. *Maybe he would abort his mission if he knew that I suspect the truth,* she reasoned. Then again, there was no way Michael would trust her, especially after their conversation over mucha.

The GPS tracker in the rover showed that he was heading in the direction of Olympus Mons, but that was amateur stuff at best; tricking a GPS tracking system was part of their first-year Intelligence training. There were other ways to track him, and if her brother was going where she suspected he was, he was in terrible danger. He sometimes put too much faith in modern technology, depended on it too much and expecting it to always work properly. He also failed to realize that most of it could be easily circumvented. Naiveté would be Michael's undoing, but Kate, on the other hand, wasn't as trusting of anything or anyone.

The rover was one of the few vehicles of its type still in operation on Mars. Centuries earlier, when the first explorers settled on the red planet, the model was considered a workhorse, built to take a beating and pressurized to Earth normal atmosphere. It provided those early pioneers with the ability to travel the rocky, rough surface. Now, though, Mars had an atmosphere, and the need for such a vehicle was unnecessary. In fact, only a few in working order remained. Those that did operated with a turbine system that tended to give off a particular heat signature. It was that signature that would be Kate's answer as to the whereabouts and plans of her fibbing little brother. Satellites in orbit were equipped with sensing equipment that would allow her to lock in on that signal and track Michael's rover in real time. As much as she hated being distracted by side quests, she had to keep him out of trouble.

It wasn't just the fact that he was family; if Michael was caught, he could blow her cover, and that was a situation she wasn't quite ready for. She knew there was a connection between Rosten and Striker. Striker's support for Rosten's family went back generations, which was no secret, but there was little to no evidence for the things she innately knew but couldn't quite put her finger on yet. Deaths and disappearances out in the blackness of space was a fact of expansion into the unknown, but the regularity left something to be considered. Transports to the outer rim disappeared too frequently, and the ability to crew those runs was only made more difficult by that publicly recognized fact.

Kate's hands played over the keyboard as she reconfigured the satellite for its new task. She placed a minor subroutine in the coding, commanding it to scan five other frequencies as well. That way, if anyone was monitoring her activity, they wouldn't be able to concentrate on one thing in particular. She pressed the enter key, and a map of the Martian surface appeared on her screen. The other five frequencies revealed nothing, but the primary one showed a small, glowing blip on her map. It was moving at a steady pace, albeit not in the direction of the dig at Olympus Mons.

"No, no, no!" She growled at the monitor. If she could have reached into the screen and pulled out that blinking blip just so she could slap the shit out of the person it represented, she would have.

Michael was heading to one of Rosten's deep space communications relay stations, and not even she had the loyalty creds to go there unescorted. *The admiral was right to send him,* she thought, because if there was any evidence to connect Rosten, Striker, and Stratton with the missing ships and dead crews, he would find it there. The only problem was that the place was equipped with better security than the Alliance capital. Everyone thought it was a low-priority station, but that was what they were supposed to think.

It also bothered Kate because it was an evidence goldmine she had intended to hit herself. If her father had waited just another week, he would have had his evidence, in addition to a living, breathing son. Kate sat back in her chair and thought about that. There were various reasons why she couldn't let her brother die. For one thing, Michael was family. For another, there would be too many questions why a close family member of hers ended up in a high-security facility. Even if that news didn't get her killed, she would never be trusted with anything again, and she'd be promptly kicked out of her comfy place in Rosten's inner circle. The point was moot though, because she wasn't going to let anything happen to her little brother, no matter how stupid he was. The admiral was not a fool, and he had to know that sending Michael up there might turn into a suicide mission; obviously, her father thought it was worth the death of his own son to stop Rosten and Striker. That alone was enough to speed up her timetable.

The first thing she had to do was catch up with the rover Michael was driving, so she could stop him from reaching the relay station. Kate hoped he'd believe that she was a double-agent and that her plan to gain access to the station was better than his. He had a head start but was still more than ninety minutes away. There was no way she could catch up to him by ground, but her ship could overtake him in minutes. The *Alexa* was a scout she'd acquired from her father when she graduated from the Academy. Evers and Tobias modified the ship and supplied the WMD she was eventually accused of trying to sell from its small cargo hold. It was fast and had some bite, but the best thing about it was that it was still all hers. The Alliance allowed her to take it, and for some reason, Rosten allowed her to keep it, even though it was kept under guard unless she requested its use. She had more than enough reason to request it now.

Time to leave, she thought as she grabbed her sidearm and headed for the door. The first thing she had to do was lose her shadow before she could make a break for the hangar and her ship. After that, she'd play the rest as it came.

"Where are you going, Dante?" asked the gruff voice behind her, a voice that belonged to her deputy. Murt was huge, and at first glance, it appeared that they'd somehow managed to squeeze an ape into a security uniform. Kate would have preferred the ape for a variety of reasons: First, he was more intelligent, and second, he simply smelled better. Murt was there for one reason, and that was to babysit and report her every move back to Marcus Rosten.

"Why do you care, Murt? And by the way, that's 'Chief Dante' to you."

It was a little game they always played: Murt would try to show that, regardless of her title, he was still superior to her. Kate, on the other hand, found it amusing to keep reminding him of just how stupid he was. Murt could probably tear her in half if he ever got his hands on her, but Kate had fought bigger and definitely brighter.

Murt let out a laugh for an answer, then plopped his large behind down on the corner of her desk. His chuckle reminded her of an old locomotive running out of steam. "Very funny, Dante. Mr. Rosten wants to see you right now."

Hmm. That's quite...unforeseen, Kate thought to herself. The "mister" was a reference to Clayton and not Marcus, whom Murt usually referred to by his first name. If Clayton wanted to see her, it could mean almost anything, from wanting company for lunch to murdering her. "What does he want?"

"Didn't say," Murt answered flatly. "He only said to make sure you are delivered to him immediately."

"Tell him I'll be right there," Kate said with a smile as she turned for the door, hoping she'd be lucky enough to make it to the hangar first.

"Wait!" Murt snapped. "Me and Costello," he said, pointing to the sergeant, who was sitting at his desk, watching a replay of some fight from the night before.

Larry quickly shut off the video and stood at attention at the mention of his name.

"We'll escort you to where you need to go. Mr. Rosten knows how…distracted you can get," Murt announced.

Kate stopped smiling and nodded. She had nothing against Costello. He was a good kid and just wanted a kiss-ass career in Mars security. He, like everyone else, was a bit star struck by her past, but he was scared to death of Murt. All Kate would do was go along with it and hope she could get to her ship and then to Michael before it was too late. The act would burn her bridges, but it could not be avoided. She hoped Evers and Tobias would understand and extract her from the situation before the shit really hit the fan, but there were no guarantees of that.

At times like that, she was truly jealous of her sister Kristin. As kids, there were the typical sibling rivalries, to the point of wanting to kill each other every now and then, but they still managed to be there for each other, whenever either of them needed help. Now, in adulthood, Kristin opted for another route aboard the *Bonaventure*, exploring the outer system and beyond. As she walked between the two large security men, Kate would have bet almost anything that her sister was having a much better time of things than she was at the moment.

Chapter 5

From the co-pilot seat on the Falcon, Kristin stared out the forward viewport at both the *Bonaventure* and the alien ship. Captain Brady, or the thing she suspected was attached to him, was on hold, waiting for an answer from her.

"Commander, the captain is requesting status and wondering why we've stopped."

Kristin nodded at Simpson and keyed her transmitter. "Sir, this is Dante. I'm having a bit of trouble with my headset. Do you mind if we go to visual?"

"We can't, Kristin," Brady finally responded after a long pause. "There's too much interference. Why have you stopped?"

Kristin looked quickly to Simpson, who shook his head. Whatever Brady's reasoning was for refusing to go to a video feed, it had nothing to do with interference. Nevertheless, she answered, "Understood, sir." She then signaled Simpson to move the conversation to the shuttle speakers. "We're having a...thruster issue, sir. Jakes tells me we have a short in one of the thruster control relays, and it's causing the system to overheat. It shouldn't take too long to fix it." She looked over at Jakes and was rewarded with a look of disbelief and a hand slapped against his forehead in disgust.

"I'll send a repair team to assist, along with an escort. We need you back here ASAP. Brady, out."

Before Kristin could protest, there was a *click* as the transmission was cut off. In a huff, she removed the headset and tossed it into the corner of the cabin. At this point, they needed information, and they needed it badly. "Tolliver, how's your patient?" she demanded.

"Still unconscious," the doctor responded from the rear of the shuttle as he set up a makeshift IV to try to restore fluids and ease her out of shock. Only three of the engineers had made it back to the shuttle from the eight-man search-and-rescue team Kristin had sent to the aft end, and Tolliver had given them all a brief examination to make sure none of the alien parasites had made it onboard, at least not attached to any of them.

Simpson and Moss came forward to join the command crew.

"He knows we know, doesn't he?" Simpson asked.

"Well, he knows we're not possessed by spiders, right, Commander?" Marshall added, casting Kristin an uneasy glance.

"I don't know who knows what. Hell, I don't even know what to think anymore," she said, her gaze still fixated on the two ships. Nothing she had trained could have prepared her for any of it. Every course she'd ever taken on first contact with aliens was theoretical at best. She was sure Kate would know what to do; her older sister always did. She also considered Kate a hero, regardless of the nasty rumors about her. Michael and Kristin both looked up to their older sister, with good reason, especially after their mother died. The admiral, their father, had sat by and watched them accuse his daughter of treason, and he did nothing to stop it. It took Rosten, a criminal, to get her out of the trouble she found herself in. Any of them—Kate, Michael, the admiral, or even that sleazy Rosten—would be able to figure out a plan for getting out of such a precarious situation, but Kate was at a loss. She looked around at several pairs of questioning eyes, all demanding answers from her, and she was ill prepared to give them any. They would die or worse, all because of her ineptitude.

"Commander," Jakes said, interrupting her self-pity, "sensors are reading a launch from the *Bonaventure*."

"What?" Kristin responded, trying to snap out of her depressed haze.

Jakes pointed to the tracking display on his board. "I've got three targets vectoring in on us, ETA eighteen minutes."

Simpson rose up and ran for his seat. He threw his body down in it and swung the tactical panel over toward him, taking note of the readout. From the look on his face, he didn't like what he saw. "The skipper lied. There's not a repair shuttle in the bunch. I'm showing a Falcon assault transport and two starfighters, closing in fast!"

"Shit," Jakes murmured as he brought the engines up to full power again.

"Jakes, what the hell are you doing?" Kristin asked.

Jakes was feeling especially angry as he pointed in the general direction of his former command ship. "There's only one reason for a Falcon and two starfighters to come at us like that, and as Simpson pointed out, it's not a mission of friendship and repair. The Falcon is carrying someone to forcibly board us. Anybody here think that's really gonna work out? The starfighters are to make sure we don't run, at least not far. No matter what, the odds aren't good for this shuttle or for us. You told me what happened to Stevens, and I, for one, don't see that happening to anyone here without a fight."

Kristin couldn't argue with any of it. Jakes was right, and it was time to act. For the first time since the whole sordid ordeal began, she finally understood with crystal clarity what Kate would do. "Everyone to your seats and strap in! This is going to get rough, boys and girls."

Jakes started throwing switches as the engines came online to full power. "Setting course at 180 degrees and engines to full."

"No, Jakes, I didn't say that. Engines to one half, and set a course for the *Bonaventure*."

Jakes swiveled in his seat to face her, his face red with the effort of holding back what he really wanted to say to his superior officer. "Commander, with all due respect, that's fuckin' crazy, a suicide mission. You're gonna get us all killed if you—"

"Mr. Simpson," Kristin interrupted, "raise the Falcon and let them know we have completed repairs and do not require their assistance. We will head back to the *Bonaventure* and dock under our own power."

"Commander? Are you s-sure?" Simpson stuttered, not sure what to do. The logical plan was to run, and she was commanding him to do just the opposite.

"Do it," Kristin ordered calmly. She then turned to Jakes and answered his look with one of her own. "You have your orders, too, Jakes."

"This is insane," he mumbled as he reoriented the ship back on course for the *Bonaventure* and the alien vessel docked with her. "I hope there's more to your plan than a death wish."

"Much more," she said with a smile as the plan began to solidify in her head. The shuttle they were in was of the same class as the Falcon and was combat ready; that would work to her advantage. "Mr. Marshall…"

"Yes, Commander?" Marshall said from his seat. He was following along, trying to read what Dante had in mind. If she had lost her mind, he would need to act in the best interests of the crew, but before committing mutiny, he had to give her a chance.

"Please take your position in the upper gun port and wait for my orders."

Marshall didn't move at first. He had a great deal of respect for his commander, especially considering the family she came from. The Dantes had a long history of pulling victory out of the backside of failure, and he had to respect that. "What's the plan, ma'am?"

Jakes swiveled around and decided to add his opinion. "I think we'd all like to know that, Commander."

The rest of the crew had stopped what they were doing and turned to listen in.

They were still fifteen minutes from the *Bonaventure*; Kristin could see the other Falcon and the two starfighters assuming escort positions next to them. She nodded at her crew and explained, "You all can see what we're up against. We were drawn out here so they could take the *Bonaventure*. The only reasonable motive for that would be so they could commandeer the *Bonaventure* to get passed Alliance security. Once they hit Mars or Earth, there will be no stopping them from spreading."

"A Trojan Horse," Moss correctly observed.

Kristin nodded. "There's no way such a huge alien ship could get through without a quarantine and major investigation. The fleet would just blast it out of space. On the other hand, the *Bonaventure* can approach either Earth or Mars unchallenged, and with those things in possession of the crew, there'll be nothing to stop them."

"So what do you suggest?" Marshall asked, glad he'd waited. Her plan was preferable to running, as he'd never been one to retreat from a fight.

Kristin brought up a diagram of the *Bonaventure*. "We have two missiles in our armament, as well as the plasma turret gun."

Simpson shook his head. "The missiles won't be enough to destroy either ship."

Kristin smiled and nodded. "I know. I want to use one missile to take out her main engine and the other to destroy the conduit relays that power her communications and sensor suite."

Jakes began to slowly clap his hands. "Bravo!" he said sarcastically. "But just how are *we* supposed to survive this kamikaze maneuver of yours?"

"Hopefully, with enough time to run and hide," she answered. "We all can't land in the hangar bay at the same time. Our escort will have to peel away sooner or later to let us land. At that time, we'll fire the first missile and take out the power conduits that run outside the bay from fore to aft. That will blind the sensors and cut off communication with the escorts. In the confusion, and with Marshall in the turret to cover us, we can head aft, for the main engine. Once we're in range, we can fire the second missile, break away, and run like a bat out of Hell. The end result is that the *Bonaventure* will be incapable of pursuit, communications, or launching any more ships after us."

"What about the escorts?" Tolliver asked. "I may not be from a military family, but anybody can see that those starfighters are faster and have more than enough weaponry to blast us out of space. Then there's that gargantuan alien ship. What if that monster comes after us?"

Jakes decided to answer for her, even if he was overstepping his bounds. "Marshall can take care of the escorts with his turret gun. Worst-case scenario, they'll be so disoriented by the lack of communications that we'll be long gone by the time they discover our position. As far as the alien ship, by the time it cuts loose from the *Bonaventure,* we'll be long gone. Did I cover all that, Commander?"

"That's a lot of fancy flying, "she calmly said to the pilot. "Think you can handle it, Matthew?"

Jakes smiled broadly for the first time. "Sounds like fun…and call me 'Matt'!"

Somehow, the fear Kristin felt melted away, replaced by a newfound confidence. *Maybe there is something to this DNA thing,* she pondered, then immediately resumed her commanding tone. "Everyone take your stations. Mr. Simpson, you are our main man on this. It's your job to keep track of everything out there and to make sure those missiles actually hit their mark. You're okay with that, right?"

"Yes, ma'am!" Simpson snapped as he locked the firing computer on all specified targets and fed the data for the escorts to Marshall in the gun turret. The multi-use turret weapon was both ground and space capable; it would serve the latter purpose on this particular assault. For their eventual escape to succeed, they had to be able to disable the escort ships at the very least.

Kristin stared at her operations board, analyzing the tactical readouts from Simpson's station. They were getting close and were currently in range of the *Bonaventure's* weapons. At that range, just one hit would leave only floating vapor and debris in its wake, and that was an unsettling thought. Part of her wanted to keep the loss of life to a minimum, but in the end, she had to prevent them from reaching Earth—or at least delay them until she could send a proper warning. Not only that, but Stevens had mentioned that mysterious Jek'Tan. He spoke the name with a bit of reverence. *Are they the true threat behind the N'Torr? First things first,* she thought as she turned her attention back to the tactical display.

"We're getting closer," Jakes reminder her from the pilot seat. He already had the shuttle on final approach, and the landing bay doors opened wide in anticipation of their arrival.

"Understood." Kristin knew the attack had to be timed perfectly. She watched as the three sensor tracks of their escort pulled away to allow the shuttle room to enter the bay. They moved themselves into a holding pattern until it was their turn to follow.

"Falcon 129, this is docking control. We have you on approach."

"Affirmative. We are on approach," Jakes answered, keeping his eye on the power conduits as they ran the length of the bay exterior. "It's now or never!"

Kristin waited till she was sure of the target, but she knew if she hesitated too long, they'd be trapped in the hangar bay, with no way out. "Stand by to fire." She took a deep breath, waited for the precise second, and commanded, "Fire! Jakes, now! Full power to the engines!"

One of the two missiles fired from the Falcon's starboard weapons pod as Jakes threw the shuttle into a high speed and turned away from the hangar. The missile struck its intended target and illuminated the hangar bay in orange fire, and that meant they also had to contend with the concussive force from the missile impact explosion.

"We have a hit!" Simpson shouted, then immediately fed the next set of target coordinates into the remaining missile in the weapons pod.

Kristin was prepared to call out to Marshall in the turret, but that was unnecessary; he was already firing at their escort, who had returned and was now in pursuit. "Jakes, get us into position to fire at the engine."

As if to answer for him, the shuttle rocked from a near miss, courtesy of one of the fighters. The burning smell of smoke wafted into their nostrils as one of the electronic panels shorted out.

Damn, Kristin thought. *We have to survive long enough to finish what we started.* "Please hold together that long," she whispered to the ship, watching some of the wires and controls melt before her. "Jakes! Hurry up, would you? We won't survive many hits like that."

"I am trying. Just a little, uh…busy right now," he snapped as he rolled the shuttle on its axis.

"Can you please keep us level," Marshall yelled from the turret. "It's hard enough to hit 'em without being caught in a damn barrel roll! Are you tryin' to get us killed or what?"

"Yeah?" Jakes snapped back. "Well, it'd be even harder to hit them if they turn us into space dust first! How about less talk and more shooting, gunner?"

Even with all the bouncing, Marshall was able to connect with the other Falcon and one of the starfighters. The Falcon had slowed its pursuit, and the starfighter was now cartwheeling off into space. The other fighter continued firing, albeit not effectively; their lack of a weapons lock was assumed to be the result of losing communication with the *Bonaventure*.

Kristin watched as Jakes tried to position the ship for their final missile fire at the engines. Docked the way she was, the *Bonaventure* at least presented a stable target for both Jakes and Simpson, who had his hand on the firing button. The blown conduit had actually done more damage than she'd foreseen, and that was good news for them. Not only were sensors and communications out, but it appeared that the feedback from the explosions had taken out main power as well, disarming the vessel of its defensive systems and weapons in the process.

She had to admit that Jakes was a master in the pilot seat. The only other person she knew who could fly a ship with such precision was her sister. Kristin could see the rear of the ship and looked back at Simpson, who nodded back at her. There really wasn't much to say; both men knew what to do.

Suddenly, there was another hit, and smoke filled the compartment.

"Fire!" shouted one of the engineers as he grabbed an extinguisher and quickly went to work to put it out.

Kristin could feel the ship slow. They had taken a hit to the main engine or one of the subsystems and were losing power. "Jakes!" she snapped at the pilot.

"I know," Jakes snapped back as he activated auxiliary power and transferred it to the engines. "Marshall! Buddy! I need you to get that fighter off our tail—now!"

"Roger that," Marshall acknowledged. "You do know that's kinda been my goal all along?" Concentrating on the targeting display in the turret, he cut loose with another stream of energy; meeting the fighter head on. The small craft disintegrated into a million small pieces and floated off. He could swear he could see a body, but tried to put that out of his mind—if they survived this, he'd mourn for his friends later.

Kristin saw the look on his face as he returned from the turret and buckled himself back into his seat.

"You had no choice," she said to him, trying to sound as comforting as she could under the circumstances.

"Did I?" He said in disgust. "Maybe he didn't have one of those things on him. Maybe he was just following orders."

"I hate to interrupt, but we are losing power fast," Jakes called back.

Simpson scanned for his target and found it. The heat from the main engines painted a steady lock. "We have a lock."

"Fire," Kristin said again. All the excitement and urgency had bled from her, leaving her empty. She agreed with Marshall and his assessment that they were possibly shooting at uninfected friends. Unfortunately, it had to be done—for the greater good. She felt the shuttle change course as it went down and to the port, away from the ships.

"We have a hit," Simpson added quietly as the light from the explosion filled the starboard viewports.

"Commander, you got a minute?" Jakes asked.

"Sure," Kristin answered, then moved up front and sat down in the co-pilot seat. "Report."

Jakes smiled and shook his head. "I've got good news and bad news. What do you want first?" he asked.

Kristin was in no mood for games but replied almost automatically. "What's the good news?"

"Well, before they went down after that last hit, our sensors reported that we pretty much accomplished what you wanted. The *Bonaventure* is temporarily out of commission."

"For how long, do you think?"

Jakes did some math in his head before turning back to Kristin. "Simpson and Moss can probably confirm this, but I'd say we're lookin' at a minimum of three days before they can repair enough of the damage we caused to get underway."

Kristin nodded. "Great. At least that buys us some time. What's the bad news?"

"Basically," Jakes answered with a laugh, "it's everything else. Communications and sensors are out. The engines took a beating, and my board's lighting up with red lights like a damn Christmas parade. We won't be going anywhere very far or very fast. Not only that, but you know the *Bonaventure* is gonna come looking for us once the hangar bay is operational."

"That it?"

"I wish," he said with a sigh. "We're venting atmosphere. It's slow, but it's something we're gonna have to worry about pretty soon. Right now, life support is compensating, but at the rate we're losing power, that can't last long."

"Recommendations?"

Jakes let out a soft chuckle again. "You might remember that I already gave mine. I thought we shoulda started running right off the bat, but right now, that's a pretty moot point. I can get Simpson, Moss, and the rest of the engineering guys together to start the repairs, but the only way I'm gonna get the leak or the engine damage repaired is to land us someplace so I can access it from the outside."

"Where do you suggest we go?"

"I'm not sure you want me to answer that."

"I wouldn't have asked if I didn't. Now where?" Kristin snapped, her patience quickly draining.

Jakes activated one of the monitors that was previously used for the currently nonoperational sensors and brought up a display of the outer solar system. "This isn't common knowledge, but there's a small decommissioned military outpost between the orbits of Neptune and Uranus. It was set up back in the early days, when the Alliance felt they needed to keep better watch on the mining colonies near the system rim. It was also a stepping-off station for ships on long trips from Mars or Earth before current engine technology rendered it obsolete."

"I thought the Alliance scrapped all those, so they can't be used by pirates or other unfriendlies," Kristin said.

"Yeah, well, the government's real good at cover stories," Jakes replied with a coy smile. "I trained out here and know for a fact that it's still there." He stared at Kristin for a moment as she bit her lip, wrinkled her brow, and weighed their options. "Listen, Commander. We don't really have a lot of choices here. Not many places within reach have the facilities to help with repairs, and I'd hate for the engines to cut out in the middle of space. At the station, we'll have auxiliary power, and at least it'll be some place to hole up till we can fix the ship and warn the Alliance that the *Bonaventure* isn't flying the friendly skies anymore.."

Kristin knew it was a literal shot in the dark, but if Jakes was right, it would be the perfect place to set down and make repairs to the Falcon. On the other hand, if he was wrong, they would be stuck in the middle of nowhere, facing a slow death sentence as their life support systems waned and the rest of their air leaked into space. In spite of the cons, it was the best plan for the moment, perhaps even worthy of a Dante. "What about the *Bonaventure*?" she asked.

Jakes thought for a moment and shook his head. "I doubt that anyone on that ship will even remember it, especially with those spider things stuck to their chests. I figure they've got more important things to worry about."

"Jakes, I don't think you understand. Is this place still listed in Alliance databanks?"

Jakes nodded as his smile faded into a frown.

Kristin shook her now-pounding head. He was right in saying that had no other choice, but if Brady found them there, they'd never survive. "Do it," she finally conceded.

"Yes, ma'am," Jakes said, then adjusted his course and put everything he had into the engines. "ETA at present max speed, about two hours."

Kristin nodded without answering and left her co-pilot seat to head for the rear of the shuttle. She wanted to talk to Tolliver about his patient and the prospect of waking her to see if she could tell them anything. At that point, any information about their mysterious enemy would be a big help and would give her something to concentrate on while the men made the necessary repairs.

She stopped briefly at the equipment locker, removed a water ration, and took a quick drink. She had forgotten how thirsty she was, but the cool liquid felt good on her parched throat. Kristin found it somewhat humorous that thoughts of her family always entered her mind during tough times. Maybe I shoulda gone into a nice, cushy Intelligence job like Mike and Kate, she mused. She thought of Kate. While her sister had gone through some pretty tumultuous times of her own, at that current moment, Kristin imagined her sitting in her office on Mars, with her feet propped up on the security chief desk and a mojito in her hand. Looking out the viewport at the visible damage, she just shook her head and laughed. "Oh, that would be the life."

Chapter 6

Time was becoming an issue for Kate as she and her escort arrived outside Clay Rosten's private quarters, if they could be called that; it was something akin to referring to the ocean as a fishing hole. She had gone with Murt and Costello willingly, albeit hoping there'd still be time to get to her ship and reach her brother. Worst-case scenario, Rosten was now aware of her undercover role and planned to kill her on sight. For the moment, there was still time to reach Michael, but only if she lived beyond the next few minutes.

The decorator seemed to be early Caligula; she was happy that she'd never been forced to go beyond the gym-sized sitting room. One thing Rosten shared with Striker was a love for antiques. In fact, the two of them had a rivalry over many of the pieces that ended up on the market. The most impressive addition had to be the waterfall that flowed from ceiling to floor.

"Sit," Murt commanded, then pushed Kate down onto the expensive couch.

"Murt," Kate said, rubbing her shoulder, "if you touch me again, I'll kill you."

"Hear that, Costello?" Murt said, letting out a brief laugh. "Little Girl Dante's gonna kill me." He then stopped and turned to face Kate, his face completely serious. "Maybe I should touch you then, so you can give it a try. Might be kinda…exciting for both of us."

"Enough of that!" snapped Clayton Rosten as he entered from the other side of the large living area. "None of that here, Murt. Just take your man and go back to the security shack."

"Yes, sir," Murt answered meekly. He, like everyone else on Mars, lived in fear of the entire Rosten clan, but the most frightening of all was the patriarch. Murt gestured Larry Costello to the door, and they both turned to leave.

"Ba-bye now," Kate said to the men, wearing a snide grin on her face. "Thank you, Clayton. I appreciate you stepping in before I had to pound him into your carpet. A big goon like that would have made quite a mess."

Rosten turned to Kate and smiled. "You're most welcome, Katherine. Murt is strong enough to do whatever I ask of him, but unfortunately, he hasn't the brains to match his brawn. He's too stupid to control himself." Rosten walked over to the bar and started to pour himself a drink. "Can I get you anything, Katherine?"

"No thank you, sir," she answered, preferring to stay clear-headed in order to help her brother. "Why do you keep him around? He doesn't do much other than babysit me and question my authority, the authority *you* gave me."

Rosten shrugged. "I don't really know. He and Marcus grew up together. For some reason that escapes me, they remain friends. My son asked me to give Murt a security job, so I did."

"You do know my job as security chief is a farce and that your son has that creature watching me every moment of the day, right?"

Rosten drained his drink in one swallow before filling up the glass with more amber-colored liquor from the decanter at the bar. "Yes, I've heard such rumors. You must understand, Katherine. The circumstances that brought you here have not placed you in a very good light with many of my people. They refuse to take orders from someone they consider a traitor, someone they believe sold out her own people prior to coming here."

Kate was about to respond to that, but Rosten held up a hand to silence her.

"Katherine, they don't know you like I did or like I do now. I know how much you hate the Alliance, and I cannot blame you after those things they made you do before the two us of reached… an accommodation. However, I will talk to Marcus and see if we can straighten this out."

"Thank you again, Clayton," she said with a smile. It wasn't a look of gratitude; rather, she grinned at the irony, for it was probably going to be her last day on the job anyway. "You wanted to see me, Clayton?"

Rosten downed his second drink as quickly as he'd gulped the first. "Yes. First, Katherine, I want you to know that you are like a daughter to me. I have something to tell you, and I wanted to tell you personally, before you hear it from the news services."

"What, Clayton? What are you talking about?"

Rosten poured another drink, but this time, he left it to sit on the counter by the bar. "It seems there was an accident on Earth, an explosion, at the Alliance Intelligence offices."

Kate felt the strength drain out of her as her throat tightened. "My father?" Her mouth was dry, as if she'd swallowed a handful of Martian dust.

Rosten nodded. "I'm sorry. From what I understand, he was in a briefing with two high-ranking Intelligence officers. The explosion destroyed the floor of their rendezvous, as well as several floors above and below."

Kate couldn't believe what she was hearing. *The admiral? Dead? But how?* She fought the tears that were welling in her eyes; it was not the time nor the place to show weakness. For years, she'd listened to her father's conspiracy theories about coups and accidents happening to those who got too close, and most had laughed them off as delusional. *Who did he talk to in Intelligence? Who would have listened to him?* "Do they know the cause of the explosion?" she asked, knowing damn well that it was an order from Striker or Rosten or maybe even that moron, Stratton, on the moon.

"No," Rosten lied. "They think it might have been an electrical fire or a gas leak, but no one knows for sure yet. I'll check my sources on Earth. If I hear anything, you'll be the first to know."

You do that, she thought, though she had every intention of finding out for herself. That was the only way to discover the truth, and only God would be able to help anyone who dared to get in her way. "Do they know who my father was meeting with?"

Rosten picked the drink up from the counter and offered it to Kate.

She shook her head, refusing the alcohol.

Rosten nodded and swallowed his third glassful down. "Why do you ask?" he inquired, with a lilt of suspicion in his voice.

Kate knew Clayton Rosten was legendary for his drinking, as well as his whoring. She felt honored, since there was no whore in sight. This drinking was a special occasion, possibly the only way he could fake any empathy for her loss. "I had a few friends in Intelligence. I'm just curious if I knew either of the two."

"Hmm. Well, I suppose we all need friends from time to time," Rosten said with a nod as he filled another glass, his fourth. He perched his body on the ornate barstool, another remarkable antique, and took a sip before setting the glass down. "I believe they were colonels, Tobias and Evers. Ring a bell?"

Kate felt the panic begin to rise to the surface but managed to keep it at a level she could control. If Tobias and Evers were meeting with her father, she was sure that meant they all suspected something. *Could the admiral have finally figured out that his daughter isn't the traitor he thought I was? Could they have told him about their plan and my part in it?* She found it difficult to dismiss it as mere coincidence that the trio of men who were all so key in an investigation of Striker and Rosten had died together in an explosion.

"No," she lied. "They probably hung out in different circles than I did." Her safety net, as well as her father, had disappeared forever, in a heartbeat. Evers and Tobias were not only her controllers; they were also the only ones who knew she was undercover and that she was not really the traitor her own flesh and blood had pegged her as. Without them to cover for her and eventually clear her name, she would continue carrying the slimy reputation of a traitor to the Alliance and a criminal. The time to grieve for her loss would come, but at the moment, she needed to concentrate on saving the living, and she had to get to Michael before it was too late. There was a high probability that if Striker knew about Evers, Tobias, and her father, he also knew Michael was on Mars, and Kate wasn't about to lose another member of her family today.

"I understand, Katherine. If there is anything I can do for you, please let me know." Rosten slowly got to his feet and put a hand out on the countertop to stop himself from falling. "Please see yourself out." With that, he turned unsteadily and made his way to the master bedroom on the other side of the waterfall. Whether there was anyone waiting for him was anyone's guess; Kate refused to speculate on Rosten's whores.

After the door shut, Kate took a second to steady her own nerves before rising to her feet. *As a matter of fact, there is something you can do for me, old man,* she thought as she opened the door and stepped out into the corridor. *You can die for me, along with Striker, Stratton, and whoever else is involved. I swear, whatever you bastards have going, I'll burn it to the ground.*

After she found Michael and got them off Mars, her next order of business would be to locate Kristin. Her father was right about two things: First, something was going to happen and happen soon; and second, she could not trust anyone. At the moment, her lack of trust was the easy part; that was really what had kept her alive over the last year, and she wasn't quite ready to let go of it.

She left the luxury building and made her way to the bay, where her ship was parked. She needed to pick up some weapons along the way; she had a feeling she would need one soon, and Murt hadn't allowed her to take one to her rendezvous with Rosten. Luckily, there were drops around the city where she managed to stash weapons, just in case things started spiraling out of control, as they were now. As much as she wanted to return to her office and blast a round into the thick skull of Murt's forehead, she knew she'd have to save that pleasure for another day. Michael was the priority now.

Rosten walked into his bedroom and shut the door behind him. He knew he'd had a bit too much to drink in front of Katherine, but he couldn't handle the conversation sober—neither what he had to tell her nor what he could not.

"Did you tell her?" asked the voice through the monitor behind him.

He turned and pulled the video screen over and looked upon the handsome face of Ethan Striker, wondering how long he'd been waiting there. "Yes."

"And what was her reaction?" Striker appeared impatient as he waited for the answer.

"She was…upset. Did you expect her to react otherwise?" Rosten looked at the picture on the screen through his bloodshot eyes and wanted to throw a fist at it. "You killed her father."

Striker looked at Rosten and shook his head. "You're a pathetic drunk," he said and took no delight in the smile that crept across the older man's face. "What is so funny?"

"Funny? Of course I'm drunk. You think I'd want to have this discussion with you sober?"

"You're right. It shouldn't surprise me. You come from a family of lushes," Striker responded flatly.

"You don't even know what a dangerous game you're playing, Striker."

"Katherine Dante is a trained Intelligence operative. *How,* exactly, did she react?" Striker asked, ignoring Rosten's remark.

"Calmly but surprised. She may have been lying about not knowing Tobias and Evers, but she hid it pretty well if she did."

Striker nodded, and a smile now crossed his face. Rosten was becoming a liability, one he'd have to deal with eventually, but for the time being, the old man still had his uses. "You like the girl. I understand that, but you know what needs to be done. Take care of it."

Rosten replied by shutting off the monitor and shoving it off the desk and into the wall, sending sparks from the broken screen. He stumbled backward and was happy the bed was there to break his fall. Drinking was a mistake, but considering that the life he had come to enjoy might quickly reach its end, he no longer cared. Katherine was like a daughter to him, even if she had been playing him. He should have been used to it, since Striker had been playing him like a fiddle for years. He was where he was because of Striker, just as his father and his father before him were; he owed the man and his family. In many ways, Striker owned him. "The bastard," Rosten mumbled in a slur.

Rosten punched up the security office on his comm and waited for someone to pick up. He was a pitiful mess; Striker was right about that. He was the most powerful man on Mars, yet he was scared to death of his immediate future, drinking himself into a stupor because he was too scared to face his reality.

Finally, there was a *click* at the other end, followed by Murt's voice.

"Don't talk," Rosten said, cutting him off, "just listen. She's on her way back to the office. Make sure no one finds the body. Then deal with the other one." He didn't even wait for a reply before he severed the connection. He wished he could feel some shred of remorse or regret, but his soul had been damned a long time ago. One more death—or even the millions more to come—could not possibly tarnish him any worse than he already was. He was as doomed as Kate was, and if there was a hell in any dark corner of the universe, he was sure he'd already bought several one-way tickets.

Chapter 7

Kate rushed through the city. The hangar bay where her ship was parked was on the other end of town, but something was very different; she could feel it, like a sixth sense nagging at her, either some side effect of her training or the paranoia that seemed to be eating away at her more and more every day. Her tail was no longer following her. The news from Rosten had rocked her to the core, especially because she knew the explosion was no accident. The simple fact that Tobias and Evers were blown to bits meant there was a very good chance they were on to her as well, and she was sure it would only be a matter of time before she, herself, ran into some sort of so-called accident she wouldn't walk away from. *Maybe he suspected from the beginning, which would explain the constant surveillance and lack of actual power in my joke of a security position,* she reasoned.

Rosten thought she was on her way back to the office, but by now, it was pretty obvious that she was heading in the opposite direction. If she was right about her cover being blown, Murt would be waiting on her, with a loaded weapon at the ready. The decision to lie to Rosten would probably cause a change of plans.

Kate checked her surroundings and noted that the closest weapons drop was around the corner. The alley she had chosen to hide her escape kit was situated between two pre-fab segments that made up the low-cost living quarters of the district; she was sure her items would never be discovered there, because even the rats and rodents avoided the place. The one disadvantage was that it was a dead end, leaving her no chance for escape if the entrance was cut off.

Her luck seemed to be holding out, for everything was right where she left it, entirely untouched. The plasma guns were in their holster, wrapped in old clothes and stuffed in the tote bag. Kate pulled them out and confirmed that each had a full charge, then strapped the holster around her waist. Her comfort level took an upturn as she moved back to the alley entrance and pressed her back against the wall.

Her years in the intelligence field presented various ways of dealing with a tail, especially a dangerous one. The timing had to be perfect. The man following her didn't have such expert training, but he was armed and presumably out to kill her.

Kate waited and was rewarded by the sight of a tall figure in a security uniform, walking across the entrance to the alley. He had obviously lost her and was looking to pick up her trail again. Of all the ways to initiate an attack, Kate decided on the easiest she could think of: She simply stuck her foot out and tripped him, causing him to drop his gun as he fell to the pavement. She watched as the weapon bounced away.

When she spun him onto his back, she recognized him as Costello and realized Murt must have left him behind after departing Rosten's. The time for pretense was over, so she quickly pulled the gun from her holster and pressed it against his temple.

"Whoa!" he cried. "Dante? Kate, what're you doing?"

He tried to push himself away from her weapon, but Kate stayed on him, pressing it harder against his skull. She reached back and retrieved Costello's small plasma pistol and stuck it in her belt. She noted that there were no registration marks on the gun, rendering it untraceable. It was obviously illegal, and it had one purpose: her death. "Drop it, Costello," she said, pressing the gun even deeper into his temple. "Time for the truth…and time is something I have very little of."

"I-I was following you," he stammered. "Orders from R-Rosten. He just wanted me to keep tabs on you. Please don't—"

She responded by smacking him on the side of the head with the butt of the gun. "I told you I have no time for your lies. Tell me another fib, and I will kill you. You came at me with your gun out. Why?"

Costello smiled and suddenly seemed quite different from the man she thought was her only friend in the office. "So you're a double-traitor then? To the Alliance and to Mars as well? It seems strange that *you* would be threatening *me* over telling lies, Dante."

"And the gun? Was that meant for me?"

"You were supposed to head back to the office. It was going to be quiet, then out to a landfill somewhere, out on the surface outside the city," Costello said with a bit of a grin. "Those orders came directly from Mr. Rosten."

Kate sat back against the wall next to Costello and tried to plan her next move. "So… You've known for a while, huh?"

Costello nodded. "Whatever Mr. Rosten is planning, I guess it was time to clean house."

Kate pointed the gun back at his head. "You're a real bastard, you know that?"

"That's your opinion," he finally said. "There's one other thing you might want to know though."

"What?"

"We know your brother is on Mars," he added. "He was supposed to be next, followed by your sister, on the *Bonaventure*. Like I said, it was all about cleaning house, with no more Dantes."

"You know about Michael?" Kate asked, horrified. *How could I have been so blind, so careless?* Now Kristin was also in danger, and it was all because of that ridiculous undercover assignment of hers. *They're all basically dead,* she thought, torturing herself. *My dad, my brother, my sister…all because of me.*

"Yes, we know. In fact, there's a squad on the way to get him."

"No!" she snapped. "I won't let it happen!"

Costello laughed, but he also seemed resigned to his fate. "So I suppose you're gonna kill me now?" he asked, milking it for all he could. "Do you really have the balls?"

"No, Costello. I'll let you keep breathing for now. Besides, I need you to tell Rosten and his retard of a son that I'm coming after him and Striker."

Costello would have said something had her gun not hit him across the top of the head, rendering him unconscious.

"Enjoy a nap first though," she said. "I have things to do." She then holstered her weapon and pulled the security officer out into the middle of the street, in full view of one of the many cameras that kept watch of the city. After dumping the body, she stared right into the camera, making certain it would verify her identity. When she was sure it recognized both of them, she pointed a finger at the camera, made a cutting motion with her finger, then pulled out her gun and put a shot through the lens. As tempted as she was to kill Costello, Murt, and then go after Rosten, she had to reach her brother first. She hoped the gesture would make them think her intention was to circle around and try for one of the Rostens. The redistribution of personnel would make it easier for her to break out her ship with limited interference.

It took only a few minutes to reach the bay and her small scout ship. The *Alexa* had once belonged to her father, but he gave it to her for graduating with top honors at the Academy. The ship was old and beaten half to death, but it was her baby. It took years of hard work for Kate to bring her up to par and make her feel like home, and Tobias and Evers upgraded everything from her engines to her weapons systems. Her quaint little antique ship was now a state-of-the-art vessel, with the claws and teeth to prove it. Truth be told, she still preferred the innocent little ship her father had given her more than a decade earlier.

There was only one guard standing by the entrance to her ship, and he looked bored with his duty. She was happy that the current Rosten regime didn't go all out to hire the qualified, for Kate had no problem gaining access. She had her security uniform on, and as the chief, getting past hangar security was seldom an issue. Obviously, the orders to have her killed hadn't yet filtered down to local law. The security man actually guarding her ship was a different mater though; she was sure had orders to shoot her on sight, and there was no time to play games or take any chances.

Stepping out in sight of the guard, she pulled her gun out and fired. The pulse round hit him in the leg, knocking him to the floor. As he fell, he let out a shrieking groan. His rifle clattered into the corner as he grabbed the blackened burn hole in his leg. Without missing a beat, Kate ran up to him and kicked him in the head, then watched happily as his eyes rolled back into his head and he slumped to the hard metal deck.

She was already in the ship, closing the main hatch, when the deck crew and hangar security arrived, attracted by the commotion. Kate quickly took the pilot seat and brought *Alexa's* engines online. She had wired the engines and flight control so it would take minimal time to get in the air; taking too long would give them the time to wheel out something that could either destroy her craft or at least damage it beyond repair. Either would result in her death, and, in all likelihood, Michael's and then Kristin's. If she failed, her entire family line could very well come to an end.

She had the engines warmed up when she noticed security wheeling out a plasma cannon and pointing it at her ship. Apparently, they were prepared for her arrival after all. One of her modifications enabled her weapons system on startup. She hit the firing stud and sent superhot bolts of plasma energy across the bay. The cannon erupted into flame and exploded, and the force of the explosion scattered security men like bowling pins.

Finally, she activated the engines, and *Alexa* rose up into the bay. Small arms fire erupted as they sought to bring her down. The armored exterior easily turned away the light armament as she turned the ship toward the exit doors. Pressing the firing button again, she sent a stream of energy at the sliding double-doors, blowing them outward and into the Martian day.

Before heading out of the bay, she keyed on her outside comm. "Tell Rosten he's next."

Her words froze security in place, just as she intended.

She switched the system off, hit her throttle, and sent the ship thundering into the Martian sky. She opened the atmospheric engines as far as possible in an effort to make up the lost ground on the security force Costello had alluded to. One of the exciting accessories her employers had provided her with was a short-range jammer. She switched it on and hoped it would keep the chatter about her escape from reaching Rosten's men who were traveling out on the surface. The only real advantage she had was the element of surprise; if they knew she was coming, both she and Michael would be dead in short order.

Kate slowed the scout as her sensors picked up the relay station below, then dropped to hover only a few meters off the ground. She was aware of the security that was used and was sure it was unlikely that they could detect her at altitude, let alone just above the ground. She was that good, and they generally were not. Rosten, both father and son, tended to hire thugs of an intelligence level that allowed them to be easily manipulated. Her sensors, on the other hand, detected the Falcon and the two support fighters on the ground outside the station, along with the rover Michael had rented. Based on those sensor readings, the engines of the three ships were still hot, indicating that they'd only arrived only a few minutes earlier. She assumed they were already searching for her brother in the communications complex. She was lucky; there were no men waiting on the ground or ships in the air. There would only be a few guards waiting with the ships, and she would handle them first.

Kate set the ship down behind an outcropping of rock overlooking the station. The automated complex was enormous, so it would take the goons some time to find her brother. She knew the kind of equipment Michael was using and knew where he could put it to the best use.

Kate shut down the engines, then headed for her quarters, shedding her skintight security uniform as she went. "Hopefully it works better as a rag," she said to herself as she kicked it into a corner of her small compartment. "Too fucking tight."

Naked and able to breathe for the first time that day, she reached for a pair of jeans and a black pullover shirt. The shoulder holster went on next, with one twin plasma pistol strapped in under each arm. Next came the combat knife that fit perfectly in a special sheath inside her left boot. She turned to her full-length mirror and examined herself from head to toe. "Ready or not, here I come," she said to her reflection as she grabbed the black leather jacket from her closet and headed for the door. Before opening the pressurized outer door to the scout airlock, she reached up between two recessed pipes and pulled down a scoped assault rifle. "Now I'm ready," she said with a smile.

Her plan was simple: She would kill everyone at the relay not named Michael Dante and live to tell the tale. Her friends and family seemed to be dying around her, dropping like the proverbial flies, quite possibly because of her. *It's time I spread a little of that around to the other side,* she thought. She'd been declared a traitor to both sides of the conflict, and she was ready to bring on some pain to the real bad guys.

Kate shut the airlock and began to make her way silently to the ships parked outside the complex. The guards had to go, for the sake of her entrance and her and Michael's eventual exit.

The wind began to pick up as she made her way down and across the rocky surface. From the increasing intensity, Kate figured she had about an hour before the storm arrived; at that point, traveling would become difficult, if not impossible. She needed to rescue Michael and get out of there in a hurry, or they would never make it. The storm would blow the Martian dust into her ship's air intakes, overheating her engines, and they wouldn't last long on the ground.

If the guards followed procedure, there would be one in the Falcon turret and one in the cockpit. At that moment, she wished she'd thought to arm herself with a grenade or two. *Then again, nothing worth doing is ever easy,* she thought as she reached the rear of the Falcon. It was a lesson the admiral had pounded into the heads of his children, though she had no intention of giving him credit for its truth.

It wasn't easy keeping out of sight of the revolving gun turret, but she knew that if the turret guard saw her, she wouldn't even feel the bolts of plasma as they cut her in half. She slung the assault rifle over her shoulder, reached into her boot, and pulled out the sharp, double-blade knife. Slowly, Kate made her way to the open hatch, keeping a watchful eye on the position of that potentially fatal turret gun. Eventually, she was close enough to look inside, where she could see the guard sitting in the pilot seat, with his feet up on the flight console. From the back of his head, it appeared to be Ferguson. She didn't like Ferguson. For that matter, she really didn't like any of them.

"Hey, Ferguson," she said quietly.

"What?" he said as he quickly pulled his legs from the console and lazily turned to face her. "Dante? That—"

He didn't have the chance to complete his question before Kate's knife spun once through the air and buried itself deep in his throat. After a short, bloody gurgle, his eyes rolled up into his head, and he fell to the deck, dead. Kate moved in and removed the knife, then wiped it on Ferguson's jumpsuit.

"Ferguson," the gruff, gravelly voice demanded from the turret, "what's going on down there? I thought you was napping. We need to stay awake, or else Murt'll have our asses for breakfast."

So, Kate thought, *they haven't yet heard anything after my escape from the city. Well, that's good.* Mason was making it easier for her. She had to quietly remove him from the turret before he got off a signal to the others. It was nice to know that Murt was leading the search; the thought of killing him gave her a warm, fuzzy feeling inside.

Kate considered the various ways she could maneuver Mason from the turret and ultimately settled on the quickest option: shutting off the power. Like the rest of the personnel under Murt's watchful eye, Mason was brutal and stupid, but most of all, he had incredible anger management issues.

"Ferguson, why'd the power go out to the turret?! What in the hell is going on, man?! Answer me, damn it!"

She could hear him removing the harness and easing himself down the ladder. While he did that, Kate went to the arms locker and pulled out a small pistol. She found herself a seat and placed the small weapon in her lap before bringing up the assault rifle and changing the setting from full auto-fire to single shot.

"If this is a joke, Ferguson, I'm gonna tear your fucking arms right outta their sock..." He stopped short of finishing his threat when he spotted the assault rifle pointed at his head. "Dante?"

"Hi, Mason," she said with a coy smile. "Look, I don't have a whole lot of time, so I'll make this short and sweet. I've got two questions for you, and it will be in your best interest to answer them."

"Nope," Mason answered, shaking his head. "I don't owe you any answers," he said, looking around, "but you owe me a couple. For starters, what the hell did you do to Ferguson? And why?"

"Now, Mason, play fair, would you? You don't even know what I'm going to ask you."

Mason gave it a second thought, then shook his head again. "And how do I know you won't kill me after I answer?"

Kate reached under her chair, pulled out the small weapon, and held it out to Mason. "Do you know what this is?"

"A stunner?" Mason asked stupidly.

"Yes! Very good," she said. She placed it in her lap and pointed the assault rifle at the big man's bald head. "I can either use that or this on you. Now, the choice is yours, hon', but you might want to consider that I am a woman who is quickly running out of time... and patience."

Mason nodded over to Ferguson again. "What happened to him?"

Kate shrugged. "I didn't like him. What's your answer?" she asked calmly; it wasn't her first time at the interrogation rodeo, and she was not in the mood for any bull.

Mason thought for a moment, and his answer gushed out of his mouth just as sweat began to profusely pour from his forehead. "Okay, fine. What do you want to know?"

"How many are in the building?"

Mason hesitated, which wasn't lost on Kate.

"Now, Mason!" she screamed, lifting the rifle and pointing it between his eyes again.

"Wait!" He rolled his eyes back in his head and counted on his fingers, like a kindergartner trying to solve a story problem. "Uh…a dozen, twelve." He looked at her and hoped she believed him. "Two from the fighters and ten others from this Falcon. I swear."

Kate nodded and lowered the gun just a little. "And how much of a head start do they have on me?"

Mason looked up at the ceiling of the transport and started to count to himself again. "About ten minutes," he finally answered, cocking his head like an obedient dog who expected a treat from his master for a trick well done. "You gonna stun me now, Dante?"

"First, take off that headset and throw it over here."

Mason obediently removed it and tossed it on the deck, right at Kate's feet.

Kate picked up the headset and placed it on her own head, over her long dark hair. "Thanks," she said as she brought the assault rifle back up.

"Aren't you gonna, uh…stun me or somethin'?" Mason stammered in a panic.

"I was," Kate said as she brought the rifle up and fired a single shot. The intense bolt of energy drilled between Mason's eyes before exiting out the back of what was left of his head, taking a fair amount of smoking brains and bone with it. "A girl's entitled to change her mind," she said with a smirk. "If you see my father, feel free to complain."

She switched the weapon back to full auto, then held the trigger down and decimated the flight controls, reducing them to a molten mess and taking the Falcon out of the equation for a possible pursuit.

Kate took one last look at the bloodstain on the deck that, only a few minutes prior, had been a living, breathing idiot. She felt no remorse, no regret for her lie or her actions. Striker and Rosten had removed any moral ambiguity when they killed her father and threatened the rest of her family. They wanted a war, and they would have it now.

She made a quick stop on the way out of the Falcon, visiting each fighter to make sure they wouldn't be flying around anytime soon. She then activated the headset, making certain that it was set to the same frequency Murt and his team were using, then headed into the building.

Her only fear was that she'd wasted too much time, and she knew that with every passing second, Rosten's death squad was closing in on her brother. Michael was very good at his job—not as good as she was but good enough to hold his ground until she caught up to them. Regardless of his experience, though, he was still facing ten-to-one odds, and with that thought weighing heavily on her mind, Kate chose speed over stealth and began to run, as fast as her legs would carry her. She was going to save her brother, and anyone who tried to get in the way of that would regret the day they were ever born.

Chapter 8

It took Michael a while as he tried to follow his father's floor plans of the complex. Finally, he found himself in the central control room. The plans he had were obviously sketched earlier in the construction phases, but they were the best the admiral had access to. Another detriment to his progress was the automated security system; cameras spied on every hallway and corridor of the complex. He had his own countermeasures, thanks to his friends in Alliance Intelligence, but he needed to be in close proximity of the devices for those to work.

Michael knew he was behind schedule; that impromptu and somewhat uneasy lunch with his sister had thrown off his timetable. It was nice to see her, but he found her Mars security uniform disturbing. She was once the pride of the Alliance and should have been the most decorated operative of all time; everyone at the time knew it, even though Kate held no decorations. Now she was a thug, just like the rest of them, and possibly an enemy as well.

He took a seat at the control panel, in an old, cheaply made chair that looked as if it had been picked up from some Martian thrift store. He guessed it was vinyl, and there were worn and torn places all over it, from back when the relay was manned by a living, breathing crew. He pulled out his data-padd and cycled through the mission briefing his father had left for him, including complete instructions as to where to place the wiretap and how to download the archived logs.

Michael reached for his pack and pulled out a small, square, electronic device, the "black box," as he called it. It only measured four inches on each side, not counting the leads that protruded from two of those sides. He put the wiretap down on the console, then pulled the cover off another panel and looked inside, knowing he had to be careful as he poked around. The electricity going through those wires was enough to electrocute him if he touched the wrong one, and he had little interest in becoming a human French fry, left to rot in that old chair.

He looked at the drawing on his padd again, trying to match the schematic up with the actual wiring harness. Finally, he found the cluster of wires he was looking for and wired the black box into two of them. Satisfied that his wiretap blended in well enough to fool the casual observer, Michael replaced the panel and moved to the next. His next task was software related and only required him to place his memory stick into the IO port and request the computer to start a data-dump to the removable drive.

Just as Michael was about to place the device in the port, he was alerted by a buzzing sound coming from his pack, indicating that someone had triggered the sensors he'd left in the outer corridors. "Shit," he said to himself as he plugged in the memory stick and set the communications storage system on download. From the location of the sensor they had triggered, he surmised that he had about five minutes before the control room door would open. He looked back at the memory stick and the reading on his download. "Damn," he muttered as he realized those five minutes might not be enough to download all the files his father and Alliance Intelligence had ordered him to obtain.

Whoever was there, they had come in a different way, or else they would have triggered the other sensors closer to the entrance of the complex. Much to his dismay, his best guess was that it was a band of Rosten's not-so-merry men, a bunch of mercenaries who preferred to be referred to as security. It was clear that they aimed to cut off his only escape, and he wasn't sure what he could do about it; that all depended on how many there were and how much time he had to waste waiting on that precious download. He watched the progress and willed it to go faster, to no avail. He also wished he had a somewhat larger and more lethal weapon than the stunner he had tucked in the waistband of his pants.

The download was 45 percent complete as he pulled up the feed from the cameras just outside the door. Michael noted, with grim satisfaction, that he'd guessed right about the identity of his guests. There, on the other side of the camera lens, was Mars Security, being led by one of Rosten's lieutenants, a waste of a man by the name of Murt. He counted ten men in all, and there was no sign of Kate among them. He pulled the stunner into his hand and debated pulling out the memory stick before it completed the download. He had no clue what that would do to the data already on the stick, though, so he decided to just leave it in place and hope for the best.

Michael was happy that he had locked the door to the control room. It wouldn't keep them out, but it would make their entrance in just a little more difficult. He was relieved when the light on the memory stick turned from red to green, signaling that the download was finally done. He reached around the console and felt around until he found the stick, then carefully pulled it out of the port. "Mission complete," he whispered, "except for that part about getting out of here alive."

From the noise at the door, he had the feeling that they were wiring the door with explosives. Michael knew he needed to find a place for cover, or else the blast would kill him before the men outside had a chance to.

"Dante!" one of the men outside called. "My name is Sergeant Murt, with Mars Security. I'm giving you one minute to open this door and come out with your hands above your head. After that, we'll come in after you. Countdown starts now."

"And then what?" Michael snapped. He hurriedly used his data-padd to call up the schematic of the complex in order to find another way out, though he wasn't having very much success. He found it quite interesting and a bit unnerving that they knew his name. It was also unusual that Kate wasn't with them, using her family connection to try to convince him to surrender. He didn't have to wait long for his answer.

"If you don't," Murt answered, "I will bury your body in the same Martian ditch as your sister. You're running out of family, Dante. First your father, then little Katie... Can you and your little sister be far behind?"

Michael slumped back against the console and felt warm, salty tears welling in his eyes. *My father is...dead? It can't be. Not the admiral. And Kate?* He'd just spoken to her earlier in the day, and he knew she was no easy kill. If they were, in fact, gone, he would deal with that after getting out of there with what he hoped was evidence enough to finish what his father had started. With the memory stick tucked safely in his pocket and the stunner in his hand, Michael contemplated how to get past Murt and the Mars Security squad. They were really a bunch of bumbling idiots, but he was sorely outnumbered, and there was only one way out of the room.

"You're lying, Murt!" Michael called out, trying to buy some time. He needed to think, though he knew every second he wasted only led them that much closer to blowing open the doors and rushing him. All he really had at his disposal was the data-padd with the complex specifications on it. Michael activated the device, but the screen was blank; somehow, they'd cut off his uplink, leaving him with nothing to fall back on.

"That don't matter anymore," Murt retorted. "In a few minutes, you're gonna be dead, and you can ask them all about it in the hell I'm about to send you to."

Ignoring the threat, Michael pushed himself across the floor to the ventilation panel and tried to remove the bolts with his fingers. He had no delusions about winning a battle against a superior force with only a stunner in hand; that sounded ludicrous, like the plot of some old-time action movie, and it wouldn't work in his current reality. If he could access the ventilation system, however, he might just have a fighting chance. The bolts that held the panel in place were welded, though, and he realized there was no way he could loosen them before the door blew in. Resigned to his fate, Michael brought up the stunner and waited. With that, the charge on the doors exploded, sending fragments speeding through the control room. He hoped that if he did find his sister in the afterlife, she wouldn't stand there with her hands on her hips spouting, *"I told you so."*

Kate rushed down the corridors, tracking the signal she received over the headset she'd pilfered from the now-deceased Mason. She overheard all of Murt's pathetic attempts to get under her brother's skin, and she almost found it laughable. Michael was no rookie, and she knew he'd set the personal stuff aside to deal with after the mission.

The explosion reached her a second later, and Kate realized that the small barrier between Murt's security team and her brother was now little more than a pile of smoking rubble. She also knew he had only a stunner, and the fight wouldn't be a long one.

When she turned a corner, she saw the first of Murt's squad. Without hesitation, Kate brought up her assault rifle and began firing on full auto. The first volley took out two of the security men before they even realized she was behind them. That unfortunately captured the attention of the rest of them, who hit the floor and opened fire with their own weapons.

Kate, already on the move, fired again and again. Two more hit the floor as the white-hot plasma tore into and through them. At her count there should be four men remaining—including Murt.

Murt heard the fire and moved into the control room. "Dante," he said quietly to himself. Their target was right: The bitch was really hard to kill.

"Problem?" Michael chimed in happily from the corner where he had taken cover. "The legend lives," he whispered to himself with a smirk.

"Nothing we can't handle," Murt answered as he gestured for Peters to outflank their opponent.

Michael watched for a moment as the security man tried to

advance along the side of the room. He then took him down in quick order with a solitary blast from his stunner. "You sure about that, Murt?"

Kate felt a bolt of plasma tear through the sleeve of her leather jacket and cursed under her breath; she loved that jacket, and she sucked when it came to sewing. Before the man could take another shot at her, she dived at his legs in a feet-first baseball slide her father would have been proud of, taking her target to the floor with a satisfying *snap* of the bone in his leg. Before he could recover, she slapped the butt of her rifle against his head and watched her opponent sag to the floor. She pulled the body on top of her as two energy bolts struck the unconscious man she used as a shield.

The security man could see she had the 200-pound man on top of her as she struggled to bring her weapon up. "Never liked you, Dante," Forster said as he pulled up his gun to shoot her in the head.

Kate stopped struggling for her own weapon and instead reached into the holster of the dead man on top of her. In one motion, she pulled the trigger and jerked her hand away as the gun overheated in the holster after firing the one shot. The pulse of energy hit the man in the chest and sent him, surprised look and all, bouncing off a corridor wall before he landed with a *thump* on the floor in a bloody, charred heap.

With a push from her legs, Kate shoved the dead, smoking body off her and shakily ambled to her feet. The blown doors were right in front of her, but as she brought up her assault rifle to shoulder it again, she noticed a new problem: There was a prominent crack in the housing that would likely cause the gun to explode the next time it was used. There wasn't much left of the doorway ahead of her, but she knew Murt and her brother were just beyond the busted frame and broken hinges. Without another thought, she pulled a plasma pistol from her holster and advanced on the room.

Murt heard the commotion outside but still had faith that his men could handle whatever they were dealing with. "Dante, I hope you don't think your rescue party is gonna make it through that door, because I'm gonna kill you before then." Murt saw Peters and noted that he bore no wounds; clearly, he'd only been stunned. "Now come on out. You've got nowhere to run."

Michael eased over and around the master control panel, holding his stunner in a white-knuckled grip. He was sure that if he could maneuver his way around the behemoth of a man, he could take him down with his stunner, then abscond his gun, which would give him a better chance against the others.

Murt had the same idea, because he looked up and noted the security man standing over him, with gun in hand. "Nice try," Murt said with a smile. "Get up."

Michael dropped the stunner to the floor and stood. When he got to his feet, he noticed the wood splinter that had struck him in the thigh. He ignored the blood seeping from the wound but placed his hand on the computer console to steady himself. "Now what?" he asked as he felt the pain surge along his thigh and into his hip. He almost smiled when he saw that Murt was having his own problems.

"Come in, sec team," Murt said into his headset. "Where the hell are you?"

"Right behind you," a female voice answered over his headset, a voice that was annoyingly familiar.

With his gun still pointed at Michael, Murt turned to face the last person he would have ever expected to see again. "Dante, you bitch. You have more lives than a cat."

"Kate!" Michael said with a smile. "This asshole said you and Dad were dead."

Kate nodded and grinned back at him. "Yeah, I get that a lot, baby brother. I figure it's just wishful thinking most of the time." She turned to Murt and leveled the plasma pistol at him. "Put the gun down, Murt, and step away. If you comply, I might just decide to let you keep breathing."

Murt looked at her and returned his own smile. "I can kill your brother long before you can pull that trigger. Am I worth it, Dante? Put the gun down, and hand over that assault rifle you're carrying."

Michael looked at her and shook his head. "No, Kate. Don't do it."

Murt pushed his gun closer to Michael's head. "Decide, Dante. Give me the weapon, or he dies."

Kate stopped and thought for a moment before lowering the barrel. "Wait! Don't shoot," She snapped as she put her plasma pistol on the table and the rifle right next to it.

Murt leaned over and scooped up the weapon. He placed his own handgun back in its holster and pointed the assault rifle at Michael instead. "You," he said to Michael, "go stand by your sister so I can keep an eye on the both of you."

Michael gave Kate a dirty look as he hobbled over to her side. "Good job," he finally said.

Kate regarded Murt with contempt as she helped her brother into a chair she pulled from the computer console. "Now what, genius? You have a decision to make, moron. What's it going to be? Put the weapon down and walk out, and I'll let you live."

The smile faded from Murt's face in the wake of her insults and threats. "That's pretty brave of you to say, coming from a pair of soon-to-be-dead Dantes."

"What do you care what I say, you mindless asshole? You are going to kill us anyway, aren't you?" Kate said, continuing the verbal onslaught. One thing she knew about Murt was that he was a vane, chauvinistic hater of women, and she was sure her plan to unnerve him would work wonders; she could tell that by the frustrated look on his ugly face. "Now, why don't you quit playing around with your little…gun and do something about it?"

"Fine. Have it your way, bitch," he snapped, bringing the rifle up and setting it on full auto. "Say hi to Daddy!"

Murt pulled the trigger, and the rifle did exactly as Kate expected it to. His fingers went one way, and the rest of Murt went the other as the force of the exploding weapon sent him flying in a crimson spray. Kate hurriedly pushed her brother and his chair over as she went down on top of him with a *thud*.

Michael fell with a groan as Kate's full weight slammed into his injured thigh. He looked over at the smoking mess that was Murt and realized that Kate had planned it all, right from the moment she'd handed the stupid goon her gun. "Gee, sis, thanks for the warning."

"Don't mention it," she said as she helped him back into the chair and strapped her holster back on. Kate pulled the knife from her boot and knelt over Murt. "You look like shit…even more so than usual, if that's even possible."

Murt held up his hands, only to notice that his right one was missing entirely and that his left was comprised of only two fingers and a thumb. Rather than moaning in the agony he must have been feeling, the man was laughing.

"What's so funny, you dumb fuck?" Kate asked.

Murt stopped laughing as blood filled his mouth. "That was really different, Dante. I didn't realize you're so…creative."

Kate noted that the shrapnel from exploding gun had penetrated his crest as well. From the look of his wounds, Murt had very little time remaining. "I told you to walk away, but you made your choice, and now…" With that, Kate shrugged and plunged the knife deep into the man's chest. "I'm full of surprises, but don't worry, Murt. I'll be sure to send some more of your friends to keep you company." She watched as Murt's eyes rolled back into his head and he let out his final gasp of air.

"You enjoyed that way too much," Michael said as she helped him to his feet.

She threw her brother's arm over her shoulder and helped him to the door. "He deserved it. Now c'mon. We need to get out of here before reinforcements show up."

Michael stopped long enough to retrieve a pressure bandage from his med kit and slap it on his wounded thigh. Once the bleeding stopped, he pushed himself away from his sister's shoulder. "I think I can make it now."

"Great. Let's go." Kate stopped when she noted that Michael

wasn't following her. "What is it? We need to hightail it out of here, little brother."

Michael looked her in the eye, searching for any sign of a lie or sugarcoating. "Is Dad dead?"

Kate stared right back at him. The weight of the day was starting to weigh heavily on her, and the adrenaline of the battle was starting to fade. "I think so, but I'm not sure." Kate looked for any sign of emotion in her brother's face but saw none. "We'll look deeper into it when we're away from here, but we need to go now."

Michael nodded and followed her out the door. "You're also going to tell me the rest of the truth, right?"

"The truth? About what?" she said, feigning innocence.

"About you and this criminal life of yours."

"Uh…sure," Kate said, her mind in overdrive as she was already planning their next step. She would stop Rosten and Striker and whoever else was involved with them, but their first order of business was to get off Mars and locate Kristin. She was sure her mortal enemies would send the entire weight of the Alliance after them both. Even if she didn't feel like a criminal before, she certainly did now.

They cleared the complex just as the storm appeared on the horizon. Kate detoured to the Falcon and cleaned out the transport of any weapons and supplies she could find.

Michael sat at the navigator station, putting the finishing touches on the repairs to his leg wound. "Kate, we need to get out of here," he said as he finished applying a fresh bandage. "You said that, right?"

Kate looked past Michael at the storm that was coming in quicker than any of them wanted to admit.

"And what about the reinforcements from the city?"

Kate nodded as she placed the plasma rifles in the same pack as the grenades and spare ammo packs. "You're right. We need to get a move-on. As far as anyone coming after us, that storm'll slow them down. We have to leave before it hits though. Won't do us any good to get caught in it too."

Michael stood and flexed his leg. There was still a bit of pain, but the meds would help. "What's our next step?"

Kate dropped the bag she was carrying and pulled her brother into a tight hug. "I love you, Michael. You don't know how happy I am to see you breathing. As for what's next, we need to head for Earth."

"Don't we need to find Kristin?"

"First, we need to find out what happened to the admiral—to Dad—and piece together exactly what's going on. That will also be a good starting point to track down the *Bonaventure* and our sister."

Kate set the self-destruct mechanism on the Falcon as they left. By the time they reached the scout, the transport was in flames. They both noted that the storm was quickly nearing, for the violent winds whipped the flames from the burning transport into a frenzy.

"Hang on a minute," Michael said before he half-ran, half-hobbled over to the rover.

Kate dumped the weapons in a rear storage bin. There was plenty of time to secure their cargo on the long trip to Earth, but at the moment, there was an urgent need to put some distance between themselves and that oncoming storm. She settled into the pilot seat and brought the scout systems online. Since they were left on standby, it only took a few minutes before the readouts switched to the green. The storm advanced, moving ever closer, kicking up dust and debris that pinged off the hull. She was right about it slowing down Rosten and his goons; radar showed them in the air, but they were cautiously hanging back from the wrath of the interplanetary Mother Nature. The filth the tumult was tossing about could easily clog intake vents, but Kate knew she really had those hurricane-force winds for keeping her enemies at bay, thanks to the resulting turbulence. Most of Rosten's men and machines lay dead and burning. The old man had few resources left, and that would make things difficult for him, no matter how badly he now wanted her dead.

Finally, Michael made his way aboard and closed the outer

airlock doors. She could hear him making his way to the guest cabin to drop off the gear he had stashed in the rover. When he was done, he walked over, still a bit tipsy, and plopped down in the co-pilot seat next to her, then snapped on the restraining harness and took the headset she offered. "I see you still have this old piece of shit Dad gave you," he said as he helped her finish the preflight procedures.

Kate smiled and nodded; the game was on. "C'mon, Mike. You're just jealous." She knew he had wanted the ship since he was little, when he loved sitting on his father's knee while they flew around in it. "You and *Alexa* were never a match anyway."

"*Alexa*?" he asked with a smile of his own. "Is that what you call this bucket of bolts? You sure it can get us past the patrol ships that I'm pretty sure your boyfriend—"

"*Ex*-boyfriend," Kate corrected.

Michael looked at her and just shook his head. "Fine. Your *ex*-boyfriend and his father, who will no doubt have ships in low orbit looking for us."

Kate smiled and pulled her harness just a bit tighter. "No problem, brother of mine. I suggest you hold on." Kate brought the engines online, and the ship hovered in place. She took a moment to load positional data on Rosten's patrol ships into the flight computer, then grabbed the two manual flight controllers from the armrests, one in each hand.

Michael didn't remember the ship being equipped with such technology. He didn't want to admit it, but he was jealous. The little ship should have been his, and Kate showed no interest in it until the admiral gifted it to her, while he practically grew up inside it. "So? We going yet or what?" He could feel the scout in the grip of the on-coming storm as it teetered from side to side in the heavy wind that blew the Martian dust into miniature cyclones.

For an answer, Kate flashed him a pearly white smile as she hit the engines.

Rather than the slow climb he remembered from when he

was a boy, *Alexa* now accelerated faster into the sky than a starfighter. "But...how?" he muttered as the acceleration pushed him back into his seat, before inertial dampeners made it a bit more tolerable.

He watched tactical systems come alive in a ship that was lucky to have a working radio in it. The course Kate had set would take them past the storm and most of the patrols. They increased speed, and the targets on the screen slowly fell back, out of range. Once they made it out of orbit and into open space, there was no way anyone would catch up to them. Only one red blip on the screen blocked their path to freedom, and rather than running from it, Kate changed course and headed right for it.

"What the hell are you doing?" he snapped at Kate. "Are you insane?"

"Watch the display," she calmly responded. "Tell me when he launches."

"Launches?!" Michael snapped. "Are you nuts? This is *not* a starfighter!"

"I said watch it, or I will hurt you."

Michael knew she wasn't kidding. When they were younger, in their mid-teens, he once made the mistake of trying to throw a punch at her. Not only did he fail to connect, but he remembered nothing about the attempted assault until two days later, when he awoke in the Academy infirmary. At that point, he made a mental note of her anger management problems and had never attempted to lay a hand on her since. He knew that when it came to his older sister, his best course of business was to simply do as he was told, so he kept his eye on the blue dot, the *Alexa,* as it closed in on the red dot, the ill-fated enemy ship.

Finally, the tactical display illuminated in red, like an ominous sign on an old videogame.

"He fired! Two targets incoming!"

Kate nodded and threw the ship into a combat roll. "*Alexa,* prepare countermeasures. Weapons to manual."

"Countermeasures ready. Weapons at your command," answered an equally calm female voice, as casually as if they were discussing a recipe for pound cake.

"Who the hell was that?" Michael asked; he didn't know what to think anymore.

Kate fired port thrusters and accelerated into a high G-bank. "Fire countermeasures!"

Michael could feel the release of two small interceptor missiles as they launched from either side of the scout. They homed in as they were designed to and took out both of the enemy missiles while they were both too far away to matter. "Two contacts. Incoming destroyed."

Kate steered back on course for the starfighter. It was visible outside the cockpit as she placed the index fingers of her right and left hands over the firing studs on her flight controls. As soon as the tactical display showed that they were in range, she fired. Twin blasts of energy lashed out from the beneath the *Alexa*, taking out the starfighter in a mixture of explosive flames and debris.

Kate deftly flew her ship right through the ball of expanding fire. The sky went from gray to red, then finally to black as they broke orbit and thundered off into space. Michael just stared at her as the tactical display shut down and folded back inside a hidden panel.

Kate popped the harness open and smiled at her brother. "There. See? I told you everything would be okay. You're big sister is *always* right, Mikey. Remember that, would you?"

Ignoring her wink and smirk, Michael just stared at the stars as his sister entered in the course for Earth. At the speed they were flying, he had a feeling the journey would take far less time than he originally thought.

Without another word, Kate stood from her chair and stretched before starting for the rear of the ship and living quarters.

Before she took even two steps, though, Michael grabbed her arm as he spun in his chair, then immediately released it when he saw the look on her face; it was very similar to the expression he'd seen before waking in the infirmary so many years earlier. "We're supposed to have that chat, right?" he asked, then immediately released her arm.

Kate stopped and looked at her arm. "Good idea, Sparky." She looked at him and could see the intensity blaring in his eyes. "Look, Michael, it's been a long day. I just want to get a little rest before we get back to Earth. Is that asking too much?" She could see in his eyes that he would not accept a delay for an answer. "Okay, fine. First a little trip to the galley for a snack, and then I'll unburden myself on you. *Alexa* can keep watch."

Michael smiled and nodded. "Fair enough. We've got all the time we need. At this speed, I figure we've still got about twenty hours. I hope the food on this tub had an upgrade too."

Kate grabbed him by the shoulder and pushed him through the door, into the small galley. "Tub? You say one more word about my ship, and the only food you'll have to worry about eating is going to come through a straw."

"Yes, ma'am," he said, with that stupid Dante grin already on his face.

Kate smiled back and started contemplating her plan. They had to be careful once they got home, for everyone would be gunning for them, from both sides of the fence. She hoped they still had some friends left, or else it would be a very short campaign. No matter how many loyal allies they had, though, Striker would be waiting for them. They had practically jumped from the frying pan and into the fire, and the heat they'd be feeling was just beginning.

Chapter 9

Earth

"Rosten, you fool," Ethan Striker growled at the video screen. "I'm going to come up to your little city and kill you." In spite of the firm threat, the thought of actually going to Mars angered him even more than Rosten and the inconvenience the man was causing. Sitting in the darkness of his office, within his penthouse, surrounded by antiques of an Earth long passed, helped to keep him insulated from a world he had no use for—at least in its present state.

"There was nothing I could do about it. Dante ran before anyone could stop her," Rosten said, with desperation dripping from his voice. As great as the history was between Striker's family and his own, he had no doubt that Striker would carry out his threat if he failed again. "It was Murt and his people. They were...incompetent."

"Of course they were," Striker agreed. "All they had to do was kill your little traitor and her brother. Your men failed, and now the Dantes are gone, along with whatever they retrieved from the relay station. Are you going soft, Clayton? Did *you* actually like her, or was this all because of an emotional crush from your degenerate offspring?"

"Ethan, I'm sorry about that," Rosten pleaded as he tried to avoid answers to questions that he knew would only dig a deeper hole for him and his family on Mars. "I can send a ship to try to catch up with them."

"No," Striker replied with a dismissive wave of his hand. "I suspect they're on their way here. I'll deal with the remainder of the Dante clan when they arrive."

Rosten nodded and could feel the sweat rolling down his face. "Is there anything I can do?"

"No, Clayton, obviously not. You've proven that already. Just stay where you are and wait for further instructions."

"Sure, Ethan. Anything you say," Rosten said as his pulse slowed in his chest.

"This is only a short reprieve for you. If this damages my plans in any way, I will see you burn," Striker said. He wanted to make sure there was no doubt as to what the penalty would be if the plans that had been so carefully laid for more than two centuries were spoiled by Rosten's lack of supervision.

Before Rosten could add anything to his already pitiful display, Striker closed the connection, and the screen went blank. "Fool," he muttered to the dark monitor before throwing it off his desk, reducing it to a heap of burning plastic and metal. Sensors attempted to compensate for the darkness by increasing the ambient, and Striker looked up and noticed that he had a visitor. "Computer, bring the lights down 20 percent."

At his command, the lights in the room dimmed, almost swallowing the silent form sitting in darkness.

"You heard?" Striker finally asked.

"Yes," came the whispery reply. "You are growing sloppy. We are too close to achieving both of our goals to allow such incompetence to sabotage what we have planned. The Dante family has been a problem for far too long. They should have been removed decades ago."

It was always like that. The voice, like an eerie whisper in the wind, made him feel something he hated more than anything else: fear. He was too powerful to be bothered with it and too important to worry about it, but there it was. Striker stared at the form, but just as every other time, it was impossible for him to discern any features. The stealth field kept him hidden, yet another wonder of the Jek'Tan.

"Admiral Dante, along with his co-conspirators, have been dealt with," Striker attempted to assure him, trying to disguise his own uncertainty. "I'm sure his daughter on the *Bonaventure* is dead as well. It will only be a matter of time before the other two return here, to Earth. As soon as they land, I will make sure they don't trouble either of us again."

"I suggest you do that. My ships will soon enter this system, and plans must be in place before that happens. It would be…most unfortunate for you if we are forced to alter out arrangement."

This time, it felt like the voice was cutting into his head like a knife, and Striker tried to rub the pain in his temples away, to no avail. "I made sure the *Bonaventure* was made available to you, but why did you need it? Haven't we sent you enough?"

"That is no concern of yours," the voice said, each syllable a threat to explode his skull from within. "Why do you care, as long as you get what was promised to your family centuries ago? We can easily go to Rosten or the one on Earth's moon if you have lost the will to do what needs to be done. Power does not come to the weak."

Striker felt the wetness in his ear; it dripped down his neck as the pain grew. "No, that won't be necessary," he relied painfully, through clenched teeth. He reached into his pocket and pulled out a handkerchief, then dabbed at the blood to prevent staining his expensive shirt.

"Good," the voice said, floating on the wind again. "You know what you need to do, Ethan Striker. Now do it!"

Striker shook his head as the pain started to fade. "Yes, I know…and I will."

Suddenly, the seat was empty; just like that, the Jek'Tan was gone.

Striker opened his desk drawer and pulled out a pain reliever. He gulped the capsule down with a glass of water he poured from the pitcher on his desk. Dealing with the alien was often a painful experience, just as it had been for his father, his grandfather, and his father before him. He didn't like the Jek'Tan, but he had no other option. They'd spent 200-plus years planning for the arrival of their race; they just needed someone to pave the way. The payment for that act of supreme planetary betrayal was simple: The Striker family would be given rule of the entire star system. *Who could say no to that?* Striker jested. *Certainly not me.*

The Jek'Tan first visited his great-grandfather on the eve of planetary war and taught him to prepare for the end, so that he and his company could rise from the ashes and take the lead in rebuilding the world. Above everyone else, the alien gods chose him to serve as the savior of his race. The aliens offered to provide the tools and the technology to clean up the radiation of a war that would claim billions; that was inevitable, they said. Afterward, a Striker heir would take his rightful place to lead. At the time, no one considered the offer to be too costly, because in essence, the Jek'Tan only required two things: The first was to allow colonization of the outer planets, with rights to their resources, and the second involved experimentation that would explore the human condition. As part of their arrangement, Striker Industries would supply test subjects for those experiments. Based on a vote by the Striker Industries Board of Directors voted, it was determined that consigning rights to the outer planets was more of a problem than supplying the Jek'Tan with test subjects. To the surprise of no one, the vote to survive the end of the world was unanimous; the general consensus was that the rights to future real estate in the solar system would be the problem of some future generation, while the sacrifice of a few meaningless individuals, little more than lab rats, was a worthy price to pay to save a civilization—not to mention themselves.

A deal was struck, and clandestine work began immediately on a massive underground complex, secretly dug out below Mt. Harvard in the Colorado Mountains. That facility would house the people and resources that Striker Industries would need to breathe life into a damaged world. At the time when the first nuclear missiles launched, there were more than 50,000 scientists, engineers, doctors, and Striker family and executives living comfortably underground, safely stashed away from the devastation and death the Jek'Tan had foretold.

Eleven months after the completion of the complex, the bombs fell. No one knew who launched the first salvo in the war, as

Moscow disappeared in a mushroom cloud, followed, some six hours later, by Washington DC. Only after that were multiple launches detected on both sides. Eventually, China, North Korea, and England joined the fray. With nuclear death raining down around them, the countries of the Middle East attempted to settle 1,000-year-old debts and disputes. In less than five days, there were more than three billion dead, and the entire planet was left smoldering and in ruins.

Like the stuff of myths and legends, though, out of the rubble rose the mighty phoenix, in the form of Striker Industries. With the help of Jek'Tan technology, they swept the globe, bringing order to chaos as they built a new world. Ethan Striker's ancestors made deals with companies in communications and construction, as the Rosten and Stratton families joined in the rebuilding efforts.

The world was a changed place, and no one had the stomach for the horrors of war again. Borders that had stood throughout history fell, as neighbors finally found more reasons to get along than to kill one another. Technological breakthroughs came almost daily, but all of it filtered back through Striker Industries, who themselves seemed under the watchful eye of the Jek'Tan.

The aliens lurked in the darkness, revealing themselves to no one else, but Striker knew they or their agents were everywhere. They only trusted their bastard creations, byproducts of their hundreds of years of experimentation on the human trash Striker Industries funneled to them. He sensed them in the shadows, like puppet masters controlling everything from behind the scenes. He sensed them in the night and in the corners of his nightmares. Like itching powder, they created a reaction without knowing where they were from, yet he knew they were there, quietly moving into positions of prominence and power. He often wondered if it was merely a product of his paranoia though, a quality that had kept him alive for all those tumultuous years. Other questions also loomed in his mind: *Would my ancestors have made their deal with the devil if they'd realized that the Jek'Tan not only want the outer planets but the inner ones as well? Then again, does it really matter, as long as I am the one at the top?*

It was then that the accidents and disappearances began. They were able to mold and influence mankind, but occasionally, an obstacle needed to be removed. Now his destiny was almost upon him. The Jek'Tan would eventually take what they wanted, and he would get the rest, along with all the power his family had dreamt about for more than two centuries. There would be no more Alliance, no more government to stand in the way. The Jek'Tan would take control, and he, Ethan Striker, would rule in their name. The Jek'Tan would cohabit and lead the human race into an enlightened future, and he would be remembered alongside Christ, as the modern-day Messiah, the bringer of enlightenment from the star gods. If a few more people had to die for him to meet his destiny, then so be it.

Striker sat back at his desk and hit a lit stud.

"Yes, Mr. Striker?" asked the voice of his executive assistant, Peggy.

"Miss Johnson, please get Mr. Gemini on the comm. I want to speak to him."

"Yes, sir," Peggy replied.

He hit the button again to end the conversation and considered Gemini, his fixer, tasked with correcting any problems that arose between Striker and his destiny. Accidents and disappearances were his specialty, and he was very good at his job. Much blood had been spilled in preparation for what was coming, and that was a testament to not only Mr. Gemini's skills but also to all those who preceded him.

They had never met before, but Ethan knew the ghostlike assassin had been removing his family's enemies and those of the Jek'Tan since the need first arose almost 200 years prior. Sometimes, he thought the body count rivaled the war, but so far, his hands and those of generations before were clean of the blood that had helped to cement his present position and his future power in place.

The mystery of Mr. Gemini was really who or what he was. Striker had his theories, the strongest of all being that it was a creation of the Jek'Tan, a being created to kill. Striker reasoned that the creature was one of many roaming his cities, the Jek'Tan's foot soldiers dispersed throughout Earth, a product of centuries of experimentation. He was not convinced that Gemini was even human, especially since the Jek'Tan had made it clear that Gemini's origins were none of his business. To them—and to Striker by association—all that really mattered were results. He only needed to give the ghost assassin a target, and then he would be free to finish his breakfast in peace.

With that thought fleeting in his mind, like so many other things he did not wish to concern himself with, a light on his console blinked, signaling a call back from Peggy.

"Sir, I have Mr. Gemini on the line," she said as calmly as she could. Peggy had realized a long time ago that every time her boss spoke with Mr. Gemini, someone subsequently disappeared.

"Send him through," Striker said, then waited to hear the voice of change in his new world.

"You needed something from us?" The voice was even and calm, as if discussing the weather or a new video review.

"Two more targets for you, both of the highest priority."

"Aren't they all?" Gemini replied without an ounce of sarcasm. "Who?"

As Striker had done so many times in the past, he placed the information in a coded electronic file and sent it to the assassin over the same line. "They are brother and sister, both very skilled, slippery Alliance intel officers. You will need to be wary of them."

There was silence at the other end of the line for several anxious seconds before the reply came. "They will be no more trouble than the others…and you will make payment as before."

Before Striker could say another word, the line went dead.

"Lights," he said, and the computer brought the lights in his office up to normal levels, allowing him to scan his office for any signs of the Jek'Tan. Striker knew he was many things to many people, but a stupid fool he was not. During all the long years of their arrangement, he had wondered who was really taking advantage of whom. The Jek'Tan was just as mysterious as always, just as they had been when first contact was made with his great-grandfather so many years ago. There was some piece of information missing; Striker could feel it. Until now, there was no real need to worry, but with the Jek'Tan on their way, maybe it was time to start. He felt change coming, along with the payoff he was promised. "Then, damn them all, the Jek'Tan can have the rest."

Next, his mind wandered back to Rosten and Stratton. *Perhaps it is time to dissolve the family partnerships of the past.* Considering that the relationships between their companies and Striker Industries went back even prior to the war, cutting those ties would be a major step. Time was running out with the Jek'Tan, and he could not afford any more mistakes. Rosten and Stratton needed to be removed, and if that required the destruction of both cities they lived in, then so be it. Once the Jek'Tan arrived, he would have no need for the resources of the moon or Mars. Both men would instantly become rivals to his powerbase, while still being an attractive replacement for him in the eyes of the Jek'Tan, and he simply could not allow that. He had always taken Stratton for an idiot, and he was sure he could manipulate him for some beneficial use, but Rosten and his family had to go, sooner rather than later. *Maybe it's time to find out just how creative the mysterious Mr. Gemini can be,* he thought with a snicker. "No one betrays a Striker, be it from this planet or any other, and lives to see the day," he told himself. If the Jek'Tan had a thought of turning on him, he would make it their last.

Clayton Rosten pushed away the communicator as if it was a dead snake that somehow threatened to strike out at him again. It was actually the same feeling he had about Striker following their call. He knew the current CEO was not stable, and his God complex, along with his connection to the aliens, made him far too dangerous. As it was, his family was practically already in control of the Alliance government. When he joined forces with the Jek'Tan, no one would stand in his way. Striker would be able to reach out to his small fiefdom and crush it without any effort at all. *To think we were all such great friends not too long ago, with a partnership that had survived an economic collapse, a nuclear war, and expansion into space,* he thought with a chuckle.

Rosten poured himself a drink and took a moment to search his own feelings. If he was anything at all, he was a good judge of character, at least when it came to men. On the other hand, Kate Dante and other women completely confused him. She had been planted in his organization as a spy, and she had managed to make a fool of him. On the contrary, Striker's motives were always as transparent as the air itself. If he were Striker, his next step would be to kill both Morrison and himself. They were the only ones privy to the great plan, or at least they had enough details to be dangerous.

The Jek'Tan bothered him the most. At first, they were means to an end, and Rosten's ancestors had agreed with Striker's. The Jek'Tan would assist with the rebuilding of Earth through advanced scientific breakthroughs; in return, the Strikers and the Rostens would provide human lab rats. It seemed reasonable, a fair trade, especially with a planet at stake. After all, the needs of the many outweighed the needs of the few.

They both mistakenly assumed it would be temporary, until Striker told them of their responsibility. Later, it was his part and Stratton's to provide manifests of outgoing flights to the rim. More and more ships disappeared without explanation, like forgotten shipwrecks on some vast sea; and, just like in mankind's seafaring days on Earth, much of the pirate problem was little more than propaganda, a scapegoat, a story invented to explain away the disappearances. It was Rosten's people and Stratton's who attacked shipping on the other side of the asteroid belt, destroying ships and leaving their crews for dead. One lie was told to cover another, perhaps a far worse one than anyone knew. Still, for all the horrible things that had already happened, Rosten knew the worst was yet to come and that it would probably engulf them all.

There has to be someone to reach out to, he thought. Kate Dante would be the obvious choice, but even after everything he thought he'd done for her—or, perhaps, because of it—she would absolutely refuse. He blamed a lot of that on his son Marcus and the relationship he tried to force on her while she was undercover.

Ideally, he would have made contact with Admiral Dante, Kate's father. "What is that expression?" he asked himself. "The enemy of my enemy is my friend." Unfortunately, the admiral and the two Intelligence officers who had placed Kate there had reportedly died in the explosion at Alliance Intelligence headquarters. "Or did they?"

Perhaps there was still someone there he could reach out to, before it was too late. By himself, he had no chance to stop or even contain Striker; he was just too powerful. The Alliance stood even less of a chance, because the cancer threatening to destroy them all was working within it. If he opened the right door, though, perhaps they could end it all, before it festered into a war none of them would be able to walk away from.

Rosten reached for the comm again and hoped the device would be friendlier to him than it had been only a few minutes earlier. It was time to do the unthinkable, to reach out to enemies who had only as much trust and faith in him as he had in them.

Chapter 10

Between the Orbits of Neptune and Uranus

Much to Jakes's dismay, finding the station wasn't as easy as he'd promised. Rather than holding steady at the coordinates he could recall, the unpowered station had drifted closer to the orbit of Neptune. The large planet held it in a gravitational death grip that would eventually pull it to a fiery death in its dense, gaseous atmosphere. Luckily, as Simpson pointed out, that wouldn't happen for several months; they had plenty of time to make repairs before going off to perform their next extremely stupid act. Moss added that they could stabilize the station if they could get the maneuvering thrusters working.

For the first time, Jakes could feel that their luck was about to change. Not only had the station drifted within cruising distance of their sputtering engines, but it looked as if it still had some semblance of power, based on the operational navigational lights that continued to blink at four equidistant points around the circumference of the old outpost.

Moss looked over Jakes's shoulder and nodded. "It looks like the solar panels are still working. There's a very good chance that life support might still be functional too."

"Get back, you idiot, and buckle in," Jakes snapped at Moss as he brought the Falcon thrusters online and began docking maneuvers. "Everyone to your seats. We might be in for a little shake, rattle, and roll here."

No one had to be told twice, as the sound of metal snapping against metal could be heard through the small ship. Kristin moved forward to the co-pilot seat next to Jakes after visiting with their guest. She was still unconscious, but Tolliver was convinced that it was due to shock and not physical injury. "She should be lucid enough for questioning in a few hours," he assured Kristin when she asked yet again.

"Hey, Boss," Jakes said as he played his hands over the thruster controls. "You still wanna be around me when I make my first mistake?"

Kristin could feel the ship shaking as the maneuvering thrusters tried to course-correct for docking. Jakes was sweating, something she didn't think their pilot capable of. "No. I was just kidding."

"Uh-huh," Jakes said under his breath. "Main engine burnout. We're on thrusters only."

Kristin tightened her belt and held on. *On the bright side,* she thought, *we made it most of the way before the main engine finally died.* It would have been a great deal worse if it would have happened during their escape or their search for the station. "Problem?" she finally asked when she noticed the look of deep concentration on her pilot's face. She actually thought twice about asking him anything, but if she was going to die, she preferred a bit of notice.

Jake shook his head as he stared at the station that was getting larger by the second in the forward cockpit glass. "Problem? What problem?" He reached over and pulled his own harness tighter, just in case.

"Isn't that station coming up, uh…a little fast?" Simpson asked from the tactical station, his eyes as wide as saucers as he stared at it.

"No, we're fine!" Jakes snapped as he reached up and threw the forward braking thrusters on full power. Everything that wasn't tied down suddenly found itself thrown backward as the inertial dampeners failed as well. "Hang on!"

The Falcon slowed as the braking thrusters worked both against the inertia of her forward movement, as well as the pull Neptune was exerting on her and the station. Jakes compensated the best he could, but he needed to match the speed and trajectory for the docking latches to align properly. Without the main engine or the dampeners, it was theoretically impossible. Lucky for them all, Jakes didn't believe in theories. He knew it would ruin everyone's day if he smashed the transport into the station, so he planned to avoid that at all costs.

Kristin watched Jakes's hands as they played over the fight console. It was like watching a skilled surgeon at work. He made one minor, precise course correction after another, and finally, the Falcon began to spin on its axis. Another abrupt thruster fire sent everyone deeper into their seats.

"Shit," Jakes mumbled as he fought to regain control.

Kristin turned to him and saw a smile creeping across his lips as the ship slowed and reoriented itself to the docking collar on the station. On the screen, the display changed to a representation of the position of the dock in relation to the Falcon's hatch.

"Hang on, everyone," Jakes warned again as the display went from green to red, then back to green again. "Docking in three… two…one…"

The *thud* of metal on metal reverberated throughout the ship as the Falcon latched on to the primitive docking collar.

"Docked and locked, ladies and gentlemen," Jakes proudly proclaimed, grinning like that Cheshire cat in that ancient children's story.

There were sounds of cheers from the back as everyone realized that whatever had happened and whatever was coming, they would at least have a bit of time to regroup and breathe again.

"Moss, is there breathable atmosphere on the other side of our hatch?" Kristin asked, knowing that if there wasn't, they would need to send a team aboard and repair those systems before actually beginning work on the damaged Falcon. That was something that would set their timetable back significantly, and she hoped to avoid anything that would squander precious minutes. "Today, Moss."

"Yes, ma'am," Moss replied. "Everything is a bit slower on back-up power, and… Wait! I am getting atmosphere on the other side of the lock. It's a bit stale and a little thin, but it's definitely breathable."

"Finally," Kristin said with a heavy sigh, "a break." She unbuckled herself from her seat and turned to the remaining members of her team. "Moss, take a team into the station and stabilize the systems. If you can manage to bring the thrusters online and stabilize our drift in a reasonable amount of time, do it. If not, don't waste time on it and just assist Jakes with ship repairs. Jakes, take whoever you need and start repairs. Tolliver, you and your people take our guest to the med-bay. The very second she's capable of coherent speech, call me. Also, I want some of your people with tech experience working on the life-support systems. I have no idea how long we're going to be here, and I'd like to continue breathing until we leave. Marshall, you and Simpson come with me to the control room. We need to access the station systems and plan our next move, whatever the hell that's going to be. Hopefully, the communications array is still operational."

There were nods and acknowledgments, but no one moved for the airlock.

"Let's get a move-on, people! We've got a lot of work to do and not much time to do it. I also want everyone armed, so remember to take a sidearm from the weapons locker."

With that firm command, everyone began to scamper. The medical team already had their patient on a gurney and had wheeled her to the hatch. Moss and his team were right behind them, carrying tool packs, and Simpson and Marshall were waiting for her. The only one who hadn't moved from his seat was Jakes.

"You waiting on a special invitation, Jakes?" Kristin asked.

Jakes swiveled to face her and shook his head. "Why do you even want to reactivate this station, if you're so concerned about wasting time? We should be putting all our effort and resources into repairing this ship so we can get the hell out of here."

Kristin shook her head and sat back in the co-pilot seat. "Normally, I'd agree, but these old stations were built to take a beating. If we can get any of the defensive systems operational, we might be able to hold the *Bonaventure* and the N'Torr off. Maybe, just maybe, we can keep them busy until help arrives. Anyway, it'd be a whole lot safer and easier to defend than sitting out there in a damaged Falcon if it comes to that."

"Okay," Jakes said, sighing in resignation. "I just hope you know what you're doing, because this place can turn into the Alamo pretty damn quick."

"Me too," she said with a smile as she stood and offered a hand to the pilot.

Jakes unbuckled and took her hand as he stood. His knees were still a little unsteady, shaking like jelly beneath his weight, but he kept that to himself as he stood. "Time to get to work."

Kristin watched him walk over to the group of technical engineers Moss had left for him. She had always liked Jakes, but after everything they'd gone through together, she now felt a deep attraction to the man. *He's a real pain in the ass,* she thought, casually gazing at him, *but he certainly has the balls to pay for it. .*

She was happy to get everyone out of the Falcon. The leak had worsened, and atmosphere was venting into space at a faster rate than before. She was also happy to see that everyone was focused on one task or another; the job at hand distracted them from the horrors that were rapidly closing in on them. She knew the aliens would eventually find them, especially after the power systems went back online. Space was too empty, and when the station came back to life and lit up deep space, it would be like a beacon, alerting the *Bonaventure* or the alien ship of their presence.

"Come on, gentlemen. We need to see if Lady Luck is still on our side," she said, then handed each of them a fresh power pack for their weapons and led them into the station.

The first thing Kristin noticed was the temperature; it was cold. The life support had been left on after the station was abandoned, but over the years of vacancy, the automatic systems had begun to fail. Consequently, the computer had to make tradeoffs to keep the station from completely deteriorating. One of the concessions it made was to cut the temperature to the bone. It was temperate enough for them to survive for a while, but they wouldn't last over an extended period of time.

"Tolliver?" she said into her headset, shivering a bit.

"Yes, Commander?"

"How do the environmental systems look? It's a bit chilly in here."

"Give me a few minutes. One of the engineers is working on redirecting power."

After a momentary pause, the lights came on, and the vents started pumping in warm air.

"We managed to redirect the solar panels and get some of the essential systems back, like life support, Commander. As far as the rest of it, that will be up to Moss. If you need me, I'll be in the infirmary, with our patient."

"Thanks, Doc. I'll stop in when I can. Keep me updated on her condition."

"Will do."

Lights illuminated the station, and Kristin finally had a good look at its condition. "What a freaking mess," she said, noticing that it hadn't been maintained or abandoned in a very orderly manner.

The command and control room looked mostly salvageable as Simpson sat at the operations console and attempted to restore systems with what little power they had to work with. He'd been taught power management at the Academy, but he usually had more resources to rely on. "Damn," he muttered under his breath.

"Simpson, what do we have? Anything usable at all?"

Simpson was so focused on transferring the power that he didn't even notice his commander behind him until she tapped him on the shoulder. "Huh? Oh! Yes, sir...er, ma'am. Sorry, ma'am."

"Wake up, Simpson. What do we have?" Kristin gestured to the console, as if to illustrate her question.

Simpson pulled up the system status display and pointed to the red and green highlighted status lights that blinked on the board like decorations on some sort of futuristic Christmas tree. Cleverly, he first directed the new flow of power to the diagnostics display; he would have no way of knowing what was out without the diagnostics computer up and running. "The lights on the display indicate the status of station systems. The green are working just fine, while the red indicates that something is damaged or powered off."

"So green is good, red is bad?"

"Yes, ma'am."

"Simpson, perhaps you can be…a little more specific," she urged, wearing a look that was far more condescending than flattering. "Believe it or not, I'm capable of understanding a few big words now and then."

"Sorry, ma'am," he said again, blushing this time. He pointed at the screen. "These systems, including sensors, weapons, and thrusters, are offline, but as soon as Moss can get me some more power, I should be able to activate most of them."

Kristin could see from the look on his face that he was hiding some sort of bad news. "What else, Simpson? What is it you *aren't* telling me? I don't like secrets."

"I'm afraid that the weapons systems won't amount to very much."

"What does that mean?"

"It means…" Simpson sighed heavily. "It seems the plasma emitters in the turrets are tapped out, and someone removed the remainder of the missiles from their launch tubes. I can power the weapons up, but there's no ammo to shoot."

In an instant, Kristin's hopes were flushed down the drain. Her plan depended greatly on being able to hold out there if necessary. Sooner or later, the aliens would find them, and they were as good as dead if they had no way to defend themselves from that inevitable onslaught.

"There is one thing we could do," Marshall said from the security console. Till then, he had remained silent, but no one seemed to recognize the obvious answer, and he was compelled to point it out.

Simpson and Kristin turned and stared at him.

"Why don't we pull the two remaining missiles from the Falcon and just load them into the station launchers? They can probably be adapted. It won't be much, but it'd be better than nothing."

Kristin was dumbfounded and a bit embarrassed that she'd missed something so simple, but Simpson just smiled and started to laugh.

"Marshall," Simpson finally said, "you're wearing the wrong uniform, man. You should have been a science geek instead of a security guy. You're a genius." He spun around to Kristin and brought up the launcher specifications. "He's right, Commander. The launchers really haven't changed much over the years. The missile style since this station's heyday really hasn't changed much either. They manufactured so many that it was easier and more cost effective to keep them in inventory than it would have been to rebuild all the launcher systems the military used throughout the Alliance. It should work."

"Finally, something. Contact Jakes and have him pull the two remaining hornet missiles from their nests so they can be installed here. Then I want you to call Moss and tell him to restore power as quickly as possible." Kristin turned to Marshall and smiled broadly, perhaps for the first time in a long while. "Marshall, my friend, you are a giant among men. I now realize why I need you around so much."

"Thank you, ma'am," Marshall said with a nod.

"Simpson, where are we with communications?"

Simpson shook his head and flicked a few switches on the board. Static screeched from the speakers in the ceiling, confirming something Kristin already suspected: They were being jammed. At least Simpson was intelligent enough to test the receiver before trying to send a message out. If they had done that, the *Bonaventure* sensors would have locked on to their location in a matter of minutes.

Kristin nodded and put a hand on the young man's shoulder. "See what you can do about comms, Simpson. There may be a time when the jamming isn't an issue, and we'll need to get a call out."

"Yes, ma'am," Simpson said quietly. "I'll get right on it."

"Very good. If anyone needs me, I'll be in the infirmary."

"Commander," Marshall said before Kristin got through the hatchway, "what do you want me to do? Everyone seems to have an assignment but me."

Kristin stopped and turned to face the large security man. "You have the most important job here, Marshall. Sooner or later, we *will* be boarded, either by alien bugs or former friends and shipmates possessed by alien bugs. I need you to set a plan in place so that we'll have a proper defense against them."

"I'll see to it, Commander."

Kristin had no doubt that Marshall would, in fact, come up with a great plan; that was the kind of man and soldier he was. Moss and Tolliver were doing a great job bringing the station back to life. The corridors were well lit and even a little warmer. The gravity seemed to have stabilized as well, a benefit of the thrusters coming back online. At that rate, though, they would show up like a light-house on a clear, dark night, beckoning the enemy right to them. *There's just one thing left to repair,* Kristin thought as she found the room with the infirmary sign outside it. They were running out of time, and she didn't have the luxury of waiting for their patient to regain consciousness. She needed answers, and she needed them immediately.

As well as Moss and Tolliver had managed to stabilize the environmental systems, the smell lingered—a combination of rusting metal, oil, and whatever decaying food was left in the unrefrigerated pantry. Her repair crews wanted to flush the garbage out into space, but Kristin didn't think that was a very good idea. Any activity, especially organic, would show up on sensors and lead their enemies right back to them, and they weren't nearly ready for company.

"Moss to Commander Dante," said the young engineer's voice over her headset.

"Dante here." Kristin was happy that, whatever the reason for the communications jamming, it didn't affect their internal communications. She didn't know what they'd do if the repair teams couldn't coordinate their crucial activities in a station that size.

"Ma'am, we've done just about as much as we can with the reactor down here. It's in really crappy shape, but we've managed to stabilize the core. There's one major issue though."

Kristin sighed. "Of course there is. What is it?"

The core has a bit of a leak, and the radiation level will eventually rise to harmful levels. She's safe for the moment, but it's taken a load of TLC just to keep her from blowing. Good news is that I did manage to repair one of the pulse cannons. I don't know how long it'll last, but I thought it might help."

"Good job, Moss. Get your teams over to Jakes and give him a hand with the Falcon." The news about the functional pulse cannon was great. It was a pretty primitive weapon, as compared to modern artillery, but with enough power behind it, the gun could do a fair amount of damage. Suddenly, an idea popped into her mind; of course it was crazy, but it was high time for crazy. "Moss, what would it take to force an overload in the reactor core and cause an explosion?"

"Hmm. I don't know. Maybe breathe on it too heavy. With it leaking like that, it might just go all by itself."

"How long till levels are harmful?"

Moss pulled out his scanner and took additional readings. "About forty-eight hours till then and another six till it goes *boom*, unless we bulk up the shielding. Why?"

The reply confirmed the facts she needed. "Thanks. Can you can rig a destruct switch to auto-trigger it from the control room?"

"Seriously?"

"Seriously, Moss."

"Sorry about the attitude, ma'am, but it was a pain just to get it up and running in the first place, but yes, I can do that. Do you need a timer?"

"Five minutes should work fine."

"Consider it done, ma'am. We'll get right on it."

Theoretically, the station was the largest weapon Kristin's crew had to work with; she hoped there was actually a way to use it as such, if the time and situation called for it. Regardless, it was good to have the option, and it would be even better with a timer that would allow them to control the diversion, giving them a small window to escape.

The conversation with Moss had distracted her, but Kristin now found herself outside the closed door to the medical facility. She pushed as hard as she could, but the door remained stuck.

"Hang on!" a voice yelled from the other side. "It's sticking due to the humidity in here."

Kristin watched as the door finally pulled open, albeit slowly and with an ear-splitting squeal. She stepped in and watched the two med techs push the door closed behind her.

Tolliver stepped out to greet her, and her first impression was that the doctor didn't look very happy. "Welcome, Commander," he said with a gesture to the medical bay, "to my little slice of hell."

"Report."

Tolliver looked at her and smiled. "Not much to say. Most of the medical equipment and meds have been removed. There were a few older-model diagnostic instruments that we're trying to make use of, but for the most part, what we have here is basically a large area with a bunch of beds. We have managed to get the water recycling systems back online, and after a few tries, it's starting to look and smell less like the station and more like drinkable water. It will probably be another half-hour or so till we have that back online. The rest of it is pretty apparent. With Mr. Moss's help, we have life support function, and most of the lights and secondary systems are restored."

"And your patient?" Kristin asked, nodding to the body on the bio-bed behind Tolliver.

Tolliver gestured for Kristin to follow him. The woman was still unconscious, but the reading on the monitor they'd set up next to the bed seemed to show that her vital signs were improving. "Her condition is improving, as are her vitals. I suggest we let her sleep a few more hours before waking her."

Kristin shook her head. "No, Doctor. That's not good enough. Wake her now."

Tolliver seemed upset that someone would attempt to over-rule his medical advice. "She was in shock. Waking her in her present condition is not advised, Commander Dante."

Everyone in the room noticed the anger in Kristin's voice, with the possible exception of Tolliver. The other med techs seemed to give them more and more space, as the reputation of anger management issues was a rumored personality issue with the *Bonaventure's* executive officer.

"Tolliver, there is a high possibility that those things from the transport ship will overrun us any minute. This woman," Kristin snapped, gesturing at the unconscious stranger, "might be our only hope. You *will* wake her, or I will relieve you of your duties and find someone else who can follow orders." Kristin did not really mean to sound as harsh and threatening as she did, but it was a struggle for her to hold back her rage. It was the one trait she had inherited from her father, though he had managed to control that nasty emotion and even use it to his own advantage; it had never been quite that simple for her.

Tolliver noticed the looks they were getting from the medical techs under his command, and the last thing he wanted was to be the center of attention, especially for bickering with his commander. He wasn't stupid; he was on that transport ship with the commander and everyone else, and he had seen, with his own eyes, what happened. He had no desire to be the next host for one of those things, and he did not appreciate the commander's insinuation that he was being careless. "Fine," he finally responded, more in an attempt to defuse the situation than to admit she was right. "You will take responsibility if her condition worsens."

"Fine," Kristin said with a nod. "Just get on with it."

Tolliver reached into his med kit and pulled out a spray injector and a small bottle of liquid marked "Adrenaline." He screwed it into the injector and placed it against the side of her neck before pulling the trigger on the instrument. The small bottle emptied with an audible *hiss* as the contents disappeared into his patient.

A few seconds later, her eyes opened, and the screaming began. "Stay away from me! No! No! Get them off me!"

Tolliver called two of his techs over and ordered them to hold her down on the bed. "Take it easy!" he yelled over her tantrum. "We rescued you. You are okay."

Kristin noticed that Tolliver was having little luck, so she decided to try her own approach. She stepped between them and pushed Tolliver out of the way. Then, with an open hand, she smacked the patient right across the face. "Lieutenant, get a hold of yourself right now! That's an order!"

Tolliver was about to object strongly to her methods when the screaming and thrashing about stopped, and his patient pushed herself back in her bed.

"Commander," she finally said.

"What did you say?" Kristin asked in surprise.

"Not lieutenant. My rank is commander, Commander Linda Stack," she said as she sat up and glanced around the medical bay. "Who are you, and where the hell am I?"

Kristin gestured for the two med techs who were restraining her to release their grip and back off. "You, too, Dr. Tolliver. Please give Commander Stack and me a little privacy."

"Not too long, Commander Dante," Tolliver said before picking up his med kit and moving off to the other side of the bay with his two techs. "We need to—"

"You need to step out for a moment, Doctor," Kristin scolded. When he finally complied, she turned to Commander Stack. "My name is Commander Kristin Dante, and I am the executive officer aboard the *USS Bonaventure*. We found you on your transport and brought you here."

"Where exactly is here?"

"One of the old decommissioned outposts, just outside the orbit of Neptune."

Stack shook her head, as if trying to understand the meaning of the words Kristin was saying. "Why aren't we on your ship?"

Kristin sat on the bed beside the dark-haired woman and tried to sum up the situation as best she could. "For the same reason you're not onboard yours, Commander Stack."

"Shit," was all she could say as she laid her head back on the pillow and stared up at the fluorescent lights in the ceiling. Warm tears rolled down her face as she recalled the horror that began several days earlier.

Kristin listened intently. The transport, owned and operated by Striker Industries, was ordered to coordinates just beyond the orbit of Saturn to rendezvous with another ship for a clandestine cargo transfer. Stack left parts of the story out, explaining that whoever had ordered them out there was "beyond [her] pay grade."

After several days of travel, the transport ship *Magellan* reached their coordinates and waited for the arrival of whoever held the cargo they were supposed to transport. Days went by, but their captain, Benjamin Merit, claimed they were running under a communications blackout. "Our orders stated that we were to stand by at those coordinates," Stack said, "until the other ship showed up. Of course there were rumors floating around among the eighty-seven crewmembers. We didn't know if we were set to meet pirates, the military, or if it was some other illegal venture. We all knew our employer wasn't exactly...always on the straight and narrow, if you know what I mean."

"I do," Kristin said. "Go on."

"Eventually, scanners picked up the ship. It was huge, bigger than anything ever recorded and definitely alien in origin. It appeared to just drift into view, rather than coming in under power, but then it went entirely motionless and just floated off our starboard bow, less than 200 kilometers away. It was just…eerie."

"I bet."

"Scans revealed nothing, and with three more days gone, Captain Merit decided to send a shuttle over to investigate the ship, hoping they'd find some sort of life-altering salvage. Unfortunately for him and the rest of the *Magellan* crew, I guess it was more life-altering than they ever could have expected."

Kristin listened intently as Stack continued.

"A salvage and engineering crew went over to the alien vessel, led by Captain Merit. Usually, the executive officer would go, but I was ordered to remain with the ship, while the captain went off in search of his fortune and glory. He assumed it was really the vessel he'd been ordered to meet. Whether or not that was true, Merit wanted to go stake his claim to whatever was onboard before anyone else beat him to it. You know, thinking back on it, I guess it's kind of funny," Stack added.

"Funny?"

Stack offered a half-smile. "They staked their claim to him instead. We lost all communications with the shuttle for more than eight hours. Suddenly, we detected that they had detached and were on their way back to the ship. We were prepared to receive them and the cargo they were transporting. The captain assured us that it was the ship we were supposed to meet, and he claimed the haul was 'wondrous.' Yes, he used that exact word."

Stack went on to explain that after the shuttle docked with the *Magellan*, she wanted to keep the crew and their cargo in quarantine, as per procedures instituted by the Alliance, but the captain overrode those orders.

"How could he do that?" Kristin asked curiously; it was, after all, one of the prime directives upon any kind of contact with an unknown and possibly alien ship. No one wanted a pathogen of alien origin to make it back to Earth; thus, every ship commander was made aware of that protocol, and it was part of his or her corporate agreements before taking command of a ship.

"He stared at me on the monitor," Stack recounted, as the tears began to fall again, "and he said, 'That is not acceptable to *us*.' The captain then used his code to break quarantine, and he and the others brought several containers out of the shuttle hangar and into the central corridor. We watched on the bridge as they opened the containers and pushed them over onto the deck."

Kristin felt Stack's hand reach for hers and squeeze tightly.

"Those things came out it, hundreds of them. All I could do was stand there and watch as they attacked members of my crew. They stuck to them, embedded in them. The crewmen creamed and fell, every last one of them. Then those nasty things just got up and moved on to others. We watched as they went through my ship and took over everyone."

"What happened next? What did you do?" Kristin asked.

Stack shook her head. "We were losing crew faster and faster, and there was nothing we could do but run to nowhere. When we heard them at the door to the bridge, most of us panicked. We were trapped, and the bridge door was the only way in or out. I had to do something, so I went to the engineering panel and told the computer to send a surge from the reactor across to the control systems for engine and flight control. I managed to fry both of the engines and the thruster controls. That was when we heard them in the ceiling panels. They started falling on us like black hail. I managed to pull one of the exhaust panels off the floor by the engineering console and roll tightly into it. I pulled the panel back over me and sealed myself in."

By now, Stack was sobbing uncontrollably, and she sat up and buried her head in Kristin's shoulder.

"I-I know it was cowardly, b-but there was nothing I could do. They were screaming, all of them, and I couldn't... There was just nothing I could do. I couldn't save them. A few minutes later, everything went quiet, like some terrible scene in a horror movie. The captain came onto the bridge and started giving orders, as if nothing had happened. They tried to get the engines started, said they had to get to Earth to clear the way for the Jek'Tan. I think that was when I passed out, and I don't remember anything else till... well, now."

Kristin nodded and pulled her hand away. Stack's eyes were swollen from crying, and her hair was a mess. "Thank you, Linda," she said, gently pushing the woman back to the pillow. "Tolliver!" she called as Stack closed her eyes.

Tolliver burst back in the room, with his med techs in tow. "Are you finished with my patient now?" he snapped. "She exhausted." He ran his diagnostics scanner over her and, despite appearances, noted that her vitals were all still in the green.

"For now, Doctor. Take care of her. Get her cleaned up and fed, then send her to the control room," Kristin responded as she stood from her seat on the side of the bed.

It all made sense now. The distress call was just a setup to lure the *Bonaventure* there to complete the redirected *Magellan* mission to take these things back to Earth. She was sure they would repair the *Bonaventure* and get underway, heading back to Earth, carrying their death cargo and with that alien ship in tow. Even if they made it to Mars, the results would be disastrous and only delay the inevitable.

"Commander Dante?"

Kristin's comm buzzed in her ear, and the voice on the other end didn't sound the least bit happy. "What is it, Jakes?"

"You need to come down to the repair bay right away."

Kristin realized then that it wasn't unhappiness she was hearing; rather, it was borderline panic in the voice of her pilot. Of everyone there, Jakes was the last one she would have expected that from, and she found that quite unnerving. "What is it?"

"It would be easier if I could explain it to you in person, Commander."

"I'll be right down. Dante out." Kristin left the infirmary and headed for the shuttle repair bay instead of the control room. She had the beginnings of a plan in her head, but she needed to discuss it with Jakes, Simpson, and Marshall. None of them were going to like it, but there really wasn't much choice. In back-to-the-wall moments like that, she always thought of her dad, the almighty, all-knowing admiral. The man was a horrible father, and her proudest moment was when she graduated from the Academy and was finally able to place a couple planets between them, but he undeniably had no equal when it came to serving as a military strategist. For the first time in a long while, she allowed herself a self-indulgent smile as she realized that if the admiral knew what she had in mind, he would be proud of her—at least just before throwing her in the brig for coming up with such a crazy plan in the first place.

I'll sure miss the old man, Michael, and Kate, she thought, *but perhaps that's the going price of insanity nowadays. A Dante saving the world? Won't that be...poetic?*

Chapter 11

The *Alexa* covered the distance from Mars to Earth in less than sixty hours, entirely unchallenged. One of the reasons for that was the unique friend-or-foe system Tobias had cleverly installed. The circuit had a chameleon-like property of rendering the ship as a friendly vessel to opponents. Only a ship in visual range could tell that there was any difference between the ship they were seeing and the one reflecting back to them over their friend-or-foe sensors.

Michael and Kate each used the time and relative safety to their own advantage. For Michael, it was a time to heal. The wound in his leg would require more than the two and a half days to mend completely, but it was enough time so that his leg would not hinder him in what they planned to do. It also afforded him time to attempt to decrypt the data he'd downloaded onto the drive. Not only did he need to find a solution to decoding the messages, but he also needed to filter out the thousands of day-to-day messages that obscured the vital information they were looking for. Luckily, the pain in his leg had no bearing on that. Kate acknowledged that he was the code specialist in the family and deferred to his talents to find the information they needed from the drive. Anyway, she had her own issues to attend to.

After leaving Mars and tending to her brother, Kate took the opportunity to, at Michael's insistence, grab a solid eight hours of sleep. She fought the idea at first, arguing that there was too much to do and that slumber would be counterproductive, selfish, and lazy—none of which she pegged herself to be. Only after assurances that he would spend every valuable moment trying to pull evidence off the drive did she finally agree.

In the end, it was probably the smartest decision she'd made in days. The nap seemed to eliminate a great deal of the fatigue and restlessness lurking in her mind and helped her push past the deaths of her father and the only two men who could clear her from the traitorous label she'd inherited. More than anything, it gave her the opportunity to begin to plan out their next move.

The first thing she attempted, after a shower and a proper meal, was to try to contact Kristin. Their little sister was the executive officer on the *Bonaventure* and always had an interesting perspective on any problem. When they were growing up, she was so much like the admiral that it came as no surprise to Michael or Kate that she could not get along with the old man. That feeling only grew worse after their mother left them. Of all of them, only their mother could dig through the layers of bullshit and stupidity under which Kristin insisted on burying herself. It didn't help that their famous father seemed to enjoy playing them all against each other. While many siblings would squabble over being Daddy's favorite, he looked at all three as little more than a family pet, and that placed a wedge between any relationships they tried to foster with each other. It was a crappy way to live, but it did allow the admiral to squeeze maximum efficiency out of all three of his kids.

They each reacted differently to his odd form of parenting. Michael held on to their father the longest, trying desperately to mold himself into what the admiral would consider not just the good son but the perfect one. The major problem with this was that their father's view of what his children should be seemed to vary daily; that was only one of his tragic flaws that drove their mother away.

Kristin emulated the legend and her perceptions of what the man was but never allowed herself to get close enough to allow him to do to her what he'd done to their mother. This ultimately molded her into something she never intended, a mirror image of the man she respected but never trusted enough to see him as anything beyond a heroic icon to her. The day she realized how alike they were was the day she requested a deep space mission. It didn't matter where or what ship it was on, as long as it got her off of Earth and far away. It seemed that luck was on her side when she was sent to the *Bonaventure,* just a step away from a captaincy of her own. Kate suspected that the admiral was silently behind it, pulling strings for his youngest daughter, even if she didn't want to accept it; she knew he'd done that for all of them, even though he would never admit to it. In many ways, he'd done what he thought was right. In the end, he ended up with three strong kids at the cost of never being able to call themselves a family.

Now, Kate was surprised that she couldn't reach her younger sister. Contacting the *Bonaventure* directly only earned her an ear-ful of static, and the Alliance military offices would only say she was on some sort of mission, under radio silence. The problem was that Kate knew the difference between the interference she was hearing and that of a ship under radio silence. Obviously, someone was jam-ming the transmission at the source. What she didn't know was who was responsible, the *Bonaventure* or some other ship. Considering that being a Dante was now an unhealthy state, as deadly as any virus in any known universe, with just as grim of a prognosis, she began to fear for Kristin's life. As much as she wanted to go search for her, Kate realized that the only option for them was to continue on to Earth and unravel the mystery they'd gotten themselves into. It would also be the best place to find out the location of Kristin and the *Bonaventure,* and they could also determine if the lack of contact with the Alliance's newest ship had anything to do with the other ship disappearances.

"Kate, get up here," Michael's voice said over the comm speaker in her cabin. "We're just coming up on the outer markers for the moon."

"On my way," Kate shot back after activating the comm on the tabletop by her bed.

Things were about to get tricky. There was a large volume of space between Mars and Earth to evade tracking, but that had dried up into only a few approach vectors that wouldn't draw the atten-tion of the Alliance military or the Stratton family on the moon. An increasing number of patrol ships were also in play, as the odds on them being discovered improved tenfold. This would render their friend-or-foe stealth system useless or maybe even dangerous if a ship compared the readings to what they saw out the window; if that was the case, they'd be boarded in an instant. Therefore, she had to take the ship in manually.

"Hey, Mike, how's it coming?" Kate asked as she walked past her brother on the way to the pilot seat.

"Fine," he said without looking up from the computer terminal he'd downloaded the call logs into. He'd been sitting there for hours with his leg elevated, trying to give it time to heal before he was forced to put pressure on it.

Kate sat down in her seat and put the communications headset on before switching off the auto-flight systems and taking over manual flight control of the *Alexa*. "Define fine, little brother."

Michael swiveled his chair around to face her. She could see the hours etched on his face, hanging under his eyes like duffel bags, evidence that he'd spent every promised minute trying to decipher the information he'd downloaded back on Mars. "I'm going as fast as I can, Kate. I've got a few things, but the sheer volume of messages is making this a little difficult for one person. They're also encrypted. I can break the code, but it changes with every subsequent message."

Kate turned back to him and smiled. "I have faith in you, bro, but we're getting close to Earth. Do you have anything so far?"

"You mean besides a migraine?" Michael asked with a small chuckle.

"Yes. Anything…weird?"

"There's a lot of chatter, but it appears that most of the communications between Striker and Rosten were transferred to a protected file named 'Gemini.' I have no idea what that's in reference to, but the file is locked with an encryption sequence I've never seen before. It's almost like he expected someone to eventually come and swipe it. There is one thing that's highly unusual though."

Kate knew her brother, who was never one to rouse too easily; if this had piqued his curiosity, it was, at the very least, something worth noting. "And what would that be?"

"There seems to be another level of comm traffic, in a far higher frequency. The Alliance doesn't even have the gear to receive that."

Kate turned back to her brother and pulled the headset off. "The military sometimes uses higher frequencies to transmit burst messages in times of war."

Michael shook his head. "I'm aware of that, but there is no war going on right now, right? Also, the transmissions weren't quick burst messages. They were sent on a loop, in a repeating format."

"Directed where?"

Michael shrugged. "I have no idea. Based on what I do have, I know it required a lot of power, and most of the transmissions were directed past any receiving stations I know of, sent out of the system. You know the oddest part of it all?"

"What would that be?"

"These higher-than-normal-frequency signals have been going on since the establishment of the relay. Someone's been sending signals out to…well, seemingly nowhere, for more than 150 years. From the old-style transmitting format, I'd say the signal could even predate the relay and originate on Earth."

"And the contents of the messages?"

Michael looked back at his computer screen and noted that most of the information was numerical. It would have been indecipherable, but there was something in the format that looked familiar. It took only a few seconds for him to recognize the pattern. "Got it! It's a repeating numerical pattern. It has to be spacial coordinates, with time and date stamps. Maybe it's a ship schedule, based on the way the numbers line up." Michael flipped through some of the other messages in an attempt to verify his theory. "Most of the other messages are the same, a tight, high-frequency beam focused out of this system, with coordinates in space, along with arrival times. There are ship names here as well."

Kate thought about it before asking her next question. "What are some of those names?"

Michael scanned the listing as he adjusted the decryption sequence. He wanted to be absolutely correct about before making any fantastic, irrational statement. "Let's see. We have, uh…the *Saratoga*, the *Shining Star*, the *Solar Belle*—"

"All famous disappearances," Kate interrupted.

"Yep, every one of them," Michael agreed, nodding his head as he stared, aghast, at the telling list. "My God. This record of ship disappearances stretches back to the beginnings of interplanetary travel."

"Can you plot those coordinates to the flight plans? Do they intersect?"

Michael punched a few numbers into the computer and waited for the readout. "Hmm," he said as he read the results.

"Well? What does it say?" Kate asked impatiently.

Michael nodded again. "They all intersect," he affirmed. "For some reason, Striker and his ancestors were responsible for the disappearances of *all* these ships."

Kate nearly jumped up and down in her seat, somewhat excited about the possibility of finally having some sort of tangible evidence she could use against Rosten and Striker. "Is it solid, enough to take to the Alliance?"

"No," Michael said with a shake of his head, defeat dripping from his voice.

"Why not?"

"I'm afraid they'll just dismiss it as circumstantial," he finally said with a gesture to the computer, "and that's not even taking into account your criminal status with the Alliance or the power of the two men you're accusing. In other words, we need something more…well, just a lot more."

"So we get it then," Kate said, turning back to her flight controls. "Dad was right all along, with that damn conspiracy theory of his. In fact, he may have underestimated the problem, and that might have gotten him killed. I'm going to finish this for him and see that everyone responsible is punished."

"Correction. *We're* going to," Michael added. He moved forward and dropped soundlessly into the co-pilot seat next to his sister. "As in *we* will make certain everyone responsible is punished. Got that, Super Sis?"

Kate nodded and was about to offer some sort of snappy retort when a blinking light on her panel caught her attention. "Strap in!"

If there was one thing Michael had learned from a lifetime of growing up with his sister, it was that it was in his best interest not to force her to bark any order more than once. As he fastened the belt, he also noted the light and realized her concern: They were being scanned by another ship. Without waiting for her next order, Michael transferred tactical to his co-pilot station and finally identified what was tracking them.

"Alliance light cruiser tracking us. Range is 12,000 kilometers to port quarter and closing."

Michael watched his sister as she handled the controls. If the cruiser decided to investigate, they would discover that they were not the transport they were tracking but something else entirely. Kate eased the controls just a point or two to the starboard, in the hopes that it would buy them a little more time or even cause the cruiser to give up on them completely. The smile on her face indicated that she was enjoying it, even while Michael was scared to death. He envied Kate and Kristin for being so at home among the stars; he had always been the landlubber of the family, much to his father's and his sisters' chagrin.

"Friend-or-foe system?" she asked.

"In operation," he said, almost in a whisper, but then he remembered they were not immersed in a heated game of golf or an old World War II submarine movie. "We are reading as an Oscar-class transport."

"Good. Keep an eye on the tactical display and let me know the instant he starts to close again," Kate ordered. She course-corrected again to extend their outward trajectory and give the cruiser more room to hopefully miss them.

Unfortunately, luck being what it was, good fortune was not always on their side.

"Cruiser's changing course. She's heading to us at one-quarter speed."

Another light illuminated her board, a notification that they were being hailed.

"Put it on speaker," Kate ordered.

"Speaker?" Michael replied, dumbfounded. "Are you insane? Why should we give him another reason to get closer? We should just run, sis. This ship is probably faster than theirs, and—"

"You're probably right," Kate agreed, "but we *aren't* faster than all of them together will be when they close in. Let me handle this, little brother. This isn't my first rodeo. Just put it on speaker."

With an exasperated sigh, Michael did as he was told

"…is the cruiser *Washington,* calling the transport ship *Hera.* Do you read? Over," repeated the transmission from the patrol cruiser that was quickly closing in.

Kate clicked on her headset and took a deep breath. "*Washington,* this is *Hera.* How are you boys in the military doing, and what can my little transport do for you?"

Michael was impressed by his sister's deep Southern accent, so much so that he almost had to stifle a laugh.

"*Hera,*" came the reply," we noticed that you instituted a change in course out of the prescribed vectors for Earth landing. Is there a problem?"

Kate pulled up the display for the friend-or-foe system and made one or two minor changes to the information being broadcast. She was about to confess to a malfunction, and she had to make the lie believable so the *Washington* would leave them alone. "No problem, *Washington*. We just have an out-of-tune starboard thruster that doesn't know when to stop thrusting," she fibbed.

"Not picking up any problems with you starboard thruster, *Hera*. Are you certain that's where the problem is?"

Michael began to feel a bit concerned, especially since the voice from the cruiser suddenly sounded far less trusting than it had before.

"Give it a second, *Washington*," Kate responded, almost cheerfully. "The problem is intermittent."

"Roger, *Hera*," the voice replied. "Wait! There it is. We've logged your issue, if anyone down there questions you. Have a safe landing, *Hera*."

Michael let out a deep sigh of relief, but that feeling quickly dissipated when he realized that, for some unknown reason, Kate would not let the issue go; the smile on his face forced him deeper into the safety of his seat. "Please don't," he begged.

"Are you sure you fellas don't wanna stop and board me? We've been in space too long, and I'd appreciate the company of some fresh faces, particularly of the male persuasion," she flirted in a drawl, even batting her eyelashes for effect.

"No, *Hera*," the voice replied. "We'd love to, but we need to get back on patrol. Thanks anyway."

"You don't know what you're missin', *Washington*. *Hera* out." With that, Kate leaned over and shut the transmission down.

"Um, which class was that at the Academy? I must have missed it!" Michael said, finally losing it.

"Just check the tactical read." Kate ordered without that smile on her face. "Where is the *Washington* now?"

Michael pulled up the readout out and noted that the *Washington* had altered its course back to its original patrol route. "Well, I'll be damned. It freaking worked. They actually veered off. I guess you got us out of that little stampede, Cowgirl."

"Of course I did, little brother. There's a reason why I'm such a freakin' legend in the intelligence community. Shut down the friend-or-foe. We're about to hit atmosphere, and we'll run dark the rest of the way."

Kate angled her small ship down toward Earth and finally into its dense atmosphere. She hadn't been back for a while, but there were some skills that just came naturally to her. As they entered the atmosphere, she altered their angle of reentry so they would seem more like a meteor than a trackable spacecraft.

"Getting a little hot in here, sis," Michael said from the seat next to hers. "This something Dad showed you?"

"The admiral was full of surprises," she replied without taking her eyes off the readouts, noting that their altitude was quickly diminishing.

"Um…I assume you're going to pull up eventually, right?"

"Meteors don't suddenly change course, do they?" Kate altered her course and headed to the Badlands, an aptly named section of the Euro-Asian continent. The Badlands had taken a beating during the war and had remained largely radioactive, due to the limited habitation there to begin with. The radiation would cover their trail as she hugged the ground below most of the radar systems still in use on the planet.

Michael understood her plan, but that did little to squash the queasy feeling in the pit of his stomach as she put the scout through its paces. He noted that the tactical display had them at 100 feet above the surface as she finally leveled off. "You gonna let me in on exactly what the plan is?"

"Sure," Kate answered as she guided *Alexa* past the skeleton timbers of burned-out forests and devastated buildings in towns that no longer existed on anyone's map as more than a warning not to enter without protective gear. "We're going home."

Chapter 12

Michael watched the landscape fly by as he pondered what "home" really was. It certainly had nothing to do with some mystical place he could get to by tapping ruby slippers together, and for him, it wasn't the stuff of "Home Sweet Home" pictures hanging on the wall. In fact, it had nothing to do with anyplace where they were actually raised. Rather, it was a codename the admiral had drilled into them, one that indicated the place his family needed to run to if they ever needed a safe house.

Years earlier, Admiral Dante had told his three children about a piece of property situated on the very tip of Long Island. It was purchased through several different aliases, and since the deed was paid in cash, it was impossible to trace it back to him in any way. He spent years modifying the property and prepping it for a time when someone in the family would require it. It was difficult for any of them to understand the necessity of a safe house then, but things had changed, and now it made perfect sense; in retrospect, many things the admiral did turned out this way. It was a testament to Kate that she still remembered its location.

"Home, huh?" Michael finally said. "You ever been there?"

Kate shook her head, a bit thankful for the distraction of the conversation after the heavy low-altitude flying. It was draining to keep her little ship so close to the ground without smashing it into anything, as was the depressing landscape beneath them. For all the miracles Striker Industries had pulled off to get the world back on its feet, the grim scenery below was a constant reminder of what they once had but had lost so very long ago.

"I overflew the coordinates a few times," she finally said as the *Alexa* finally burst from the English coastline and darted across the Atlantic Ocean, "but I've never had the guts to actually stop for a visit. It felt like I was daring the gods to give me a reason to put the place to use. Looking back, I guess I should have stopped by. Dad... er, the admiral... Geez," she said, shaking her head in frustration with herself. "You know, I don't even really know what to call the man anymore. Anyway, he found out I flew over, and he went bat-shit crazy. He told me if I ever did it again, he'd pull any and all of my flight privileges, then and in the future."

Michael shut his eyes and nodded. "Funny how he got that way. I guess it's easier to reflect on him now that he's gone."

"He's not," Kate snapped. "I need evidence too. I won't believe it till I see a body!"

"Kate..." Michael tried to sound as calming as he could, under the circumstances. "Look, you really need to let this go. I read the report. The explosion took out three floors of Alliance Intelligence HQ, and there's proof that he was inside and signed in on one of those floors when it happened. He's gone."

"Not till I say he is," Kate insisted before she turned back to the controls and watched the waves roll by below them. Striker Industries and their subsidiaries had used their new processes to clean the land, but the results were far less positive in the oceans of Earth. In spots, life still managed to find a way, but in other places, the sea was as dead as a puddle of mud on the moon.

"Wait!" Michael snapped suddenly. "I'm picking up a large metallic object, twenty-two kilometers west of our position and closing."

Kate looked to the skies. "Where?"

"No, under us. I think it could be a sub."

Kate cursed under her breath and considered their options. The only thing that could have tracked them was something in-visible, something lurking under the surface. There weren't many submarines in operation anymore, but they still existed and were used as early warning systems. "Gee. The Dante luck is strong with us today, huh?" she said in a bit of a sarcastic huff. She knew if she tried to gain altitude, the *Alexa* would show up on every tracking system on both sides of the Atlantic, and without the friend-or-foe system on, they were appearing as the scout ship she was sure everyone was still looking for.

"They're trying to contact us," Michael said as he listened to the voice coming over his headset. "It's a U.S. sub, the *Silverfish*, on patrol. They're demanding that we identify, or they'll shoot us down. I've got a feeling they've already identified us though. What should I tell them?"

Kate flicked a switch on her panel and accelerated to the north. "Don't tell them anything. I'm jamming their transmissions."

"They're firing!" Michael exclaimed. "Two contacts, both surface-to-air missiles, and they've got a damn lock too!"

"*Alexa*," Kate said calmly, "prepare countermeasures and interceptors."

"Yes, Kate," the robotic female voice immediately responded.

"What about the sub? They may fire again."

Kate knew her brother had a valid point, but she wasn't prepared to sink a U.S. vessel and litter the already filthy ocean with the bodies of more than 100 innocent men and women in the process. "I'm not going to kill everyone on that ship!" she yelled. "Hell, I may actually have slept with a few of them."

Michael stared at her in disbelief before returning his gaze to the tactical display. "Missiles are closing…300 meters…250…200…"

"*Alexa*, stand by for countermeasures and interceptors," Kate ordered. "We need to make this look good. Michael, you may want to tighten that safety harness of yours."

Michael had no idea what his sister had in mind, but again, he wisely trusted her judgment and did as he was told. "We're at 150 meters…100…50…"

"Now!" Kate snapped out. "Fire countermeasures and interceptors!"

Without waiting for an answer, Kate threw the small scout ship into a dive, heading straight for the ocean surface. Chafe and flares fired out behind the *Alexa* as the countermeasures gave the missiles something new to lock onto. Two interceptor missiles fired from an aft weapons pod and destroyed both missiles as the *Alexa* hit the water with a splash and went under.

"What the hell?!" Michael snapped.

The scout continued its descent, until it touched down on the sandy ocean floor.

"*Alexa*, status report."

"No damage," replied the voice. "We are water tight, but I would not recommend more than thirty minutes of submersion."

"Affirmative," said Kate in agreement. "How are you doing, Mike?"

"What the hell did you just do? How are we underwater?" Michael asked, looking through the cockpit window for cracks and wondering why they weren't filling with water.

"Well, basically, we took out the missiles and are now faking our death," Kate said with a victorious, satisfied smile etched across her face. "As far as the how, you do remember who owned this ship previously, right?"

Michael nodded; he should have known the admiral had built that little aftermarket addition into his private scout ship. He turned his attention back to the tactical display and could see the sub resuming its course, obviously duped into believing they'd made the kill. "They're moving off. You're a maniac, but I love you anyway."

Kate responded with a wider grin. "What are big sisters for?" She reached over and fired the thrusters briefly to get them off the bottom. When she was happy they were a safe distance away from any rocky outcroppings, the rear thrusters came online, supplying them with enough power for forward movement through the murky water.

"I can't believe you kept this from me."

"Get over it," Kate said with a dismissive laugh. "I think we've given them enough distance. Let's try this again. *Alexa*?"

"Yes?" replied the computer.

"Adjust friend-or-foe output to Pattern Six please." Kate put down the data-padd she'd pulled out from under her seat and fired the thrusters. Seconds later, they were back at 100 feet and again heading west, toward the East Coast of the United States.

"What is Pattern Six?"

"Well, as of now, we have the return pitter-patter of a flock of birds," Kate answered with a shrug. "Only eighteen minutes remaining before we reach the eastern seaboard, we hopefully won't need our feathered friends, but it'll keep any other ship busy guessing."

"Good idea."

Thankfully for both of them, the quick trip to their destination was both quiet and uneventful. Michael had returned to the computer, and the system was still deciphering the information from Mars.

Kate remained in her pilot seat and watched as the U.S. coast filled her cockpit window. She checked her chronographer and noted that sunset was only a few minutes away. She set the flight controls back to manual and hovered over the northern tip of Long Island, Shagwong Point specifically, at the northern tip of Montauk State Park.

She found the house right where she remembered it from her training flights during her Academy years. It was isolated and far away from normal traffic, but there was nothing remarkable about it. In fact, the house resembled every other beach house along the coast, yet their father had determined it was the perfect place to hole up. Kate moved slowly over the house, only relying on thrusters, searching for a place to land.

Suddenly, the entire ship was blinking with lights, and the autopilot kicked on.

"*Alexa*," Kate snapped, "why have you taken control?"

Before the computer could respond, the forward monitor came alive with the admiral's voice. "Don't be alarmed. I have detected the *Alexa* and have taken over landing protocols. Control will be returned to you after landing has concluded."

In awe, she looked from the admiral's face on the video to Michael's beside her, then back to the video as the ship descended.

"Look! Down there!" Michael said, pointing.

The area was covered by debris, leaves, and sand, but it was coming alive with a circle of bright, blinking lights. The ship settled down softly within the circumference of the lights and rested there for a brief second before the pad started lowering slowly into the ground.

"Holy crap," Michael stuttered.

Too stunned to utter a word, Kate watched as the lights on the surface slowly dimmed and the *Alexa* descended deeper into the ground. Suddenly, the lift they were on came to a stop, and more lights activated, revealing that they were in a small, underground hangar.

"What now?" Michael asked.

In answer to his question, the monitor came alive again with the face of their father, Admiral Dante. "What you do now, Michael, is collect your things and leave my ship for the house. All home systems are now operational. Further instructions await you inside."

"You mean *my* ship, Admiral Facsimile," Kate answered.

"And take your sister with you."

Kate was about to say something, but the monitor went out again.

"Now I know why my period of grieving will be brief," Kate said as she powered down the *Alexa* systems. She only left the engines on standby, in case they needed to make a fast getaway; the place might have been their so-called home, but she didn't trust it just yet.

Michael stopped briefly to grab the intel from Mars and his pack but was the first at the hatch. Kate took her time packing light, with the exception of the plasma pistol at her hip and another assault rifle flung over her shoulder.

Michael just looked at his well-armed sister and shook his head. "You are aware that we're in our father's house, right?" he said, pointing at the weaponry she carried.

"Incorrect," she answered as she hit the airlock door. "We are in our father's *home*. There is a difference. We need to be ready for trespassers."

The outer hatch opened, and two steps later, they were on the hangar floor. The air smelled a bit musty, and even with the vents blowing in recycled air from the surface, it felt more like a tomb.

"Doesn't look like anybody's been here for a while," Michael said, verbalizing the same thought his sister had.

Kate looked around and was practically mesmerized by what she saw when the lights came up. All along the walls of the hangar were rows of weapons, everything from energy-based plasma and old-style lasers to racks of antique military assault rifles with extra magazines. "Wow. I guess Dad figured it was all going to go to hell," she said in wide-eyed amazement. He's got enough arms here to start a small war."

"Or end one," her brother added.

"True. Look over there." Kate pointed to an open door, obviously an elevator. "Come on."

"Think it's safe?" Michael asked as they approached it and looked inside.

Kate shook her head and laughed. "Didn't you just say a minute ago that this is our father's house? What's there to be afraid of, right?"

"Right…I guess, but—" Michael said, but before he could say another word, Kate stuck out her right hand and shoved him in ahead of her.

"See? Wasn't that easy? Push a button."

Michael looked at the three buttons on the panel. The bottom one was marked "Hangar," the middle said "Ops," and the top was labeled "House." He decided on the "Ops" button, and the door shut so the lift could rise. For an elevator that had missed more than a few service calls, the ride was surprisingly quiet and quick. One level up, the doors opened to reveal the nerve center of the admiral's secret safe house.

"Wow. Look at all this," Michael whispered as he took in the state-of-the-art computer and communications equipment in the center of a room, ringed with monitors that displayed information of all types. The systems activated as soon as they stepped off the elevator.

"Dad was busy."

"No shit," Kate said as she pulled the long sheet of plastic off the operating control boards in the center of the room. She looked them over before pulling a chair over and sitting down. From what she could see, the screens revealed everything from local security sensor readings to sensitive communications on and off the planet.

"If Striker knew Dad had access to all this, they would have killed him long ago."

Kate nodded. "No wonder the admiral placed so much validity on his suspicions," she said, pointing at all the monitors that ringed the large room. "A lot of that evidence filtered through here."

Michael nodded and plugged the drive from Mars into one of the control input terminals. He grabbed a chair and swung it next to the panel, where he punched commands into a keyboard. One of the monitors switched over to the task of decrypting the rest of the communiqués from the Martian relay station. "I always trusted Dad's suspicions and thought them to have value. It was you and Kristin who suspected he was crazy. You two put too much weight on Mom's thoughts on the issue, and you were too busy resenting him because all this made her leave."

Kate nodded and pushed herself away from the panel. "Guilty as charged, though I'm sure Kristin's got her own reasons. What are you doing?"

"These computers are more powerful than the one on that designer ship of yours. I should be able to decrypt it faster here, then run it though the databanks for a match."

"Well," she said as she finally stood and headed for the elevator, "see what you can find. I'm going to head for the top floor and see what other surprises the admiral arranged for us."

Michael smiled before turning his head back to the keyboard. "Go ahead. I'll be up in a little bit. I wanna see what else I can find."

"Great." Kate pushed the button on the elevator panel and waited for the door to open. "Don't take too long. I want to be on the way to the capital in the morning."

The elevator stopped, the doors whooshed open, and Kate stepped in. The floor choices were before her, and this time, she chose the "House" button. The door closed, and the elevator ascended briefly before opening.

Kate was engulfed in darkness as she stepped out. "Lights," she said, and the newly activated computer recognized the command. When the lights came on, she realized she was in the living room, which had obviously been decorated by her father's heavy hand; he was definitely not into minimalist décor and appreciated vintage and retro things. The admiral had kept the look of the small house pretty much the way it was intended since its construction more than 200 years ago: the couch, chairs, and tables were all either exact replicas or original antiques. She had to hand it to him, because even the plastic covering on the furniture seemed authentic.

Kate made her way to the kitchen and noted that the faucets and electric stove now worked, as did the empty refrigerator. She checked the cupboard and found a case of emergency rations, none of them past their expiration dates. While they were not exactly gourmet foodstuffs, they would at least quiet the rumbling of her stomach, but she decided to hold off until Michael came up from the ops center.

Her brief tour of the rest of the house was uneventful. There were three furnished bedrooms and the standard one and a half baths, but she found no real surprises. Knowing the admiral the way she did, though, it was difficult to imagine that there was nothing hidden there; secrets were factored into his DNA.

Outside, the grounds were made up of overgrown grass and weeds behind the house and the sandy beach and ocean in front. The best feature of the house was the seclusion it offered; there wasn't another building as far as her eyes could see. She did find sensors all around the property, extending out into the grasslands of the former state park and a fair distance out into the surf. She was sure all of that tied into a security panel inside, equipped with a biometric scanner to keep track of anyone who stepped foot anywhere on the premises. As far as she knew, her brother was watching her at that very moment.

Kate walked to the side of the property, the place where the landing pad had summoned the *Alexa* down to the bay. She noted that the pad was buried in overgrowth, debris, and sand again, probably because the surrounding fans had camouflaged it so it wouldn't be visible from the air; she didn't really see the point, as she couldn't imagine there would be much in the way of air traffic at that point. The true mystery, considering the size of the hangar and ops center, was how he had managed to keep it secret during its construction. Another truly amazing thing was that there were two other landing areas around the house. Either there were two other hangars, or the hangar they were in was much larger than they first assumed. All in all, her father had created the perfect safe house. Satisfied that they were secure, Kate went back in the house and shut the door, convinced that they had nothing to worry about.

"Hello, Katherine. How are you?"

With a gasp and a hand darting up to her chest, as if to still her racing heart, she turned. There, right before her, stood a man she thought dead, Admiral Nicholas Dante. "Dad?!" she said, shaking her head. She didn't know what else to say until she heard the laughter coming from the couch.

Michael was sitting on the plastic, with his hands on a keyboard that had appeared out of the table.

"What the hell is going on, Mike?!" she snapped. He was very lucky he was family, or she would have shot him right then and there for giving her the fright of her life.

"It's only a hologram," Michael said, struggling to stop laughing. "There were instructions downstairs. The computer is programmed with his voice and some of his memory patterns as well."

She looked at him and winced. The holographic representation of the admiral was almost perfect. "So this thing can really respond to questions?"

The hologram watched her as she walked around to examine it; the expression on its face was pure Dante, as was the attitude. "Yes, Katherine, I can respond. Also, please keep in mind that there is enough of your father in me to give you a bad day."

"Great," Kate mumbled as she plopped down next to her brother on the couch.

The hologram disappeared, then rematerialized in a chair opposite them. "It is nice to see both of you. I'm sure you are curious as to why your father would create a hologram in the first place."

Michael nodded. "Yes, you could say that. It seems a bit, uh… self-serving."

"This whole place does," Kate chimed in. "What's going on? I was told that you—the *real* you—are dead."

The hologram nodded solemnly, as if grieving the loss of his creator and the effects on his children. "My program was linked to the communications net. When sensors acquired enough proof of the death of Admiral Dante, I was activated. We hoped the two of you would remember this house and come here. Admiral Dante wholeheartedly believed you would need a place like this, a place to regroup, so he had it constructed from a budget that I believe was supposed to be delegated to the construction of a communications platform for deep space flights."

"That explains the electrical equipment. No one would suspect."

"Correct, Michael," the Dante image said with a nod. "It also made the small reactor buried in the sand a few miles down the beach more believable. You are totally self-sufficient here. Behind the pantry, you will find a freezer full of food." The hologram stopped and looked around the room before looking back at Michael and Kate. "I don't see Kristin. Where is your sister?"

"We were hoping you could tell us," Kate answered. "The best we can find is that her ship is out near the rim, running dark."

The holographic admiral shut his eyes and appeared to be locked in deep concentration. "Scanning all communication frequencies." Its eyes finally opened, but his blank expression was not readable or helpful in the least. "Military communications traffic regarding the *Bonaventure* reported the ship going dark more than sixteen hours ago, on orders of Captain Brady. Prior to that, he sent a report to Alliance Fleet Command regarding a signal his ship received. They were going in to investigate, but there's been no word since. Fleet Operations has tried to raise them to counterman the run-dark protocol and discover what is happening, to no avail."

"We need to find out what Striker is up to and if the *Bonaventure* is involved," "Kate added. "Is there anything else?"

The hologram shook its projected head and gave them the same look the admiral had given them often, whenever he was disappointed in them. "Your ship was identified over the Atlantic by a submarine. I see that they attempted to shoot you down. They now show you as destroyed but can't seem to locate any wreckage. They have a capture or shoot-on-sight order for both of you. Truly, didn't we teach you better than this?"

"Who signed off on that order?" Kate asked. "Was it General Martinette?"

"Yes," the hologram acknowledged, surprised that Kate was able to figure it out on her own. "How did you know, Katherine?"

"The admiral—the *real* admiral—surmised that Martinette is in Striker's pocket. He called the man 'General Marionette' because he was sure he was just a puppet of Striker's and Rosten's. He probably has large enough of an ass for both those bastards to fit in a hand. Looking back on it, it makes sense now. Someone as connected as Martinette could easily hide the disappearances of all those missing ships. I'm pretty sure he had something to do with the *Bonaventure* too."

"Okay. So what's the next step?" Michael asked.

Kate moved off the couch and headed back to the kitchen, then stopped and turned as she reached the doorway. "I don't know about you, but I'm going to hit that pantry, then get a good night's sleep in one of those bedrooms. Tomorrow is going to be a big day."

"When are we leaving?"

Kate laughed and shook her head. "I never said *we* are going anywhere tomorrow, little brother. *I* am going," she continued, her voice growing more serious. "You can stay here with Holo-Dad and all this equipment and finish decoding the Mars intel. It wouldn't hurt if you could locate our little sister while you're at it. I think she owes me money."

"But—"

"That's an order!" Kate said, cutting off his protest. She knew he wanted to go with her, and under normal circumstances, she would have welcomed the help from such an experienced field agent, but nothing about their situation was normal. "Listen, Mike, I need you here for the data, but more than that, I need you here for backup, to pull my butt out of the fire I know it's going to land in. If you can't, then I need you to go find Kristin and stop whatever it is that Rosten is planning."

The hologram was the first to agree. "She's right, Michael. It's a very sound strategy indeed."

Kate shook her head and looked back at her brother. "Well?"

Michael couldn't argue with the logic of it; he was the only one left who knew that things were not quite right. "Fine. Just don't eat all the food back there."

"Agreed," Kate said with a smile. "Just do me a favor and shut Holo-Dad down before you need even more therapy." She saw Michael smile at that, and she grinned back at him, happy that everyone knew what role they were there to play.

Kate located the pantry and looked behind it. She half-expected to find an old-style icebox, so she was relieved to discover a stasis freezer. The atoms in the food were frozen by streams of magnetic energy, which kept the food from spoiling. Not only were the results better at a fraction of the power, but the food was ready to eat as soon as it was removed.

She searched through a drawer marked "Deli" and pulled out some ham and Swiss cheese. She then made a sandwich on a roll she found. The pantry and freezer were very well stocked, but she was highly disappointed by the lack of alcoholic refreshments. It came as no surprise though; her father always preached that alcohol slowed the mind and the body and had no place in the grand scheme of things. What he didn't realize was that there was a time and a place for almost anything, booze included.

Reluctantly, she grabbed her sandwich, a bottle of water, and a small jar of pickles and headed up to one of the bedrooms. Unlike the well-packed living room, the bedroom was Spartan in its furnishings, with only a bed, a chair, and a desk. She sat on the bed and laid her plate down, then unscrewed the lid from her water bottle. *Ironic*, she thought, *that after 200 years, the most effective design for a bottle of water is still a plastic, screw-off top. I guess some things never change.*

She took a bite out of the sandwich and was rewarded when her stomach faded from a lion's roar to a kitten's purr. As she ate, she thought about what she'd said to Michael. Nothing she had told him was a lie, unless it was a lie of omission. There were good reasons for him to stay there, but there was one reason she had left out: Michael was and always had been a more honorable person than she was. No matter how messed up the system was, even if it cost the life of his own father, it would all work out well enough in the end. His happy, orderly world involved evidence and arrests of anyone involved, because that was what their Daddy would have done. The admiral would have arrested them and let the system sort it out because that was the orderly way, the way he and Michael always tried to handle things. They refused to admit to anyone, including themselves, that the people who created the system could be criminals.

Kate knew her plan was easier. She didn't want to arrest anyone. She just wanted to burn their house to the ground, with all of them in it. The reason she didn't want to take Michael along was because she knew she might fail and not make it out alive, and he needed to survive to continue the fight.

She pushed the sandwich to the side, suddenly devoid of appetite. She would have smashed the bottle of pickles against the wall, but the smell of the juice would have made her gag, and she was in desperate need of uninterrupted sleep. No matter how it all turned out, it was going to be a long day, quite possibly her last. The last thing she wanted to do was spend the night trying to protect her nostrils from the invading stench of salt and vinegar.

Her possible doom wasn't the happiest thought to fall asleep to, but it was all that spun through her head as she finally dozed off.

Whether it was the sandwich she ate before bed, the leftover adrenaline from the prior day, or the sense of impending doom she felt about the next day, Kate wasn't granted a very restful night's sleep; if the clock on the wall could be believed, she'd gotten only five hours of it, most spent tossing and turning. A trip to the bathroom and a hot shower—her first with real water in a long time—went a long way toward bringing her back to life.

Back in her room, Kate discovered a shirt hanging in the closet, along with a pair of jeans. They fit perfectly, and she quickly shimmied into them. She buckled her holster snugly around her waist, snapped one of her throwing knives to her right wrist, then looked in the mirror hanging above the desk and proclaimed herself ready for war.

She walked past her brother's room and noted that he was still fast asleep. She hoped his interactions with the hologram had done him some good. In some ways, it was nice to have access to a lesser version of him, one who was more Dad and less Admiral. It was for the best that he was sleeping; she had no intention of waking him up, and she'd never been good at goodbyes anyway.

At the bottom of the stairs, she looked around the living area and let out a deep sigh. The place was the manifestation of what her father thought a home should look like. She had to give him credit for trying. It was something he should have put into place years before, without making it so much of a secret. "Home shit home," she said to herself as she wheeled around back to the elevator, only to find herself face to face with the hologram of her father.

"Are you going somewhere?" he asked in that commanding tone of voice that held her in awe when she was a child but now only boiled her anger to the surface.

"Get out of my way," she answered, even though she knew she could probably walk right through him. "Tell Michael I'll contact him when I have something."

The hologram wouldn't budge an inch. "I agree with your reasoning for not taking your brother along, as well as the reasons you and I both know but did not voice."

Kate's rage sent a stream of bile up into her throat, one that tasted something like Swiss cheese. The hologram version of the admiral seemed to know what buttons to push, just as the living one did. "How the hell do you know what I did not voice?"

"Katherine," the projection began, its voice was cool and even, so much so that for a quick second, Kate was lost in the illusion of the thing as her father, "my personality matrix was derived from Admiral Dante's own brain patterns. If anyone or anything can come close to understanding his feelings and thoughts, it is me. The admiral confided in me, shared his personal thoughts regarding a number of topics. Our conversations sometimes lasted all night."

Kate laughed but tried to keep her volume low enough so as not to wake her brother. "I know my father loved the sound of his own voice, but this is ridiculous."

The hologram shook its head. "No it isn't. He used me more as a sounding board than just a macabre reflection of what he wanted to hear. However, he did talk about his children more than anything else. He hoped you would find yourselves and the qualities that make each of you unique individuals in the world. I do know more than you would think about his views. He wanted you to take care of your siblings and do the right thing."

Kate nodded. "And that's exactly what I've done, what I'm doing now. If you have my father's thought patterns, you know there are things I may need to do that Michael or even Kristin will be opposed to. What would the real admiral say to that?"

The hologram pondered her question for a moment. It could have just been accessing its databanks, but Kate thought the process was something a bit more sophisticated, as if it was searching for the correct way to form its opinion. "I stand corrected," it finally said, "as would your father." A smile formed on its face, and both the words and the facial gesture took Kate by surprise. "He would tell you at this point to do whatever you feel you must do. More than anyone else, he trusted you to do the right thing, and he loved you more because of it."

Kate felt tears in her eyes and finally understood why her brother was so fascinated with the construct. "Anything else?"

The hologram pointed to cabinet on the wall. "Please open that."

Kate obediently opened the cabinet and noticed that it was full of keys.

"Take the one on the second row from the bottom. The vehicle is in the garage. He was sure you'll approve of it."

"Thanks," Kate said as she stared at the keys she held, "but you didn't answer my question. What else would he have added?"

The hologram nodded and smiled again. "I do not need to extrapolate an answer to that. Admiral Dante anticipated the question, and I was ordered to offer you a direct quote."

"What quote?"

The hologram paused again; this time, based on what it told her, Kate knew it was attempting to download information directly rather than forming an answer of its own. "Katie," her father's voice said, not a holographic reproduction, "I hope you like the stepdad I left for you. It may not be me, but it is as close as technology would allow me to get over the short time I had to program it and get the house ready for you and the others. I programmed it to anticipate many of your actions and questions and to respond in the way I might have responded myself. There is one thing you must understand though. I never doubted your loyalty, not for a moment. For that lack of faith in you, I apologize, but if you have gotten this far, I'm probably dead. Thus, there is little I can say that will help you from where I am now. If my suspicions are true, then there is something out there, something worse, something to which Striker and Rosten pale in comparison. I trust you, Katherine, to do whatever you feel is necessary. You, unlike Michael and Kristin, have the Dante gene in you that will equip you to do whatever needs to be done to finish your mission. Kate, do whatever necessary to stop Striker. Kill them all if you have to. I love you. Take care." With the last word, the hologram nodded at her and vanished, leaving Kate alone.

Kate felt her knees go a little weak as the voice from beyond gave her the last bits of a father she had never even bothered to dream about having, and it only took his death to bring her to that conclusion. All of a sudden, everything became very personal.

The two-car garage was situated next to the house. The door was overgrown with weeds, but they were easily cleared away to reveal a handle with an old-fashioned lock. She pulled out the set of keys the hologram had provided for her and inserted the smaller of the two in the lock. Rather than unlocking the door directly, the key released a panel with an eyepiece, a standard retinal scanner. She placed her right eye over the scanner and stepped back as the garage door began to rise.

Inside, Kate could see one four-wheeled vehicle under a heavy cloth tarp. Her heart skipped a beat when she pulled the tarp away and laid eyes on the 200-year-old, pre-war Mustang Cobra. For the first time, one of the relics brought back serious memories of her father. The Cobra was his baby, the only real concession her mother had allowed him to indulge in. She ran her hand across the black metal body and noted that the baked-on polymer shell had held its finish far longer than she ever would have expected it to. The coating was a prototype at the time of its creation, but it was now a staple for most of the Alliance space fleet. It was practically indestructible. *And very shiny,* she thought with a smile.

Kate weighed the key in her hand and felt thirty-plus years of memories flooding back in, some good and some not so much. She remembered the rides when she was eight and how she enjoyed the time with the admiral, but she also remembered trying to take the car for a joyride at eighteen, without permission, and her father turning his back on her when he found out. The car was full of memories, and now there it was, right in front of her, with the key practically burning a hole in her trembling hand.

The garage itself had an automated vehicle maintenance system, so she was sure the car was all gassed up and ready to go. Her father loved his antiques, but he knew when it was time to trust the tools of a more modern world. Clearly, the Cobra had been well cared for throughout all those decades, like some precious thing in a museum.

The door opened with a turn of the key, and she could smell all those missed years in the scent of the leather and plastic of the interior. As she slid into the driver seat, Kate couldn't help but wonder if the car was the sum total of her warm memories regarding her father. First, he had passed on his personal scout ship, and now she had the keys to his Cobra. *Maybe it's time to reevaluate my feelings about the man,* she mused.

Kate put the key in the ignition and paused. She found herself actually nervous at the prospect of starting such a symbol of her past. *Funny,* she thought. With all her near-death experiences on and off the planet, that car was what made her nervous. Pushing that thought aside, she turned the key and listened as the ancient but powerful V-8 engine roared to life. The dashboard instruments glowed red as the tachometer revved up at the touch of her foot on the gas pedal. She half-expected the hologram to appear, or at least to hear some sort of audio message warning her to drive safely, without a scratch, or she'd be in trouble. No such thing happened, though, so it appeared that she had all the blessing and advice she was going to get. Considering that her father was probably dead, the post-mortem gift was totally unexpected.

With no reason to waste any more time, she put the Cobra in reverse and eased out of the garage and into the early-morning air. Kate remembered that her father had adapted the car for off-road driving, with thicker tires and an enhanced set of shocks. She would have no problem heading west, to the capital. She put it in gear and headed out toward the main road. It wasn't the most inconspicuous form of transportation she could have chosen, but it would make a statement in more ways than one. She looked in the rearview mirror, casting a glance at the house as she drove away. She hoped it wouldn't be the last time she saw it or her brother again.

Sentimentality and emotion were the first two lessons taught to Intelligence agents at the Alliance Military Training Academy. The reason they were taught that before anything else was because, while there were various ways an agent could die in the field, one or both of those would generally be the cause. They dulled senses and clouded the mind to dangers lurking in an agent's surroundings. That was, in fact, the reason Admiral Nicholas Dante had been somewhat of an enemy in his own house more than he was a beloved parent. He always attempted to make his children aware of these dangers, even before the Academy, hoping they would learn a life lesson that would keep them alive.

Whether it was the stress of the past several days or the sentimentality brought on by a cherished memory, Kate missed the rising sun glinting off the lens of the multipurpose sniper scope and the assault rifle it was attached to.

The man holding it was dressed in a black leather jacket and dark glasses. The weapon he held wasn't military issue, nor was the ultra-quiet whisper cycle he stood next to. As opposed to the antique Mustang, his weapon and mode of transportation were both state of the art. His targets had separated, something his employer had assured him was not likely. Now, he needed further instructions, and that didn't sit well with him at all.

He mounted the bike, placed the safety helmet on his head, and pulled down the visor. He then reached to the side of the helmet, pressed a code, and waited for a response.

"Yes?" said the voice in his ear.

"You were right," he said, watching the Cobra in the distance through the enhanced optics in the helmet. "They settled into the beach house late last night. However, contrary to what you told me she would do, Captain Dante has left the house without her brother. What are your instructions?"

"Follow her," the voice replied. "I want to know where she goes and what she does."

The cycle started silently, as the electric motor was dampened by sound-absorbing material that kept the vibrations to a minimum. "Striker wants her and her brother dead. Should that not be my primary mission?"

"No. Just follow her...and stay close," the voice calmly said. "I will try to send some more of our people out to watch Michael and the house. As far as the kill order from Striker, I'm sure you will address that when the time is right. Don't screw up, Morrison. Out!"

With a significant change in orders that significantly altered his previous instructions, Morrison brought up the tracker he had placed in the vehicle before the Dantes' arrival. It clearly showed Kate Dante heading west, toward the capital. The cycle accelerated along the sandy beach, staying out of range of the house security systems as his pursuit began.

He decided that for the time being, he would obey the instructions to follow her, but whether the old man at the other end of the line approved or not, he would deal with Ethan Striker's contract in his own way and in his own time.

Chapter 13

Kristin finally made her way down to the shuttle repair and maintenance bay. The route she took wasn't as direct as it might have been, due to her discovery of a section of the station that had been open to space, possibly from a meteor collision. Backtracking, she eventually discovered a safer path and saw the room designation over the hatch. She pressed the door release and watched as it swung to the side, releasing the agonizing groan of rusted metal. She stepped in to find everyone standing around in a circle, with Marshall pointing his assault rifle at something sitting on the deck. "What's going on here?" she asked.

The group parted, to give her full view of the object that was so captivating their attention.

"Shit," Kristin snapped and instantly pulled her own gun out and took aim at the alien spider. "What the hell's wrong with it? It's not moving."

Jakes stepped forward and prodded the creature with his own assault rifle but garnered no reaction from the thing that had threatened all of them and taken their ship just a short time ago. "We found the slimy bastard when we were cleaning out the main engine exhaust. It musta found its way into the engine when we severed the connection to the transports airlocks. This one managed to grab hold of the manifold. Either it got hit during our escape or maybe when the engine blew. The question now is what you wanna do with it. If you opt to flush it out the airlock, you'll get no argument from me, Commander."

There were nods of agreement from the others, with the exception of Moss, who had been assisting with the Falcon repairs.

"Mr. Moss, you have a different opinion?" Kristin asked. Her own opinion was derived from something her father had taught her long ago: "When in combat, don't waste any resource that may grant you a better understanding of your enemy."

Moss knelt down next to it and pulled out his scanner. He shook his head before pulling a pencil out of his uniform breast pocket and poking the thing around what they assumed to be the mouth. He shook his head again and sighed as he spun it around in a circle. Whatever its outer shell was made of, it offered very little resistance as it rotated twice before coming to a rest. With the pencil back in his pocket, Moss turned to face his commander. "Well, ma'am," Moss said, then hesitated a bit, as if he was searching for a way to give an answer in a way that Commander Dante and the others would understand, "this thing shouldn't exist. Its DNA isn't consistent with anything in the scanner databanks. Hell, it isn't even consistent with itself. I'm sure if Doc Tolliver examines it further, he'll confirm that. Also, Commander Dante, I'm picking up artificial elements in its makeup. Believe it or not, the thing is part machine, a freaking robo-spider."

Kristin took the scanner and examined the readings herself. "It doesn't make any sense. According to this, it's not even real. There are no internal organs, no central nervous system, nothing. How is it possible?"

"It's not. It's insane. First the thing was alive and taking people over, and now it's just...this," Marshall chimed in. "Y'all remember what it was like when it was alive, right?"

"Right, but look at it now," Moss said as he took the scanner back. "There's not a mark on it. It looks perfectly fine. Something had to render it inactive, power it down or something."

Jakes looked at Moss, then over at Kristin. "The question of the day is still yours to answer, Boss. Wat the hell do we do with it?"

Kristin thought it over for a few seconds and decided that nothing about the situation had made her change her mind from her earlier assessment. "Moss, rig some sort of containment for it, just in case it goes zombie on us and returns from the dead. Then I want you and an armed escort to take it down to Doc Tolliver and his team. You two figure out what makes it tick. Got that?"

"Yes, ma'am," Moss said enthusiastically as he grabbed two engineers to help him complete his task of containing and transporting the alien creature.

"Marshall..."

"Yeah, Boss?" the security man said as he straightened to attention.

"Go with the kid and make sure everyone gets where to where they're going—preferably all in one piece. Don't take any chances. If that thing decides to respawn, destroy it."

"Then what?" Marshall asked curiously.

Kristin smiled. "Then, big guy, I want you to go to weapons control and figure out how to use what works. Also see if there's anything else that can be done with the rest of this antiquated mess if it comes down to combat."

"Affirmative," he said with a nod, then moved off in the direction of Moss and his men.

Kristin then turned to the last piece of her current puzzle. Jakes had gone back to the Falcon, with clipboard in hand, and was busy with his checklist of working and nonworking ship systems. "Report," she said. "What's our condition?"

Jakes looked from clipboard to the shuttle and back again. "I've got 'er as patched up as I'm gonna get with the equipment we've got available. I can fiddle with the systems a bit, but for the time being, I've done all I can. She'll either fly or she won't. I patched the hole in the hull, so life support shouldn't be an issue. The main engines are at about 75 percent, but I wouldn't push 'em too much. I'm still a little worried about the hull damage, though, especially around the engine exhausts. I machined them as well as I could to get them in working condition, but we're working with old, crappy equipment, so the ride might tend to get a little rough at higher acceleration. Fortunately, the seatbelts still work."

"How about weapons?"

Jakes took a deep breath and let it out slowly. "More like a lack thereof," he said, shaking his head as he scanned further down his clipboard. "The four remaining missiles have been removed and installed in the launchers, as you instructed. The only remaining on-board weapons are the two forward plasma cannons, as well as a set of countermeasures and interceptors in the rear. Good news is that the plasma cannons are fully operational, but to take full advantage of those, we'll have to face something head on."

"Well, that's good news," Kristin said, releasing a deep breath of her own.

"Commander, I hate to pry, but what is your plan exactly?" Jakes asked in a low tone, trying to keep the conversation between them. "You know Brady will find us eventually, whether he had one of those things attached to him or not."

Kristin nodded. "I know. We need to get word out on what's out here. How much time do you think we've got before *Bonaventure* is operational?"

Jakes thought for a moment. "The damage was substantial. I figure she's got her thrusters back online by now, and I'm sure they've cleaned off enough of her launch bays to send fighters out after us, but I'd say it'll be at least another forty-eight hours before they even attempt to fire up those engines. Don't forget, Commander, that Brady's baby has enough fighter support to blow us to dust, while we've got very little to fight them off. How do you intend to get word out, by the way? We're being jammed."

"You sure you want to hear the details?" Kristin asked quietly.

Jakes just nodded and leaned against the Falcon hull for support. He knew whatever she was going to say would be interesting at the very least, and his curiosity was piqued.

"All right. First, we put up a little fight, and then we surrender and invite them aboard."

Jakes shook his head and laughed. "*That's* your plan? Hell, I'd rather jump out an airlock in my undies than let them grab hold of me."

"Oh, I forgot to tell you. That wasn't the part I thought you'd hate," she said with a smile.

"Oh, hell no," he said as it finally dawned on him.

"Yep," she replied. "As soon as enough of those things are on-board, I'm going to blow the station and destroy as many of them as possible."

"And how does that help us get a signal out?"

"You use the diversion to get the Falcon as far from here as possible, at least out of range of the jamming, so we can warn the Alliance."

"Kristin," Jakes pleaded, "you can't do that. You'll die in the blast."

"Nope. Not part of my plan to die here," she said with a nod. "It's your job to get everyone else off this piece of rusted metal. There only needs to be one finger on the arming switch."

"But you'll—"

Kristin cut in, shaking her head and smirking at him. "Don't forget, Moss rigged it with a five-minute delay. That's plenty of time for me to get a little…creative. You don't have to worry about me, Jakes."

"Forget worrying. I'm staying behind with you."

Kristin smiled and gave the pilot a hug. "You know you can't, but I appreciate the gesture."

"Fine," Jakes finally conceded. He decided not to get misty-eyed about it, but he knew there had to be something more he could do. "I don't have to like it though."

"I never said you do, but I would think trying to squeeze a bit more power out of the Falcon engines would be a better use of your talents."

"Hey, I can multitask with the best of them, Boss," Jakes replied with a smile. "By the way, if we get through this—and that's a big damn if—would you mind if I buy you a drink?"

Kristin was touched. The pilot was a bit older than her, but he was also attractive, with a delightful sense of humor and personality, and she couldn't deny that there was some connection between them. "It's a date, but first the engines. This is all a one-in-a-million long shot, and we can't waste any time. If anyone needs me, I'll be back in the control room."

"Yes, ma'am." Jakes turned back to the engines and picked up his clipboard again. He'd squeeze as much power as he could out of the pile of scrap metal and keep his promise to her about shaving some decimal points off her one-in-a-million estimate. It was the least he could do for family.

Chapter 14

It took Kate a while to acclimate to the feel of driving the Cobra, but once she did, it became the only part of her trip she would enjoy. The route west, to New York City, took her through Long Island and the former boroughs of Brooklyn and Queens—or at least what was left of them. The war had left most of the real estate in ruins and uninhabited, and the decimation only grew worse the closer she got to the Alliance capital and ground zero.

There had been a priority during the reconstruction after the war, and the survivors rose from their bomb shelters amidst the destruction. Resources were stretched unbelievably thin, giving Striker Industries the perfect opportunity to play the role of triage nurse; thus, only that deemed necessary for the survival of the populace and Striker Industries was rebuilt, while the rest of the world still lay beneath layers of radioactive ash. It was possible to actually determine the blast or kill radius and the path of the fallout by looking at the destructive pattern. People, descendants of the original survivors, still lived out on the tip of Long Island, as the fallout from the bomb used on New York blew more to the west than out to sea. Damage was at a minimum there, but it increased in proportion the closer one got to the city.

Several times, Kate had to backtrack and seek alternate routes, due to the burned-out skeletons of cars and trucks that were caught on the roads at the time of the blast. It made for a rather eerie, apocalyptic labyrinth for her to maneuver. Whether it was a result of the electromagnetic pulse or the concussive shock and heat of the nuke, the vehicles were frozen in place forever; in most cases, the skeletal remains of their occupants were still sitting in their seats. With ground travel almost impossible and the danger of radiation constant, Long Islanders had turned to the sea to transport goods to market in the city and bring supplies back to their homes. The Alliance eventually established air transport and cargo drops for the more isolated areas.

The depressingly long trip was only a reminder of her hatred of Striker and the way his family had used their newly conjured resources to build a new world on the bodies of the dead. The dead couldn't speak for themselves, but she intended to give them a voice, even after all those years. It took six hours—three miles forward and two miles back—before she found herself on the final approach to the capital. Halfway through Queens, radiation levels started dropping to normal, and the first signs of civilization began to appear as the roads cleared. Homes along the way now appeared lived in.

Most of the Brooklyn she remembered from the history books was gone, flattened by the bomb that took out Manhattan. When Striker Industries began the rebuilding of that once-thriving metropolis, he first reestablished it as the financial capital of the free world, then again as the capital of the new Earth Alliance. They also used Manhattan Island to reignite the faith of humanity, to give them hope that the infrastructure and system could be restored. Most of the city was rebuilt in the updated image of the one destroyed in the 2,500-degree nuclear firestorm. The concrete, glass, and steel were replaced by a stronger version of what was there before. What had no place in the new order were the people who made the city more than the sum of its tall, pretty buildings; they were really viewed as insignificant, no more valuable than the cockroaches, rats, and pigeons that had once festered in the cracks and crevices and sewers and walls.

Manhattan was rebuilt in the image envisioned by the Striker of the day and his family. At first, it was designed to recapture the business it represented, but it didn't take long for it to become the political center of the planet. At no time were people allowed back in, except for those the Strikers deemed worthy; all others were turned away. The rejected and neglected hordes settled on the western side of Brooklyn and Queens, near the rebuilt bridges that only allowed a select few in. Soon, Striker Industries took advantage of them as well, and low-cost housing was created for the workforce that was required to keep the city running.

The brownstones of Park Slope, Brooklyn somehow found a way to survive the destruction of New York. Some were more than 100 years old at the time of the war and managed to maintain their resiliency to exist, in spite of anything foolish mankind threw at them. They only fell when the bulldozers purposely knocked them to the ground to make room for the low-cost homes to house the working masses who came in search of the hand-to-mouth life amidst the ruins of the beaten world. Sadly, that was all the higher anyone's dreams stretched anymore, except for those privy to the favor of Striker and his ilk.

Kate drove past the flimsy buildings and tried to imagine those old brick homes that were literally constructed one on top of the other. She shook her head at the incredible contrast in the way these people lived compared to those beyond the bridge. Her life as the child of a fleet admiral had given her more than a pass on that type of life; it had given her a way of looking at things, a perspective that only an epiphany of such magnitude could erase.

As hard as it was, she tried to push those thoughts deeper into her mind as she looked for a safe place to leave the Mustang. The bridges were equipped with more than toll booths now; in this new world, they were manned by armed guards tasked with inspecting the identification of every vehicle or person entering or leaving the island. Striker valued his security, and she was sure she was at the top of every most-wanted list of every agency on the planet. For her, any security checkpoint would be bad news.

Finally, Kate found the place she was looking for, an alley between two of the cleaner buildings she could find. She checked to make sure no one was watching, then turned in and went as far off the street as she could maneuver the Cobra. She popped the small trunk, pulled out a fitted tarp, and used it to cover the car. *Hopefully*, she thought, *no one will stumble down here and find it.* She also grabbed the binoculars, knowing they would come in handy. Before closing the trunk, she noticed a blue and orange cap with "NY" embroidered on it. The wide brim would offer some cover of her face, so she quickly took it out and tried it on. Since it bore the initials of the city, Kate theorized that it was probably fan gear or perhaps that it belonged to one of New York's pre-war sports teams. After all, the admiral was a sucker for antiques, and they were much harder to come by after the ancient internet was dismantled, along with access to EBay; so much of history seemed so absurd now.

Covering and locking the vehicle only took a few minutes, and she soon found herself staring down both ways on an empty street. She needed to find a point where she could reconnoiter the bridge and the security on it. If she waited until morning, it would be simple to gain access to the city, with the help of the morning influx of workers. Unfortunately, she couldn't wait that long.

After a brisk walk to the Brooklyn shoreline, Kate found herself in direct view of the bridge. The toxic sea water between her and her destination was a greenish-brown color and was, in all probability, at least somewhat radioactive. She was also sure the chemical content consisted of far more than H2O. In fact, she was surprised it wasn't glowing and squirming with microscopic terrors. Swimming would not be her solution; if the smell was any indication, such a bath would probably prove fatal.

She zoomed in on the Brooklyn Bridge with the electronic binoculars. It had been rebuilt as part of the Manhattan reconstruction project, and materials were incorporated to its new construction that made it stronger and sturdier than the one that was originally constructed in the nineteenth century. Kate also noted that security on the bridge was just as state of the art as the structure. There was no way she could cross the bridge on foot, because they would surely recognize her and either take her into custody or shoot her on sight. She was no fan of either and preferred another solution, a more subterranean one. Unfortunately, she would need Michael's help to accomplish it.

Under the streets of New York and branching though the infrastructure of the other four boroughs was a system of subway tunnels that were used for transportation before the war, during the war to shelter some of the population, and after the war as a means to transfer materials to and from the island. If those tunnels were still accessible, Kate was sure she would find one she could use to walk right under the noses of the guards on the bridge and the shoreline on the other side. It wasn't difficult to miss the security posts every 200 or 300 meters on the water's edge facing Brooklyn and Queens. Michael would be able to pull up the tunnel schematics and point her to the one that would give her the best chance. The hardest part was overcoming any grudge her brother was temporarily holding.

Michael had opened his eyes twenty minutes after Kate had left the house and had searched all three levels to make sure she wasn't doing anything she wasn't supposed to, which was often the case with her. It took him half that time to realize that the thing she should not have done was leave the house in the first place. She hadn't even bothered to wake him, and to make matters worse, she'd commandeered their father's Mustang. He didn't know what bothered him more, the fact she'd left without a word or that she'd committed grand theft auto. *First she gets the scout ship and now the car? Geez.*

"Just great!" he screamed to no one in particular.

The hologram had formed again and just stood watching him.

"And you? Couldn't you have stopped her or, at the very least, woken me up so I could have done something?" All of a sudden, all the reasons why his sisters didn't like him came to the surface.

The hologram pointed to the chair and gestured for Michael to sit. "You really need to calm down, Michael."

"Why? Because *you* think I do?" Michael said, but he eventually gravitated to the chair and settled into it. He didn't know if it was because he wanted to or if it was simply the effect of his father's voice on him. *Kate might be right,* he realized. *Maybe I do need therapy after all for these damn Daddy issues of mine.*

"Very good, Michael. Take some time to think and clear your head. I was aware of what Katherine was planning. She ordered me not to wake you, and that it was for your own good."

Michael shook his head and pushed himself deeper into the chair. "And you believed all that?"

The hologram nodded. "I understood her reasoning."

Michael just shook his head and left the chair for the elevator.

"Where are you going, Michael?"

Michael stared back at the projected copy of his father and shook his head. Without a word, he got into the elevator and shut the doors behind him. "You've gotta be kidding me," he fumed.

The doors opened to the ops area, and Michael took a seat at the computer and went back to work on the Martian communications files. At that point, the best use of his time was decoding those files, rather than seething about his inconsiderate sister and the holographic father who was obviously taking her side.

A few hours later, he'd found the sub signal used by Striker and Rosten and then the actual coded messages between them. A few hours of decoding gave him his first breakthrough, as he discovered the actual cypher they used to scramble the messages they sent. It would only be a matter of time before he could apply the decoding cypher to the transmissions and find the information they needed. The bad part was that he had to wade through more than a century of stored messages, beginning at the time the relay station came online and stretching all the way to the present. One thing he appreciated was the absence of the hologram. He was starting to realize why everyone other than him had always found the admiral so annoying.

It didn't take him much longer to find what he was looking for. "Shit," he muttered to himself as he slumped back in his seat after scanning some of the more recent communications. He had to read their content three times before he could accept that his eyes weren't playing tricks on him. "Striker, you self-serving, insane, evil son-of-a-bitch!" He knew he needed to get the shocking intel to the proper authorities, but he had no idea who among them could be trusted. Most of the Alliance officials he knew, in both military and civilian circles, were mentioned in the messages. Michael wondered what Striker could possibly offer to someone for help in destroying the world. Whatever the case, he had to get the vital information to Kate, and he hoped she'd know what to do with it. Suddenly, his problems with his sister and father faded well into the background.

He looked over at his headset and noted that it was blinking. *There is a God,* he thought, assuming it had to be Kate checking in. He grabbed it and stuck it in his ear, and the action activated the comm. "Kate, I'm not even gonna ask why you left without telling me," Michael started. "I just heard the world is ending soon."

"Michael, I don't have time for a lecture. I need your help."

Michael couldn't believe his ears any more than he could believe his eyes earlier. "Did you hear what I just said? I deciphered enough of the communications from Striker to his little peer group to prove that he's going for a coup that'll put us all six feet under."

There was a long pause before Kate came back on. "I'm sorry, Michael. It's been…a day. I realized a while ago that Striker and Rosten are planning something big, bad, and ugly. That's why I have to find a way into the capital, and that's where you come in. Can you help me or not?"

"Are you nuts, sis?" Michael snapped. "Security at the city gates is pretty unbeatable. They've got all the bridges covered, and the subways are booby-trapped. There's almost no way in."

"Almost?"

"Yeah," Michael said, finally giving in. "There are—or at least there were—tunnels that Intelligence cleared in case of terrorists overtaking the capital. They planned to use them to sneak ground troops in, if that became necessary. I have no idea if they sealed them or increased security. They may be flooded, for all I know."

"But there's a chance, right? Do you have access to the underground schematics?"

With a sigh, Michael walked to the house computer system with the knowledge that his father was connected to almost every database and server in the star system. It only took a few seconds for the computer to spit out the fifteen-year-old plans and blueprints. The only danger was that a lot could happen in fifteen years. "Okay, Kate," he said slowly as he thumbed through the tunnel diagrams, "I found an old set. To be honest with you, though, I don't know if the information is worth risking your life."

"What do you mean, not worth it?" Kate retorted. "You just got done telling me that the world's going to end."

"Good point," Michael agreed. "Hang on."

He let his hands play over the keyboard as he overlaid the plans over the original pre-war configuration, then used his Alliance Intelligence Service password to access all the emergency routes his department had detailed before they were shut down. The next thing he processed was current security patrol patterns, checking for cross-matches with the schematics. He knew it was a risk, because they would flag and trace his code, since he was listed on the same capture order as Kate. It would take them a while to track him to this particular house, but they were relentless and would eventually find him. Nevertheless, as he and his sister agreed, the time for playing it safe was over.

"Got it!" he snapped into the headset a few minutes later.

"What?"

"You need to head north, on York Street," Michael said, reading her the data off the screen. "The Alliance kept one of the tunnels free of debris as a way into the capital, in case they had to send troops or one of us operative types in undercover."

Kate pulled out her comm and checked her GPS. She was only about a half-mile or so south of York, which computed to either a short ride or a brisk walk in the dark. The patrols, both on the ground and in the air, seemed to have increased, almost as if they knew she was in the area. "Thanks, Michael. What's security like at the station entrance?"

Michael looked at the screen and read the security schedules. "You're gonna have to take it easy. I'm showing a lot of activity for a decommissioned station. They may know you are in the area, so be careful."

"Thanks, *Dad*," she sent back to him sarcastically. "I'm going to make my way up there on foot and leave the Cobra here."

"Take care of that car. It was supposed to be mine. Call me when you're in the tunnel, and I'll try to help you navigate it," Michael said, just as a search notation on the screen caught his attention.

"I don't remember Dad giving you a car," Kate argued.

"Yeah, okay," he finally said, as if he wasn't paying any attention to a word she said. "Just get back to me when you're in the tunnel…and please don't get yourself killed on the way. Out."

With that, he clicked off the receiver and turned back to the mysterious word that had come up on the computer screen, the same word that had manifested itself 582 times in the transcript conversations between Striker and Rosten but not between anyone and Stratton on the moon or, for that matter, Striker with anyone else.

He had a little time before any search party would show up looking for him. Fortunately, the security software his father had installed on the computer was first rate and easily created 100 cloned server addresses all over the planet; thus, it would take a long time to finally narrow down his location. That gave him the window he needed to discover the significance of that word looming on the screen before him: "Jek'Tan."

Chapter 15

Kate made her way through the dark streets of the west side of the borough of Brooklyn, trying her best to stay out of sight from the surveillance cameras and security patrols. Most of the area was rebuilt after the surprisingly small amount of blast damage it had suffered during the early stages of the war. If she remembered her history correctly, the bomb that had hit New York was low yield but dirty, with an electronic pulse that erased the financial data from all but a few of the Big Apple's well-shielded computers. Luckily, there was enough redundancy built into the system that most of the data lost was recoverable, at least eventually. While that did nothing to save the residents of the Brooklyn neighborhoods closest to Manhattan, it did preserve most of their property and the infrastructure.

The restoration still took decades. Many of the homes and storefronts were returned to what people assumed were the classic design, what they looked like before the nuclear blasts hit them. The sad part was that most of it was a façade, just for show. The homes didn't house anyone, and the stores were just glass and metal decorations, like a Hollywood movie set, commemorating what had been there before. The people resided in tall projects, with apartments stacked one on top of the other. Food and clothing was distributed on the lower floors in shops run by Striker and his cronies. Manhattan was the corporate headquarters of Striker Industries, so it didn't take much convincing to have New York City declared the new capital of the United States and then the Alliance, especially with a hole in the ground where the White House used to sit. The horrible thing was that there were faux cities like it all over the world, as well as off it as well.

Kate heard chatter and footsteps approaching her. She reached for her gun but then thought better of it; the commotion of a firefight would draw too much attention. If stealth had not been an issue, she would have just gone up to the bridge and knocked. She looked quickly and saw that one of the phony houses had an equally set of phony stairs leading down to a door that likely led to a basement or a lower-level apartment of some kind.

As quietly as possible, she ducked down the stairs and pushed her back tightly against the corner of the door, where the rust-free hinges met the newly cleaned concrete. It was amazing how pristine and immaculate things remained when no one was around to tarnish or use them. She listened as the two uniformed men discussed everything from sports to the weather. One of them was actually making fun of the other for "not getting any," and Kate surmised that if the so-called "any" was anything like him, he was a lucky man indeed.

Eventually, they passed, and Kate once again continued her trip north, to the York Street station, making the occasional detour to avoid the cameras that kept watch on the streets at night. The team she'd managed to avoid a few blocks earlier was the only one patrolling on that clear night. She did note that the closer she got, the more cameras there were, and that slowed her progress significantly. Other than the cameras, though, the rest of the trip seemed clear of patrol. After the importance Michael had put on the York Street station as a clandestine point of entry to the city, she found it hard to believe that there weren't any checkpoints or guards at the entrance. All she saw at the corner of York Street was a set of stairs leading down to where the F subway line from Brooklyn to Manhattan had its last stop before heading under the East River. With an APB out on her and Michael, she would have thought security would have been tighter, but their foolish oversight would be her gain.

She pulled her gun out and held it tightly in front of her as she descended into the dark abyss below, an abyss that had once teemed with commuters and beggars and prostitutes. The first thing she noticed was the temperature. Without the mammoth fans of yesteryear, the station held in the warmth of the late spring day like a sauna. The stagnant air and lack of circulation made the tunnels feel like more of an old nineteenth-century coalmine than the primary transportation hub for the people of the city.

Kate re-holstered her weapon and removed a small flashlight from the inside pocket of her jacket. Due to the immense size of the station and the complete darkness, her light did very little to illuminate her surroundings beyond a few yards in any direction.

"Michael? Are you there?" she said into her comm.

At first, all she got back was an earful of static.

"Michael, I'm in the station. Where do I go?"

"Kate…breaking up… Get…trap…" was all she could make out before the static gobbled up the transmission entirely. It was not interference caused by the concrete and steel construction of the station; rather, someone was using an electronic jammer. She knew it was because of her, because there would be no other reason to jam an old subway tunnel.

She felt the darkness all around her. It was almost like a living thing, whose sole purpose was to suffocate her, to sap the life right out of her. She looked back at the entrance and the moonlight that streamed down, casting a ghostly glow. She decided a retreat might be in order, but she stopped when she heard the clomping of boots moving quickly at the top of the stairs and when she saw shadows playing on the walls at the bottom of the staircase. She finally understood why Michael had said, "Trap," because she'd clearly walked right into one.

There wasn't much she could do about it at that point. Her exit had been cut off, and she had no desire to fight a superior force or one that outnumbered her. Kate was sure their orders were to take her alive if they could. Knowing what she knew about Striker and Rosten, she guessed that someone out there had orders to fire as soon as she showed her face. Her only viable option was to continue on as planned and hope that whatever was lurking in the tunnels ahead was easier than what lay in wait for her above ground. It really was a choice between two evils, and the gripping darkness was the far lesser.

She pulled the gun again, lifted it to eye level in front of her, then turned and headed down the out-of-order escalator, heading in the direction the ancient signs pointed to for the actual train platforms and the tunnels. From the noise coming from behind her, she determined that the men had entered the station and were quickly closing off her escape points. They were coming after her, albeit slowly, as if they were herding her into a particular location. Nevertheless, all she could do was continue on.

At the bottom of the metal staircase was a landing, as well as another set of stairs made of concrete. Over the stairs was a sign that simply read, "Manhattan." She shined her light down into the darkness and heard the sounds of little feet scampering somewhere beyond the reaches of her light. "Great. Rats," she said quietly to herself.

As if the darkness wasn't enough, she now had to deal with rodents scurrying about. As bad as things were, she had to remember that the vermin in the tunnels did not possess plasma pistols or the orders to kill her on sight; all things considered, they were preferable to the vermin lurking behind her. The temperature was on the rise again, though, making the lack of air seem even more stifling than before. With a force of will born more out of self-preservation than anything else, Kate walked down the remaining stairs and found herself on the train platform.

At the edge, she shined her meager light down the tunnel in both directions. No matter which way she pointed it, the darkness swallowed the small light she carried, refusing to clearly answer the question of which way she should go. Again, she was assisted by a marquis hanging over the platform, a sign that designated the lines that passed through the station, as well as another "Manhattan" notice.

She hoped down on the tracks and jumped at the small, dark shape that skittered over her foot and hurried down the other side of the tunnel, squeaking angrily at her. She heard the footsteps above her head again; her pursuers were getting closer, even if they didn't seem to be in too much of a hurry. They hadn't come down to the platform yet, but she knew it was only a matter of time before they did.

Which direction? she thought. It was a 50/50 shot, down in one direction or the other. The only way she could not go was back up the stairs, because that would be the end of it. Suddenly, she felt a bit of a draft wafting in from one of the tunnels, a welcome breath of not-so-fresh air. She knew it had to be coming from the tunnel under the East River. Whatever the environmental reason, that would be her chosen path, if only because she needed to find a cooler place before the subway tunnel became her smothering tomb.

Before heading off in that direction, Kate removed her jacket and tied it around her waist. The sweat was pouring down her face, and the last thing she wanted was to be dehydrated when she met up with whatever was probably waiting for her farther down the line.

With gun in one hand and light in the other, she picked up her pace and started toward the city. Behind her, she could hear that her predators had made their way down to the platform, but they seemed to be reluctant about chasing their prey any father.

Well, that's one bit of luck, she thought to herself as she used the little light she had to guide her through the darkness.

Morrison stared out of the fourth-floor window of one of the old but renovated pre-war buildings that sat across the street from the York Street station, using the enhanced optics in his helmet to watch the inept security men trip over one another like newborn chicks in a box. He had to admit to himself that Dante had guts to try to go through the tunnels to get into the city, especially knowing that everyone on both sides of the law was out to kill her.

He understood her reasoning though. Of the four ways in— sea, air, bridge, and subway—the tunnel offered the least amount of risk. Striker knew she was coming, and the timing was just right to trap her underground. Letting them get away with that wasn't part of his plan though. Kate Dante was his mission, and he wasn't going to allow Striker's goons to beat him to her.

Getting by them wouldn't be an issue. The helmet actually contained its own cooling system, as well as infrared and light-enhancing capabilities. Not only would he be comfortable, but tracking his target wouldn't be an issue. He had a reputation to uphold, and he had no problem with removing some of the pawns who'd clumsily made their way into the station behind her.

Morrison checked the plasma pistol in the shoulder holster under his black jacket, then left the empty apartment and made his way down to street level. His black outfit and helmet allowed him to fade into the darkness a bit, camouflaging him as he made his way to the entrance to the station.

The streets were clear at the moment, as most of the action was subterranean at the moment. Down the stairs he went, using the darkness and the moon-hiding cloud cover to his advantage. He first spotted two guards by the turnstiles at what appeared to be the only entrance to the tunnel. Morrison pulled his combat knife out of his boot and held it at his side as he approached them. Surprise and stealth were typically part of his arsenal, but he had fallen behind Kate Dante, and he needed to catch up with her as quickly as possible. The last thing he was going to do was let two bumbling idiots get in his way. He pressed a button on the side of the visor and felt the warm, heavy air hit him like a hot towel before a shave. It was more important to flash the fools a friendly smile than to keep his visor down.

As soon as they saw him, they dutifully brought their assault rifles up.

"Stay where you are!" the guard on the left yelled. "This is a restricted area. Why are you out beyond the curfew?"

Morrison looked at them both and smiled. It was dark down there, even with the lights they'd set up to assist in their search. "Easy, guys," he said, with a bit of a stupid laugh. "I was on the way home, and… Well, my bike broke down. I saw the lights down here and thought there might be a crew working late. Do you have a comm I can use to get my wife down here to pick me up?"

The two guards looked at each other and nodded, but it wasn't because they believed his bullshit story.

"Turn around and put your hands against that wall," the one on the right said as he shouldered the assault rifle and approached.

The other guard continued to point his weapon in Morrison's direction. "What are you really doing down here? Don't you work for Striker?"

Morrison waited till the guard was almost on him and at his most vulnerable. He started to put his hands up, but stopped halfway and kicked out with his right foot, catching the man's thigh right below his body armor. The snapping sound of breaking bones brought only a moment of glee to him before he turned and fired his knife at the other guard, catching him in the throat as he brought his weapon up for a shot. He looked down quickly and noticed that the guard was going for his sidearm, so he easily broke his wrist with one quick downward step of his heavy, booted left foot. The man screamed in agony, but Morrison quickly kicked him in the side of the head; it wasn't enough to render him unconscious, but it did stop him from making too much noise.

Morrison lowered his visor again and was rewarded with cool air. After taking a second to suck down a lungful, he pulled the whimpering security guard into the corner and sat him up like a broken doll on a shelf; he'd been taught never to waste a source of intelligence.

He frisked the wounded man and made quick work of removing all weapons and communications devices. In the darkness, Morrison could see the man regaining consciousness, and he didn't appear happy.

"My friends are going to kill you," he said with a sneer.

"Well," Morrison said, pointing at the other guard lying in a growing puddle of his own blood, with the knife still buried in his throat, "you appear to have one less friend. I have two questions for you. First, do you wish to come out of this alive?"

The guard said nothing but did attempt to spit at his capture.

"Screw you!" Morrison responded by punching him in the side of the head.

"Yes! Yes, I wanna live!"

"Fine," Morrison said through the speakers in the helmet. "Then my second question should be easy for you. How many men came down here with you?"

The response was silence, something Morrison had very little time or patience for.

Morrison used the enhanced mode in his helmet and located the fracture in the guard's thigh bone. He hadn't caught it for a full break but had managed to split it almost apart. "Now, we're going to try again," he said. He grabbed hold of the man's thigh at the point of the fracture and put pressure on it.

The pain on the guard's face was evident.

"If you scream, I will take that knife and gut you like a fish before your friends get here." Morrison planted his booted foot on the man's throat and applied just a small amount of pressure, just enough to silence him. "Nod when you have something worthwhile to say. If I don't like it, I will introduce you to your liver."

Without a second of hesitation, the wide-eyed guard nodded.

Morrison removed his boot from the man's bruised throat.

"How do I know you won't kill me?" the man asked, his voice raspy at best.

"How could you say that?" Morrison said through the helmet speaker, trying to sound hurt. "Don't I look trustworthy?"

"No!" he replied as he saw the boot coming back. "Eight... er, seven!" he corrected, looking over at the dead man on the floor. "There are seven men out ahead of us. Really!"

Morrison nodded. "How do I know *you* are telling the truth?"

"Take the scanner from my belt." He gestured with his working hand. "They'll all show up on it. Please, mister!"

Morrison bent down and removed the small device from the guard's belt. He examined it and noted the eight little dots on the display. What concerned him were the two just a short distance ahead of them, down the tunnel. One had to be Dante, but he had no idea what the other was; he could only see that it was huge and closing with her. Before the man could make a comment, Morrison kicked him in the head. *There, buddy. A concussion is better than dead any day, and that'll shut you up for a while.*

He grabbed his knife, wiped the blood off on the dead man's uniform, and grabbed the assault rifle from him before taking off in a dead run down the dark corridors, toward the stairs that led down to the platform. He did not have the luxury of time, so he had no need for stealth either. He simply bounced down the stairs and put one quick shot into the head of the guard on the platform. He hoped the others didn't hear the shot from his energy weapon, but he knew that in a moment, it wouldn't make a difference.

Kate stopped short when she heard what she thought was the sound of a plasma weapon being fired. She shook her head in confusion. It could have been a number of other things down there as well, anything from a rat to a falling piece of the original construction material. It was odd that she'd heard only one shot. Fighting the urge to direct the light behind her, Kate focused it instead down the tunnel and what lay ahead. From the number of steps she'd taken, she calculated that she'd already passed the halfway point.

Kate stopped walking and took a breath. The temperature was oppressive, and her discomfort was only exacerbated by the humidity of the water pressing on the concrete ceiling. The trek over miles of rotted tracks and vermin was not easy. Her legs felt weak, mostly from dehydration, since she'd been sweating profusely from every pore in her body. Again, it was only sheer force of will—that

Dante will she'd inherited from the admiral, like it or not—that kept her aching legs moving. She took a deep breath, wiped her forehead, and started again.

Up ahead, she saw an unexpected flicker. There was always a chance that the light had been left by some irresponsible maintenance worker, but she doubted that. Kate was never one to dismiss anything as mere coincidence, especially when her head was on the chopping block and countless executioners were after her. As quietly as she could, she lifted her pistol from her holster again and slowly moved toward the light. What she saw left her somewhat speechless.

In the center of the tracks sat a large, padded chair, next to a small table with a lamp on it, connected to a portable battery. It was a surreal scene, a pre-war living room, right out of the pages of some pre-war magazine of Middle American home decorating. She immediately recognized that it was not the doings of a maintenance team, but it was a recent development in that dark pit. Whoever sat in that chair was still there somewhere. She felt the chill in her bones through the sweltering heat of the subway tunnel, almost a precognition of looming trouble. She knew that whatever or whoever was coming, she didn't have to wait long.

"Hello, my dear," said a voice from the darkness.

Kate finally realized the reason for the odd scene: It was bait, and she'd fallen for it. Standing in the light while her mystery man was camouflaged by the darkness was something her father would have chided her for, a stupidity she should not have tolerated in herself. "Hello," she finally responded. "Who are you?" As she asked the question, she slowly started backing out of the light, hoping to make herself less of a target. She also wanted to entice her opponent to be a bit chattier so she could gain a better idea of his position.

"Please stay in the light," the voice commanded. "If you don't, I will shoot out your knees."

Kate looked around, darting her eyes in every direction; the voice seemed to be coming from everywhere. There was no easy way for her to pinpoint a reasonable location for a shot. For now,

Kate decided to play it his way and stopped backing away. "Fine. I've stopped. Who are you?"

"Thank you," the voice said, sounding pleased. "My name is Mr. Gemini, and I have been waiting for you. Please take a seat. After your long walk, I'm sure it will be a comfortable change for you."

Kate sat in the chair but kept her weapon in her lap. She found it interesting that Gemini didn't ask her to drop it. "What do you want, Mr. Gemini? There are men behind me, and we don't have much time."

The laughter caught her by surprise before he continued, "I assure you, Captain Dante, I have all the time I need."

Kate felt herself shiver. She knew if she wasn't careful, she wouldn't be leaving the chair, let alone the tunnel. "And what would that be, Mr. Gemini?"

"Please, Captain Dante," Mr. Gemini responded coolly, "you know full well what this is. There is no point in playing coy with me."

Kate looked into the darkness and realized that the mysterious Mr. Gemini was toying with her. She was suddenly keenly aware of how a mouse must feel face to face with a cat. "Then just get it over with. Why all the games?" If there was one thing Kate had learned from her father—and there were actually man—it was that there was no such thing as an unwinnable situation. No matter how tight the trap was, there was always a way out. She just had to bide her time and look hard enough for it.

"Captain Dante, I get so few opportunities to talk to my... assignments. I also received a request from Ethan Striker to inquire as to your knowledge of his affairs. I suppose it is safe to assume that you will not cooperate with me on that."

Kate shook her head and immediately knew who the mysterious Mr. Gemini was. "You're a coward."

There was a bit of a pause before the voice responded. By the tone of it, Kate's statement had caught him by surprise, at least momentarily. "Why would you say that?"

Kate smiled; she had finally found the chink in the killer's armor. "Because I know who you are."

"And who is that, Captain?"

Got you! Kate thought to herself. "You're the kind of bastard who kills by remote, the chicken-shit type who never has the guts to look into the eyes of the people whose lives you end. That's what you are, all you are. Why don't you find your balls, and then we can discuss a retraction?"

There was silence, followed by laughter, albeit a bit more restrained than before. "We all have our various functions, serve our various purposes, Captain Dante. Mine is doing what my masters require of me, whether it is deemed heroic or cowardice by others. It is why I was created."

Wait. Created? That makes no sense, Kate thought as she heard a heavy sigh from the darkness. She tightened her grip on the plasma pistol in her lap.

"There are reasons my masters think it wise for me to make use of my talents in secret, but perhaps you are correct in your assumption of my character. To someone so unaware of the truth, I suppose it might appear that I am a slight bit less than what I actually am. Maybe it's time for a fresh start. You can be my first, Captain. The last Dante I ended was deprived of that privilege."

"Bastard," Kate said to the shadows. "I'm going to kill you."

"I don't think so, but you are welcome to try. Please stay seated. This will only take a second."

Kate watched as a figure began to appear from out of the darkness. It was tall and thin and clad in some sort of silver environmental suit. At about three meters tall, its thin legs and arms were longer than normal, but its gait was graceful, almost fluidic as it came closer. The helmet was entirely solid, so much so that Kate wondered how the hell Mr. Gemini could see. She watched at the long arms reach up to the helmet and pop the two fasteners over each shoulder. The hands grasped the helmet and lifted it off, then dropped it to the debris-strewn floor.

"Is this better, Kate Dante? I can now look you in the eye as I rip your spine from your body."

Kate's mouth dropped open as she gawked at the thing that stood before her. The body was alien enough, but the head was even more grotesque. It had the appearance of a leather mask wrapped tightly around a bare skull. "What the hell are you?" she gasped out through tight lips.

"Me?" Mr. Gemini asked. "I am your future and the future of your race. The Jek'Tan have foretold it." He shook his disgusting head. "They are the true masters, not Striker and his pathetic primitives. I admire your prowess somewhat, so I feel you should know before you die, Katherine Dante. This is nothing personal."

Kate raised her plasma pistol and pointed in at her huge opponent.

Mr. Gemini's mouth pulled into a parody of a smile, and the sardonic laugh came again. This time, without the helmet, it sounded far more alien. "Put down your toy, and I will make your death painless—an easy end of the day for both of us."

Kate lowered the gun. "Who or what is the Jek'Tan?"

Mr. Gemini shook his head. "The rulers of the universe, my creators. I have killed for them and Striker in secret, and now our time is over."

Kate watched as Mr. Gemini approached her. She quickly brought the gun up and fired a shot directly at the charging thing's chest, where a normal man's heart would be. The energy blast bounced off the silver suit and impacted the concrete and steel retaining wall of the tunnel. "Shit," she choked out as Gemini grabbed her around the neck and threw her like a ragdoll into the table. Kate spat blood as she rubbed her neck. *So far, so good,* she thought, determining that she had no broken bones yet, but she probably wouldn't survive another attack.

"I told you that would not help you," Mr. Gemini angrily snapped. "Do you see my eyes? *They* see you!"

Kate could see the twin black orbs as they regarded her. She'd gotten under the creature's skin, so that was at least something to be proud of. She heard him growl and charge again. "Hey, ugly!" she wailed.

Mr. Gemini stopped his charge and regarded her for a moment with utter contempt. He realized in that quick second that he had let the human appeal too deeply to his vanity.

Kate took that short moment of his introspection to release her throwing knife into her right hand and heave it. The knife spun completely around once before lodging its blade deep in Mr. Gemini's black right eye.

The creature roared in pain as he clawed at the handle of the blade lodged deeply in his right eye socket. Kate took a running start and delivered a flying kick to the middle of his thin chest. The impact sent Kate to the ground, but the tall monstrosity stumbled backward, until it stood beneath heavy support pylons that reinforced the tunnel wall and ceilings. He landed with a *thud* as his hands finally found the blade. He pulled it out in a gush of dark fluid. In one motion, Kate pulled grabbed her pistol from the floor and fired at the supports above Gemini's head. First one shot hit, then another, and then another in succession. Finally, there was a flash and a concussive shock as the ceiling supports came crashing down, bringing with them tons of concrete and steel. The debris rained down in a destructive storm of rock, wood, and steel, burying the creature with crushing force.

Kate pulled herself back to the chair and collapsed into it with a sigh. "Oh, what a day," she said with a smile. One thing had slipped her mind, though, and it was pretty important.

"Drop the gun and raise your hands!"

She looked up and saw seven of the same security guards she'd avoided earlier at the station entrance. Much to her dismay, Gemini had delayed her long enough for them to catch up. She looked at them and shook her head. "You've got to be kidding me." She dived off her seat and fired her pistol, taking out one of the guards as she took cover behind the cushioned chair.

The next thing she heard was the sound of an assault rifle, followed only by silence. It was deafening, but she risked taking a quick look above the chair.

The entire security squad were scattered about the floor, peppered with red, seeping holes. Sitting over them was a figure dressed in black, wearing a dark helmet with its visor down and holding an assault rifle sitting in his lap.

"Drop the gun," Kate snapped. *Great. Another freak in a helmet,* she thought, leveling her weapon at the strange figure.

He didn't drop the weapon, but he did move it aside so he could stand. He held his hands out to her, palms up, then raised them to his helmet and popped the latches on the side.

Kate watched the helmet come off, fully prepared to blast whatever it revealed. She had to admit that the face she saw was the last one she would have expected to encounter. "Cole Morrison?"

Morrison smiled and took a bow. "Happy to save you, sweetheart. By the way, your daddy says hi."

Kate dropped the pistol and tried to stand. "He's still alive?"

Before Morrison could respond, a cracking sound came from the ceiling, and more of the supports crumbled and collapsed. This time, water started to pour in with it, first at a slow rate and then faster and faster, as more and more of the ceiling caved in above them.

He put the helmet back on and grabbed Kate by the arm. "C'mon. We need to get out of here."

Without another word from either, they both darted down the tunnel toward Manhattan, with the East River right behind them, literally lapping at their heels.

Chapter 16

"No, no, no!" Michael screamed at the computer screen. Sensors had registered gunfire and explosions in the subway tunnel, midway between Brooklyn and Manhattan. Now they were picking up a breach in the tunnel wall and water pouring in, and there'd been no word from Kate since she'd gone into the tunnel and the jamming had begun. Security was all over the York Street station like ants on a picnic, and that just so happened to be Kate's entry point to the island.

He felt helpless. His sister was missing, and he was stuck on the far tip of Long Island, with no way out other than the scout ship in the underground hangar. It would be fast to travel that way, but he knew his ass would be shot out of the skies before he ever made it to Queens. He was landlocked, homebound, and he had to make the best of it, at least until he found out her condition, though he wasn't sure he really wanted to know.

The other thing was that reference to the Jek'Tan. Not only was it connected to Ethan Striker, but it also went much further back. There were references to the Jek'Tan in Striker's communications and assorted databases going back to before the war. It seemed an interesting coincidence that Striker Industries, which had proven to be a reasonably successful company in the years before the war, had begun to achieve unmatched success only three years before the first bombs dropped, at precisely the same time as the mysterious Jek'Tan started showing up in communiqués from Striker's C-level staff.

There were also records at the time of disappearances prior to, during, and after the war. Every time a plane disappeared in the wild blue yonder or a ship vanished at sea without so much as an oil slick, stock in Striker Industries increased, as did their predictions of global destruction. Later, people began disappearing off the streets in great numbers, and like the planes and ships, none of them were ever found again.

As the foretold nuclear Armageddon approached, the political interests of the Striker family moved them deeper and deeper into the realms of the rich and influential. When the war came, all the horrors Striker Industries promised came with it, and the Strikers became the poster boys for rebuilding the human race. Breakthroughs in the Striker R&D Department came quickly, and more and more astonishing advances helped drag mankind out of the radioactive mud and into the future. After that, the connection remained quiet for about seventy-five years, until Ethan Striker and the Jek'Tan reestablished their connection. That just so happened to be the same time when mankind began to look to the stars for further expansion. As the human race moved to the stars, or at least the moon and then to Mars, the Jek'Tan followed, and more disappearances and accidents were left in their wake.

Death and destruction followed Striker and their connection to the Jek'Tan. People died while Striker Industries worked to turn the entire world—or worlds—into their own image. To say they were the root of all evil was putting it lightly, according to the evidence in the system. The only question was the identity of the Jek'Tan.

"Shit," Michael cursed the computer again, shoving the keyboard away in disgust. His father loved antiques, and that monotonous keypad was one of them.

"It is pretty circumstantial, isn't it?" the hologram of his father said at his side.

"It was enough for you...er, for my father, I mean. Wasn't it?" Michael pushed himself back into his chair and nodded to the readout on the computer screen. "He always knew about this, didn't he? It was why he went on his crusade, and it is what got him killed, reduced to...well, you."

"Michael," the projection countered as he sat down in the holographic chair that appeared out of thin air, "he followed the path he believed in. Didn't he teach all of you to do the same?"

"Scan all databases and news reports. I want to know any news about Kate, immediately and in real time." Michael then turned his attention to the TV monitor and the local news reports.

The hologram began to fade, then solidified again. "I have no information on Kate, but I have information on Kristin."

Michael swiveled around and could see by the projected look on Holo-Dad's face that the news was not anything worth being happy about.

"Per an Alliance update," the hologram said, "the *Bonaventure* has been listed as missing. Fleet Operations has sent out ships to look for her."

Michael let his face fall into his cupped hands and felt tears beginning to well in his eyes. "Not again," he said. He was all too aware of the pattern of disappearances, and he was pretty certain no trace of the *Bonaventure* would ever be found—or his sister with it.

Ethan Striker watched those same news reports in his penthouse office. With the help of the Jek'Tan, he was able to track Dante and her brother from Mars to their landing on Long Island. From there, it was easy to follow her into the city and to her eventual destination, the York Street station. Mr. Gemini had taken it upon himself to set up in the tunnel, with the idea that they would manipulate her right into his hands.

Striker had long since given up on an allegedly accidental death for Kate Dante; at this point, he just wanted her dead and out of the way. Once she was eliminated, her brother would be next. The Dantes had become the bane of his existence, and they needed to be exterminated.

He looked back at the screen and turned up the volume: "We are repeating our earlier announcement. There has been an altercation at the old York Street subway station. It appears that one of the retaining walls under the East River has given way, and sources tell us that the station is now flooding. Crews have been dispatched to the scene. We are cautioning that anyone in the area of the York Street subway station in Brooklyn should stay away from the—"

Striker muted the report and picked up his comm. He punched in his contact number for Mr. Gemini and awaited his response. When there was no answer, Striker disconnected and stared at the transmission from the scene. They were bringing his men out of the station on stretchers. Most were wounded, and none of them were female. *Could Gemini have possibly failed?* he had to wonder, looking at the carnage before him. In more than two centuries, a failure on Gemini's part had been considered unthinkable. *Is it possible that the lunatic dropped and flooded an entire subway tunnel on Dante?*

"No, no, no!" Striker shouted, shoving everything off his desk in anger, like a child throwing a temper tantrum. Whatever had happened, he knew he had to reach the Jek'Tan and tell them. They wouldn't be happy if something happened to their pet killer, but they would be even angrier if he withheld information from them.

Striker picked up the comm again and called capital security. They needed to mobilize against Dante, if she wasn't buried in the subway, before she ruined everything he'd worked so long and hard for. It was also time to send a team after her brother. Panic carried a bad taste, and he didn't like it.

"Where is he?" Striker asked himself quietly as he watched everything play out on the local news. He controlled the news media to a certain extent, but there were things that even he couldn't keep under lock and key.

"Gemini is dead," said the windswept voice from the back of his office. "You have killed him."

"Killed him?!" Striker snapped toward the sound of the voice. "How did *I* kill him? I wasn't even there!"

"The Dantes never should have been allowed to leave Mars," the voice answered. "Nevertheless, he was but a tool. His brother will finish his mission."

"Brother? What brother?" Striker concentrated, making an attempt to see behind the veil of energy that so effectively hid the Jek'Tan. There was a shape there, he was sure, but he couldn't determine what shape that was.

The sound that came next cut right through to his brain. It was the Jek'Tan equivalent of laughter, and there was nothing funny about it.

"Do you think us so foolish that we would have but one? They were created as twins to serve us, linked by a telepathic bond you cannot comprehend, and we have since created them from the human clay we have been molding over time."

"The experiments!" Striker mused. "Clay? That's what we've been to you all this time, isn't it? That's why you needed the... volunteers."

"Yes," the voice replied. "Your people were helpful. The humans you and your family have provided over the years have afforded my race the raw biological materials necessary not only to create something superior but also to sustain our lifeforms. For many thousands of your years, the Jek'Tan have been on this ball of mud, experimenting and evolving your race as it suits our goals or needs. As I said, we require tools, and we have many."

"Why are you really coming here?" Striker asked, finally understanding the full brunt of panic and hating it all the more.

"Because we want the rest." The voice was calm, as if remarking on a warm spring day over a frosty glass of lemonade. "Our work here will soon be concluded. We only desire to reclaim our assets, sanitize this miserable world, then continue onboard our ships to find new races so we can also help them to perfection."

Striker felt around in his desk drawer and finally found his small emergency plasma pistol. "Why should I help you anymore?" he demanded.

The Jek'Tan rose a foot off the ground and floated above the carpeted floor, then approached the desk.

Striker tightened his grip on the weapon. He had no way of

knowing what it would do to a Jek'Tan, if anything, but his plan for the day did not include dying there.

"You should help us because you are not a fool. You will either assist us in managing our human resources or you can become one."

The intensity of the anger accented each word as it beat into Striker's head like a hammer on a nail, but he still managed to hang onto the gun. "It was my destiny!" Striker cried as he jerked the gun from the drawer and pointed it at the shimmering alien. "We had an arrangement!"

"So you are a fool, as were your ancestors. The agreement was only meant to last until the necessity of it and you expired. You and I are really not that different, Ethan Striker. Like you, the Jek'Tan is but a cog in the great galactic machine. We all have a part to play, and for the plan to succeed, we needed your Earth. For that, we thank you."

Striker felt himself wavering between fear and anger. The first he had no experience with, but the second he was a master of. "You do need me, or you wouldn't have bothered asking for my help. You still need someone to control the Alliance military. If your ships approach without clearance or someone to grease some palms, they will blow every Jek'Tan ship out there to dust."

"Yes, to maintain the illusion, we did require your assistance, but understand that your primitive ships are no threat to us. We will have to make do, as you humans say. If we must, we will sweep them aside and take what we need from this ball of dirt, this Earth of yours. It will not be ideal, certainly not our first choice, but if we have learned anything from you and your ancestors, it is wise to have a back-up plan."

Striker began to sweat profusely, till several beads grew on his forehead and dripped down onto his nose. How can this shimmering thing speak to me in this manner? He was the ruler of an entire star system. "I have the weapon," he stammered. "What is stopping me from shooting you and warning the Alliance military about the threat you represent? Then I can be the hero."

"Him," was all Striker heard in his head as he turned to the open door.

"Mr. Gemini, you know what to do?"

"No! Stay back! I am the ruler of this planet. I say who lives and dies." Striker aimed at the silver-suited figure and fired. The energy pulse bounced off the reflective coating of the second Mr. Gemini's silvery suit and put a smoking hole in a wall on the other side of the room. Striker continued to fire as the giant approached him.

"Ethan, this is for the best," the Jek'Tan said soothingly. "You will thank me after."

Striker didn't bother listening as he jumped from his chair and tried to find a way out of his office. It was insulting to think he would die in a room he considered impregnable. He fired at the tall, thin creature until the charge in the weapon was exhausted; only then did he throw the weapon in defiance. He watched as it bounced off the silver material and landed on the ground. "Killing me won't help you!" he snapped as he pushed his back against his antique oak-covered wall.

"Who said anything about killing you?" Mr. Gemini chimed in as he grabbed Striker by the throat with the long, slender fingers of his right hand.

Striker tried to say something, but he couldn't seem to get enough air into his lungs to utter a sensible syllable.

"Don't worry. You can talk later. Perhaps we can discuss the death of my brother." With that, Mr. Gemini opened the fingers of his right hand and produced a black box.

Striker watched in horror as the box seemed to grow eight legs, all moving with purpose. Had he enough air in his lungs to muster one, he would have produced the loudest scream of his life. He felt weak and dizzy as the stranglehold the creature had on his neck prevented blood from reaching his brain, barely feeling the eight legs dig into his flesh as the box between them seemed to eat its way into his chest. He felt the pain clawing deep, into his core and whatever soul he had left, and then he felt nothing at all.

Mr. Gemini lowered the body of Striker Industries CEO Ethan Striker back into his chair. He and the Jek'Tan watched as the body shook and convulsed while the N'Torr exerted dominance over its new home.

Finally, the shaking ended, and Striker's eyes opened to look at Mr. Gemini and then the Jek'Tan. With a smile, "Master," was the only thing it said as he buttoned up his blood-covered shirt. He knew he'd have to change before he went out amongst the sheep, but that could wait till the creator and his minion departed.

"Welcome to the world, my child," the Jek'Tan said warmly. "I need your help, for we have much planning to do. It appears that our peaceful occupation here will soon be over. Make ready for the others."

"Yes, my creator," he said, his smile decidedly out of place with his host's last memories. His creator had asked him for help, and there was no way he could refuse, especially after being given such a nice, warm home. "It is my honor to serve."

Chapter 17

Fifteen years ago, the Alliance military put contingency plans into effect regarding potential terrorist takeovers or other overt threats directed at the planet's new capital city. With the Brooklyn and Manhattan Bridges rebuilt, as well as local water traffic, Manhattan became less like an island prison and more like the center of commerce that it used to be prior to the war. While they were easily patrolled and controlled, there was always a chance that enemy forces could take control of these key access points. In response to that, the military and civilian authorities, in secret, rebuilt and maintained one subway tunnel for entrance to the city, in case of emergency.

The Army Corp of Engineers, along with Alliance military, equipped the tunnel from the York Street station with additional supports to hold the weight of the water above and to maintain structural integrity in case it needed to be used for an armed incursion into the city. Eventually, other contingencies came about, and they replaced the tunnel. It was then closed and decommissioned only five years after its renovation. Fortunately for Kate and Morrison, the tunnel systems still functioned.

"What the hell are you doing here?" Kate snapped as she ran. Her legs felt like lead, and her breath burned in her chest, but it was better than what was behind them. *Maybe bringing the roof down on that creature was not the wisest thing to do,* she thought.

"Stop!" Morrison yelled back in response as he came to a halt and began feeling along the wall.

"Why? What are you doing? I don't know about you, but I'm in no mood to end up like a drowned rat down here." Kate asked, pointed behind them. As the sounds of falling rock and metal increased, so did the rushing sound of the water bursting into the tunnel. It had gone from a trickle to a raging current, and it was getting closer.

"Hang on," Morrison said. He moved the helmet visor back down and scanned the wall. "Here!" He reached into the wall and turned a hidden knob.

Kate's eyes widened as she heard the sound of a motor coming to life. The tracks pulled apart, and a small, six-seat, open-air car rose from the ground.

"Get in!"

Without a word of protest, Kate jumped in, and Morrison joined her. He shoved the simple throttle control forward, and the car rolled about six feet, then came to a rest.

Kate noticed the water starting to lap at the sides of their alleged rescue vehicle. "Tell me you have this figured out," she said.

Morrison refused to answer immediately; instead, he moved under the throttle lever and pulled off the maintenance cover. He finally said, "This thing has been down here since they renovated the place. Between the heat and humidity, I'm not surprised it crapped out." He pulled out a section of wiring and handed it up to her. "Here. Hold this and grab hold of something. There's gonna be a kick."

Kate took the wire harness and tossed it into the seat behind her. She knew what he was attempting to do and grabbed the armrests while pushing her knees into Morrison's side, hoping to help hold him in place, even though he was much heavier than she was. "Ready," she said as the radioactive, odd-hued water started to climb up the sides of the car.

Morrison pushed the throttle ignition wires together and sent full power to the motors. The whine of the motor climbed, and the car bolted forward, gaining speed and leaving the water behind.

Kate was pinned into her seat like a vacationer on a roller-coaster, but her knees held Morrison in place. She looked ahead and saw the lighted area ahead. "Morrison, ease up on the throttle! We're coming up on the next station. We must be under the capital."

Morrison nodded and began to pull the wires apart. The car slowed and coasted into the Grand Street station. She noted a bit of an incline, as well as other tunnels branching off in various directions. Hopefully, they'd seen the last of the flood waters.

"You okay?" he asked as he collapsed into the seat and removed his helmet.

Kate nodded and pulled herself up to the platform. "I suppose you want a thank-you or something."

Morrison shook his head and ran his hands through his dark hair to wipe off some of the sweat and water that had soaked it. "Dante, needless to say, I know better than that. This isn't the Academy anymore. No reason for me to kiss your pretty butt. Here. Hold this." This time, he handed his helmet to her, then boosted himself to the platform before he took it back.

"Morrison, don't sell yourself short," Kate said, wearing a big smile. "Some of my favorite Academy moments involved you kissing my butt...and then some."

It was Morrison's turn to smile. "And what would your daddy say about that, little lady?" he retorted in his native U.S. Southern drawl. "If I recall, the admiral didn't much like me. As a matter of fact, I remember he transferred my to a listening post on the far side of the moon just to split us up."

At the mention of her father, Kate fell back onto one of the station supports. Suddenly, the facts smacked her right in the face. Her father, the almighty Admiral Dante, was dead, and no one had clued Cole Morrison in on that. "Dad's dead, Cole," she said flatly. "He was killed a few days ago, with Evers and Tobias. They were murdered by that creature I killed in the tunnel."

Morrison sat next to her, held her chin, and lifted her head so he could look into her eyes. "Listen to me, and listen carefully. No one is dead—not your father or Evers or even that little bastard Tobias. They're all alive."

Kate was shocked, but in the end, she knew her old man was too big of an ass to die that way. As far as she was concerned, he was as resilient as the cockroaches that had survived the war, and that wasn't the only similarity she found between them. On many occasions, she had wished she could squash him with her boot, too, and she knew many others held the same opinion of the man. "What are you talking about? On Mars, Rosten told me they were killed in an explosion at Alliance Intelligence HQ. I saw the report on the news."

Morrison shook his head and laughed. "The news? Really, Kate. Years and years ago, the so-called 'news' reported that Martians love strawberry ice cream. When was the last time you saw one enjoying a sundae?"

She laughed. "You have a point."

"Anyway, the three of them discovered that an attempt was going to be made on your father's life. Striker decided to take out Evers and Tobias because he knew they were the only connection to your assignment on Mars."

Kate shook her head, feeling as if she was the last one to be let in on some inside joke. "You knew I wasn't a traitor?"

Morrison nodded and was about to say something, but she interrupted him.

"How about the admiral? Did he know too?"

"He didn't know a thing about it till you left with Rosten and his dipshit son for Mars. Evers and Tobias briefed him after the attempt on their lives. That sorta convinced them that your father's concerns carried...a bit of weight."

"And my brother, Michael?"

"Your father sent him to Mars to find some more tangible evidence against Striker. At the time, he had no idea about your assignment, so he really had no way to warn your brother that you are a friendly. Funny though..."

"What?" Kate asked, not finding much laughable about it.

"He didn't really put much faith in Evers when he told him you were undercover."

"He didn't?" Kate suddenly felt a lump in her throat, the manifestation of the hate she had felt for her father more than once.

She knew he had trust issues, but the whole thing was ridicules.

"He became a believer when he found out about your escape. You left a bit of a mess on Mars," Morrison added with a smile. "We tracked the scout to the house on the tip of Long Island and figured this would be your next stop."

"How did he track my ship?" Kate asked, pushing him away. "I went over *Alexa* a hundred times. There are no tracking devices anywhere. Where did he put it?"

"Dante, it was the *admiral's* ship at one point. He had it installed in the engine core, in a safe spot almost anyone would overlook."

"The bastard," she said quietly to herself with a smile. "The old, sneaky bastard. No wonder he wanted me to have his ship. Even his heirlooms have a freaking agenda."

"Yeah, well, he always does everything with purpose. Can't say I fault the man for that," Morrison said. "When I found out Striker had tracked you with some weird alien tech and put out a kill order on you and your brother, I went to the house and watched it until you left."

"You little son-of-a-bitch!" Kate snapped as she hurried to her feet. The left cross she threw to his jaw communicated her feelings better than her words ever could.

Morrison stood and glared at her as he rubbed his chin. "Hey! What was that for?"

"You had *me* under surveillance and didn't say anything!"

Morrison watched to make sure Kate wouldn't try a second punch. "I was under orders."

Kate pulled back a fist and thought about pummeling him again, then thought better of it. "Whose orders? Last I remember, you worked for Striker."

"I was undercover too, right out of the Academy. Who do you think provided the admiral with intel about the attempt on his life? Who else could have told him you were heading back from Mars with a damn price on your head?"

Kate stopped for a moment and held a hand up to quiet him. "Wait. You said Striker was able to track us, right?"

"Yeah. So?"

"Does that mean he knows where the house is? My brother is still there!"

Before Morrison could answer, they both heard noise from above, coming from the entrance to the Grand Street station.

"We've gotta get outta here before they cut us off." Morrison made a grab for Kate's hand, but she pulled away.

"We have to warn Michael, Morrison," she snapped, refusing to move.

As the sound of footsteps grew closer, Morrison put his helmet on and activated the sensors. "Kate, we can warn him as soon as we're clear. Right now, we have to run. They'll kill us, and besides ruinin' my day, that's not gonna help your brother one iota. Now let's go!"

Kate knew he was tracking the intruders though the helmet, and he was right in his summation of the situation. If they died, it wouldn't help anyone but Striker, and she refused to be a martyr on that slime-ball's account. The house was equipped with its own defense system, and her ship was docked there. "Fine! Lead the way, and take me to my father. We need to have a chat."

Morrison was a fan of famous battles throughout human history. There was always something to appreciate in every simulation, but he had no intention of landing in the middle of a Dante family argument. "Right this way, ma'am," he said, offering a wink she couldn't see behind his closed visor. He knew the layout of the station like the back of his hand. The Alliance engineers had installed a back door, and unless something was parked outside it, he knew it would allow them to avoid any patrols.

He pushed open a door, revealing a ladder. He could see through the light-enhancing feature of his helmet that there was a hatch and a keypad at the top. He quickly hopped on the ladder and motioned for Kate to follow. As they climbed, he thought about the woman behind him, and he fondly remembered what they'd shared together at the Academy. Those nostalgic thoughts were quickly let go, though, when he reached the last rung on the ladder; Morrison was all business when he had to be. He punched in the four-digit code he'd acquired from the admiral and was rewarded with a sharp *click* as the lock gave way.

Morrison slid the circular hatch cover out of the way and climbed out, then, like the gentleman he always tried to be, helped Kate through the narrow exit and opened his visor. He couldn't help but look at her as memories of those Academy years came rolling back, no matter how hard he tried to swallow them.

"Whew. It feels a whole lot better out here," she said and took a deep breath of the cool night air, a relief after spending so long in the stagnant, smoldering tunnels. "What are you looking at?" she asked as she dusted off her pants and jacket

"Nothing," he said with a flirty smile. He couldn't think of a more beautiful woman, even if she was covered in dirt and scratches.

"Morrison, don't be a jerk," Kate spat, words that immediately jerked him back to the present. "Just take me to the admiral. I'm sure he has the number for this house."

Morrison nodded and pointed north, somewhat sad that his little daydream was over. Kate Dante had ruined it, just like she tended to ruin most relationships she'd ever had, simply by opening her pretty mouth that was gifted with spouting some of the ugliest things.

Chapter 18

Michael looked at the screen and finally realized the identity of the mysterious Jek'Tan. From what he could see, they were extraterrestrial beings, the source for every little innovation Striker Industries pushed out to fix the planet. The computer continued working overtime, digging even deeper into the communications files and recordings he'd copied from the relay. He watched as historical archives connected to news reports and intelligence data, revealing links between the aliens and the missing ships and people.

"Oh shit," he finally said as everything became transparent. Everything achieved in that relay, either by Rosten or Stratton, was insurance against Striker, if they needed it. All the accidents were assassinations, and there was a list of them right before his eyes. Striker was protecting his deal with the Jek'Tan and, just as his ancestors did, carefully orchestrated the removal of anything or anyone who dared to stand in the way of it. "The little bastard wanted to be king, and he traded the lives of thousands to land his sorry ass in that throne," he said, resisting the urge to punch the monitor. "The Jek'Tan gave him their secrets, and Striker gave them…people?" he said with a gasp.

Michael dug even further and found a note from one of Striker's ancestors, the one who had made initial contact. He speculated that it was, in fact, the Jek'Tan who started the war, by striking at both Moscow and Washington with nukes supplied to them by the strong military arm of Striker Industries. One thing was apparent from the very beginning: Regardless of the promises of power and dominion over Earth by the Jek'Tan, not one Striker—even going back to the first—actually trusted the aliens to keep their word. There was something missing though. "There had to be more of an end game," Michael calculated. "I mean, why would the Jek'Tan keep this thing going for two centuries? For primitive space technology and their crews?" He shook his head. "Nope, that doesn't make sense. There has to be…more."

Nevertheless, he had made some very interesting discoveries, and he needed to get the information to the Alliance as soon as possible. Despite his father's lack of trust in the government, he was sure there had to be some official who would listen to him, especially with everything he had to show them. Michael pulled out a portable computer drive and linked it to the input/output port on the computer. He would leave the house, but the evidence was going with him. Unfortunately, the alarms signaled that he'd run out of time.

Michael looked for the source of the high-pitched klaxon that threatened to burst his eardrums. It didn't take long to find the answer: The perimeter alarms had detected intruders within their range. Someone had found him, and he had a very good idea that his visitor was sent by none other than Ethan Striker, if not the devil himself. Sensors detected the three jet-copters coming in low over the Atlantic as they reached the beach.

"The defensive systems are activated with that red button on the right side of the console, Michael."

Michael looked at the hologram and did as the projection suggested. When he pressed the red button, the alarms ceased, and one of the cameras turned to reveal a surface-to-air battery rising from the sandy beach. The copters hovered momentarily before attempting to settle on the sand. The defensive gun opened up, and one of the copters took a direct hit and exploded before it reached the ground. Fragments and debris from the explosion hit the copter next to it, sending it to the beach in a fireball, burning but surprisingly intact. The third copter fired on the defensive battery and disabled it with a volley of wing-mounted missiles as the house shook from the impact.

One copter was down and burning, but the other two had landed outside the perimeter of the house and were quickly disgorging armor-clad troops. Michael reached over and armed the minefield that surrounded the house. It was not a permanent solution, but it would buy him a little more time to think of a way out. Sensors registered three detonations as a trio of unlucky men met mine. That seemed to take a little of the urgency out of the attack as the others hurried to scramble out of reach of the mines.

Somehow, they'd found the surveillance cameras his father had placed around the property and were in the process of taking them all out. All Michael had left were the sensors; all visual tracking was lost. Still, he didn't need sensors or cameras to know what they were doing, because the sound of gunfire echoed down the elevator shaft to him. They were firing into the house, with no idea that he was actually under it, and they were using that time to work their way through the mines.

He turned to the hologram of his father, who was starting to flicker along with the lights. It appeared that they'd discovered the generator and had found a way to shut it down. As the systems began to shut down to preserve power, only the emergency lights illuminated the place.

"They are in the house," the hologram said, stating the obvious as emergency doors slammed shut. "I have sealed access to the lower levels. This will slow them, but they will breach it eventually. Michael, it is time for you to go."

Michael waited until the light on the stick flashed a steady green before pulling it from the computer. Not only had he downloaded the evidence he needed, but he'd also copied most of his father's files, as well as the hologram's personality matrix. He was not going to lose the admiral again, real or not. The simulation was also based on his father's mind, and he saw no harm in having one of the planet's premier tacticians at his disposal. Holo-Dad or not, he still had plenty of great advice to offer.

One thing his father had taught him was to never leave intel for the enemy when retreating from a previously secure position. With that in mind, he pulled a wired package out from under the console and slapped it on the data storage drives that stored everything his father had amassed on his conspiracy. The explosive was small but powerful, was more than enough to destroy everything in the room, including all the sensitive and mostly ancient equipment. He armed it with a flip of a switch on the small remote he pulled from his pocket. All he had to do was press it again, the entire second level would be blown to smithereens, along with a good part of the first and third.

"Hope you don't mind me cleaning house before I go, Dad," he muttered with a smirk. He turned to the elevator and saw the hologram of his father gesturing for him to hurry; the dwindling power was beginning to take a visible toll on the imaging projectors, and it was becoming difficult for the hologram to retain its form.

Michael stopped in front of the representation of his father and saluted. "Thank you, sir," he said with a smile, feeling tears in his eyes.

"Go now, son," the projection replied as it returned the salute. "Hurry…" was the last word it spoke before the power demand forced it to shut down.

Michael hurried into the elevator as an explosion in the house blasted the heavy emergency door at the entrance to the shaft. The door opened at the third-level hangar, and he spotted the *Alexa*, parked right where he and Kate had left it. He took one last look around at the weapons; they were all still locked in their racks, and he was disappointed that he didn't have time to load them onto the scout ship. Their father had amassed enough of an arsenal to defend a small army, but since he was actually lacking that army, he had little use for so many armaments. Still, like the intel, he wouldn't leave that for the enemy either.

Michael climbed aboard the *Alexa* and dropped his gear into the co-pilot seat before buckling himself into the pilot station. He looked over the scout controls and realized it was essentially the same ship his father had used to take him on rides as a boy, more or less. There were a few new buttons on the console, and he had no idea about their functions, but all he needed at the moment was flight.

He found the engine controls and attempted to bring the engines online. When they didn't activate, panic set in. If Striker's goons found their way down there and discovered him in the ship, they would have many options as to how to end his life, and Michael wasn't a fan of any of them. It finally occurred to him that Kate had some sort of artificial intelligence (AI) built in, perhaps to prevent her little brother from taking a joyride on her ship. Unfortunately, he desperately needed a ride now, and joy had little to do with it.

Before anything else, he looked at the chronometer; that told him the troops had had enough time to make it to the second level. He pulled the detonator from his pocket and pushed the button again. The explosion brought down a sizable chunk of the ceiling but very little else. Now it was time to turn his attention back to the ship.

"*Alexa*, can you activate the engines please?" he asked out loud, hoping the computer personality was monitoring the cabin and wasn't programmed to hate him.

"You are not Kate Dante," *Alexa* responded in a female voice. "This ship and its AI are programmed for her use only. Please identify, or I may need to take further measures."

Wait. The ship is…threatening me? Damn it, Kate! Michael shook his head in disbelief. He knew Kate was a stickler for security, but that was just insane. "My name is Michael Dante. I am the brother of Kate Dante, and if you don't give me flight and weapons control, neither of us will ever hear my sister's voice again."

"Scanning," *Alexa* responded. "I have detected armed men in the level above, attempting to descend. It appears your assessment is correct. Until the emergency has subsided, I will provide you, Michael Dante, with manual systems control over flight and weapons systems, as requested. Protocols to protect this craft have been activated."

Michael heard the engines coming online just as the first trooper burst through the elevator doors. *Great. They must have slid down on the elevator cable to get here.* He grabbed the controls, rotated the nose and the wing-mounted plasma cannons toward the elevator, and fired. He took out two of them, while the others took cover in the small elevator car.

Without missing a beat, Michael rotated the scout again and opened fire at the stacks of weapons lined up against wall, blasting them all with the streams of energy. "*Alexa,* scan the level," he ordered. "Is there another exit point?" Michael was sure his thoughtful father, always a stickler for details, would not have left the clunky elevator as the only entrance and exit. He had to have thought of an escape route for situations like this one.

"There is an exit 1.3 miles distant, at a course of .75," the AI replied. "No lifeforms are detected. The exit appears safe, Michael Dante."

"Great. Here we go." Michael turned the ship toward the coordinates *Alexa* had provided, firing again at the open elevator door as he rotated past it. The hangar was dark now, with only the blasts from his weapons lighting the way. He wished he could see where they were going, but had to trust that the AI was leading him in the right direction. With her thrusters activated, the scout accelerated into the darkness. Finally, and much to his relief, he spotted the moonlit opening at the end of the tunnel and guided the ship toward it, breaking out of the darkness and into the sky.

He hadn't forgotten the two surviving jet-copters on the beach, so he fired two missiles from the rear weapons pod. He didn't remember the scout ship having a weapons pod of any kind, but on this day, the alterations sure came in handy. The missiles each struck a copter, lighting the beach up in an enormous inferno, like a bonfire gone mad.

Taking a deep breath, Michael wiped his sweaty hands on his pants and guided *Alexa* safely out into the night. He decided to head over the Atlantic for a bit to throw off tracking, then take her low, just as Kate had done, retracing his way back to the mainland.

He could take the ship all the way into the city, but he knew he'd be shot down long before they made it. What he needed was a secluded place to set down, so he could try to reach Kate. Hopefully, her plan to take the old subway tunnel into the city hadn't gotten her killed.

Chapter 19

Eluding the authorities was trickier than either Kate or Morrison had considered. They cautiously poked their heads out of the sealed grating, into what, several hundred years earlier, was once a bustling, busy Chinatown. Unlike the Brooklyn shore, very little effort had gone into rebuilding what was once a landmark section of lower Manhattan.

The devastation of the past was a depressing reminder as they pulled themselves out of the tunnel. Morrison crouched and felt under the recessed edge of the hatch to activate two buttons, then quickly stepped out of the way of the closing doorway. Underground, their trail would effectively end at a ladder to nowhere.

Most of the area, all the way down to the East River, was littered with debris and rubble, like the ruins of some ancient civilization, except for the broken wires jutting out here and there. The steel skeletons of buildings that had been brought down by the nuclear warheads remained as a testament to mankind's stupidity—or at least that was the bullshit story perpetrated by each and every male Striker who refused to put a dime of funds or effort into its rebuild. It was easier to take the altruistic route and call it "a memorial to the dead" than to make it home for the living.

They cleaned, sanitized, and made it part of the capital tour for the masses, as if the thousands who had died long ago still cared. Kate knew better; it was simply an ego stroke for big-headed, self-serving cowards who didn't give a damn about the people who once lived there and were gone in the flash of a nuclear hell. As sanitized as the area was, Kate could almost still smell the blood and singed flesh, a stench that would forever stain those streets and ruins, the burning death of long ago that would never be erased.

Morrison tapped her on the shoulder, distracting her from her grim thoughts, and pointed down the recently paved road at the rotating lights of the security forces still searching for them both above and below ground. The smooth road they stood on, paid for by contributions from Striker Industries, were excellent for the tourists and their cameras but offered little or no protection from the enemy who was quickly closing the gap between them. To make matters worse, Morrison pointed upward at the beating sound in the air.

"Jet-copters," Kate uttered as the new set of lights in the air added to their misery. "We'd better find some cover." She knew if the copters got too close, there'd be no place to hide from the infrared sensors that would detect their body heat signatures. "How about back down the ladder?"

Morrison shook his head. "Too late for that. The passage is sealed. There! Let's make a run for it." He pointed to a building that seemed to be less damaged than the neighboring structures. "The roof is partly metallic. It should block the temp sensors—or at least confuse them. It's our best bet for the time being."

Kate nodded and grabbed Morrison's hand. They crouched low and tried to stay out of the line of sight of the troops in the road before deciding to make their move toward the building. She had no idea what purpose the building had served before the war, but if they reached it before they were noticed, it would possibly save both of their lives. From the engine whine and the lights in the sky, they could tell the copters were getting closer. They needed to be inside before the lights or sensors spotted them.

When they finally reached the building, Morrison tried the door, only to find that it would not budge; either it was locked in an effort to keep the curious tourists out, or else it was still welded shut from the nuclear blast that had decimated the area 200 years ago. He picked up his assault rifle to use as a club to batter the door down, but Kate held out a hand to stop him, knowing the noise might get them caught. Morrison nodded, thinking better of his actions, and gestured to the door. Kate looked it over and banged on the upper left corner, where it met the burnt frame. A chunk of the frame splintered off, and the stubborn door finally opened with a slight *squeak* that reminded her of the nasty rats in the sweltering tunnels below them.

She smiled and gestured toward the door with a sweeping motion of her hand. "After you."

Morrison tried to resist, but the smile came out in spite of his attempts to hold it back. "Smartass."

They entered the building and noted the lack of anything inside. That came as no surprise, as most of the buildings were just shells of what they once were. There was no sense in maintaining the inside that no one was allowed in to see. From the looks of the walls, though, it appeared to be a restaurant. The ornate patterns in what was left of the paint suggested some sort of Asian cuisine; of course, all that information did for Kate was to make her stomach rumble. She turned to Morrison and noticed that he placed a hand on his tummy, probably thinking the same thing.

They found a wall at the far side of what was the large dining room and sat with their backs against it, positioning themselves so they could see outside without being seen by any patrolling troops. Now, it was just a matter of waiting and hoping that no one would check that particular building.

"We need to get out of here," Kate said quietly as her patience ran thin.

"Hang on," Morrison said, pointing up at the whining sound and the searchlights that illuminated the area in front of their hiding spot. "The copters are making a final pass."

"Final?"

"Yeah, final," Morrison answered as the light started to grow fainter. "Two passes are standard protocol."

Kate tried to amble to her feet, but Morrison pulled her back down. "Why—"

"Quiet," he whispered as they heard footsteps coming toward the door. Morrison motioned for Kate to take a position to the right of the entrance, while he took position to the left. He held the tracker he'd obtained from the security man in the tunnel and noted that two targets were approaching. They'd obviously been ordered to complete a thorough building-by-building search, regardless of the sensor data from the copters.

They waited on either side of the entrance as Morrison watched the blips get closer. He looked up at Kate, then clipped the tracker back this belt and ran his right hand across his throat. Kate nodded and readied herself as he held up his hand and put his fingers down in a countdown from five. At zero, he balled his fingers into a fist. At that precise moment, the door opened, and both men stepped in, holding their assault weapons out in front of them, with not too much conviction. They walked side by side, somewhat nonchalantly, as if confident that they would find just an empty building like all the others.

Kate wanted to laugh at the stupidity in their careless formation but avoided the urge, knowing that chuckle would be her last if she set it free.

Both Morrison and Kate struck at the same time, using the same maneuver they'd learned in their basic combat lessons at the Academy. It was over quickly. They pulled the two roughly into the building with their own weapons, knocked them to the floor, and then punched them hard in the sides of their heads. Within seconds, they were dragging the two unconscious men away from the doorway and into the former restaurant.

They looked at each other and smiled.

"Are you thinking what I'm thinking?" asked Morrison.

"I hate to say it, but I think so. Give me a hand here."

Kate and Morrison stripped the unconscious capital troops and shrugged into their uniforms the best they could, considering the difference in the size between them and the two men lying on the floor. Morrison's was a tight squeeze, while Kate's had room for two of her.

"Well? How do I look?" Kate straightened up and tried to smooth the wrinkles out of the oversized uniform and affix her helmet on her head.

Morrison tried not to laugh but failed miserably as he looked at her. "You look great. Really." Morrison's uniform fit a bit better, as did the helmet. He tucked the other helmet into his pack, disappointed that it didn't match his disguise, since he knew it would prove much more useful than lackluster and ill-equipped hardhat he now wore. "Let's go."

With their visors dropped, they could see other members of their squad farther down the street, searching other buildings, but the jet-copters were nowhere to be seen. They assumed the vessels had exhausted their fuel and had returned to their base to refill their tanks.

"Three and Four," a voice said in their helmets, "what took you so long? It's just one building. Get over here, damn it. This isn't a field trip."

Morrison and Kate looked at each other and shrugged. They needed to get away before someone noticed they weren't the Three and Four their commander was looking for.

"Affirmative, sir," Morrison answered, trying to imitate the voice of the man who'd donned the helmet a few moments prior.

"Now what?" Kate asked.

Morrison pointed to the ATV across the street and smiled, hoping their luck was changing. The vehicle was the size of a pre-war Jeep and was used for officer transport. It would be missed but not until it got them away from there and deeper into the capital.

Kate hopped into the driver seat and put the vehicle in gear.

Morrison threw his pack into the back seat and joined her up front.

"Hang on," she wisely advised.

Just as wisely, Morrison heeded her advice and grabbed the metal windshield frame as the ATV rolled away from its former owners and the place that was once Chinatown.

The further north Kate drove, the more the city seemed to come to life. The first thing they passed was government housing for military personnel, as well as Alliance security. Morrison pointed to a side street, and Kate drove down it. When they reached the end of the street, she shut down the engine and removed her helmet. As far as Morrison was concerned, no matter how many layers of dirt, grime, and sweat she was covered in, Kate Dante still shone like a beacon in the night.

"We can't depend on the ATV anymore," he said to her as he ditched the helmet and the uniform and replaced it with what he wore before. "They've probably reported it missing by now."

"You do know where we go from here, I hope," Kate said as she removed the baggy uniform and replaced it with her black leather jacket. "I need to find my father and warn my brother."

"The admiral's safe house is a mile or a mile and a half northeast of the capital and midtown Manhattan. On foot, we can be there in an hour."

"Works for me. Let's go."

They stuck to the shadows as sunrise introduced what they hoped would be a better day than the one they'd just endured. Manhattan seemed to wake up with the dawn as merchants opened their shops and support personnel came from the surrounding boroughs to the east, as well as the rural areas to the north of the city. Technology and the graces of civilization were still a privilege, a luxury reserved for the big-city elite, but they still depended a great deal on the manpower and the farms of those who lived outside the suburban areas. If nothing else, the war had drawn a bolder line between the classes, creating an even wider divide between men like Striker and everyone else.

Eventually, they saw bigger buildings and more expensive clothing, but instead of heading to the heart of midtown, toward

Striker Industries headquarters, they headed east, toward the discolored water. Kate watched as Morrison put his visor down. She still wasn't 100 percent certain of Morrison's loyalties, regardless of their last twelve or so hours together. Kate Dante did not give trust away to anyone so easily, and her hand never strayed too far from her weapon, even if he did keep looking at her like a puppy after a chew toy.

Above their heads, the jet-copters continued their patrol of the city. Whether it was standard operating procedure or the hunt for them was still on, they continued unabated.

Morrison raised his visor and moved ahead. "We're almost there," he assured her as they continued to walk.

Kate pulled her gun and pointed it at his head. "Stop, Cole. We're running out of land. I know you think pretty highly of me, but I can't walk on water." Remnants of FDR Drive stood before them, and after that, there was only the East River, along with the bridges that linked them back to Brooklyn and Queens.

Morrison stopped and turned back to look at her with a scowl. "Put the gun down, Kate. If I wasn't with you, I'd have handed you over way before now."

"I've seen you using that helmet radio of yours. Tell me what we're really doing out here, Morrison." she demanded, feeling her old trust issues rising to the surface again. *Damn you, Admiral*, she thought. *Your DNA and your behavior have made one nasty little messed-up concoction out of me!*

Morrison took his helmet off and dropped it to the ground. "Kate, I *am* with you. If you don't believe me, go ahead and pull the trigger." He pointed ahead of them. "I wish you'd trust me, though, if only for a few minutes more. If I don't come through for you, then you can feel free to shoot."

Kate thought a moment before lowering the gun, but she didn't bother to place it back in her holster. "Don't think I won't. Move it."

They both continued to the East River shore. Over the years, both the shoreline and the famous FDR Drive had receded back to the ocean, creating a bit of a beach. Unfortunately, there was no sunbathing, due to the toxicity of the water; no one was about to don a bikini and hop into the water when it reeked of death and was teeming with bobbing dead fish.

Morrison stopped at the water's edge and picked up a stone, then tried to skip it across the blackness. "Hmm. Never was very good at that. I guess you're gonna have to shoot me now," he said, raising his arms like a man under arrest.

Kate shook her head and felt the gun growing heavier in her hand. "Morrison, what is this?"

Before he could answer, a rumbling came from the water, and the cunning tower of a 200-year-old submarine poked out of the murky depths.

"About time," Morrison said, putting his hands down. "C'mon, Kate. We haven't got much time before security picks the sub up and redirects the copters."

She looked out at the sub, and the shock on her face said more than any verbal reply ever would. "How?" she stuttered.

Morrison pulled a tarp off a small, hidden boat and gestured for her to hurry. "Come on. I need your help getting this into the water."

Kate holstered the gun and helped Morrison maneuver the thing into the toxic drink. The electric motor poked out the back, and the boat went rigid as it hit the wet surface. They both climbed in, careful not to splash themselves with the poison, and Morrison activated the motor and steered with the rudder that poked out the back.

Morrison steered toward the sub as Kate watched the city recede in the distance. Men on the deck hurried to help them as they pulled alongside the huge craft. They lifted Morrison and Kate over and onto the deck of the sub before firing on the small motor craft to send it to the bottom of the river.

They were quickly ushered through a deck hatch and into the underbelly of the submarine. The sound of men running and alarms signaled to Kate that they were preparing to dive before they gave away their position. Everyone onboard was garbed in an Alliance Fleet jumpsuit, and each moved about with purpose.

"This way, Captain," one young ensign said, then led her in the opposite direction from where another led Morrison.

Weird, Kate thought, the only word that came to mind as she looked around. The vessel was over 200 years old, yet Morrison's people were using it as a command post. It wasn't hard to see where it was retrofitted and where new tech had supplanted the ancient electronics used in its original construction.

They stopped outside an unmarked cabin, and the man signaled for her to wait as he entered and shut the door behind him. About ten seconds later, he opened the door and gestured for her to enter. "This way, ma'am," he said to her before moving out of her way.

Kate walked in and turned to see the ensign shutting the door behind her.

"Hey, Kate," a familiar voice said from the desk in the room.

Kate's eyes began to moisten as she wordlessly walked over to the desk where the two men sat. Both her brother and her father, of all people, stood as she approached. "Well, I'll be a son-of-a-bitch," she said quietly.

"Hello, Katherine," the admiral said, smiling and holding his arms out as if he expected a hug from his eldest daughter.

Kate refused the embrace and instead offered him an open-handed smack across the face.

"Kate!" Michael snapped. "What the hell are you doing?"

She looked at her father, who was rubbing the side of his red face in confusion. "You fucking son-of-a-bitch!" she cried as the anger welled up inside her. "I thought you were dead."

"Kate, stop! You can't just—"

She pointed at Michael, wearing an expression that screamed, in no uncertain terms, that he should stay out of it. She then turned her furious gaze back on the admiral. "Are you a hologram, or is this really you?"

The elder Dante shook his head, confused for a moment, but then he finally understood. "No, Kate, I'm the real thing. The red cheek ought to prove it. I'm sorry I couldn't get in touch with you after the attempt on my life or even after Tobias and Evers finally broke down about your undercover assignment. They said it might blow your cover. Then we started talking and found out that we all had the same suspicions. I'm sorry, Kate, but by then... Well, things had taken on a life of their own, and I had to sidestep one shit-storm after another. Surely you understand—"

"And Morrison?" Kate asked, cutting him off. "You sent him to babysit me?"

Admiral Dante sat back down and shook his head. "He was there as backup and nothing more. His orders were to watch you and stay out of your way, unless you needed him. He was only to assist if life and limb were at stake."

She stared at her father and realized she had forgotten how old he was. She had never really thought of him in terms of his chronological age. Nicholas Dante was a force of nature to her, and he typically carried himself like a man half his age. Now, though, he looked like a tired old man, and she felt like a queen bitch for being so harsh with him. She then pulled herself away from her father's wrinkled face and cast it on her brother. "And you?" she demanded. "How the hell did you land on this relic?"

Michael could see that the fireworks between his father and sister had finally fizzled out, so he sat back down. "They sent an assault team to the house. Unfortunately, there isn't much left of it, but I managed to escape with the evidence, the hologram, and—"

"My ship, I hope," Kate interrupted.

"Yes, *your* ship," Michael added snidely. "*Alexa* is fine. I landed outside of Babylon, and the hologram set up an interface that allowed Dad to track us. He contacted me, and the sub met me out in the Atlantic. It's a prototype developed to carry out stealth missions in enemy waters. The admiral and his friends in Intelligence retrofitted it with updated systems and weapons, and they've been avoiding Striker ever since."

"Great," Kate replied with a sigh. "Where is my ship now?"

"We had a helicopter bay without a copter," Admiral Dante replied, "so there was plenty of room for the scout."

"Dad, I have to hand it to you. I never saw the sub coming," Kate said, then finally gave him the hug he wanted. "It's an antique like you, but I suppose you both have value," she conceded. "I'm so happy you aren't dead, and this little family reunion is nice, but now what?"

Dante held his daughter in a tight, warm hug for the first time in two decades, and he felt himself gaining strength from it. *Hmm,* he thought, curious about his own reaction. *Maybe I'm actually becoming human in my old age. I suppose I'll have to check into that later.* When he finally disengaged from her, he hit the intercom on his desk. "Captain, bring us around the island and have senior officers convene in the wardroom for a meeting." He pushed the intercom button again to end the conversation, then looked back at his daughter, whose twisted, contorted, hateful expression had melted into something a bit softer. "Kate, my dear, I do believe it's time we all compare notes. Let's go."

Chapter 20

It was standing room only in the wardroom, and Kate was the last to arrive. After her tunnel-rat adventure, all the combat and the narrow escapes, she'd insisted on stopping for a five-minute shower and clean clothes before joining the command crew. When she stepped into the tightly packed room, she saw the admiral and Michael sitting at the table, with Evers, Tobias, Morrison, and Captain Murry, the commanding officer of the sub. She was glad to see they'd saved one seat for her, and she quickly sat down in it and nodded at her former commanders. "Nice to see you gentleman are still alive and kicking," she said. "Of course, it would have been nicer to have a little support when all of Mars was out there trying to kill us."

Evers was about to make a comment when Tobias held up a hand to quiet him. "Kate, by the time Mars went sour, we had plenty of our own problems here to contend with. We met up with your father and traded information on our current situation, including your assignment on Mars and his theories on Striker. We barely got out of our offices before the explosion blew it to bits."

Kate nodded and pounded a fist on the table. "I know all about that. Rosten showed me the news footage. Nevertheless, you still managed to put Morrison on my ass. You could have brought us in at any time, but you left us out there as bait. Tell me that isn't true, damn it!"

"We did what we could when we could, Kate," Evers chimed in.

"I found the thing that tried to kill you...or rather, he found me," Kate added. "It was some sort of alien hybrid. It wanted to kill me for sport, instead of the accident it planned for me in the tunnel."

Admiral Dante watched the exchange and leaned over to whisper something to Michael.

On cue, Michael nodded and activated his computer connection.

"So you met Mr. Gemini," the admiral interrupted. "The rumors about him are almost as old as the Alliance itself. He kept coming up in communiqués from Striker. Usually, a call about Gemini ended in the death of someone somewhere up the food chain, but we've never had any eyewitness reports to go on. What did the bastard look like, Kate?"

Kate looked at her father and closed her eyes. "Well, he was wearing a silver suit that reflected most of the energy from our plasma pistols. He was tall and thin, with dark eyes and a slit for a mouth, but his hands were the strangest thing, with these long, thin fingers. He was almost indestructible—almost."

"How did you kill it?" Tobias asked.

"She dropped a tunnel on it," Morrison answered for her with a laugh. "She blew out the supports and buried it in a few metric tons of rock, along with half of the East River."

At that point, every eye in the room fell on Kate.

She just shrugged and continued, "He also mentioned something about his masters. He called them the Jek'Tan, said they were his creators and that they would rule the universe. Anyone?"

Admiral Dante cleared his throat and stood from his seat at the table. "In information I've put together from both Alliance Intelligence and communiqués Michael so skillfully downloaded from the Mars relay, we've found more than one mention of the Jek'Tan. It seems that Jek'Tan communications generally coincide with the disappearance of ships on planet prior to space travel, or spacecraft near the rim of the system in the present. There are strange reports of missing persons as well."

"The two are tied together," Michael added. "I've got evidence that the Strikers—the current one and one or more of his ancestors—traded locations of ships and transport schedules to these Jek'Tan for whatever they needed to get a foothold in this system. Evers and I also took the investigation back pre-war."

Evers activated a control, and another screen lowered from the ceiling. "In some old NORAD tracking files, we discovered that the detonations that took out Washington and Moscow at the beginning both originated from space. Neither was fired from a land-based platform, according to the radar telemetry we discovered. That information was buried for more than two centuries. We found clues alluding to that deception in our research into the communications relay."

"Are you saying these Jek'Tan started the war?" Admiral Dante asked, astonished by the new findings.

"So it appears," Tobias said, pointing to the tracking display. "Contrary to popular opinion, leftover angst from the Cold War had little to do with the decimation, Admiral. Neither we nor the Soviets had anything to gain by destroying both capitals. It had to come from space, and the only feasible conclusion is that the Jek'Tan started this war."

Dante couldn't believe it. "So they started a war, then stayed in the background while Striker Industries took credit for rebuilding the planet? Why?"

"Shit," Kate said, just a little too loud. "They wanted the people. The Jek'Tan could have had their fill during the insanity after the war, but unless they did something, their subjects would be tainted with radiation and eventually die. Any further study or experimentation on us would be useless."

"And how do you know any of this, Kate?" Tobias asked, arching an eyebrow at her.

"The thing in the tunnel, Mr. Gemini, called the Jek'Tan his creators. I'm thinking he meant that in the literal sense. His parts may or may not have originated on this world, but whatever created him, my guess is that it had nothing to do with evolution. That silver suit seemed to be more than protection. I'm guessing it was part of his skin as well. They created a pretty efficient killer, like some sort of deadly, almost invincible cyborg with an attitude."

Michael nodded and pulled up several files about the missing ships and their crews and manifests. "Then it all makes sense. These documents were recorded and transmitted between Striker Industries and Mars. They coincide perfectly with the ships that have disappeared over the years."

"Our guess," Evers continued, "is that they contributed ships, while Stratton supplied mineral resources and helped bury the evidence."

"So Rosten knew about the disappearance of the deep-space transports as well?" Kate reasoned.

Admiral Dante nodded, then asked his daughter, "Do you think he was aware of the Jek'Tan connection?"

"I don't think so. The one impression I got from Rosten was that, as much as he's in it for himself, he'd never do anything that would compromise the Alliance. We're the only thing standing between him and Striker."

"But what about the *Bonaventure*?" Michael asked. "Dad, Kristin's ship has gone off radar. Could they be connected somehow?"

Admiral Dante shook his head. "I'm not sure. Since our alleged deaths, we've fallen out of the loop. Striker controls the flow of information, and we know very little regarding the *Bonaventure*. We have attempted to communicate with her, but we've received no answer."

"There's got to be a way to find out. Can't we send another ship out there? I can take the *Alexa* out." Kate wasn't even sure that what she was suggesting was possible, and even if it was, she was sure it wouldn't be their first priority. *What's one little sister after all, in the grand scheme of things?* she thought sarcastically.

"As much as I'd love to send the entire fleet out in search of the *Bonaventure* and your sister, Katherine, there are far more pressing issues at hand," the admiral answered.

Kate winced a bit; she could see from the look on his face that it wasn't an easy thing for him to say.

"We have a new emergency," he said.

"And what is that?" Kate asked, knowing it had to be crucially important for him to put a hold on any search efforts for his own daughter.

Admiral Dante gestured over to the sub CO. "Captain Murry, the comm-screen please."

"Aye-aye, sir," the bearded man said as he pressed a touch-sensitive switch on his side of the table.

Kate observed the captain and found him to be a rugged, handsome man, though he appeared to be in his late forties or early fifties. She thought the slight gray in his beard gave him the distinguished look of a man who belonged on the sea. The smile vanished from her face, however, when she saw who had appeared on the monitor. "Rosten?"

"Hello, Kate, gentlemen," he said.

Clayton Rosten's smile was warm, but it did nothing to detract from her desire to kill him. She stood from her seat and stormed over to her father. If there was any question as to her feelings regarding Rosten, they all disappeared with her quickly melting smile. "What the hell is the meaning of this? That man is a criminal, yet you're all chatting with him like he's done nothing."

"Kate," Rosten said from the screen, "I am trying to make amends and help the rest of you stop Striker and Stratton from this maniacal little plan of theirs. Please give me some credit, darling."

"Dad," Kate implored, "don't listen to him! He's a murderer. He's responsible for all those ships disappearing and probably the *Bonaventure* as well."

Admiral Dante stood from his chair and met his daughter's glare with one of his own. "Katherine, sit back down in that seat, or I will have you removed and confined. Am I clear?"

Morrison watched Kate as the muscles in her neck and shoulders violently contracted and released. Finally, the red in her face began to fade a bit, and without another word, she slumped back into her chair.

"Very wise."

Kate looked at Rosten and studied his face that bore none of the self-righteousness he had displayed at their last meeting on Mars. "Fine, but this is a mistake."

Rosten looked over at her, and his face softened even more. "Kate, what I tried to do for you, I did because I care. I had no other motive. For what it's worth, I am sorry. I was wrong to support Ethan Striker and his foolish goals, and I can admit that to you now."

"You expect me to believe that?"

"Kate, you can believe whatever you wish, but it's true." Rosten looked back up at the admiral, then at Evers and Tobias. "Gentlemen, we are ready whenever you give the signal."

"Ready for what? What is he talking about, Dad?" Kate asked.

Rosten smiled at her sudden confusion before looking back at the admiral. "My ships and security forces are already on their way to the moon. They should be there in a matter of hours, and—" Clearly Rosten was distracted by someone off screen. "What?" he asked, looking at the data-padd the person had handed to him. He then glanced back up at the admiral. "Gentlemen, I'm afraid I have some potentially bad news. It seems deep-space tracking has picked up four large targets entering the system. They have set a course for the other ship that has remained near the orbit of Neptune. I believe the Jek'Tan are on their way. Now transferring telemetry."

Murry split the screen that Rosten inhabited and brought up the deep-space tracking data streaming in from Mars. The screen showed that four additional ships were indeed making their way to join up with the one already represented on the screen. The readout also showed a much smaller reading below the original.

"Could that be the *Bonaventure*?" Michael asked. "The size is about the same."

"The ships I have left aren't enough to stop such an invasion," Rosten said quietly. "Computer projection puts them at sixteen hours from Earth."

"We need the Alliance fleet on our side," Dante said to the table.

"Martinette has control of the fleet," Tobias answered slowly, "and the orbital weapons arrays."

"And Striker has control of Martinette," Evers finished grimly. "Our forces are too split up to deal with this. The Jek'Tan will probably take this planet without firing a shot."

"I will go after Striker and force him to release control of the ships and the array," Kate said with a nod.

"No," Morrison countered. "You'll never get past security. In fact, it's so tight there that you won't even get by the automated system before it sounds the alarm. They'll get you before you even get close."

"Then what do we do?" Kate asked, running out of ideas and time.

Admiral Dante started to laugh, something his children found odd for the man they knew as their father. "It's staring us in the face, boys and girls," he said. "We simply go after Martinette."

Tobias and Evers nodded and smiled at that idea.

"That might work," Tobias finally said. "We have no control or authority to affect security at Striker Industries, but we do have all the security codes for Alliance Military Command."

"We can get you inside without a problem," Evers agreed. "The rest will be up to you."

"What if we can't convince him?"

Admiral Dante stood and straightened his uniform. "Don't forget that I'm a fleet admiral. I'll get the ships, but I can't guarantee that they'll be enough to battle those five mile-long monstrosities coming for us. We need those weapons satellites online. That information transfer to Martinette was probably what motivated Striker to make the attempt on my life."

"What makes you think your command will be acknowledged by the fleet captains?" Kate argued. "Without the authentication codes, they won't even respond to you. I'll let you know when I have them."

"You can't go in there without backup, Kate," Morrison snapped as he got to his feet. "Like you said yourself, even you can't walk on water."

Kate just stared at him.

"You're not going alone…and that's final," he said.

Before she could utter a word in defiance, they all turned to see the admiral nod. "Done. You two are off then. Take the scout. It is still programmed with my command codes, so you should have access, unless someone changed them." The last part was delivered to both Tobias and Evers, who simultaneously shook their heads and quietly uttered, "No."

"Admiral, what about me?" Michael asked. "Do you want me to go with Kate and Morrison on the mission?"

"No, son. I want you and the intel twins here to go through all that evidence you brought back and condense it to something I can release to the media, a nice little nugget of shock and awe that will damn Striker and his followers forever."

Michael smiled, loving the idea of that. He was capable with guns and ammo, but he could do far more damage with a keyboard, and his father knew it.

"That's it then. Everyone get moving."

As Kate and Morrison passed Admiral Dante, he grabbed her arm and pulled her back into a forced hug. "Be careful, my dear, but know that you have to finish this quickly. The faster I have those codes, the more time I will have to intercept the alien ships before it's too late to stop them."

Kate hugged him back, then broke free. "Yes, sir. We'll get this done."

"No rulebook either," her father said with a smile. "Do whatever you feel is necessary. And as for you," he said to Morrison, "keep her safe, or the two of us may have to have another discussion, perhaps even worse than the one when I heard you two were dating at the Academy. Am I understood?"

"Yes, sir," Morrison answered, just a few shades paler than when he'd first started for the cabin door.

Kate watched Cole walk into the corridor, then turned back to her father. "What did happen that night? He never told me."

"Let's just say Mr. Morrison has every incentive to make sure you live a nice, long life."

Kate couldn't tell if her father was smiling, so she just walked off and headed for the launch bay and a reunion with her ship. She could hear Murry's voice over the old speaker system as he ordered the ship to the surface, the deck pitching up a few degrees to confirm it.

She found the small launch bay and the *Alexa* parked under the watertight doors. The hatch was open as she approached it, and she noted the crate sitting on the deck by the doors. "What the hell is this?" she asked Morrison, who was buckling himself in.

He had strapped the sensor helmet to his head but had the visor up. "Weapons," he responded simply.

"Mind telling me what sort of weapons?" Kate asked as she took the pilot seat and snapped the shoulder and lap restraints in place.

"All of them," Morrison answered as he lowered the visor and brought the ship systems online.

Kate nodded and released a sigh as she activated her flight and weapons control systems.

"This is *Alexa*. We are ready for launch."

"Stand by, *Alexa*."

Water poured into the bay as the twin airlock doors pulled open, revealing blue skies as the sub settled to the surface. Kate poured power into the vertical thrusters as the scout rose up into the sky high above the Atlantic. She stared up into the deep blue and puffy clouds and said a silent prayer that they would see them again tomorrow. Without a word to Morrison, who appeared to be napping, she switched to atmospheric flight and set course for the mainland. *God help anyone or anything that gets in my way,* she swore. She had her daddy's permission to kick some ass, as well as that Dante iron will of hers, and nothing was going to stop her until she got what she needed.

Admiral Dante watched the scout ship fly off and wondered if he would ever see it or his daughter again. As soon as the small ship was clear, the bay doors closed, and the submarine once again submerged out of sight of the world that had abandoned it as a workable concept. Dante looked again at his latest project and accepted a timeless truth: *Even old things have their uses.*

He'd found the sub berthed in New London, Connecticut. It had escaped the fate of so many other warships of its time by running silently under the ice for the duration of the war, testing prototype systems. When they found the world at war, they returned home to be with their families. Before she left for the icepack, the *Tigershark*, as she was named, was a state-of-the-art warship, one of the best of her time. When Dante spotted her via satellite, it didn't take much effort to salvage and update her systems. The hard part was finding and training a crew, but that turned out to be easier than he initially expected. Deep-sea exploration was an art only enjoyed by a few, but he managed to find them.

Captain Malcolm Murry had served with Dante, both in space and below the seas, and Dante couldn't think of any better hands for the *Tigershark* to be in. It was an underwater starship, and he commanded it as such. In fact, Captain Murry was the first he reached out to after the attempt on his life, and the lives of Evers and Tobias. Now, Murry had given him complete command of his vessel.

Dante watched his son Michael, along with the two Intelligence officers, attempting to craft their evidence against Striker into some sort of usual media. He had friends among the captains of the Alliance fleet, but he wasn't sure if any of them would disregard orders from Martinette and swing their loyalty to a presumed-dead admiral, the father of two alleged traitors. He had to have something solid to put in front of them. "Gentlemen, we are running out of time," Dante said to the three men.

"Admiral, this may take a while," Evers said before turning back to his screen with Tobias and Michael.

"You have thirty minutes to get me something I can use to sway those ship commanders," Dante said, pawing the bottle of pain relievers that sat before him with the glass and pitcher of water.

"Dad, we need more time than that."

Dante looked in his son's eyes and shook his head. "Michael, if I can't get the fleet to intercept those ships at Mars, it really won't matter. We'll all be dead."

Michael just nodded and went back to work on assembling the data.

Dante hated putting pressure on his son and daughter, but he had no choice. His suspicions went back years, but now they had only hours to deal with the consequences.

At that moment, he missed Kristin most of all. Of all his children, her mind was the most like his, and it would have been nice to bounce a few things off her. He felt a little helpless where his other children were concerned. Dante was usually aware of where all three of them were, but now he had no idea where his youngest was or if she was even still alive. *This parenting thing is truly a bitch,* he silently fumed.

Chapter 21

Kristin was angry, but there it was on the scanner, as big as life and about as crappy. The four alien ships entered the system with all the grace of lumbering elephants. Unlike the first ship, there was no attempt to mask the approach. From the course plotted by Simpson, they appeared to be meeting the first ship, which had broken contact with the *Bonaventure*. Computer projections determined the next destination as Mars, followed by Earth. The *Bonaventure,* on the other hand, had changed course and was in a standard search grid. It didn't take a genius to know who they were searching for.

Kristin dropped down into the seat next to Simpson and dropped her face into her hands. Her long blond hair had fallen out around her face long ago. With the heat and humidity in the station, she'd given up trying to control it. *Wow. Look at this rat's nest. Kate would have one big laughing fit at this bad-hair day of mine,* she mused. Her older sister had teased her since they were kids regarding the almost pathological lengths she went to take care of her blond locks. Thinking of Kate made her think of Michael and the admiral, but suddenly, she was struck with the somber thought that she might never see her family again.

The news of the alien fleet also eliminated the possibility of taking it and the *Bonaventure* out. The jamming continued, as did the increase in background radiation from the damaged reactor core. They still had another thirty-two hours to go before the levels would become harmful, but sooner or later, it would come down to a choice of how they wanted to die: trying to make a run from the *Bonaventure* and ending up as hosts for one of those spider-things or succumbing to radiation poisoning before going up in a big explosion when the system could no longer manage to control the breach that was slowly killing them. At least before this latest update, she had a plan to distract both ships long enough to free Jakes to alert the Alliance.

"Commander," the voice of her chief medical officer called over the comm, "can you please come to medical?"

Simpson turned to her and shook his head. "Good luck."

Kristin smiled. *In about a day, this will all be over, one way or another,* she thought to herself. Of course, from the looks of those alien ships, it would probably be over for Earth as well. "Luck? I doubt it. Let me know if anything gets worse while I'm gone."

Simpson nodded and turned back to the tactical display.

She passed the recreation room on the way to medical and saw Jakes with a cup of coffee in his hands. "Everything okay?" she asked as she took a moment to stick her head through the doorway.

Jakes took a last gulp from his paper cup before crushing it and tossing it to the floor. "Doubt it. Simpson told me about that quartet of alien ships. So much for that suicide mission of yours. Your father would not have approved anyway."

"And how would you know what my father would or would not approve of?" Kristin asked, wondering where Jakes was going with it.

"Well, now I let the cat out of the bag," he said with a smile, "the admiral sponsored me for the Academy when the Alliance wouldn't touch me with a ten-foot cattle prod. When I was about fourteen, a patrol found me in the capital, scrounging for food for my mother and brother. There I was, with no ID or work pass and an attitude bad enough to earn me a well-deserved beating seven nights a week. You know how things are in the capital. I was a nonperson in a land where people like Striker decide who or what you are."

"So what happened?"

"There were five guys on patrol. They wanted to take me to a detention center, but I protested a little too much, and they didn't like it. To teach me a lesson, they took turns beating me until there was very little left. I spent three weeks in a local clinic, with more broken bones than I thought a human body could hold. Hell, I hurt in places where I didn't know I had places. Anyway, when I was released, I tried to find my family, but Mom was gone. I never saw her again. My brother said she went on a food run and just never came back. I was forced to turn to a life of crime to feed my brother and me. It was mostly small-time stuff, nothing violent. I thought I was a goner when I got caught trying to pickpocket an Alliance fleet admiral. I had no idea he was so…famous. You might recognize his name, Commander *Dante*," he said with a wink. "Instead of turning me in for what would have been another beating and maybe some jail time with types they tell teenage boys to avoid, he offered—or should I say threatened—to send both me and my brother through school, then to the Academy. He told us it would build character, and he reminded us that our options were pretty limited. I took him to my brother, and… Well, as they say, the rest is history. So, yes, I do think I have some idea what he would or would not approve of, Boss…and I owe him a great deal."

Kristin knew everyone's bio, but that part of Jakes's history had been dutifully excised at a high level, an easy task for a fleet admiral. "I'm sorry."

Jakes shook his head and smiled. "Don't be. After all, it was your father who saved my brother and me, and now and again, we do what we can to repay a little of that debt."

"Did he order you to keep an eye on me?" Kristin asked, not sure if she should be mad or flattered.

"No," Jakes said, trying not to act too humble. "I knew who you were, and when I heard you were assigned to the *Bonaventure*, I had the admiral pull some strings. Face it, darlin'. We're about as close to family as you can get without a blood test."

Kristin was speechless. She'd never heard that story from anyone, not even her father. Jakes owed his entire life and his brother's to the admiral, who'd rescued the little street urchins from a far worse fate. *Maybe we've underestimated his heart*, she thought. *Maybe he actually has one.* Before that day, she really couldn't be sure. "Listen, Jakes, we'll talk later. I need to go see Tolliver."

"Mind if I tag along? I might learn something. The Falcon is as ready as she's gonna get, and until your launch order... Well, I've really got a whole lotta nothin' to do."

Kristin was about to refuse his company, but she realized she had little reason to, other than the fact that she was uncomfortable after his revelation. "Sure."

"After you then," Jakes said with a smile as he gestured toward the hatch that opened to the corridor.

It was a short walk to the infirmary. Kristin was happy that the former Commander Stack had found a white coat and was assisting Tolliver.

Tolliver was standing over an isolation tank. Inside the tank was the spider, currently in the shape of a disk. "You're late, Commander," he said to her without turning from the tank.

"Doctor, to say I've had a bad day would be an understatement," Kristin said to the back of his head, not really caring if he turned to face her or not. "Please tell me what you've found."

Tolliver gestured to the tank.

Jakes looked at it from a distance, as if he wasn't so sure about it.

"Are you happy, Mr. Jakes?" Tolliver offered sarcastically. "The isolation tank is quite secure."

Jakes nodded but his hand never left the butt of his gun. "So far, so good, Doc."

"Tolliver, today please."

"Yes, Commander Dante," Tolliver continued. "I ran every test I could think of in this limited environment and found nothing. Then I just turned up the force field while I prepared the next test. Then this happened."

Tolliver turned a dial at the side of the tank, and a steady *hum* filled the small medical bay. They watched as the disk suddenly reacted, growing larger, and eight legs jutted from the sides.

Kristin watched as the thing started to transform in front of them. Jakes pulled his plasma pistol out and took aim, just in case.

"Please," Tolliver said, trying to calm them. "I assure you it's quite safe. Ms. Stack, please power down."

Stack did as she was asked, and the legs retracted back into the re-formed disk.

"How?" Kristin asked. "And no games. I'm in no mood for magic tricks…unless you can levitate us out of here to someplace safer, maybe halfway around the galaxy."

Tolliver smiled as if he was hiding a secret. "I didn't add anything to the tank," he said, "but it does have to do with something that exists in the environment here."

Jakes nodded and holstered his weapon. "The radiation leak! They're vulnerable to the neutron radiation leaking from the reactor core, right?"

"Correct," Tolliver said with a smile. "The worse the leak gets, the greater the effect on the creature. On the outside, they appear as solid as you or me, but their energy signature seems to exist on more than one level at the same time. The neutron radiation given off by the core is powered by a combination of artificial elements created due to their inexpensive but highly charged radioactive fields. It's a dirty byproduct, just waste that is generated by the fusion core of the reactor. It seems to disrupt their biological systems, rendering them inert and, with longer exposure at higher levels, dead."

"Could we use it as a weapon?" Kristin asked, grabbing at straws.

"The only issue is that the radiation must be present in a large enough dose to take effect immediately. When the source of the radiation is shut down, they recover quickly, and they are not happy when they do."

"Question," Stack piped up from the corner. "What if we could set off a pulse of neutron radiation at a high level? Could we fry it?"

Tolliver nodded and went back to the controls on the isolation tank. "Ms. Stack, you might just be on to something." He grabbed dark glasses from an equipment bag and handed a pair to everyone present. "Let's see if we can exterminate a spider, shall we?"

Kristin grabbed his hand at the last minute. "Wait! Is there a way to kill it without killing the host?"

"Doubtful, but let's give it a try." Tolliver dialed up the neutron charge on the tank to levels just below lethal. "Glasses up, folks." He then boosted the force field power to both revive the creature and protect them from the radiation blast.

As he amped up the power, the creature came back to life with crazed intensity and violently attacked the sides of the tank.

"Three...two...one!" Tolliver hit the button, and a bright green flash enveloped the tank.

The spider stopped its attack on the tank, twitched, then lay still. They all watched as the legs quivered once before falling off and turning to dust right in front of them.

For the first time since they'd left the *Bonaventure*, Kristin felt like they had a chance. "Can this be replicated on a larger scale?" she asked hopefully.

Tolliver thought for a moment before Jakes interrupted, "Moss can probably tell you better than I can, but I'm sure our only source is the reactor."

Kristin pulled out her comm and called Moss, then quickly explained everything to him.

"Commander, like I said, it's been hard enough keeping this thing from blowing. We can do it, but I'll have to set that self-destruct as a shaped explosion and vary the power level so we get the right amount of radiation flowing where you want it into space. I just need the level from the doc."

"Tolliver," Kristin asked seriously, "are you certain this won't do any permanent damage to the human host?"

Tolliver nodded. "If the legs withdraw like they did in the test and we get to them in time to administer an anti-radiation shot, then yes, it should work."

"*Should*?" Jakes snapped. "You mean you're not sure?"

Tolliver looked at Jakes and shook his head. "I don't know about you, Pilot, but this is the first time I've ever done this. It should work. That's the best I can do."

"We have no choice, in either case. Everyone, let's get started…and, Jakes, make sure the Falcon is ready to go ASAP. We're getting the hell out of here," Kristin said as she headed for the door.

"Where you going?" Jakes asked.

"I've got to make a call," she said, and then she was gone. Her old suicidal plan had managed to morph into a brand new one, albeit one that was a little more promising. With any luck, the day might have a happy ending after all. *And even if it doesn't,* she surmised, *no one will be around tomorrow to complain about it.*

Jakes caught up with her halfway down the corridor and grabbed her arm. "You are not seriously doing what I think you're about to do, are you, ma'am?"

Kristin jerked her arm away and turned angrily.

Jakes recognized the expression and released her arm; he'd seen that same look on her father's face plenty of times.

"Let's get one thing straight, Jakes," she spat. "Beyond the fact that I outrank you, I also really don't care about your relationship with my father or the blood oath you seemingly swore to keep me safe. There are five very large, very bad ships full of death heading to my home, and I will try anything to see that they don't get there, even if it costs the lives of everyone here. If we can take back control of the *Bonaventure* and her weapons and maybe, just maybe save a few of our friends in the process, I will do it. Do you know why? Because—"

"Because it's what the admiral would do," Jakes finished. What she said was a verbal smack to his face and a blow to his ego, but Kristin Dante was right: It was a duty they owed their shipmates and their oaths to protect the Earth and the Alliance.

"That's right," she said in agreement. "This is the same idiotic, backs-to-the-wall plan my father would endorse. Look, we're all dead if we stay, and we're probably dead or worse if we try to make a run for it. This is it." Kristin stopped her rant when she saw the smile creeping across Jakes's face. "What's so funny?"

"You."

"Me?" she asked in surprise.

"Yes, you. I wondered why you and the admiral never got along, at least as far as he would tell me. The answer is now pretty obvious." Jakes stopped and waited for her to take the bait, which she quickly did.

"And why is that?"

"Because you are just like him," he finally answered. "You two are like two peas in a pod, but you're also like similar poles on a magnet, pushing each other away. I don't know about your brother and sister, but you're the admiral's little girl through and through… ma'am."

Kristin forced herself to smile. She had a retort, of course, but it was better to save it for another time. Changing the subject, she said, "I need you to do something for me."

Jakes stood at attention and nodded.

"Round everyone up and get them back to the Falcon ASAP. As soon as everyone is onboard, you get out of here, regardless of how far into the repairs you are. Brady will find us sooner rather than later, and I need you and the others to find someplace to hide until we see if this stupid plan of mine works. If it does, move in on the *Bonaventure*. Work with Simpson to plan the best course away from the station. Go somewhere out of range of the radiation from the main force of the blast. Find Moss and tell him to meet me in the control room. He should be done calibrating the blast radiation and the detonator by now."

The look of concern painted Jakes's face with wrinkles he didn't even know he had. "What about you?"

Kristin pulled Jakes to her and gave him a hug and a kiss on the cheek before stepping back. "I'm a bit late on my check-in with the captain. That detonator only has a five-minute fuse, if that. If this works, you're going to have to board the *Bonaventure*, assess the condition of the crew and the bugs, then take control of the ship. Your orders will be to pursue those alien ships and do whatever damage you can to them until the rest of the fleet shows up."

"Wait a second. It sounds like you're not going to be on that Falcon with us."

Kristin nodded. "I may not. Things could…go wrong. For one, the radiation leak may have drifted out into space, to the point that it might affect them enough to avoid contact with the station. There is also the leak itself. It may not cooperate and blow like it's supposed to. There are probably a hundred other factors to worry about, but this needs to work on the first try, even if all the kinks aren't worked out. I need to get them all close enough so the radiation from the blast will have a chance, regardless of what happens to me. If it doesn't work, it might be preferable to getting captured. If I order you to leave, you leave. Understood?"

"Understood," Jakes answered reluctantly, "but if it works, I will come back for you."

"If you insist. Now get going. You have your orders." Kristin only walked ten feet down the corridor before she heard Jakes yelling something to her. It sounded a lot like "*You're gonna make it*," but she couldn't be sure of his words or his prognosis. Without turning back, she pushed the smile down deep and made her way to the CIC room.

There was no way to judge the reaction she might get from the thing that was Captain Brady. It had his memories and experiences, but the real question was whether or not it harbored his instincts. Only the next few minutes would tell.

She reached the control room a minute and a half later and took a seat at the communication control console. The jamming sent from the *Bonaventure* was modulated toward higher frequencies, the kind that needed to travel the length of the system in seconds rather than minutes. The short-range stuff still worked, but the danger was that if the *Bonaventure* was monitoring, they would pick up the low-band transmission and track them with no problem. Stealth was critical before, but now it was just the opposite. She needed to bait them in just far enough that a core explosion from the station would incapacitate the things attached to them, giving the shuttle time to board the ship and retake it.

She saw Moss at the door. He was about to say something, but she held up her hand to silence him as she switched on the transmitter. "Dante to the *Bonaventure*," she said into the microphone on the console. "Come in please."

There was a brief moment of static before the voice came on. It was eerie to hear the voice of her captain and friend and know it was an alien and not truly him. "Commander?" Brady said over the speakers. "Nice of you to report. I assume you realize that you are… quite late."

"Yes, sir. I do. Sorry about the delay." Acting had never been Kristin's forte. She'd been a straightforward person for most of her life, and with the exception of a few regrettable incidents, she had tried her best to avoid lying. At this particular moment, she had to be more like Kate and Michael. They had somehow found a way to lie for a living, and if they could do it, so could she. "I know you're looking for us, and I know why."

"Do you? Do you really?" the voice spat back. It sounded like Brady, but the tone hid something sinister.

"We found a gateway station outside the Neptune orbit. It's venting atmosphere, and the Falcon was damaged when we ran."

"Are you telling me you have no way out?"

"Yes, sir."

"Are you asking me to rescue you?" Brady asked with what Kristin assumed was an approximation of a laugh. "It would suit the Jek'Tan well to simply leave you all there to die, would it not?"

"We'd be useful to you," she added, trying to make it sound as if they were worth saving, "maybe even without acting as…hosts."

"How so?"

She smiled when she realized she had his attention; he seemed at least curious enough to listen to her proposal, so she thought it up in a hurry. "You know who I am, who my father is, correct?"

"Of course."

"Then you know I can help you get what you want. All I ask is that you spare my crew here, that you rescue us before the environmental systems are gone." She hoped the Jek'Tan would jump at what seemed to be a low-risk, high-return option. Unfortunately, they had more than a dozen other bodies to use, so she wasn't sure she had enough cards to throw on the table.

There was a moment of silence before the voice of Captain Brady returned. "We agree to your proposition. Perhaps you do have value, and our sensors have confirmed your position at the gateway station near Neptune, as you said. We will set a course for you, but know that if this is a deception, we will see that you regret it."

"Thank you, sir," Kristin said, trying to sound as relieved as she could.

There was a flash of static through the system. "Don't thank me, Commander Dante. When this is over, you may wish that I allowed you and your shipmates to die in the vacuum. I will remind you once more. If this is a ruse, I will destroy you, the station, and every living thing onboard. Understood?"

"Yes, sir," she answered.

The transmission went dead as Brady closed the channel.

Moss walked over to her at the communications console. He looked as pale as death, mirroring what they all knew was likely their fate, perhaps within the next hour. "Commander, I rigged the detonator and increased the shielding around the leak, as ordered."

"Where's the detonator?"

Moss motioned for her to follow him to the ops station. He pointed to an illuminated switch on the control panel, then pushed it, causing the button next to it to blink red. "The system is armed. Push this blinking one here, and five minutes later…*boom!* Once you push it, there is no way to reverse it, so you have to be sure when the time comes."

"Great," Kristin said as she stared down at the button and the blinking red light. "Thank you, Moss. Now go gather your gear and join the others in the Falcon."

"Yes, ma'am," Moss said. He turned to leave, then stopped and turned back to her. "Commander?"

"Yes, Moss?" she asked, looking up from the button.

"Is this going to work? I have plans for about an hour or two from now," he said with a forced smile. "Maybe some lunch."

"I hope so, Moss," Kristin answered with a bit of a laugh. "I'll tell you what. If this all works out the way we want it to, meet me at the *Bonaventure* café, and I'm buying. Now get the hell out of here… and tell Jakes I sent you to remind him of his orders."

"Yes, ma'am!" Moss snapped to attention, smiling broadly for the first time that day.

Kristin returned the smile and watched the hatch shut behind the young lieutenant. It was nice to give someone something to look forward to when things got bad, to spread a little hope around, no matter how false. It gave them all something to live for in the end. Hopefully, in a few hours she'd be able to keep her word to Moss, but more than likely, neither would be alive for that or any other meal. A lot of it depended on how well the shielding around the leaky reactor kept the radiation from being noticed as a threat.

She looked at her chronometer and realized that in less than half an hour, that question and all others she had at the moment would be answered, or else they'd be all too dead to care.

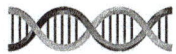

Captain Henry Brady was a prisoner in his own head. He could see and hear normally, but he was otherwise powerless as he sat in his command chair on the bridge of the *Bonaventure*. The thing that had him was dug into his chest like a Louisiana tick, and the same held true for the rest of his unfortunate crew. It was constantly in his head, rummaging for information that would help it become more him.

The only thing they were not aware of was that the exchange of information went both ways. Every time they dug into his consciousness, he was able to access a small part of theirs as well. They were Jek'Tan, or at least created by the race of extradimensional beings who had taken his ship. Their creators bioengineered them with their own DNA, then reengineered them over and over again for thousands of years, until they ended up in their present form. They were like an intelligent virus, living off a host organism and then reproducing in order to continually repeat the cycle. Unfortunately, the host died at that point, but more of the creatures were created. He had no delusions of survival; Brady was sure he was not going to get out of it alive.

They'd discovered the huge ship floating just outside the orbit of Jupiter. It was like none they'd ever seen before, and it appeared to be alien in origin. In a moment of careless, egotistical judgment, Brady had led another shuttle over to the ship himself. It only took his extraordinarily gifted tactical officer a few minutes to gain access, and a few minutes later, they were all piled inside. .

It was dark, and with the exception of an unnerving clicking noise, it was silent. It was like walking through an ancient Egyptian tomb, as there were obscure markings on the walls and ceilings. As antiquated as it seemed, the technology was far more advanced than anything developed on Earth; conduits of liquid light carried energy and then re-formed into something else, but none of them had any clue to what end. It was that strange thing that allowed them to advance as far as they did. The clicking eventually moved off into the distance, and Brady was sure any noise was worth following, especially since the odd conduits seemed to be lighting the way there as well. He had no idea until later about the magnitude of that mistake in judgment.

Several minutes later, the lights lured them into an enormous chamber with an almost cathedral quality to it. There was a chemical smell there, almost like burnt plastic. As soon as they entered, the passageway sealed behind them and the lights went out. They each carried emergency lights, but the darkness actively devoured any light further than a few meters away.

The clicking that had been intermittent earlier grew louder and louder, until it was almost deafening. When the noises finally stopped, a portion of the chamber illuminated. In the glow was a humanoid figure, seemingly floating. The light followed it as it approached. From what his landing party was able to make out, it was thin and humanoid in shape, but it was shimmering in almost the same liquid energy as the conduits they'd seen on the way. There was no way to decipher any of its features, other than an approximate shape and size. Whatever it was, it was quickly coming closer.

It stopped and hovered just a few feet from them. The intensity of the shimmering energy grew as it got closer, before it abated to a mute glow.

"Who are you?" Brady asked slowly. "My name is—"

"Your name is Henry Brady," interrupted the alien, "and you are the captain of the USS *Bonaventure*." The voice sounded far away, as if it was carried to him on the wind. Considering that the alien was not more than five feet away and there was no breeze, it was quite unusual.

Brady saw that one of his security men had a hand on his weapon. He held his own hand out and gestured for the officer to stand down. He then turned back to the alien and shook his head. "How do you know that?" he asked. "I-I don't understand."

The shimmering gained a little intensity as the alien regarded him. "Understanding is not required, Captain Brady. We are the Jek'Tan, and we have come a long way to visit your people."

"How do you know of us?" asked Lieutenant Brandt, the science officer.

"We have known of your race for centuries," the Jek'Tan said in almost a whisper. "There are Jek'Tan there now, working alongside your kind. We have come to share our many wonders with you. It is fortuitous that you have arrived to escort the Jek'Tan the rest of the way to your planet."

Brady smiled and thought about the career boost he'd lucked himself into. He might not have made first contact, but he would be remembered as the captain of the ship that escorted their alien visitors. "But we didn't come out to escort you," he said. "We were out looking for a missing transport."

"We all know why you are out here," the Jek'Tan said. "We required your presence. The ship you are searching for was necessary to accomplish that."

"You are responsible for the missing ship?" Brady looked to his security man, who pulled his weapon out. "Why?"

The Jek'Tan glowed brighter, and the bothersome clicking ensued again. "Because we required your ship."

"Captain," Brandt interrupted nervously, "radiation levels are off the charts."

The clicking seemed to be coming from all around them, and it was getting louder.

"You said we?" Brady asked, reaching cautiously for his own weapon.

Suddenly, other shimmering humanoid shapes came into view, surrounding them.

"Captain, what now?!" the security man called out over the sound of the clicking.

"Let us out of here," Brady snapped, with his gun suddenly pointed at the Jek'Tan, "I don't want to hurt you."

"You won't hurt anyone, but we have need of you," the Jek'Tan said in words that seemed to float in the nonexistent wind.

The lights came up in the large chamber, and what Captain Brady and his team saw froze them in place. The source of the clicking was suddenly very obvious. The things looked like spiders, as each had eight legs that met in a round, black body. Their legs tapped in place, as if they were merely waiting for an order to attack.

"Everyone, weapons out!"

Without hesitation, the team of six pulled their weapons and pointed them at the mass of clicking creatures.

Brady turned his gun on the Jek'Tan in front of him. "What are they?"

"They are Jek'Tan, as we all are, albeit altered to a form that fits our needs. We like to…create things."

"This doesn't need to get violent," Brady said nervously. "Just open the door and let us out, and we can go our separate ways and end this peacefully."

"Peace?" the Jek'Tan said, the intensity of its shimmer causing it to pulsate. "You are right. I, too, have grown tired of this banter. We need peace. My children, they are yours. Do not kill them."

With that, the mass of spiders moved in on them. The six humans fired their weapons, and the arachnid-like things fell in great numbers, but in the end, there were too many of them. In no time, Brady and his team were engulfed.

And that was that, Brady said in his head as he watched the *Bonaventure* view screen through eyes that were no longer his own. For a second, he forgot that any thought he had was easily read by the thing that clung to his chest. It laughed at him, regarding him as a simple vessel and nothing more.

Brady thought of his conversation with Kristin Dante, during which the creature had hijacked his mouth and voice. She was giving herself up, and that was nothing like the Kristin Dante he knew; it was nothing like any Dante anyone knew. Kristin would not go down without a fight, and if he knew that, so did Junior in his head. He tried to communicate with the other Jek'Tan though the parasite, but it would have nothing to do with him other than to steal whatever information it wanted. *I just want to die,* he thought, *but I'll take some of these bastards with me. There has to be a way.*

"No way," the voice said in his head. "I will drain your energy, and then there will be more of us. That is what we are. In the meantime, we will hunt your friends and destroy them, just as we have destroyed you."

The laughter pushed Brady deeper and deeper into his own mind. He needed to hide his thoughts, or else he would be their end, rather than the creature within him. Kristin Dante was the only chance they had, and if DNA was any clue as to the potential outcome, then his life and the lives of the others couldn't possibly be in better hands.

The Jek'Tan were on the bridge, supervising their puppeteers, guiding them in every decision they made. Brady's parasite would probably not trust Kristin to follow through on her surrender, but one question remained: *Will the Jek'Tan?* Kristin was right in saying she had value; she was the daughter of an admiral after all. The only real question was whether or not her value as a captive outweighed her danger as an adversary, and only time would tell what their decision would be.

Chapter 22

With the help of Evers and Tobias, Michael had already released an edited version of the audiotapes incriminating Striker, Rosten, and Stratton of capital crimes against the Alliance. Those tapes had gone directly to reporters in the news media who were not beholden to Striker Industries or Ethan Striker for anything. When contacted for comment, which happened almost immediately in the media frenzy, Striker claimed that the recordings were "fake," the accusations "groundless and improvable." Hopefully, though, it was enough of a wedge to give Kate and Morrison an edge, as well as his own attempt at securing command of the fleet if they weren't successful at obtaining the satellite or fleet authorization codes.

Now, Nicholas Dante had the wardroom all to himself—or at least the room with a split-screen communication with the commanding officers of the Alliance's four cruiser-class ships. If he had to sum up the conversation in one word, it would have been confusion. He had blown up the chain of command, and that resulted in the spectacle of officers with twenty years or more of space experience under their belts refusing to budge without confirmed orders from their fleet commander, Martinette.

"Williams," Dante said, addressing one of the captains, "you know who I am, correct?" Captain Anthony Williams was one of the more seasoned of the bunch. Dante knew if he could convince him, he stood a chance of swaying the rest.

"Yes, sir," replied the captain of the cruiser *Dakota*. "You appear to be Admiral Nicholas Dante."

Dante looked at the screen and wanted to punch a hole through it. "What do you mean, I *appear* to be, Captain?"

Williams shook his head. "Sir, you were reported dead a few days ago. Not only that, but this signal comes without an authentication source, on a frequency other than that of Alliance military. I'm sure I am at great risk for even talking to you, Admiral Dante, if you are even really him."

Dante grabbed a cigar from the box he'd brought with him. Smoking was a disgusting habit, one he thought he'd given up years before, but it did manage to keep him calm. Drinking, on the other hand, was something he'd promised himself never to return to, and that was one promise he meant to keep. He lit the cigar and puffed smoke into the oxygenated air of the sub, hoping the scrubbers would remove the odor before Murry saw him with it or, quite literally, caught wind of it; the man was a prude when it came to vices. "So you recognize me as Admiral Dante, your superior officer?" he asked.

"Sir, it doesn't matter what I think. Without authentication from General Martinette or the command codes, there is nothing I can do."

Dante watched as Williams tried to play both sides of the fence by acknowledging Dante yet refusing to accept his orders because of military protocol. "Great," he said in disgust as he flicked ashes onto the carpet that stretched from wall to wall in the wardroom. "Didn't you see the news report about Striker?"

"Yes, sir," Williams answered with a nod, "but Mr. Striker, no matter his crimes, is not my commanding officer."

"Damn it, Williams!" Dante snapped. "Haven't you seen the deep-space scans and the five large targets approaching Earth? Are you just going to sit there and do nothing, like your three other friends?"

"Yes, sir," Williams finally said, clearly about two seconds from ending the conversation. "You are correct. Our deep-space scans report five inbound targets, but as I said, without confirmation from General Martinette that the targets are hostile, I cannot proceed with an intercept. Until then, I can do nothing. I am sorry, sir."

With that, the channel closed not once but four times as each ship captain decided that following orders over evidence was how they intended to handle the situation. To a certain extent, they were doing the right thing by not accepting his ID as authentic without confirmation, but their own sensors were telling them of the approaching hostiles, so their adherence to the rules over the obvious was a bit much. Dante's only hope now was that Kate and Morrison had better luck with Martinette than Dante had with the general's subordinates.

Kate maneuvered the *Alexa* over the Alliance Military Command (AMC) landing pad and waited for the automated system to recognize the ship as her father's. It would then take control of her flight systems and bring her down into the hangar. The only problem was that they should have already, but nothing had happened. "Morrison," she snapped before sending an elbow into his shoulder. "Wake up. We have an issue."

Morrison opened his eyes and noted that they were still in the sky, floating above the AMC building, rather than inside, where the admiral said the automated system would deposit them. "Huh? I-I thought we'd be on the ground by now," he said sleepily as he shrugged his helmet on his head and dropped the visor. "Someone revoke your dad's parking pass?"

"Yeah, that's what I'm thinking. Maybe he's got unpaid parking tickets. *Alexa*," she said to the computer, "run a perimeter scan." Before she could complete the thought, red lights lit up the tactical display.

"Warning," the computerized voice said calmly. "We have a perimeter alert. Please activate weapons and defensive countermeasure systems."

"Jet-copters coming in from the north, east, west, south," Morrison said before Kate could get the information from the tactical display. "Damn. They're trying to fence us in."

"Yeah, I got that part," Kate snapped as she set the controls back to manual. "Hang on!"

Needing room to maneuver, Kate pushed the scout into a straight-up, high-speed vertical climb. The copters attempted to follow, but they were designed for atmospheric flight, while the scout was a thing of space; her inertial dampeners allowing for quicker turns that would have turned an unprotected pilot to paste.

Suddenly, the tactical display illuminated again, this time with multiple targets.

"They're all firing," Morrison said. "I guess they're jealous of your smooth moves. Eight missiles incoming."

Kate ignored the chitchat and watched the missiles as they closed. The weapons were equipped with tracking systems that were not at all concerned about how fast they had to turn. They were in their element, and they'd catch up before the *Alexa* reached space. Kate took the controls while Morrison activated the countermeasures.

"Keep us steady," Morrison snapped. "I just need another second. There!" He hit a switch, and there was a soft *click* as the rear weapons pod discharged two interceptors. "C'mon!" he screamed at the tactical display as the tracking showed the interceptors closing in on two of the incoming missiles.

Suddenly, there was a bright explosion behind them, and then two of the incoming vanished from the screen, leaving six in pursuit. Morrison pressed another button on the countermeasure panel, and flares leapt out of the underside of the scout. Two other missiles locked on those flares and exploded. Suddenly, their problem was cut in half, but four were still on their tail and closing.

"Now this, I can work with," Kate said with a smile as she reversed direction and sent the small ship into a dive.

"What the hell are you doing?" Morrison snapped, grabbing hold of his armrests and making sure he was locked securely into his seat.

Kate didn't bother responding as she sent the scout straight at the copters, forcing the missiles to change course to keep up with her. The less maneuverable copters tried to get out of the way of the scout as it blew past them. In the process, two of the hostiles drifted into each other, colliding into a fireball, while the other two headed in opposite directions as the remaining missiles followed the hot wreckage of the other two copters into the ground.

"Nice," Morrison said with a smile, "but the other two are about to open fire."

"Not if I have anything to say about it." Kate then opened up on both copters with the twin plasma cannons just below the engine pods on either side of the cockpit. The twin bolts of energy ripped into both remaining jet-copters, turning them into flaming debris. "You were saying?"

"Now what?" Morrison asked.

"I'm done!" she snapped as she directed the ship toward the bay doors. "We have no more time to play nice." With a free hand, she targeted the landing bay and fired. The beams made contact with the doors and played across them for the briefest of moments before exploding. Kate judged that the hole she'd made was just large enough to drop the scout through.

Unfortunately, weapons batteries ringing the bay doors began to track them.

"Ground-to-air about to fire, Kate!"

Kate only half-heard Morrison's warning as she increased the speed of her dive, to the point where the guns had trouble tracking her. "Here we go!"

"Shit," Morrison said under his breath as he noticed the building coming up very quickly. "You gonna pull up sometime today?"

"Nope," Kate said as she fired two quick shots at the weapons batteries, taking them out as the scout shot past their range, down the bay entrance, and into the building through a center transport shaft that connected each floor from the roof landing pad to the basement hangar.

"You're nuts, you know that?"

Kate smiled and pulled out of the dive, setting the *Alexa* to hover. "I don't have time to be sane. What floor is Martinette on?" They had come in at Floor Eighty-Six and had not stopped the dive for another ten floors. Now she had to find the general.

"I'm querying your dad's database," Morrison said as he read the display in his helmet. "He's on…the thirty-eighth."

Morrison didn't need sensors to know that they'd dropped into the middle of a hornet's nest. Alarms and flashing red lights seemed to announce their arrival to the entire building as he read off the floor numbers on the inside of the shaft.

"Another four floors, and we're there. I assume you've got a plan once we arrive, right?" he asked through his open visor.

"Sure I do," Kate whispered as she lowered the ship the four floors and rotated so they faced the elevator doors.

"You know there'll be a welcome party on the other side, right?"

"Yup, but I've got a little housewarming present for them. If I were you, I'd get ready to move for the hatch," Kate suggested as she stopped the rotation and fired the plasma guns at the doors. They exploded inward, throwing to the floor a half-dozen armed men, and sent the others in the corridor running for cover. With her finger on the trigger, Kate continued to fire through the door, causing secondary explosions throughout the building.

"Kate, stop!" Morrison snapped as he watched her clear the corridor beyond the door.

"Weapon up and get to the hatch," she ordered as she guided the scout to the recently blasted entrance to the thirty-eighth floor of the building. Moving her hands quickly over the controls, she allowed the computer to take control of the ship, maintaining its position by the door, and their escape route. "*Alexa*, Omega Protocol in thirty minutes. Acknowledge?"

"Acknowledged," the ship's computer replied.

Kate took one last look around her ship, then turned to Morrison. "Time to go."

Morrison grabbed a handful of grenades before throwing an assault rifle to Kate. She slung the powerful weapon over her shoulder and took two grenades for herself as Morrison opened the hatch and looked out at the wreckage and the corridor Kate had cleared of hostiles.

"Ready?" he asked.

Kate checked the charge on the weapon and brought it down and into firing position. "Yes. Let's move."

They both leapt onto the smoking platform and moved cautiously into the smoking corridor. There were a few bodies lying amidst the destruction, but Kate had no idea whether they were dead or alive. Like Morrison, she felt bad for firing on men who were only doing their jobs, but the stakes left no room for sentimentality. Either they accomplished their mission, or everyone on Earth would die. In the end, anyone who stood in her way—simply obeying orders or not—was counter to her mission. She would do whatever needed to be done and deal with the consequences later.

Morrison had his visor down and scanned the corridor for hostile forces. "Clear."

Kate moved out first, with Morrison covering her rear; it was not the time to get shot in the back, for that would only end their mission and be personally embarrassing. She checked the names on the doors and finally found the one they were looking for: "General George R. Martinette."

"Down!" Morrison snapped as he whirled around and took down two troopers who were closing on them from behind. They had attacked them from one of the rooms off to the side, which they'd retreated into when the doors exploded.

Morrison reacted slowly as the doors to the personal elevator opened and three more security men came running out, already firing. Kate pulled out one of her grenades and threw it in their direction. The men noticed the incoming grenade, but in the tight corridor, they had nowhere to escape to. The blast made chopped meat of all three of them.

"You're welcome," Kate said as she pulled a small beaching charge from her belt and fastened it to the general's door. "Stand back." It only took a quick moment to arm the detonator she carried. The red light on the small box stayed steady, indicating that the explosive was armed.

Morrison took the advice as they both ducked into one of the offices across the hall. The shaped charge was designed to blow outward, with very little of the explosive force coming back on them, but there was always the possibility of painful, dangerous debris and shrapnel propelled by the force of the explosion.

Kate slowly counted down. At zero, she pressed the button on her detonator. The explosion blew the old wooden doors off their hinges and sent them flying into the large office area. They were both in the office before the smoke cleared.

It wasn't the two old-style, bullet-shooting handguns in the general's hands or the presence of Ethan Striker that dampened her day; rather, it was the creature she thought she'd killed the day before, in that tunnel under the East River. Seeing him standing there in front of her quickly took Kate's day from bad to worse. She turned to Morrison and saw that his gun was down, and he seemed to be fiddling with something on the side of his helmet. "Great," she muttered. They were outgunned and seemingly outnumbered, and her partner looked to have given up without a fight.

"I killed you already," Kate said quietly to the tall form in silver. "I dropped a tunnel and half the East River on your skinny head. Why aren't you dead?"

The face regarded her as one would look at an insect before stomping on it. It might have been alien, but there was no mistaking the anger it was trying to suppress inside. "It was my brother you killed, and I will enjoy your death at the proper time."

"Gemini?" Morrison said with a laugh. "The twins, as in… two of you. Now I get it."

"Captain Dante," General Martinette said, interrupting in his deceptively warm, Southern drawl, "how nice to finally meet you.

Your father and I have often talked about your once-sterling career with the Alliance. I suggest you both place your weapons slowly on the floor, or else my men or my two little antiques will end you, perhaps a bit prematurely, if my tall friend has anything to say about it."

Morrison removed his helmet and laid it gently on a small antique table in front of him. He nodded to Kate and placed his rifle, sidearms, and grenades on the floor, then took a step back from them.

Kate stood rigidly for a moment as she considered the pros and cons of a firefight. She assumed she could take out one or two of them, but the odds of her nailing either Martinette or Striker were poor at best. Against her better judgment, and knowing she was about to commit a failure that her father would probably find unforgivable, she did as she was told and placed her weapons in a pile next to Morrison's. The only thing she managed to retain was the knife in the spring-release clip on her wrist. That gave her a little comfort, even though it was no match for the armament they faced.

"Good," Martinette said as a smile spread across his bearded face. "Now have a seat, both of you." Martinette pointed to a conference table, and Kate and Morrison sat down. He then motioned for Mr. Gemini to cover them, though it seemed to be somewhat pointless.

"General," Kate said as she sat, "we need the authorization codes for the fleet. There's an invasion on its way to Earth, and all our forces are locked into orbit. Don't you see what that thing is?"

"That thing, as you put it, is a brother. We all serve the Jek'Tan, and you may as well, if you survive today. There really is very little that either of you can do at this point," Striker said as he took a seat across from them at the table. "The ships of the Jek'Tan will be here in a matter of hours, and then this will all be over. Even the general now understands, don't you, Martinette?"

Martinette placed his two guns on the desk and sat as well. "Are you both insane? Those ships will be the salvation of this planet. Who do you think brought us back from the brink when the war nearly destroyed this planet? The Jek'Tan helped rebuild in secrecy, and now they're coming here to take control and bring us into the galactic family of worlds so we can be a real Alliance."

"You idiot!" Kate snapped. "They're coming to kills us. Ask your friend Striker here. I bet he conveniently forgot to tell you that it was the Jek'Tan who nuked us in the beginning. They started the war just so they could get a foothold on this planet until their ships could come and finish the job."

Martinette shook his head. "Lying is not becoming, Dante. They helped repair this planet after we almost destroyed it. We did this to ourselves."

"Maybe we poured a little salt in it," Morrison added, "but the first shots were theirs."

"Very, very good, Kate Dante," came the windswept voice from the other side of the room.

"Creator," both Striker and Mr. Gemini said, bowing their heads in reverence. "We are your servants."

Kate and Morrison turned in the direction Striker and the tall alien killer were staring at. The form was humanoid, but it seemed to shimmer a bit, almost like a mirage in the desert heat. It rose several inches in the air and approached them, stopping just a few feet from the table.

"What are you?" Morrison asked as he tried to identify features through the haze.

"You're a Jek'Tan, right?" Kate responded.

The figure continued to float, and there was an almost supernatural ethereal quality to it, but Kate and Morrison knew they were dealing with no semblance of an angel. "You are correct, Kate Dante. I am Jek'Tan. I had to make myself known to you out of respect for your intuitive abilities. For 1,000 of your years, we have occupied your world, guiding you to best prepare for the events of today. Not once, in all that time, have we encountered anyone intuitive enough to finally understand our true purpose."

"What is that supposed to mean?" Kate asked, trying to get as much intel as she could while biding her time. She had one last card up her sleeve, and she was eager to play it.

The Jek'Tan paused for a moment as he came closer, as if to study her. "Kate Dante, the Jek'Tan has been many things to many planets over the course of our existence. We are an old race, born before your star shone in a primeval Terran sky, and we will long outlast this star, even when it is nothing but a memory in our own collective consciousness. We created wonders on our planet before we went to the stars, yet we were still… I believe you would call it bored. We ventured out into the galaxy and met hundreds of different species, but we found them lacking."

"Lacking in what?"

"In everything, Kate Dante," the Jek'Tan continued. "We considered ourselves the pinnacle of perfection as we traveled from planet to planet, dimension to dimension. We were dominant over all, and we found many deficiencies in the species we visited, so we fixed them. That, in turn, provided us the raw materials to fix others along the way."

Kate looked at Mr. Gemini, then at the shimmering form of the Jek'Tan. "Fixed them how?" she asked, just beginning to understand.

"We reworked their DNA and improved them as a species. Sometimes we introduced the DNA of others we had met, combining them to produce something completely new. The Jek'Tan finally found perfection in a non-perfect galaxy by creating it ourselves. We found our purpose, a solution for an imperfect universe, as well as a cure for our boredom."

"And Mr. Gemini? Is this overgrown tinman one of your cocktail creations too?" Morrison asked snidely, looking at Gemini as if he was the vilest thing on any planet.

The shimmering of the Jek'Tan brightened a bit, like a proud parent beaming over his son. "Yes he is," the alien warmly responded.

"He is a mixture of several different races. Traits required for him to be what he was designed to be were incorporated into his making."

"And what was he designed to be?" Kate asked. She felt her anger boiling within her, and that helped to push the panic and fear behind a closed door in her brain. "A killer and an assassin?"

"Yes, Captain Dante," the alien responded matter-of-factly. "From his modes of vision to his acute hearing and mastery of weapons, we created him and many others to serve a specific purpose. I am sure you understand that even the best of hobbies grows tiresome over time. We needed a change. Instead of just altering the inhabitants, we decided to influence their societal paths as well. We took planets and pushed their inhabitants from one scenario to another, all while continuing our research and experimentation. We have always been a patient race. Some adapt very well to our influence. We destroyed your planet, and in two of your centuries, you are reaching for the stars. You humans are the culmination of what we have been searching for."

"Is that why your ships are coming?"

"Yes. We have ended our social experiments on your race, and it mustn't go any further," the Jek'Tan answered as his shimmering became a bit muted. "When the Jek'Tan ships arrive, we will harvest all we need from your people, then move on. We may require another century or two of continued experimentation here, but as I said, we are a patient race."

"You won't get away with this," Morrison said defiantly.

"We will fight you." Kate felt the need to do something, but she knew Gemini would probably kill her before she even stood from the chair she was confined to.

"If you are referring to your fleet, it will be destroyed in orbit. They are of no consequence."

"What is the meaning of this, Striker?" Martinette challenged. "Is this one of the Jek'Tan you said are to lead us to our destiny? Is Dante right? Did they instigate the nuclear war? Now we're nothing more than spare parts and junk DNA to them?" He picked up one of the guns from the desk and pointed it at the shimmering form.

Finally, Kate thought, *something is sinking in.* "General Martinette, they are going to kill us all. You need to do something."

Martinette looked at Kate, then turned toward Striker, then shot his eyes back to the alien. "In a second, Dante. No one move, especially you, Gemini. You all have been playing me for a fool, Striker. All these years of watching my friends die to protect your secret? No more!" Then, before anyone could move or utter another word, he fired two shots at the Jek'Tan.

The Jek'Tan simply floated in place as the two metal slugs went right through it and embedded in the wall by the doorway.

"How?" Martinette asked, staring, dumbfounded, at the weapon he was holding.

"We are multidimensional beings, General Martinette," the Jek'Tan explained. "We exist in several dimensions at any given moment. Your weapon cannot kill what the projectiles cannot hit. It is… an inconvenience that you now know the truth. You could have continued to be of use a short while longer, but now you are a liability."

Martinette thought of the mistake he'd made as he backed toward his desk. He needed to get out a warning to the fleet and activate the satellites. He couldn't kill the Jek'Tan, but he hoped he could at least deal with Striker and Gemini. He had to try a bluff. "You all need to drop your weapons and surrender," he said as he backed toward the comm system built into his desk. "Right, Dante?"

She looked at him and was about to say something, but the general nodded, then stared at a picture on the other side of the office.

"We cannot allow you or anyone else to order out your ships," the Jek'Tan said slowly. "They are no match for us, but a battle would be senseless waste of our resources and our investment, as well as our time. Lives will be lost, but they would only be yours. Mr. Gemini?"

Martinette turned as he felt the cold steel of the barrel of the gun he'd left on the desk. His mistakes were piling up at an alarming rate as he saw the long, thin fingers pull the hammer back. "Someone will stop you," he said, pushing himself to attention.

"No they won't," Striker said with a laugh as Mr. Gemini pulled the trigger.

In a flash, the gun went off again, this time decorating the walls with the brains of Alliance General Martinette.

"That was pleasant," Mr. Gemini said, wearing a sick grin as he put the gun back on the desk.

"You bastard," Kate said quietly but in no way trying to hide her rage. It wasn't that she felt anything for Martinette—far from it. In a way, he had paid for his sins against humanity. Instead, she grieved for the missing codes that would keep the planet undefended until it was too late. *There was something though.* She looked toward the other side of the room at the picture of his wife and son that hung on the wall. He knew he was going to die, but he made a point of looking at that picture. She checked her wrist and noted that the timer of her Omega Protocol was running down; she had only two minutes and counting. It was time to make a move.

"Apologies," the voice of the Jek'Tan said, drifting over to them, "but that was necessary. When a part serves no useful purpose and becomes a danger to the wellbeing of the whole, it must be removed."

"You didn't have to do that, and you're wrong about one thing," Morrison said with a snarl.

"And what is that?" the alien asked curiously.

"It'll be you who loses."

"We will see, Cole Morrison. We will see. Kate Dante, I have confided in you as a sign of respect. You have done well, and my only regret is that I will not be leaving here with your DNA. You would be a nice addition to the new Mr. Gemini or perhaps a female version of him."

"What is your will, creator?" Mr. Gemini asked of the shimmering form that was the Jek'Tan.

"You know what must be done. Then leave this place with Striker and prepare for our arrival." With that, the Jek'Tan shimmered brightly one last time and vanished.

Striker looked on with interest. They were truly a joined entity. The thing that was attached to him controlled his body, but deep within, the mind of Ethan Striker watched what played out as if it were some late-night drama from the golden age of television. The paralysis gave him a sense of freedom he had never felt before. He knew it might eventually kill him, but like everything else that had tried in the past, he hoped to overcome it. *What is that old adage? What doesn't kill you makes you stronger?* Somehow, by taking him over, the Jek'Tan had helped him to find great strength.

Mr. Gemini once again picked up the antique handgun from the desk and examined it closely. "Primitive firearm, but like Martinette, it had its uses. You killed my twin, Kate Dante, and for that you will die painfully. I felt him die. I felt the water fill his lungs and the stones crush him to paste. For that, I will make you watch your partner die, and then it will be your turn." He then casually walked over to Morrison and put the gun to his head. "Captain Dante, do you have anything to say before this man's brains join Martinette's on the walls?"

Kate nodded and turned to Morrison. She slowly counted down in her head as she smiled at the thing that would kill them both. "Cole, remember when I said back at the Academy, that the only way we would last as a couple was if you paid attention to everything I told you to do?"

Morrison shook his head in confusion. He was about to be killed by a tall, thin nightmare in shining armor, and Kate Dante was dredging up their old love life. "Kate?"

The countdown reached ten seconds.

"Just pay attention."

"Time to die, Cole Morrison," Mr. Gemini said calmly.

"Duck!" Kate screamed as she lashed out with both feet, hitting the thing in the most twig-thin part of his leg. She was rewarded with the *crack* of Gemini's breaking bone and the *thud* of Morrison hitting the floor.

Zero...

At that point, all hell broke loose as the *Alexa* opened up with her guns. The streams of energy again ripped down the long corridor and into the office, blasting apart walls and furniture as the onslaught continued.

Morrison rolled on top of Kate, using his body as a shield until the barrage ended. "What the hell?!" he barked.

"Get off me!" Kate yelled, shoving him.

Omega Protocol had functioned perfectly. *Alexa's* orders were to lay down fire at her current position and maintain it for ten seconds. She looked around the office, and it appeared to have worked better than she'd planned. Mr. Gemini was now in several pieces. His silver suit could turn away small arms fire, but it couldn't disperse the heat from the ship-mounted weapon. It eventually shredded and fell away, and the next few shots sent him to join his brother.

Morrison rifled through the debris and carnage, searching for his helmet. The helmet had taken a hit, but it really looked no worse for the wear; the same couldn't be said for Ethan Striker. "Kate, over here," he said slowly.

Kate was busy examining the family photo Martinette had gestured to. "In a sec," she answered, poking around the edges.

"Now please," he said, with more urgency in his voice this time.

She nodded and pulled the picture away from the wall. Behind it was a small personal safe. She heard Morrison clearing his breath and turned to him. "What?"

"C'mere," he said slowly. "You need to see this."

Kate walked over to see what her partner was looking at, and it just so happened to be the body of Ethan Striker. One of the plasma bolts had struck him in the chest and neck, nearly taking his head off. She'd seen what weapons could do to a human body and was prepared for the damage, but this was something she didn't expect. His shirt had opened up, revealing something black clinging to his chest—something that was moving. They both watched in awe as eight appendages, seemingly there to hold it in place, pulled out of the body.

"Holy crap," Morrison said as the appendages turned into the legs.

The thing appeared to be heading for Kate, but he kicked it into the corner of the room, giving Kate time to retrieve the assault rifle she'd earlier dropped to the floor. The thing seemed to hone in on Morrison this time, but Kate brought the gun up and blasted it into dust.

"What the hell was that?" Morrison asked.

Kate shook her head. "I don't know, but my guess is that it was directing Striker."

"That could explain a lot."

"Yep, but I just don't know for how long." Kate poked the dead thing with the barrel of her gun and noted that it appeared both organic and mechanical. "It's dead now. Morrison, there's a safe back there. Do you have another charge to get it open?"

Morrison found his pack, retrieved another charge, and placed it on the safe. They both hid behind the general's desk as they set it off. Once the door was open, Kate pulled out papers of all types. She perused them quickly and found the arming codes to the satellite defense grid.

"No fleet authorization codes?" Morrison asked.

Kate shook her head. "Nope. We're screwed."

Morrison shook his head and smiled. "Maybe not." He handed her the helmet. "Put this on and hit play on the side."

Kate put on the helmet and pushed the button. She watched their entire experience in Matinette's office, recorded through the camera and sensor systems. "Morrison, I never thought I'd say this, but you're a genius!" she squealed, grinning beneath the visor. "You may have just saved us all. We need to get this to my father." She opened the visor and handed it back.

"He should have it already. The feedback to the admiral should have been live." Morrison stopped talking as he adjusted the sensors. "We've got company coming. We need to leave."

Kate picked up their weapons from the blood-soaked floor and turned to give Martinette one last look. Despite his act of loyalty in the end, she had no sympathy for the man. For the cost of her feelings, he received far more than he deserved. In fact, the three seconds she lamented over him was more than a traitor to humanity was entitled to.

With the satellite codes in her possession, they made their way quickly down the corridor and back to the still hovering *Alexa*. While the elevator was nonoperational, the stairs were still working, and they both heard the *clip-clop* of heavy boots climbing them. Morrison stopped by the door to the stairs and flipped a grenade inside; they were pretty far away, but it would slow them down without killing them.

Finally, they made their way back to the *Alexa* and shut the door behind them. They dumped their weapons and jumped into their flight control seats. Kate set the ship back to manual and grabbed the control stick. The *Alexa* began to climb through the shaft, faster and faster with each passing second.

"What about the copters? I'm sure there will be more than a few waiting for us when we get out."

Kate only half-heard him, for she was too busy concentrating on the task at hand. Her hands tightened their grip on the flight controls, and the *Alexa* built up more speed.

"You're gambling that nothing is camped out right above us, aren't you? I hope you're right, Kate."

He's right about that, Kate thought. The exit was right before them, and she knew the timing had to be perfect. If there was anything at the mouth of the entrance, she was certain the explosion would be spectacular.

The *Alexa* burst out of the shaft, into the afternoon sky. The tactical scan revealed six jet-copters approaching and another two closing. Without missing a beat, she switched from atmospheric thrusters to sub-light engines. As they climbed, the G-force pushed them both back in their seats, as the internal environmental systems struggled to keep up. The sky went from blue to black as they left Earth's atmosphere behind them.

"Where are we going?" Morrison asked, happy to see Earth in his rearview mirror. He knew how lucky they were to even have made it that far. .

"I'm heading for the fleet."

"The fleet? Are you insane? We just broke out of Alliance military HQ, and you wanna party with their space fleet?" Morrison ripped his helmet off and dropped it to the deck. After a few days of wear, the inside was getting a little ripe, to say the least.

Kate shook her head. "If the admiral was able to convince them with the recording of Martinette and we can show them the sat codes, we'll be okay."

"You're kidding me, right? That's a pretty damn big if, Kate." He tried to laugh it off, but it didn't matter whether they were blasted out of the sky or out of space; in the end, dead was dead. "The odds are just as good that they'll fire on us. What do you suggest we do if that happens?"

"We'll soon find out, because there they are," she said, pointing at the fleet that was looming ever larger in the cockpit window on their approach. "I suggest a prayer that my father was convincing."

Chapter 23

With a bizarre fascination, bordering on obsession, Dante watched the entire drama play out in Martinette's office. Back when he first began to suspect Striker and his connections to Rosten and Stratton, he never would have guessed that the real enemy wasn't even of his own planet. He knew Striker was a criminal and that he'd murdered his way to some sort of endgame that would put the Alliance in jeopardy, but never would he have dreamt that his plans included a deal with aliens for the genocidal conquest of his own race. Morrison and Kate were right about one thing: The Jek'Tan wouldn't get away with harvesting an apple from his world, let alone the entire human race. Still, there it was on the screen before him, as were the incoming ships on the tactical display.

He had to hand it to Cole Morrison: The man was a genius to have activated the broadcast element in his helmet and set it for a live feed back to him. He watched as Morrison and his daughter stood at the mercy of the Jek'Tan. There was very little he could do about it but hope they survived. His eldest daughter always seemed to have back-up plans to her back-up plans, something he was sure she inherited from him. The recording ended with the plasma fire, he assumed from the *Alexa*, hitting the helmet and knocking it from the perch Morrison had put it on. He didn't have it all, but he had enough to send to the fleet. He hoped that and the sat defense codes would be enough to motivate them. Michael had transmitted the recording over every Alliance military frequency; now he just had to wait for an answer from them now.

"Admiral..." Murry's voice came over the speaker in the wardroom.

He was still sitting with Michael, Evers, and Tobias, and they all looked up at him at the sound of the sub commander's voice.

"We're getting a response from the fleet, sir. Transferring it to your screen."

It was Captain Anthony Williams of the *Dakota* who came on the viewer. "Admiral, we don't know what to say. The other captains and I watched the recording you sent over and were shocked by what we heard and witnessed. We still can't believe General Martinette had any part in this."

Dante shook his head. "Neither can I, Captain Williams. Now, based on this new information and the fact that my daughter has retrieved the codes for the defense satellites, will you and the other captains assist with the defense of this planet and meet the threat?" Dante then waited as Williams was handed something from somewhere off screen. He recognized it as a communiqué of some kind.

Williams read it, then handed it back and turned to the viewer again. "To answer your question, sir," Williams began slowly, "I have just been handed orders from both Alliance Military Command and the Alliance Council, instructing that the fleet be placed under your command. They have all witnessed the tape, as well as the carnage that resulted in its acquisition approximately thirty floors above their heads, and they have agreed with your assessment regarding the threat to the planets of this system. The fleet is yours to command as you will, Admiral Dante," Williams finished, offering a salute.

Dante shook his head. *Oh how quickly one rises from the grave,* he thought with a smirk. "Better late than never."

"What are your orders, sir?" Williams asked.

"Ready your ships for combat, Captain," Dante ordered. "Send a shuttle for me. As soon as I board your *Dakota*, we will be on our way."

"Yes, sir!" Williams said, then again snapped to with a salute, then went off air. He returned only a second later. "Excuse me, sir,.."

"Yes?"

"It seems we have a ship approaching, scout class. I'm told it's Captain Dante and Commander Morrison, requesting permission to dock."

Dante slipped back into his chair, releasing a heavy sigh and wearing a satisfied smile. He looked over to see that his son had the same stupid look on his face. He rationalized that grinning was never an easy task for any of his relatives, and he had to blame that on genetics too. Tobias and Evers simply nodded, which didn't surprise him. "Captain, please allow my daughter to dock," he said. He then thought about that for a moment and quickly changed his mind. "No, belay that order. Tell her I said to come down here and pick me and my staff up. I want a fighter escort with her, just in case there are any trigger-happy idiots about who haven't heard that the kill-on-sight order has been canceled. Understood?"

"Yes, sir," Williams responded smartly. "Anything else, Admiral?"

"Yes. Get word to AMC to issue a red alert to all Alliance military and civilian forces throughout the system. We're going to need all the help we can get, because if we lose this little skirmish, there will be no place in space we will be safe from these Jek'Tan."

"Yes, sir. We'll be ready when you arrive."

Dante nodded and closed the communication. "Well, gentlemen, we are a go."

"You're back in charge again," Michael said, still holding tightly to the smile and the feelings that produced it. "Do you think we have enough to stop them?"

"I hope so," Dante responded, but his smile was now a thing of the past.

"It's a shame we don't know the status of the *Bonaventure*," Evers added. "We could really use her firepower."

Dante had been thinking of that same thing, along with wondering about the status of his daughter. At the moment, the five Jek'Tan ships were in the vicinity of the last reported position of Kristin's. Either they were fine or they weren't, but until he saw a body, he would go with the former. "We deal with the cards we're dealt, gentlemen. Please get whatever you need to bring and prepare to depart. Kate will be down in a few minutes, and I don't like to make her wait. As you saw from the tape, she is easily pissed off." *Just like her father,* Dante mused, a thought he knew was likely echoed in the heads of many in the room. He then closed his eyes and considered what was at stake and who would be dead or alive come this time tomorrow.

Kate and Morrison watched through the small cockpit window as they got close enough to the lead ship to realize it was the *USS Dakota*, the flagship of the fleet. The good news was that no one had taken a shot at them yet; the bad news was that no one had offered them permission to enter the hangar either. "Surely they saw the recording from Martinette's office by now. Why is there still an issue?" she said to no one in particular. She would have contemplated it further if not for the ear-shattering sounds of the perimeter alarm.

"She's launching fighters!" Morrison snapped from his tactical display. "We've got three of them on an intercept course. Wait…. There's a transmission coming in from the flight leader."

"Come in, *Alexa*," a voice said over the radio. "This is Flight Commander Scott. Please respond."

"Well?" Morrison said with a nervous smile, lookin over at Kate and shrugging his shoulders. "They wouldn't call to talk before shooting us, would they?"

Kate shook her head and activated the comm in her headset. "This is *Alexa*. What are your intentions, Commander Scott?"

"Captain Dante, my orders are to escort you to the surface to retrieve Admiral Dante and his staff."

"Do you believe him?" Morrison asked.

"Don't be stupid!" Kate switched her comm back on as she watched the fighters take position in a typical escort formation around her ship. "Where did these orders originate from?"

"They were handed directly to me by my CO, Captain Williams. He received them verbally, directly from the admiral himself, ma'am," Scott said, waving at her from the cockpit of his fighter. "Oh, Captain Dante, there is one other thing I need to pass along."

"Go ahead, Scott."

"Captain Williams asked me commit it to memory, just in case of a trust issue. The message is from Admiral Dante. He said, 'If my trust-issued daughter does not believe this is genuine, tell her that her brother and I are smiling, and we think we broke our faces.' Does that mean anything to you, ma'am?"

Kate nodded and smiled as Morrison looked at her and shook his head. "Has to be him," Kate said. Smiling had never been his forte; there was barely a rumor of it among all who knew him. "Yes, that is sufficient, Commander Scott. We appreciate the company."

"Great news, ma'am. We have the admiral's current coordinates. Keep up, and we will cover you. I was also told to tell you that we have a war to fight and to, uh...'move your ass,'" Scott added. "Sorry, Captain. Those are his words, not mine."

"Acknowledged," Kate said quietly. "*Alexa*, out." She then turned the scout for the atmosphere and accelerated to keep up with her escort. Her father was right about there being no time to waste. Win or lose, she'd already decided that all of her DNA would stay with her, but she intended on spilling a lot of the Jek'Tan's.

She also thought about her sister, Kristin. They weren't the closest siblings in the galaxy, but she was family, and Kate wasn't about to let anyone lay one finger or one blast or one spider leg on her little sister. She would find her, regardless of what it took. She could think of no better time or place for a real family reunion, and with any luck, she hoped she'd stumble upon the *Bonaventure* as well. It was time for all of them to move their asses, and after 200 years of unknowingly serving as puppets on a string, it was also time to kick some, no matter how shimmery it was.

Ten minutes later, her father and the others were onboard. Seating was limited on the scout, especially *Alexa*, so it was somewhat difficult to endure the cramped ride up to the *Dakota*.

Kate shook her head as she followed the escort back to their ship. "Maybe it would have been better to wait for a shuttle, Dad," she suggested. "More leg room."

"Just fly the damn ship, Katherine," said the admiral. "No one promised us a luxury cruise."

She laughed, as she thought that the coincidental atmospheric buffeting was just a bonus.

Soon, they were in the blackness of the space, with the submarine and the ocean it rested on visible only on her ship's sensors.

Eventually, the fighters peeled away, as they had their own military bay to land in. Kate adjusted her course to that of the main landing doors as they slid open atop the *Dakota*. While not as large as the *Bonaventure*, the ten-year-old space cruiser resembled, in both in size and construction, a cross between the submarine below and a pre-war aircraft carrier. With a main gun facing forward, as well as secondary weapons along the rest of her hull and a squadron of space fighters, it was hard to believe there was anything out there that the ship and its four equally equipped sisters couldn't handle. Hopefully, it would be enough, especially once they joined up with Rosten's ships—or at least those he had left after tending to Stratton on the moon.

She thought about Rosten and how he'd worked himself out of the 200-year-old pit he'd managed to dig into. In her eyes, after what she'd seen on Mars, he was just as evil as Striker. For now, the admiral needed him, but after all of that was over, she had every intention of going after the old man and his degenerate son, even if she had to deal with them herself. Kate had learned many things, and one of them was that it was sometimes necessary to go rogue, no matter who did not like it.

She watched as the landing bay doors pulled apart and the blinking lights inside directed her to the place where she was to set her ship down. Easing back on the controls, she fired the thrusters and slowly landed *Alexa* exactly where instructed. From the outside, the hangar seemed to have a small footprint, but on the inside, it somehow proved to be much larger, with facilities for servicing ships much larger than her own. She and Morrison powered down the systems and waited until everyone gathered their possessions and gear. Within minutes, the outer doors were closed, and the bay pressurized.

When the doors opened, everyone headed out onto the deck. Kate waited and watched as the bay hatch opened, and in walked Captain Williams and a small honor guard.

"What's the problem?" Michael asked from behind her. "Adding antisocial to your list of personality quirks?"

"No, bro," Kate said, pushing herself back into her pilot seat and putting her legs up on the flight console.

"You know, if the old man saw you with your feet up like that, he'd bust you," he said semi-seriously as he sat next to her.

"I have the pink slip in the glove compartment," she said with her eyes shut. "My ride now—and he's got a bigger one to worry about anyway. Let him enjoy the moment. I'd only ruin it for him."

Michael lightly punched her in the arm. "Why would you say that?"

"Have you forgotten?" Kate yawned. "I'm the traitor to the Alliance."

"Stop that," Michael snapped. "That's over and done with. You were undercover, and everyone will know the truth in time."

"I guess," she said, shrugging.

"There something else?" Michael probed.

Kate realized her little brother was getting better at reading people, and she hated that, because it meant she had to stop treating him like the dorky kid brother and more like an equal. There was something else, but she wasn't sure if she wanted to tell him or not. "Yeah, there's something," she finally admitted.

"What?"

"I'm going to bounce soon, and... Well, Dad's not going to like it."

"Why? Where are you going?"

Kate opened her eyes and sat up in her seat. "Michael, Kristin is still out there, and knowing Dante luck, she's probably hip-deep in all this crap. I'm not about to fight a battle millions of miles away from our sister if she needs us. The admiral has a battle group with him now, a whole fleet. He's not going to miss me and my little *Alexa*. As soon as I can leave, I'm out of here."

"You mean we," Michael said quietly, placing a hand on his sister's shoulder.

"Hey! You two aren't going anywhere without me," came the voice from behind them.

"Morrison?" Kate snapped. "How long have you been back there?"

"Forgot my lucky paperclip or something," he said with a smile. "Anyway, I repeat, you aren't going anywhere without me."

Kate shook her head. Her seat suddenly felt even more confining than the one in Martinette's office. She made a real effort to jump out of it, for she felt as if they were ganging up on her. "Look, I can't ask you guys to come with me. In fact, I outrank both of you. I can officially order you both to stay...and to shut up about it too."

"Shut up about it? Kate, we are obligated to rat out anyone who intends to go AWOL. We'd have to turn you in to the higher authorities, right, Mike?" Morrison said. "That means tattling to Daddy Dearest."

Michael glanced at Morrison, then over at Kate before shrugging. "How can I follow the orders of a deserter? Do you have a choice?"

Without much to say in response, Kate did what anyone else would do in a similar situation: She growled at both of them, went to her small quarters, and slammed the door behind her.

Morrison patted Michael on the shoulder with a large hand. "Well, that went well."

"I don't know about that," he said as he pushed Morrison's hand off his shoulder. "We probably would have been safer joining the fleet to fight that quintet of five-mile-long invading alien ships. You know how Kate is when she's mad. Plus, we have no idea what's out there…or what happened to Kristin or the *Bonaventure*." With that, Michael headed for the door to join his father, leaving Morrison alone to wonder if it was such a good idea after all.

"Those Dantes are crazy," he said, "but maybe that's why I want to be like one…and liked more by one." He smiled at the thought of her covered in the filth of the subway tunnel, aiming that gun at him as if he wanted to do anything scandalous to her. The fact was, he wasn't done watching out for Kate just yet, whether she liked it or not.

Chapter 24

Twenty minutes later, Kate, Michael, and Morrison walked into the crowded briefing room. The admiral was at the head of the table, concluding his combat briefing with Williams and the captains of the other three ships, as well as Military Command and the Alliance Council. Rather than looking for seats, they decided to stand against the wall, out of the way but accessible if they were needed.

The plan was to make their stand near Mars, where ships from the various colonies were assembling. Kate was surprised to hear that even Clayton Rosten would have a vested interest in the outcome, as his loan cruiser would be made available. All other defensive resources Rosten claimed would be held back for defense of his city, in case the Jek'Tan broke through the Alliance front. As far as Earth was concerned, the only things left for defense were the satellites in orbit and the various global militias.

Damn, Kate thought. *If this war comes down to atmospheric combat, we're already lost.*

The admiral used edited footage from Martinette's office, as well as select audio recordings from the Mars communications relay, to paint a bleak picture of where the Alliance stood and what would befall them if they lost the inevitable battle. There was very little to say after that and certainly very few questions. The enemy was an unknown, their ships and weapons a complete mystery. Only a trial-and-error battle would afford them any useful tactical answers.

When everything that needed saying was said, the feed to the Alliance Council and Military Command was closed. The five captains of the fleet stood and saluted, and, with the exception of Captain Williams, returned to their ships. Their orders were to leave immediately upon their return. Williams finally saluted and left as well, as he had his own ship to prepare. He would retain command of the *Dakota* while the admiral had overall command of the fleet.

Kate watched her father closely. For a man his age, he never looked more alive, but the effort left him exhausted. He was only a few years from retirement, and she naturally worried about the effect that the battle and its associated pressures would have on him. She also knew that she could never have such a conversation with him, and she already knew how he would respond: *"I only need to live for the next twenty-four hours. I think I can manage that."* That was another problem she would deal with when she had to and not before.

Morrison nudged her and nodded to the admiral, who was still sitting at the large table in the center of the room, going over specifications of each and every ship that would be involved. Michael nodded as well, but his was a telling gesture that indicated that it was time to tell their father about their quest to find their sister.

"All right!" she snapped at both of them. It was similar to all the moments Kate had hated the most growing up. She always felt awkward going to her father to ask his permission for anything, especially something she already knew he would deny her. It was yet another cause of her rebellious nature. Unfortunately, there was no way for her, Michael, and Cole Morrison to sneak off this ship without everyone knowing. She actually needed his permission, even if it killed her to ask for it.

She sat down next to him at the table and waited for some form of acknowledgment of her presence. She waited, waited, and then waited some more. As the child of a military officer, especially one so high ranking, she had learned never to interrupt him when he was busy, and he was busy often. Unfortunately, if patience was a virtue, Kate would never be considered a very virtuous woman. Throughout her childhood, that impatience and her propensity to interrupt had resulted in numerous groundings, but they were well-received lessons for her younger siblings. As far removed as she was from the possibility of grounding at this point, the training still stuck with her. Time, though, was something she had in very short supply, and she had even less patience.

"Dad, you got a second?" she finally asked as her patience timer rang off the hook.

"Yes, Kate?" Dante answered in the monotone voice she remembered from her childhood, without ever taking his eyes off the computer screen in front of him.

"I need to ask you something. It's important."

Dante continued to read from his screen, and Kate's awkwardness only grew heavier. Finally, he pushed the screen to the side and turned to her. "What is it, Katherine? Is something wrong? I have a lot to do and not much time to do it."

"I know," she said, eager to get to the point. "I need to leave, Dad." *There*, she thought, *out in the open and ready to get shot out of the sky like a duck in a hunter's sights.*

"Why?" he asked. "I… We need you here. I need you all here."

Kate looked at her father and began to see some of the cracks in his armor that the others failed to notice. As much as he was reveling in the moment of his one last brush with destiny, Holo-Dad had been right: Admiral Dante needed the strength his children gave him. In a lot of ways, all her trust issues came from him. "I need to find, Kristin," she answered quietly. "She's lost in all this with the *Bonaventure*. She's my sister and your daughter, and if you want us *all* here, I need to find her. She might need my help."

Dante reached over and squeezed his daughter's hand in his, then performed yet another miraculous smile. "Kate, I know I was hard on you during your youth, but I want you to know I couldn't be more proud of the person and the officer you've grown into. You're right. You do need to go find your sister. She's in trouble. I feel it. Remember, while we Dantes are a force to be reckoned with individually, together, we are a force of nature. Go find Kristin…and take that lot with you," he said, gesturing toward Michael and Morrison. "I'll make sure to save some Jek'Tan ass for you to kick when you get back. From what I've seen, you do that pretty well."

Kate leaned over to her father and squeezed his hand, then gave him a kiss on the forehead. "You know, old man, you surprise me more and more every day. I love you."

Dante smiled and pulled his hand back. "Just get out there and bring that little girl back with you. That's an order, Captain."

Kate stood from the table, smiling but with a tear rolling down her cheek. "I'll do that, Admiral. You have my word on it… and a Dante's word is… well, you know." To punctuate her point, she gave him the first salute that either could remember, then walked back to the others.

"One other thing, Kate," Dante said from behind the screen.

"Sir?"

"I want *my* scout ship back in one piece too."

"*Your* ship? But—"

Michael and Morrison each took an arm and dragged her out of the briefing room before the argument could ensue. They hurried to the landing bay listening to Kate's complaints every step of the way. They decided to take turns making fun of her, in the hopes she'd shut up.

"That goodbye brought a tear to my eye," Morrison said with a wink.

Michael was laughing too hard to talk much, but he still managed a jab. "I told you you're his favorite. Just don't tell him about the Cobra. By the way, where is that car?"

"Quiet down, both of you," Kate whispered, hoping no one overheard their chiding. "We're here." She had made it to the landing bay without killing either of them, and she considered that a major accomplishment.

They entered the scout, and Kate plopped down in the pilot seat and started preflight checks for launch. She was pleased to find that the flight crew of the *Dakota* had managed to resupply her weapons and defensive systems.

When she heard bickering, she looked up to find Morrison

and her brother fighting over the co-pilot seat. "And just what are you two doing?" Kate asked calmly.

"He wants the seat," Michael finally said. "Can you believe that?"

Kate looked at Morrison and shook her head. "Can't one of you be adult enough to take a step back?" she said, hoping one of them would take the hint. "We need to leave before we end up in a combat zone. Kristin is out there, and you two are in here acting like little boys fighting over a toy. Now sit your asses down before I kick them both! We've got no time for pissing contests."

Morrison picked up his hands in a gesture of surrender. "Fine," he said and settled for the tactical station to the side. "I guess I'm the adult here." He set his trusty sensor helmet beside his seat before strapping himself in and transferring the defensive subsystems to his board.

Michael was just about to complain about something else when Kate shoved a finger in his face and pointed to the co-pilot seat. "You wanted the seat, right? So sit in it!"

He started to offer some sort of backlash, but he realized he was acting like the typical baby brother and quickly held his tongue. Not only that, but the look on her face convinced him to sit quietly.

"I don't want to hear another word from either one of you until we've launched."

Kate adjusted her headset and keyed the comm system on. "Flight Control, this is *Alexa*. We are ready for launch."

The response was almost immediate: "*Alexa*, this is *Dakota* Flight Control. We have your traveling orders. Stand by while we depressurize the bay and move you into launch position. Please keep in mind that we usually don't do this while underway."

"We have a vacuum in the bay," Morrison said from his station.

They felt the deck shift as they were moved into position to launch. When they were finally in position, the metal clamps that had held the scout in place during high-speed travel withdrew.

Kate brought the main engine online, along with her ship thrusters, and she hovered in place as the bay doors slowly pulled apart. "Thanks, Flight Control. *Alexa* departing."

"Good luck and good hunting, *Alexa*," the voice came back with a slight Southern twang to it.

"You too, *Dakota*," Kate said as she applied vertical thrust at full power. She didn't want to get sideswiped by the rear-mounted communications dish of the cruiser. When she thought there was enough vertical separation, she veered to the starboard and brought *Alexa's* main engines online.

Her engines were very similar to the larger FTL drives built into the *Bonaventure*. While it would take the fleet almost two hours to get to Mars, at their present orbital coordinates, she could make it to the rim and back in less time than that, and the *Bonaventure* could do even better.

"So? What's our course?" Michael asked. "The transport was listed as missing somewhere around Jupiter. Could the *Bonaventure* still be in that area, or do you think they've moved on?"

Kate thought about his question for a minute before responding. "Let's assume the *Bonaventure* ran into trouble. That would explain the loss of communications, since they disappeared two days ago. Considering drift, they could be anywhere from Jupiter to Uranus. Then again, what if they were being pursued by those large alien ships and had to find someplace to lie low? Where would you guys go?"

"Well," Michael said slowly, using the computer to check relevant points in the outer system, "there are a number of mining colonies in the databanks, but I don't think Kristin or Brady would bring trouble to anyone's doorstep."

"I doubt they'd run to the decommissioned mining colonies," Morrison added. "Those asteroids are a real bitch to reactivate."

"Maybe one of the rest stations the Alliance set up for trips to the rim?" Michael suggested. "Those wouldn't take too long to power up. There are probably four or five rest stops out there."

"No," Morrison disagreed, shaking his head. "There really isn't much to them, especially now, since most have been stripped for parts or used for target practice."

"How would you know that?" Kate asked.

"Because my brother and I trained out there, and… Well, we occasionally took a liberty or two with the junk left floating around."

"Wait a second," Michael said as he turned to face Morrison. "Didn't the Alliance sign a treaty with the outer system miners that prohibits the military from setting up an outpost in their mining zone?"

"Yep, but the military didn't care much when transports started getting shot up," Morrison explained. "The trust between the military and the civilian sections of the Alliance always left much to be desired. They established the outpost, and for the better part of a decade, it served its purpose and kept an eye on everything going on out here. Then a corporate mining vessel—from Turner Mining, I believe—stumbled into it, and the Alliance military had no choice but to shut it down as if it didn't exist. Part of the decommissioning deal with Turner Mining was that they would never admit that it existed, but it does."

"And how does that help us?" Kate asked.

"My brother is stationed on the *Bonaventure*. I'm certain that if the shit hit the fan, he would head for the safest, most unknown port-of-call he knew about." Morrison unbuckled his seatbelt and crouched between Kate and Michael. "Since the military and civilian authorities have no idea that this place even exists, it's where I would go."

"Do you happen to know the coordinates?" Michael asked as he prepped the jump drive and nav board.

"I just might," Morrison said with a grin. "What do ya say, Boss?"

Kate took a deep breath and let it out slowly. "I guess it's as good a choice as any. Let's do it."

Morrison closed his eyes as he tried to remember the coordinates from his last stay there.

"Well? Do you remember or not?" Michael finally asked.

"Hang on!" Morrison closed his eyes tighter and tried to picture the nav display in the ship he'd flown out there about six years earlier. He grabbed a piece of paper and started writing numbers on it. When he was done, he handed the paper to Michael.

"Are you sure about this?" Michael asked nervously.

"Definitely," Morrison said, then went back to his seat and fastened his safety belt. "Well, it's more like, uh…probably 99.9 percent."

Kate shook her head. "Great. We'll end up in the sun, but program it in anyway. It's a big system, and we're looking for a small ship. We're going to need all the luck we can get."

Michael transferred the numbers into the navigational controls, occasionally stopping to scold Morrison for his awful handwriting. When he was done, he looked at his sister and shrugged. "Your guess is as good as his. Numbers are in, and I've corrected for gravitational drift. For all intents and purposes, we're good to go, sis."

Kate gripped the controls and said a silent prayer that the coordinates would lead them to Kristin, as well as another regarding the new drive, which had never been used at full power. The coordinates would lead them someplace near Neptune if the nav was reading it correctly. If the drive didn't explode, she estimated twenty-eight minutes till they reached their destination.

"Hang on, guys," she said as she eased the drive up to full. "This might get a bit bumpy. Three…two…one…" she counted down. At zero, she applied full forward thrust, and the stars disappeared for a brief moment before reappearing as the *Alexa* flew faster than she had ever flown before.

Kate finally released her grip on the controls. When autopilot took over, she unbuckled and started for the rear of the small ship.

"Drive is working within specs," Morrison said before he noticed her heading for the back. "Where are you going?"

Kate turned back to them and smiled. "I need five minutes of shut-eye, and then I'm going to assemble every piece of offensive weaponry we have onboard. I don't know what we'll find, if anything, but I want to be prepared. I suggest you two do the same. And, for God's sake, play nice! You don't want to wake Mommy up from her nap."

Without waiting for a response, she shut the door to her cabin behind her and grabbed the painkiller for the headache that was starting to become an issue. One thing was certain; She was not about to go to war with a migraine. She finally understood why the aliens attempted to take the *Bonaventure* off the board. She was the fastest, most powerful ship the Alliance had ever produced, an unknown that the Jek'Tan probably feared. Not only did she want to find Kristin, but recovering the *Bonaventure* could mean the difference.

She had also promised the admiral his youngest daughter back, and nothing was going to prevent her from keeping her word—not the Jek'Tan, that agonizing headache, or even the two immature children she'd brought with her. She only hoped her father would still be alive to see it.

Chapter 25

Kristin sat at the controls and did her best to wait for the inevitable arrival of her ship and crew. Patience had never been attributable to anyone in her family, but the wait gave her time to float between the different control consoles in an effort to prepare for what needed to be done when the *Bonaventure* arrived. There was just too much to do all at once. She needed to adjust the radiation flow in the core to keep it from spiking, and she couldn't give the Jek'Tan any indication of what her plan was until it was too late. Not only that, but she had those sensors to deal with, as well as communications, weapons control, and, of course, the detonator.

By now, she assumed the Falcon was some safe distance away, hiding until she triggered the big light show. They knew their orders. She, on the other hand, knew her responsibilities. Right now, that was to give her command the best chance of survival. If the Jek'Tan were capable of drawing on the memories of Henry Brady, they would know she wasn't about to go down without a fight. It was up to her to try to lure them close enough so she could trigger the blast. The only problem was that she didn't have enough arms to do what she needed to do.

"Commander, I thought you might need some help."

Kristin looked up from the console and was shocked to see Simpson standing in the doorway. "What the hell are you doing here?!" she spat. "Get your ass back to the Falcon and get the hell off the station right now!"

"Sorry, ma'am," he said, "but the shuttle is already gone. Permission to help the commander, ma'am?" he asked with a crisp salute.

Kristin looked at the young lieutenant and wanted to knock him to the deck. She wasn't happy that one of her officers had decided to blatantly disobey orders. "Why, Simpson?" she asked. "Why are you here? Odds are that neither one of us is going to get off this rotted metallic junk heap in one piece."

"Well, we drew lots on the ship to see who would help you. Everyone knew this was too much for one person."

"And you lost?"

"No, ma'am," Simpson said with a smile. "I won. I thought I'd have to fight off Moss and Marshall, but Mr. Jakes broke us up."

Kristin was touched at the display of loyalty from her people. "You still haven't answered my question. Why?"

Simpson simply shrugged. "It seems like the right thing to do, and to be honest with you, ma'am, every person on the Falcon believes they will see you tomorrow on the *Bonaventure*. Moss and I are keenly aware of the complexity of what you are attempting, and it stands a greater chance of success if you have an extra hand or two. Besides, he said something about you owing him lunch at the café."

Kristin nodded and admired the young officer's dedication, but the faith he and the others had in her seemed a bit misplaced. It appeared that her last name always inspired more in people than her résumé ever had. She wouldn't disappoint any on them, and perhaps that would be all the added motivation she would need to actually pull it off. "Okay, Mr. Simpson," she said with a smile, "please take tactical and weapons control. We don't have much time."

Kristin sat back and tried to adjust the radiation flow. The needle was climbing, and she needed to increase the power to the force fields that held the core together and the radiation leak to a minimum. In addition to trying to keep the Jek'Tan from reading those levels, she also desired to minimize the harmful effects on them; if they just so happened to get out alive, she didn't want either of them to grow an extra nose or die of some sort of cancer.

An alarm sounded as the tactical display jumped to the main view screen in front of them.

"Perimeter warning," Simpson called out. "I'm tracking multiple targets."

"Define multiple," Kristin ordered.

Simpson studied the readings before throwing it to the main screen. "It's definitely the *Bonaventure*, and she's being escorted by a squadron of starfighters."

"Hmm. Not very trusting," Kristin said quietly to herself.

"I would agree, ma'am," Simpson said as he fine-tuned the tactical display on the monitor. "He seems to be holding back."

"Is he within range of the radiation blast?"

"No," Simpson answered as he put the range projection on the display. "He needs to cross another 20,000 kilometers for the radiation levels to be anywhere near where they were to that N'Torr in the lab. Just FYI, ma'am, we're well within his attack radius. He can fire on us anytime, with certain success."

"Great." Kristin realized that that very moment was what she'd been afraid of since the beginning. Through the N'Torr's interface with Brady, the Jek'Tan knew—or at least highly suspected—that she would not keep her word and surrender. "Damn. Where is the love anyway?" she half-joked, knowing she had to try something else. "Dante to *Bonaventure*," Kristin said into her headset. "Come in, *Bonaventure*."

"Hello, Kristin," replied the voice of Henry Brady. "It's so nice to finally find you."

What was it Dad always told me? The admiral had a headful of analogies for basically every situation, and he loved throwing them at his children. *That's it!* she thought, picturing a juicy worm on a sharp hook. *You can catch almost anything if you have the right bait.*

"Sir, we've been waiting for you," she said, as innocently as possible. "This station is really unstable and can go at any time. You need to come get us."

"Kristin, the Jek'Tan have five very powerful ships heading to Earth. They are not going to share their culture or their advancements or help you to ascend to greatness in any way. We are going there to subjugate and experiment on your people leading to the eventual extinction of your race, and when the creators are done with Earth, whatever rubble and bio-waste is left will be promptly incinerated. Please tell me again why I should bother keeping you or any of your people alive. You are nothing more than a non-essential loose end."

Kristin sat back and pulled the headset off. He was right: She didn't have one bargaining chip, nothing she could offer that would make a difference one way or another. They could keep the *Bonaventure* right where it was and watch as the station tore itself to bits, or they could simply fire a few missiles their way. There were no more cards to play. *Or are there?*

"Fine," she finally said. "You paint a very bleak picture of the future of my species. We do have a fleet that will fight you…and maybe even defeat you."

"That will never happen. We will sweep them aside as easily as the Falcon you tried to hide," the voice said, a bit agitated.

It was then that Kristin knew she had planted the seed; the creature now realized its creator might just be beatable after all. The N'Torr were so religiously captivated by the Jek'Tan that they saw them as all powerful gods. She hoped that was something she could use. She didn't really enjoy exploiting religion and faith, but bait was bait.

Wait. What did that thing just say? The Falcon wasn't destroyed…was it? If that was the case, then everything was lost. Nevertheless, Kristin had no choice but to play it out to the end and hope for the best, and she had one last ace in the hole.

"There is one thing you will lose in our destruction," she declared.

"And what is that?" the creature responded, its curiosity piqued.

"We have a weapon that will destroy both the N'Torr and the Jek'Tan," she said, as casually as if she was announcing the weather.

"Ma'am?" Simpson stuttered, obviously confused by the revelation.

Kristin raised a hand to silence him.

After a brief moment of no response, Brady's voice argued, "It is not possible. Captain Brady would be aware of such advanced weaponry. Are you trying to tell us that you created it on your little metal lifeboat?"

"That's exactly what I'm saying, spider-boy!" Kristin barked. "Now prepare to die!" With that, she cut off the transmission, satisfied that the insult and threat would buy her at least a minute or two. She turned to Simpson. "Listen closely. Bring up two of those missiles from the Falcon onto the launcher and prepare to fire."

"Yes, ma'am," Simpson replied as his hands went to the weapons control. "If you don't mind my asking, though, what are we doing? If what he said about the Falcon is true, we're done."

"Not yet, Simpson. I'm going to bait him in. After you fire those missiles, I need you to track them," Kristin began. "Then—"

"But, ma'am," Simpson interrupted, "those missiles won't do any harm to the *Bonaventure*. She could just shoot them down with a couple of interceptors."

"Listen to me, Simpson. As soon as you see a detonation, I'm going to drop the shields on the core to a level just high enough to keep it from blowing. Then I'm going to raise the shields."

"Oh!" he said as it dawned on him. "So you're gonna try to convince them that what they feel from the radiation generated by the core are really just the missiles?"

Kristin nodded. "That's the plan. I need to make them think there is something worth their time here so I can get them closer in order to detonate."

"Brilliant, Commander." Simpson brought up missile tracking and locked it on the *Bonaventure*. "Weapons are armed, and tracking is locked. Ready to fire."

Kristin put her hands on the shield controls. At the moment of detonation, she would drop the shields around the core. It had to be done carefully; too little would offer no effect, and too much would send the station up in a cloud of debris, with the ship out of range. "Fire!" she called at precisely the right moment.

The tracking lit up on the display as the two red blips reached out in search of a target. Kristin rested her hand on the shield control for the reactor core and waited for the missiles to detonate.

"*Bonaventure* is firing. Detonation!" yelled Simpson.

The tactical readout showed two beams of plasma energy reaching out for the missiles, intercepting them, then blowing them to vapor. Kristin quickly lowered the shield on the reactor and watched as the needle climbed slowly into the red danger zone.

"Radiation increasing!" Simpson noted from the environmental computer. "We are reaching tolerance levels."

Kristin waited just a few more seconds before turning the shield power back up.

"Levels still climbing, but we are below lethal levels."

"Great," she said. "Let's see what they think of that."

The bait was out, and it was time to see if the fish were going to bite. There was nothing left but to see if the effect of the radiation was worth the risk they'd taken.

Brady watched the view screen from deep within his own head. He had no idea what Kristin was up to when he saw the two missiles. The N'Torr kept prodding, looking for answers to questions he knew nothing about. The weapons closed, and he could feel the arrogance of the creature as it looked at his second-in-command as nothing more than an annoyance and a liar. *Is Kristin Dante bluffing for some reason?* He had no idea; that was the answer the alien possessing him had to accept as fact just before they detonated the incoming attack with a blast from the forward plasma array.

He saw the detonation splash across the screen, then felt the weirdest thing. For just a moment, a few blissful seconds, he was in control of his own body again, and the Jek'Tan who had supervised from the bridge had vanished. He looked around at his bridge crew, and they all seemed to be feeling the same thing.

Brady could feel the N'Torr's legs still holding on to his body, albeit not as tightly as before. He had to remove it before whatever was in that missile wore off and it exerted full control of him again. He reached under his uniform and began to pull the thing out, one painful leg at a time. He got to the third leg before the hole that had swallowed him before took him again. It was so fast, so immediate that he barely felt the legs tighten, but the two he'd pulled out quickly reinserted themselves into the flesh of his chest. The N'Torr again exerted its control over him, though there was one big difference: The arrogance and certainty it felt before was replaced with panic and fear.

How do you like it, alien? Brady cried out in his mind.

There was no answer as the N'Torr turned his head, looking for the Jek'Tan who had been with them but had now vanished. Alone, and without guidance from its masters, the N'Torr-possessed bridge crew sat in silent dread that their gods had deserted them and were not coming back.

Brady laughed out loud in his mind at the creature which, just five minutes before, had been so certain about the extinction of the human race. Now, they were almost catatonic. He hoped Kristin could replicate whatever she'd done, because he would use that time to rip the creature off him and take back his ship.

Kristin watched and waited, but nothing happened—or at least nothing she could see. There was only silence. If the neutron radiation from the core had any effect on them, it was hard to tell. The *Bonaventure* just sat there, but the fighters moved into a tight formation around the ship, offering another level of protection.

"What now?" Simpson asked as he moved to stand behind her chair.

"I don't know," Kristin answered, as it wasn't exactly the outcome she'd predicted.

"Look there, on the screen." Simpson pointed to the tactical display that had suddenly gone dark.

Words appeared, somehow without an incoming signal of any kind. It was a message, and the meaning was clear: "Surrender the weapon, and we will let you live. Decline and die. You decide." It was also just as obvious who sent the message.

"Jek'Tan," Kristin said slowly. "Simpson, it looks like we finally got their attention." *Amazing*, she thought. *We went fishing for minnows and landed a shark.* Now it was time to try to land her catch. Her father was right again, but the rest was up to her. "Simpson, send them a message via the same frequency," she ordered, then took a moment to compose her thoughts, pondering a game that was played a long time ago, to test the nerves of two opposing drivers.

"What's the message, sir?" he asked, his hands ready on the keyboard.

"Come and get it," she said smugly.

"Done."

"Ever play chicken, Simpson?" Kristin asked as she threw her headphones on top of the console.

"I've read about it, ma'am, but no, I haven't."

Kristin took a deep breath and let it out slowly. "Me neither, but you know what? It's going to be fun to see who blinks first. Stand by on the detonator timer, because we're reeling in a big one."

Chapter 26

The explosions and radiation surge lit up the sensor systems of the *Alexa* as she passed the orbit of Saturn. The scout slowed and adjusted course as alarms blared, alerting the crew to the anomaly.

"Michael, are you reading that?" Kate pointed to the sensor display and the increase in radiation.

Michael ran a scan and nodded. "It's a neutron surge."

"Wasn't neutronic waste a byproduct of those cheap reactor cores the Alliance used years ago?" Kate asked.

"Ya know," Morrison added, "that military station I mentioned ran on a neutron-based power system. The ol' chief engineer went insane trying to keep the core shielded."

Kate nodded and adjusted course. "There were two explosions before the radiation surge. Hopefully, it wasn't your station breaking up. Altering course."

"Switching to stealth configuration," Morrison said as the *Alexa* became virtually invisible.

Kate increased speed as they closed on the source of the explosions. She looked at Michael, who was trying to make sense of the readings coming from the sensors. Under normal circumstances, such a look on his face would have gone unnoticed, but Kate knew every expression her brother's face could produce, and this one cried confusion when they had no time for such a thing. "What's wrong, Michael?" she asked.

"Well, I'm picking up the station. It's still intact, believe it or not. I've also got a large contact matching the profile of the *Bonaventure*. She's got a fighter squadron of four in a tight formation around her. I-I don't get it."

"What's that?" she asked.

"It's the *Bonaventure*, and she appears intact."

"We should try to raise them."

Michael shook his head. "Hold on," he said. "Something isn't right."

Morrison came up front and looked over Michael's shoulder to examine the data. "I've never seen a formation like that. Brady would never orchestrate it. The fighters are too damn close to the ship."

The tactical panel began to emit an unusual tone.

Morrison hurried to the console and stared at the readout. It was a communications stream, being piped through the tactical systems. He adjusted the controls, put on a pair of headphones, and smiled. "Whoa. I haven't seen this in years, since intel training," he said out loud. "I'm getting a tight-band laser communications stream, directed right at us."

"Where's it coming from?"

"Let's find out, Kate. Transferring signal to audio."

Morrison switched the mysterious signal to the cabin speakers. At first, all they received was static, until he tuned in the transmission just a little tighter.

"Unknown ship, this is Falcon 249. Please identify yourself," said the voice over the static.

"Track it," Kate ordered. "I have no idea how they can see us when we're in stealth mode, but I don't like it."

Michael began to adjust the sensors. "I think I know how they found us," he said, pointing out the window.

There was the Falcon, sitting about a kilometer in front of them.

"Geez, what a mess," Kate said as she moved the *Alexa* a bit closer. "Looks like she's been in a hell of a fight."

Michael nodded and ran scans. "My obvious question is why? With all that damage and the *Bonaventure* floating not too far away, why is she out here at all?"

Morrison sat back in his seat and played the message over again. The voice sounded oddly familiar, and it suddenly dawned on him why. "Falcon 249, this is the Alliance scout ship *Alexa*. Is that you, Jakes?"

There was silence on the line for just a moment before Morrison got his answer. "Cole? Oh my God, little brother, is that really you?" the voice cheerfully questioned. "You're the last poor soul I'd expect to see out here. What are you doing in that scout, kid? It looks a lot like the one the admiral used to fly back in the day."

Kate and Michael both looked at each other and shook their heads before turning together to stare at Morrison.

"Your brother?" Kate asked. "Really?"

"Who's that I hear?" Jakes asked.

"You're right about the ship," Morrison sent back. "I'm here with Kate and Michael Dante. We're actually out here looking for their sister Kristin and the *Bonaventure*. What's going on out here, bro?"

For two minutes, Jakes transmitted his account of what had transpired over the last few days, including Kristin's plan before they were ordered to leave and what had taken place just a few minutes earlier. To say it didn't go over well with the rest of the Dante family would have been an understatement.

"How could you let her stay?" Kate snapped angrily into her headset.

"Do you think I *wanted* to let her?" Jakes snapped right back. "Maybe you've forgotten who and what Kristin is. Not only is she my commanding officer, but she's also a Dante. If you can tell me the name of more stubborn bunch of people, then please do." Jake waited a second or two to let his words sink in, then continued, "It's too late to take any of it back now. We need to get in there and get her out."

Kate knew he was right, and they had to take action in a hurry.

"Sensors are showing that the Jek'Tan are coming for her and her weapon. When is she planning on detonating the core?"

"What? Moss, are you sure?"

Kate noted that the conversation was within the Falcon and waited for a reply. "Jakes," she finally interrupted when her short patience ran out again, "what's going on?"

His tone was somber when he finally explained, "She activated the timer about thirty seconds ago. It's set for five minutes, and then the station goes up, with a neutron radiation surge directed toward the *Bonaventure*. *Alexa*, we are heading back to the station for pickup."

Kate looked at her brother and Morrison, who both nodded and tightened their seat restraints. "Negative on that, Falcon," she said as she transferred power to shields and weapons. "My sister gave you a mission. We will attempt rescue."

"You sure, Kate?" Jakes asked quietly. "I don't wanna be the one to tell your father that I watched all his kids die today."

"Even if we fail," Kate replied, "the plan might still succeed, in which case you need to get your ship back and assist against the invasion on Earth. My father still needs you. Now hang on. You're wasting my time." Without another word, she shut down the channel and activated the main engines. The ship roared away, leaving a surprised Falcon in its wake.

"Stealth mode and weapons online," Morrison stated firmly, with his mind set on the task at hand. If there was anyone out in the universe that he would gladly die for, it was the Dantes. "Either way, this is certainly gonna be interesting," he said.

"So what's the plan, Kate?" Michael asked as he located the docking bay on the station. They were heading right at the *Bonaventure* and her fighter escorts from the rear. So far, the stealth systems seemed to be functioning properly and keeping them off the starship sensors.

"The plan?" Kate said with grim determination and a side of anger. "Shock and awe. That's what the plan is."

The *Alexa* made up ground quickly on the *Bonaventure* and the fighter escort. Her more detailed plan was to slow them down with a little damage and a lot of confusion. Since they couldn't see the *Alexa* on their scanners, the *Bonaventure* would be blind to her approach and attack. She hoped the confusion and chaos would allow them to reach the station and rescue Kristin. It was truly their only option, and they were quickly running out of time.

"Locking weapons!" Morrison said.

"Only superficial damage, Cole," Kate reminded him, "just enough to confuse. If this works, we're going to need that ship."

"Right," Morrison said as he hit the trigger. "Missiles away!"

The *Alexa* was so close to her targets that the two missiles she fired impacted almost immediately. The first was targeted at a spot near the *Bonaventure's* rear weapons pods, while the second was on course for one of the fighters. They watched as the missiles hit their targets. The first explosion lit up the rear of the starship, while the second created a dust cloud where a fighter had once been. The outcome couldn't have been better as the fighters that remained scattered. The *Bonaventure* momentarily lost control, ramming another fighter and sending it spiraling off into space.

"We're running out of time! More speed, Kate!" Michael yelled. "Two minutes, forty-five seconds until detonation."

"Two fighters have regrouped and are trying to intercept us," Morrison added from tactical. "They probably picked us up on visual."

"I'm too busy up here," Kate snapped as she added rear navigational thrusters to the mix. "You take care of it!"

Morrison didn't need to be told twice; he quickly released two interceptor missiles from the rear weapons pod. While they were mainly used for stopping inbound missiles, they would work in a pinch in taking out two light starfighters. They caught up quickly and destroyed one outright, while damaging the other enough to halt its pursuit.

"Michael, send a message for Kristin to meet us at the landing bay right now," Kate ordered as she noted the temperature gauges for the engines and thrusters approaching the red line.

Michael adjusted the ship comm to broadcast on every channel it could and activated the microphone. "Kristin, this is Michael," he said frantically. "Are you there, sis?"

Kristin and Simpson sat and watched everything play out on the tactical display. The Jek'Tan had taken her up on her invitation or her threat, depending on one's perspective. As soon as they were within the blast radius, she set and activated the five-minute timer. Both of them realized that since there were no ships in the bay and the Falcon had their orders, there was nothing left to do but wait for certain death when the core blew. Now, she watched as something exploded at the rear of the *Bonaventure* and the fighters started disappearing from the tactical display one by one. It wasn't going to be the biggest surprise of the day.

"There's an incoming message," Simpson said, shocked, as he walked over to the comm station.

"The Jek'Tan?"

"No," he said, and a smile suddenly crept across his face. "It's...something else. Listen."

When he put the signal on audio, Kristin heard the sweetest sound she could think of in her twenty-eight years of life: "Kristin, this is Michael. Get down to the landing bay right now. Kate and I are coming to get you."

"Michael? But...how?" She grabbed her headset and put it back on her head. "Mike, we're on the way," she cried into it. She pulled it off again and threw it to the deck. "Come on, Simpson. Let's get the hell out of here."

Simpson was already up and out of his seat, and he quickly followed her as they ran for the small hangar. "Eighty-four seconds till detonation," he said. "Was that your brother and sister?"

"Faster, Simpson!" she called out over her shoulder. "Yes, and it's probably past my curfew. Now, less talking, and more running."

"Yes, ma'am!" Simpson ran for all he was worth. He would have reported the spiking energy reading, due to the shields coming down around the core, but he didn't see the point at the moment.

"There!" Kristin said as the bay control room door opened before them.

Jakes and Moss watched as the *Alexa* missiles blew out the rear weapons pod of the larger starship. It thundered past on its way to the station, leaving one of the four fighters as nothing more than an explosive cloud of dust and debris and another flying off out of control. The other two fighters, though, remained in pursuit of the scout ship. If they didn't do something, the starfighters would easily catch up and happily blast them out of space.

"What's our status?" Jakes asked Moss, as the story looked pretty bleak based on the host of red lights on his board.

Moss shook his head and handed Jakes his data-padd. "Life support breach in the rear is patched, but we're leaking like a sieve. Power to life support is draining, and we're on auxiliary power already. Unfortunately, that's not gonna compensate for the loss."

"How long?" Jakes asked as he looked out at the *Alexa* and the two fighters in pursuit.

Moss shrugged as he took the padd back. "Fifteen or twenty minutes, tops, till system failure shuts off life support permanently."

"Is that enough to get to the *Bonaventure* if the plan works?"

Moss shook his head. "I'm not even sure we have enough shielding to survive the radiation surge when that reactor blows. Not enough power in life support to hide, and not enough for the shields to protect us from the blast. The radiation exposure will be lethal."

Jakes nodded and turned his chair to face the remaining crew. "You've all heard our predicament. We don't have enough life support to hide and wait out the blast, nor do we have enough shielding to protect us."

"Not much of a choice," Tolliver offered from the rear of the ship. "We can either die of suffocation or radiation poisoning and suffocation. I really don't prefer either."

"We do have one other play," Jakes said with a smile, "but only if you all agree to it."

"And what would that be?" Marshall asked from his seat at tactical.

"Moss, give me an engines and weapons status," Jakes said.

Moss looked down at his data-padd and smiled when he realized what Jakes had in mind. "Engines and weapons operational, at least mostly. Let's do it," he said, happy at the thought that Kristin would live to have another drink, even if he didn't.

"Do what? What is he talking about?" Tolliver finally asked.

"Yes, let's," Marshall said, wearing his own smile as he turned back to tactical and fired up the weapons systems.

"What?!" Tolliver demanded again, a little confused and growing angry at being left out.

"All right," Jakes said, "all in favor for spending our last minutes making a difference and protecting our commander's ass, say yay."

Jakes and Moss smiled as the remaining crew of Falcon 249 voted unanimously, even Tolliver, who was still wearing a dumb look on his face while he raised his hand and yelled his yay.

Swiveling his seat to face his flight controls, Jakes throttled the engines to full and set out in pursuit of the fighters closing on the *Alexa*. "Everyone, it has been an honor to serve with each of you," he said as the Falcon picked up speed.

No one was happy with the noises their ship made as it died, but they all knew they'd probably be dead long before the structural failure tore them apart.

"Now, target those fighters, folks, and let's get to work."

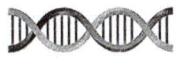

The *Alexa* was closing with the station, but the doors were still shut.

"Michael, I need those doors open," Kate ordered.

"Gimme a second." Michael had the specs for the station on his screen, including the remote door codes.

"We don't have a second," she snapped. "Hell, we don't have half a second. Open them now!"

"There!" Michael said proudly as the doors began to obey.

Kate pulled into the bay and set the ship down as Michael pressurized it. "Cole, open the door!"

Morrison unbuckled and dived over for the hatch release. The hatch swung open, and he waited for the third Dante to enter.

"Twenty-six seconds," Michael added.

"There they are!" Morrison shouted.

Chapter 27

"I'll be damned," Kristin said as she recognized the admiral's former scout ship and her sister's new ride. "Run for it, Simpson!" When they reached the door, Kristin gave the young lieutenant a push from the rear. She ran inside and shut the hatch behind her. "Hey, Kate. Does Dad know you have his ship?"

"Shut up and find a place to sit," Kate said with a smile as she activated the thrusters and turned to face the door.

Suddenly, without warning, the bay was rocked by explosions.

"Is that the core going?" Michael asked Kristin as she found a place to hold on to on the deck floor.

"No," Morrison responded. "That's the *Bonaventure*. The Jek'Tan don't seem to be waiting anymore."

"It's not working," Michael said as he tried the code for the bay door again. "Power to the door is down!"

Ignoring him, Kate, fired multiple blasts from the plasma cannons at the door. Finally, it blew outward in an explosion of metal and unvented gases. "That's the way to do it."

"Five seconds to detonation," Simpson said as he looked up from his data-padd.

"Shields on full!" Kate screamed as she pushed the engines to full burn from the standing start.

The *Alexa* shot out of the bay and into space. The inertial dampeners had a difficult time keeping up, keeping everyone pinned in place, but little by little, they gave in, and the pressure relaxed.

"Where is that explosion?"

Simpson looked at the padd and shook his head. "Moss! His calculations for the timer must have been off."

"That would not be a good thing," Morrison added from tactical.

Simpson stood and walked over to look over the tactical display from over the man's shoulder. "The *Bonaventure* is in pursuit. Should I fire on her?"

"Not yet," Kate answered as she tried to evade the incoming fire that played across her shields. "We need the ship intact."

"You're assuming that the core is going to blow and that the *Bonaventure* will not blast us to dust in the meantime."

Kate knew Michael was right: It all depended on the ability to blow the core and send that pulse of radiation toward the ship that was now after them.

"I have another reading, the Falcon."

The shuttle came from out of nowhere as Jakes turned and rolled between the *Alexa* and the *Bonaventure*. The Falcon executed a loop and began to fire its plasma cannons. Shields on the larger ship held as it fired at the scout once again.

"Shields are dropping," Morrison said grimly.

Another shot hit the *Alexa,* and small electrical fires erupted throughout the ship. Simpson and Kristin found the fire extinguishers and attempted to control the fires.

Kristin watched as the Falcon continued to fire; their depleted weapons had very little luck against the shields of the larger ship. She gasped as she noticed the hull damage and wondered how anyone could be alive inside.

Suddenly, there was an explosion of light as the Falcon took a hit and started spinning, end over end, into space.

"Jakes!" Kristin screamed. "Why?"

"Kristin," Jakes said over the damaged speakers, "most of the systems on the Falcon were damaged after we left the station. Fighters attacked and damaged us pretty badly. Life support's almost gone, we're leaking atmosphere, and we've got no more shields. There was no way we woulda survived the pulse. You need to finish this for us." There was a blast of static that drowned out his next few words, but he continued, "I told you I'd keep you safe. Tell my brother I'm sorry. He'll know why. I love you both."

Another blast came from the closing *Bonaventure* and struck the Falcon again. This time, with their shields down, the effect was devastating.

"No," Morrison whispered to himself as he watched the smoke coming from the charred hull breach on its port side.

Kristin just put her head in her hands and cried. With the Falcon opened to space, there was no hope for survivors. Kate and Michael looked at her in concern; in all the years they'd known her, she had never allowed herself to cry in front of anyone, not even them.

"The *Bonaventure* is inbound," Michael said, knowing they were seconds from death.

"Commander," Simpson said as he looked carefully at the data on his padd, "radiation readings are climbing."

Suddenly, there was a bright, intense explosion of light, and the station ceased to exist. The core explosion tossed the *Alexa* around like matchstick in a hurricane, but the remaining shields were able to absorb most of the radiation before they blew out.

Kate crawled back into her seat. She saw that Michael had hit his head on the nav panel, but he seemed all right as he pulled himself painfully back to his own chair. "Everyone okay?" she asked as she assessed the damage.

Everyone nodded, but Kristin and Morrison looked more than a bit upset.

"Michael, check the Falcon for life signs."

Michael ran his hands over the sensor panel and looked away, grimly shaking his head.

Kristin wiped her tears away and stared out at the wreckage of the Falcon floating off in the distance. "What's the status of the *Bonaventure*, Michael?" she finally asked.

"Kristin," he said as he stood and put an arm around her shoulder, "I'm so sorry."

Kristin shrugged out of her brother's grasp, turned her back on him, then stared out at the *Bonaventure*, which had stopped dead in space. "I asked about the status of my ship."

Michael let her go and went back to the sensors. He could see Kate checking *Alexa's* systems, but Morrison wasn't in much better shape than Kristin. "Power systems active, and I'm getting sporadic life signs throughout."

"Kate," Kristin said as she stared at the floating starship, "move us closer to the *Bonaventure*. They should all be inactive now. We need to move in and take control of the ship while we still can."

"And if they're not…inactive?"

Kristin shook her head, her voice grim. "If they're not, it won't matter. If that's the case, we'll be lucky if they blow us out of space. We'd never get far enough fast enough. Either way, we need to take advantage of this possible break."

Kate nodded and brought the engines back online. The damage to the main drive system was evident, but they were functional enough to carry them to the *Bonaventure*. She knew her sister was correct in her assessment of the situation: There wasn't enough left to make a run for it. "Morrison, are you okay? I need you on this," she said. There would be time for grieving after, but at the moment, they needed to act.

Morrison sat on the deck with his head in his hands. "My brother was my only family, and now he's just…gone."

Kristin knelt down next to the broken man and pulled his hands from his head, revealing a tear-stained face. "Cole," she said as soothingly as she could, "he told me about you and what you went through growing up. He told me you saved him, and he just saved all of us. Please don't let their sacrifice be in vain. Help me kill the bastards who are responsible."

Morrison looked up at her and nodded. "Okay," he said as she helped him to his seat. He ran through a few system checks and nodded to Kristin, letting her know he was functional enough to do what needed to be done. "Weapons and stealth systems are down, but tactical and tracking scanners are operational, though barely."

"Kate, we need to move in while we can," Kristin said as Michael let her take his seat.

"Hang on," Kate answered as she applied thrust. The *Alexa* shook as the engines sputtered and finally caught. She could smell the metallic scent of burnt wiring and circuits, but her damaged ship began to slowly lurch toward their destination.

Michael had moved from the seat next to Kate and over to the engineer station, where he monitored the ship systems. "Kate, the engines are about to seize. You'd better shut them down."

Kate nodded and switched off the main drive. She would have to take them the rest of the way on thrusters. Her poor *Alexa* had given her all for the mission; she just had a little farther to go. "Where are we going?

"Head for the cargo bay," Kristin said, pointing below and off to the starboard of the main landing bay. She leaned over and triggered a burst from the nav sensor. "I'm sending a command override."

They all watched as the bay doors slowly slid open.

"Can you get us in there?"

"Watch me," Kate answered as she tightened her grip on the control stick. With only thrusters, she positioned the *Alexa* for entry through the tight entrance of the bay. The bay was not designed to accommodate anything the size of *Alexa;* it was created to facilitate the receipt of satellite packages and small cargo deliveries when the main bay was occupied.

They heard the sound of metal on metal as the *Alexa* scraped through the bay entrance. Somehow, Kate managed to keep her word and maneuvered the ship inside. Thankfully, since it was her maiden voyage, there was no cargo. She settled down in the center of the bay as Kristin triggered another signal that caused the doors to slide shut. As soon as they were closed, sensors detected their arrival, and filled the cargo area with oxygen.

Circuits began to short circuit as Kate shut down the power to the damaged systems. Smoke filled the ship, and the main lights went out, quickly replaced by dimmer emergency ones.

Kate looked around at the damage and shook her head. "The admiral is going to kick my ass for this," she said quietly to herself.

Kristin was already out of her seat and into the weapons locker. "Everyone take something. In fact, take as many as you can carry. I've got no idea what we're going to find inside."

Morrison went to the locker and handed Michael and Kate a weapon before taking an assault rifle. Michael took his weapon and hit the release on the hatch. The door slid open, and he stepped out into the cargo bay with everyone else behind him.

Kristin took the lead quickly, holding her weapon in front of her. The look in her eyes made it clear that she was ready to fire first and ask questions later. She reached for the door control, but Kate grabbed her hand.

"Are you sure you're ready for this?" Kate asked her younger sister.

Kristin nodded and pushed the button. The door slid back as she stepped into the corridor. "We have nowhere else to go at this point, do we?"

Knowing she was right, everyone followed her into the corridor. It only took a moment to find the first body. It was a cargo tech, a small woman lying on the deck with a small pool of blood beneath her. Kate knelt by the corpse and gently turned her over. The woman's uniform was ripped below her chest where the N'Torr had grabbed hold and attached, but now there were only ashes beneath her.

"Michael..." Kate gestured for her brother. "Get over here with the medical scanner."

Kristin looked at the woman and shook her head slowly. "Ensign McGiver. We never really spoke, but I promised them all."

Kate stood out of the way as Michael held the scanner over the prone form. "She's still alive!" he said, looking back up at Kate. "Her vitals are a bit in the red, but she's slowly stabilizing. I think she's gonna be okay." He reached into the med kit and pulled out some disinfectant spray and a bandage to dress her wounds.

"We can't do that for all of them," Morrison said. "It'll take too long. There are bodies all over this ship."

Kristin nodded in agreement. "You're right. We need to get to the bridge."

"Let's get moving," Kate said as she helped Michael to his feet. "She should be okay. We need to get control of the ship and check on the command crew."

They headed for the transport tube and used it to reach the bridge. The doors opened to reveal a scene similar to what they'd witnessed in other parts of the ship they'd traveled through. The command crew was unconscious on the deck, bleeding from wounds similar to those of the ensign.

"The captain!" Kristin snapped as she ran over to where he lay beside his command chair. "Michael, bring the med kit."

Michael turned Brady over and saw the same dust under him, the ashy residue of the N'Torr from the radiation wave that had hit the ship. He noted that the shields were up, but the pulse still penetrated in sufficient strength to kill them. He pulled open the uniform and treated the wounds. When he was done with the physical damage, he reached in and found the smelling salts. It was a pretty primitive method, but he hoped it would work. He broke it open and held it under Brady's nose.

The captain coughed and opened his eyes, and his hands immediately went to his chest. His sense of relief when he didn't find anything there was evident. He looked up and saw Kristin kneeling by his side. "Commander Dante?" he said weakly. "As I live and breathe. You're one tricky officer. I take it that radiation surge took care of our infestation issue?"

Kristin looked down at her captain and smiled. "Yes, sir. Bugs are gone. Cleanup by broom and pan."

"Congratulations for outthinking your alien-possessed skipper."

Kate knelt down next to him and smiled. "Captain Brady, we're going to need your ship."

Brady looked over at Kristin, who was smiling as well.

"My sister, sir," she said.

Brady nodded and looked back to Kate. "Kate Dante? Aren't you a criminal and a traitor to the Alliance?"

Before Kate could answer, Kristin interrupted, "Not today, sir."

"I was undercover, Captain," Kate responded. "If we survive the day, everything will be explained. There are five huge, dangerous Jek'Tan ships headed for Earth. My father has the Alliance fleet of however many other ships he could find, and they're going to meet them around the orbit of Mars. We need to get to them with this new weapon my sister and her people discovered. It may be the only way to defeat the Jek'Tan."

Brady nodded and looked again at Kristin. "Captain Dante, I'm looking forward to that explanation, but for now, Commander Dante, take over."

"Yes, sir!" Kristin turned to Morrison and Michael. "You guys need to get as many of the engineering staff on their feet as possible. We need to get underway ASAP."

"And me, Captain Sister?" Kate said with a grin.

"You and I need to get the bridge up and running. We also need to figure out a way to generate another blast wave without destroying this ship along with it."

"Commander, now that you mention it, what happened to the Jek'Tan?" Brady asked as he pulled himself back into his chair. "When the N'Torr controlled me, they were always by my side. Did that radiation exposure destroy them too?"

"If they're based on the same biology, it might have affected them the same way as the N'Torr," Morrison added. "What did that alien say to us in Matinette's office? They're multidimensional beings? Maybe the neutron surge disrupted their stability or sent them someplace else."

"Then that's our priority," Kristin said. "You guys get the crew on their feet and get us moving. We need to get to the fleet before they destroy it and Earth."

Morrison and Michael both nodded, then took the transport tube back to engineering, leaving Brady, Kristin, and Kate behind with a slowly recovering bridge crew.

Kate sat at the ops console and brought the engines online. "No reason to hang around here," she said as she set course for the fleet. She looked over at Kristin and shook her head. "I'm sorry, Kristin. When everything is over and done, we'll come back and retrieve the Falcon."

"Thanks, sis," Kristin said as she leaned over the ops chair to give her a hug.

"What was that for? Not that I'm complaining."

Kristin released Kate and sat down in the nav seat next to her. She reached over and confirmed the course to Mars. "I just…wanted to apologize for being such a bitch."

Kate fired up the drive and set it on auto as the *Bonaventure* altered course and gained speed. "Under the circumstances, it's understandable."

Kristin laughed. "No, I mean…since I was a kid. You and Michael came out here to find me and my ship. I just want to thank the both of you while I still can."

"Okay…and agreed," Kate said with a smile. "You *were* a little bitch growing up. As far as the rescue is concerned, that's what family is for."

"The admiral is going to be pissed about the scout."

"Yeah, I know, but one piece of Armageddon at a time please."

Chapter 28

Rosten sat back in his office on Mars and waited for whatever was going to happen in space above his city. With the exception of the five massive alien ships looking to end all human life in the system, he had to say it had actually been a very good day.

Rumor had it that Ethan Striker was dead, and his holdings had been seized by Alliance forces because he and his family had been implicated in the alien invasion that was currently in progress. His own ships had gone after Stratton at Lunar One, as agreed to in his deal with the Alliance Council, but by the time they arrived, Stratton had cleared out to some undisclosed location. With the help of his people on the moon, he'd secured all the assets and contacts Stratton held and was now in the process of buying out Striker Industries, since their company stock had fallen through to the center of hell. It appeared that stock prices reflected the stability of a company conspiring with aliens to turn their entire race into experiments in DNA research. No one wanted any part of them, especially when their stock became almost worthless in light of their diabolical deeds going back centuries. They were easy pickings without their charismatic CEO malevolently pulling the strings behind the curtain.

It was just Rosten's luck to be in the position of the king of the hill of a civilization about to be wiped out by the same twist of fate that had actually given him reign in the first place. His ships were back in time to rejoin the Alliance fleet. It was the largest collection of military spaceships in the history of the human race, and it still might not be enough to turn the tide. He looked out his window at the city he and his family had built from the ground up, from nothing but the red Martian dirt, and he realized that all of it could be gone in the next few hours. Dante had told him the Jek'Tan would reduce his city to dust, along with everyone in it, before moving on to Earth. He had never been a fan of the military or of the Dante family, especially after Kate Dante's betrayal. Now, he found it insane that a Dante held the key to his future.

Nicholas Dante stood on the bridge of the *Dakota,* looking admiringly at the fleet he'd help pull together on such short notice. It didn't matter what their affiliation was, pirate or private; as long as they carried armaments and were crewed by human beings, they were welcomed with open arms. The only thing he was missing was the *Bonaventure* and his family.

He'd tried several times to reach the *Alexa,* but those calls had gone unanswered. Normally, that would have worried him, but he had absolute faith in his children. Apart, they were great, but together, they were truly unbeatable; if his older daughter and son had found their sister, he knew there was nothing he needed to worry about. It would be a shame for Kate to miss the fight; win or lose, it promised to be epic.

He looked out at the ships again. At first, most wanted nothing to do with the Alliance. That wasn't really surprising, since some were smugglers and privateers; just days before, they'd been shooting at each other, and now they were set to fight together to defeat a common enemy. They only had to hear the recordings once to pledge their loyalty for the sake of the one-time battle. As part of the human race, they were all targets, just like everyone else. He had no idea how they'd react once the fighting began, but any damage they could inflict on the enemy would be welcome.

The only real regret Dante had was Rosten. He hated dealing with that slimy piece of crap, but such desperate circumstances bred desperate acts. In exchange for Rosten removing Stratton, coming clean about Striker, and contributing his ships to the fleet, the Alliance promised to pardon him for past deeds. In a number of ways, they had just traded one problem for another, but if they ultimately won, it would all prove to be worth it.

"Admiral," Williams said from his command chair, "are you okay? Sir?"

Dante was suddenly jolted back to the here and now. He'd been lost in thought, and that was something that seemed to be happening all too frequently as of late. He'd forgotten his pills in his quarters and reminded himself that he would need them before the battle began. The doctors had given him a diagnosis, but the name of his illness had been given to him too long ago for him to even try to remember its overly long name. They assured him that the symptoms would worsen over time, and he would slowly lose the things that made him the man he was. First were the issues with concentration and balance. The later stages would bring pain as the mass in his head increased in size. The only one who knew the truth, outside his entourage of trusted physicians, was Michael. He knew that of his three children, his son was the most capable to handle his affairs after he was gone.

After all those years, it was hard to imagine that he would suffer such a fate. It wasn't that he feared death—far from it. It was the way he was going to die that bothered him most. He was a warrior, and some badly replicating cells in his head had no right to take him in such a meaningless way, but it was what life had chosen for him. In the end, it was inoperable, and he was terminal, but his meds would keep him focused enough to do what he had to do. Regardless, he had enough to get through the next few hours; he had to, for if he didn't, they were all lost.

"Yes, Captain?" he said.

"Sir, sensor scans of the area show that the five Jek'Tan ships have crossed the asteroid belt. ETA on Martian orbit, four hours."

Dante shook his head. "They should have been here already! Something has happened to make them overly cautious." *Is that you, Kate?* he thought. *Did you do something to shake up the opposition?*

"Word from Martian Defense Forces are that atmospheric and starfighters are ready for launch, and missile batteries have been armed, sir," Williams added.

"So, that's it then, Captain," Dante said as he sat at the executive officer station. "There's nothing left to do but wait."

Brady stared at the tactical display Simpson had placed on the main view screen. The *Bonaventure* was moving at full speed, gaining quickly on the Jek'Tan fleet, but they would still be at least thirty minutes behind by the time they reached Mars. They had managed to bring most of the formerly N'Torr-possessed crew back to normal functioning, but a portion of the personnel was still out of commission due to adverse reactions of their separation. They were lucky to have enough manpower to maintain the ship.

"Can we contact Admiral Dante and the fleet, Lieutenant?" Brady asked, needing to know what was happening before they engaged.

Simpson looked at the most recent damage reports. The engineering crews had just started repairs on the long-range communications systems that were damaged during their own attack on the *Bonaventure*. "Not yet, sir. We have crews working on it, but they don't think it'll be up and running by the time we reach Mars."

Brady shook his head. When the N'Torr broke connection with him and died, he thought their problems were behind them, but the problem didn't really go away; instead, they just morphed into other problems. Kristin was a godsend, and what she and her away team did would earn her a commendation, a promotion, and probably her own command; she was certainly her father's daughter. Then there was Kate. Until today, he'd held on to the fact that she was some sort of villain, as she'd been pegged by the Alliance as a criminal and a traitor. Now, he knew better. She was the reason Kristin and Simpson were still alive and why he was still in command of his body and his ship. If they survived the day, he would almost consider a transfusion to fill himself with that magic Dante blood.

Right now, they were in the briefing room with the heads of both science and engineering, trying to work out the next stage of their plan. He hoped they could conjure up a little of that Dante magic one last time.

At first glance inside the *Bonaventure* briefing room, the last thing anyone would think of was magic. Arguments were waged around and across the table. Joining Kristin, Kate, and Michael was Ted Parsons, Chief Engineer, and Silvia Jenkins, Tolliver's former assistant and next in line as medical officer. The only one without an active argument supporting his own plan was Michael Dante, who had somehow taken over the role of referee in the ongoing game of stupid.

Morrison would have been at the table as well, but the death of his brother had hit him hard. He decided to take it upon himself to get the *Alexa* back on her feet. It was something he told them he needed to do, and it was something he wanted to do alone.

"We need a viable plan," Kate said to the assembly, "and you people are telling me we don't have one?" She was so frustrated she was about to take her gun out and shoot them both.

"Captain Dante," Parsons tried to explain, "the neutron radiation waste product we need, at the intensity you're looking for, is impossible to create. It was phased out of the reactor cores of all Alliance ships more than twenty years ago."

"How about the older ships in the fleet?" Kristin asked. "Someone out there has to be using older tech."

Parsons shook his head and pointed to a graphic on the screen, illustrating the specifications of some of the older ships in the Alliance. "Even the older vessels, those with suitable cores, are equipped with too many safeguards to build up an explosion large enough to do any real damage. There just isn't any time for them to retrofit their current power systems."

"Face it, Commander," Jenkins added, "you lucked out on that old station with the right combination of core size and lack of mandated safeguards. You were just in the right place at the right time." She pointed to the specs and shook her head. "Unfortunately, there are no military outposts with a reactor old enough and with the right materials at its core to generate what we need to take out all five ships."

Michael watched as Kate and Kristin tried to understand why it was so impossible to re-create a relatively simple primitive energy blast with the modern technology onboard the *Bonaventure*. The impasse had almost reached an unbearable point when the solution hit him. "I have an idea!" he tried to shout above the insanity, but either no one was listening or no one could hear him. In response to that, he stood and threw his data-padd against the far wall, shattering it into several expensive pieces.

"Michael, what the hell are you doing?" Kristin asked of her usually restrained older brother.

Thrilled that his temper tantrum had finally garnered someone's attention, he said, "I know exactly where we can find a large enough, old enough reactor—at least one that might work. Unfortunately, you're not gonna like it.

"Michael," Kate said in frustration, "it has to be better than this. Just spill it. What have you got?"

Michael took a deep breath before answering, "We give them Mars."

Everyone stared at him in disbelief, some with wide eyes and some with rolling ones.

Michael ignored their whispers and stares and continued, "The only reactor I know of is the one that powers New Earth City… on Mars."

"Wait a second…" Jenkins snapped as she stood from her seat and pointed a well-manicured finger at him. "Are you suggesting that we trigger an explosion from a power core that sits below the feet of a 100,000 people? That's insane."

"Sit down!" Kristin ordered. "Michael, we can't just set off a nuclear blast under a population center."

"Wait…" Kate responded before Michael could say anything. "The Jek'Tan plan to attack Mars regardless of what we do, and Earth will be next. They want the populace as both N'Torr bait and spare parts for the Jek'Tan experiments."

"So you're saying we should sacrifice our own people to defeat the Jek'Tan?" Jenkins questioned, like a dog with a bone; there was no way she would give her approval to a plan so drastic. "Can they be evacuated?"

"To where?" Michael asked. "What do you suggest we do with them, Lieutenant, escort them to Earth? That would be a waste of time, considering that Earth is the aliens' next stop." Michael shook his head and softened his tone a bit. "Look, I understand that your love for Mars and your loyalty to Clayton Rosten would make anyone feel as you do," he said calmly. When she attempted to respond, he interrupted, "If I'm saying anything that's not true, please let me know. You grew up in New Earth City, and Clayton Rosten sponsored you for the Academy. Is that not a fact?"

Jenkins was speechless, and her face flushed with anger. A moment later, she started, "Yes, but—"

"Lieutenant, you are dismissed," Kristin stated bluntly, cutting her off.

"What?! You can't do that," she stammered. "The captain wanted me here, and—"

"That's nice," Kate said. "Why don't you go to the bridge and tell him that?"

"But—"

Kristin stood and walked over to the *Bonaventure* science officer, until they were standing nose to nose. "I gave you an order, Lieutenant. Either you follow it, or I'll have security haul your black and blue ass down and throw it in the brig."

"I'm not black and blue," Jenkins said a second before her brain registered an understanding of the statement. "Yes, ma'am," she finally said, then turned and headed from the briefing room.

Kristin sat back down in her seat and turned to Michael. "I hope you have a plan. The captain will never endorse the destruction of New Earth City with all those people living there."

"Of course I have a plan," Michael finally said, "sort of." It was really still forming in his head, but he knew if they could communicate with the fleet, it stood a chance. "It depends on getting a message out to the fleet as soon as possible," he said. "We can do this and keep civilian casualties at a minimum."

"Michael, we don't have all day," Kate said slowly. "What do you have in mind?"

"Don't you all see it?" he asked with a smile, feeling he'd finally bested his brilliant sisters, at least a little. "We have a fleet of ships above Mars and more than five hours till the Jek'Tan arrive. The power station is far enough away from the city that with the dome up, it might survive the blast."

"But there's the radiation," Parsons interrupted. "The plant is approximately seven kilometers from the city, and we can probably direct much of the explosive force away, but the neutron radiation at those levels will kill any living thing. Not only that, but the EMP from the blast will fry most of the unprotected circuitry."

"What about the dome?" Kate asked. "Will that offer any protection?"

Parsons checked his data-padd and did a bit of math before answering. "Whatever's farthest from the blast will probably survive. Anyone in the docks or cheap housing won't stand a chance."

Michael thought about that for a moment. "The fleet can evacuate a significant percentage of the population, at least temporarily, until the levels decrease to normal."

"What about the rest? There aren't enough ships in the entire system to carry more than 100,000 displaced people."

"Parsons, you are quite the pessimist, aren't you?" Kate said, giving him her trademark dirty look. "Unfortunately, they'll have to hole up in the center of the city the best they can."

"And if it doesn't work?" Kristin asked.

"You all know the answer to that better than I do."

They all knew Michael was right. If the plan did not stop the Jek'Tan, it really didn't matter where the population of New Earth City died.

"There won't be much time to evacuate the city, and we also have to convince Clayton Rosten. We're probably going to need his engineers to help us work this out in the few hours we have left," Parsons said, with his hands clasped in front of him. "Either way, this is not going to be easy…and that's a fact, not pessimism."

"But is it *possible*?" Kristin asked. "I need to take this to the captain, but before I do, I want to know what all of you really think."

Parsons thought about it for a second, then nodded. "It's possible, but it will be at great risk to the civilian population, as well as the ships that have to evacuate them."

Kristin reached over and pressed a button on the table in front of her, opening a channel to the bridge. "Simpson, this is Dante. Do we have long-range communications?"

The reply came back quickly but wasn't the positive response they were looking for. "It'll be about eight hours before that is restored. Sorry, ma'am."

Kristin shut the channel and looked at everyone at the table. "There you have it, folks. There's no way to get a signal to the fleet to begin the evacuations. We have no time to implement this. I need to tell the captain."

Kate shook her head. "Wait, Kris," she said. She then pulled her personal comm from her belt and flipped it on. "Cole, are you in the *Alexa*?"

"Yeah, Kate," Morrison responded. "I'm working here. What do you need?"

"How much have you got done?" Kate asked. "Are the long-range comms fixed?"

"Most of the fire damage came from blown circuits," Morrison reported. "I replaced most of the destroyed boards, and I should have her flyable in an hour or so. To answer your question, comms are up right now, as are *Alexa's* main drive systems."

"Thanks, Cole," Kate said cheerfully. "Michael and I are on the way down."

"Michael and you?" Kristin asked. "What will I be doing?"

Kate was sure Michael's plan would work, but time was running out, and it required them to be in too many places at the same time. "You are going to the bridge to fill Captain Brady in on our plan. The rest of us—you included, Parsons—will call the admiral, then take the *Alexa* to Mars. If Morrison is right and the main drive is operational, we should be able to sneak past the Jek'Tan ships and prep the reactor."

"And the *Bonaventure*? You do understand that we can get to Mars faster than the *Alexa* can," Kristin interjected.

"The Jek'Tan will pick up the *Bonaventure's* engine signature. There's no way for you to get past them, but the *Alexa* and her stealth systems can. You guys have an important part to play in all this. You need to keep track of the bad guys and hit them hard from the rear just as they engage the fleet. We know that they can be disoriented when the attack pattern is not what they expect. Hopefully, that will buy us some extra time for the evac and the reactor modification."

"That's insane," Parsons told them all.

"Yeah, but it just might work," Kristin said. "Now raise Dad and let him know what he and his fleet need to do. I'll brief the captain and give him our recommendations. This is crazy, but crazy's all we've got right now. Let's do it."

Without another word, everyone left the briefing room. Kristin headed for the bridge, while the others went to the *Alexa* in the cargo bay. The ball was now in Admiral Nicholas Dante's court, and if there was one person who could make it happen, it was him.

Chapter 29

Dante sat in the briefing room and ordered the computer to lower the intensity of the light in the small room as he tried to massage the pain from his head. The dim lights made it easier to deal with, but the throbbing agony was becoming more of a problem every day. He was happy he took the call from Kate and Michael away from the judgmental minds of the captain and bridge crew of the *Dakota* and spoke to them in private.

He was also happy beyond words that his children had, at least so far, managed to remain untouched. It would have made him even happier if they would have stayed aboard the *Bonaventure* and set a course for deep space, on the quest for entirely new lives elsewhere; as much faith as he had in Kate's suicidal plan, there was always room for error and death, and he had subjected his children to too much of that already. He didn't argue with his daughter, though, because her plan was the only one they had, and she wouldn't have listened to him in the end anyway. Now, he only needed to sell the insanity to the fleet and Rosten. Clayton was about to suffer significant losses to his assets, and he wasn't going to be happy about it. Just like Goldilocks in the fairytale, Dante had a feeling someone would be sleeping in Rosten's bed that night.

Kate would be there within the hour, accompanied by the chief engineer of the *Bonaventure*. They would supervise the modifications of the reactor and its detonation when the Jek'Tan settled over the city. He hoped Kate and Michael were correct and that there would be enough room in the fleet to get everyone off planet.

"Captain Williams, report to the briefing room," the admiral said into the comm. It was time to work miracles before he spoke to Rosten.

The man was a crooked bastard and a criminal, but he knew an opportunity when he saw it. *How many men can turn down the opportunity to become the savior of humanity?* With Striker and Stratton gone from the landscape, the PR alone would be of enormous benefit. There would be cities named for him across the Alliance. Now, if only he could get Rosten to buy it all.

Dante watched the *Alexa* set down in the landing bay. The ten minutes it took for him to brief Williams was enough for him to head off to alert the other ships that it was going to be standing room only onboard their vessels soon. The evacuation of the city went on as per Alliance regulations regarding procedures in times of emergencies; far and away, this was a confirmed emergency.

His call to Rosten was more a courtesy than a requirement. If Rosten went along with it, things would go easier. Initially, he opposed the evacuation and insisted that they would attempt to ride out the blast behind the dome if they had to. By the time Dante finished his sales pitch, Rosten was still opposed but agreed to help facilitate the evacuation for the safety of his citizens.

The ship had touched down, and Kate, Morrison, and Michael walked out of it with what he assumed was the engineer from the *Bonaventure*, Parsons. He didn't see Kristin, so he assumed she had duties to tend to on her own ship.

Kate smiled and waved at her father as she exited the landing bay. "Hi, Dad. Good to see you."

Michael sneaked in a handshake, and the engineer followed suit.

"Nice to meet you, Admiral Dante," Parsons said with a hearty handshake.

Dante nodded, then turned back to his daughter. "Evac is in progress, and I gather that you and your team are on the way down to the reactor?"

"Yes, sir," she said quietly. "I don't even think we'll be here for more than a minute or two before we head down. How did Rosten take it?"

"How do you think? In one day, the poor bastard saw his partners either dead or fleeing for the hills and the crown handed to him for the kingdom, and hours later, we told him we're going to nuke his throne right out from under him."

"Dad, Rosten knows the score," Michael said. "He's just looking for a higher road to negotiate from. I'm sure he's got a comfy bunker set up for himself at Lunar One when the Jek'Tan come. I'm also pretty certain he's already arranged caterers for the victory party at his triumphant return if we win."

"It doesn't matter, Michael," Dante said with the hint of a smile. "If the Jek'Tan get past us, they'll find him eventually. It won't take much."

"True."

Dante walked over to Morrison and put a hand on his shoulder. "Son, I heard about your brother. I am so sorry for your loss. Jakes was a wonderful boy and a good son. I will miss him too."

Morrison nodded as the admiral pulled him into a tight hug.

Kate stood with her mouth agape, looking over at her brother as the hug released. They wiped their eyes and nodded to each other before her father turned and walked down the corridor and out of sight. "C'mon, Cole" she said soothingly. "We've got work to do. We'll wait for Parsons in the *Alexa*."

Morrison nodded and headed back to the ship.

Kate turned to follow, but Michael caught her hand, holding her up. "What is it?" she asked.

"I know you. You're going to make a big deal out of this. Don't."

Kate shook her head. "I don't know what you're talking about."

Michael followed Morrison into the ship, but Kate stopped and thought about what her brother had to say. Something was wrong with her father; there was never such a change in a man without a damn good reason. She decided that if they were all alive the next day, she would find out exactly what that reason was.

The *Alexa* descended to the surface, near the power plant outside the city. Michael pointed out the ships of every type and size as they passed them on the way down. The evacuation was making slow progress, and with less than two hours to go, the odds that they were going to get everyone out in time was becoming less of a certainty. Three cruisers from the admiral's fleet set down outside the city limits, picking up far more passengers than the shuttles could. Kate adjusted course and brought her own ship down outside the reactor.

They left the *Alexa* and were greeted by the unhappy staff members of the plant. "Not only does the plant power the city," one worker told them, "but also the atmospheric processing plant as well." Kate knew it didn't matter if Mars was made as inhabitable as it was centuries earlier, as long as the Jek'Tan were stopped there.

In the control room, the engineering crew was joined by Parsons, who took command of the reactor preparation. To Kate's surprise, Clayton Rosten and his son Marcus were right in the middle of it.

"Hello, Katie," Marcus said, wearing that twisted smile he seemed to favor. "You always seem to appear at the worst times for my family."

"Marcus," his father said, pushing him aside, "we're all on the same side right now. We must leave Kate Dante to her discretions, at least for the moment." He extended a hand to Kate and looked at her with an obviously manufactured smile. "Please accept my apologies on behalf of my son."

Kate looked at his hand with a feeling of disbelief, especially after the events of a few days earlier. She felt the hatred for this man well up in her, far beyond that for the Jek'Tan. She soon found her hand unconsciously tightening on the pistol at her hip. He had tried to have her and Michael killed, and now he wanted to make friends.

Michael was talking with Parsons when he glanced over and noticed his sister with Rosten. He recognized the look on her face and the fact that her right hand had strayed to the butt of her sidearm. As much as he would have rejoiced to see Kate kill both Rostens, it was neither the time nor the place to settle old debts. "Kate!" he called out to her. "Parsons wants to patch into *Alexa's* nav computer for orbital data so he can regulate the blast parameters." When she didn't acknowledge his call, he tried again, a bit louder this time. "Kate!"

Shocked out of the trance she seemed to have fallen into, she pulled her hand from the gun and backed away from Rosten and his son.

Michael walked over to Rosten and nodded to his sister as she spoke to Parsons. "Stay away from her, both of you."

Marcus made a move to intimidate Michael, but his father held him back. "Don't think I've forgotten either one of you, Dante. One day, I will bury you and that bitch sister of yours."

Michael shook his head. He found it unfathomable that Rosten's son would try to pick a fight with him just hours before the entire human race would be forced to fight for its existence. "I'll make this quick, I don't have time for anything more. You may not believe me, and I really don't care, but I just saved your lives. You will both stay away from my family forever, as well as anyone or anything associated with this project. If I find that either one of you or any one in your employ is in violation of that, I will see to it that you have an up-close-and-personal view of this reactor as it blows. Whether you will be breathing at the time will be entirely at my discretion. My family is very important to me, Mr. Rosten, just as yours is to you." Michael repeated his terms as he glared at them both. "Do we understand each other?"

Marcus Rosten was about to blurt out something stupid when his father held up his hand to quiet him. "Yes," Clayton Rosten answered through clenched teeth. "We understand."

Michael smiled and nodded. "Very well, gentlemen. In that case, our business here is concluded. Please have a nice day…and do try to stay out of everyone's way."

The Rostens watched as Michael sauntered off to join his sister and Parsons before the three of them went into the power plant.

"How can you let him talk to you like that?" Marcus said as he felt every muscle in his body tighten.

"Shut up, you stupid little shit!" Rosten snapped, then smacked his son across the face. "What possessed you to antagonize the only people who can possibly save all of our lives? You need to watch your mouth, before someone named Dante shuts it permanently. Just get to the ship. We are leaving here before the fireworks begin."

Marcus rubbed his cheek and forced himself to calm down. "Where are we going?"

"To Lunar One. Where else?" Rosten said quietly, so no one else could hear them. "I hear there is a vacuum in leadership there—no pun intended."

"And the Dantes?"

"If this works…well, tomorrow is another day," Rosten offered pragmatically. "If their plan fails, it really won't matter, will it? Now go." Rosten stopped to take his last look at what his family had built, then shrugged. *Perhaps it is time for a change of scenery,* he thought as he followed his son out the door and into the Martian air.

Kate adjusted the remote interface to the *Alexa* computer for Parsons as she watched Michael enter the reactor control room. She wasn't happy that her brother had intervened in her confrontation with Rosten and his son, but she didn't know what she would have done if he hadn't. As much as she wanted to shoot them both, it probably would have been the wrong decision; no matter how good it would have made her feel.

"Are we going to be ready in time?" Michael asked.

Parsons nodded as he took the data-padd from Kate. "We've got about ninety minutes, so we're cutting it close, but one way or another, it'll be ready in time. The reactor is old, but the new Alliance-mandated safeguards are making it difficult. To be honest with you, it'd be easier to blow up the capital than to try to cause a meltdown and explosion here. I'm missing Lieutenant Moss. He died on the Falcon, but he was the young engineer who modified the core on the station to explode. He knew these systems inside and out."

"We have faith in you, Parsons," Kate said, placing a hand on the man's shoulder.

"Thanks," he said with a hopeful grin and a thumbs-up as he went to the control board and sat down.

"What's your problem?" Michael whispered to his sister.

"I didn't need your help with either Rosten or his offspring," she whispered back. "I can take care of myself."

Michael nodded and poked her in the shoulder with a stiff index finger. "You can take care of yourself too damn well! None of us need Rosten provoking you into a fight. You do know that's what that bastard son of his was trying to do, right? Kate, there's too much riding on all this for anyone to have to deal with your crap or theirs." Kate tried to say something, but Michael stopped her and continued, "Hold up. I'm not finished. Besides the fact that the human race might soon be over, you are my sister. Even though I'd like to beat my head on a wall sometimes because of it, I would go to the grave protecting you, Kristin, and even Dad—just like he would for us."

When he brought up their father, Kate nodded and changed the subject. "What's wrong with the admiral, Michael? I'm tired of trying to guess. Tell me, or I'll beat it out of you, in spite of the wonderful and tender monologue you just put me through. I know you know, so just spit it out."

"Let it go, Kate."

Letting it go was the last thing Kate had any intention of doing. She'd already been deprived of the chance to unleash her fury on the Rostens, and she was not going to be deprived of the information she now sought about their father. "I will stand here in your face until you answer my question, Michael."

"Dad's dying," he finally blurted, knowing her threats were never idle. "There. Are you happy now?"

Kate had suspected it but didn't want to believe it, so the news hit her hard. This was to be her father's victory lap: win the war, leave stuff for his kids, say goodbye to friends, and then move on to the next realm. "What's wrong with him?" she asked as she stared into the distance.

Michael shook his head and wiped his eyes. He'd been living with that sad secret for almost a year now, and he almost wished his father hadn't entrusted it to him. It felt good to let someone else in on it. "The doctors told him the scientific name for it, but you know Dad. The name wasn't as important as the details. Basically, he has a cancerous tumor in his brain and a few small lesions that have spread to his brain stem. The symptoms are poor concentration, impaired motor function, and headaches. Before you ask, it's inoperable. I've taken him to enough specialists to know that."

"Why didn't you tell me?!" Kate snapped, not caring who heard her. "He's my father too!"

"I'm sorry," Michael said through tears of his own. "Dad told me not to. He's gonna be pissed that I told you now."

"You're sorry?" Kate snapped, then smacked him in the face. "You little shit. When this is over, we're all going to sit down and discuss this. Does Kristin know?"

Michael simply shook his head as he rubbed the red mark on his face.

"Good. At least one of us can remain relatively sane until this is over."

"I'm sorry," Michael said again as the tears led to a nice cry for the both of them.

"Come here," Kate said softly, hugging him close. "Don't do this anymore, okay?" She found it amazing and disturbing that the admiral somehow managed to control them, even though he was miles away in orbit, with a tumor in his head. "Let's get this done and make him proud." She could feel her brother nod, then pull away.

"Captain Dante, Commander Dante," Parsons said timidly, "I have a report for you."

Kate was so involved in the emotional rollercoaster with her brother that she hadn't even heard the engineer approach. "Report," she finally said, as she and her brother switched on their professional personas. She was certain there would be more than one personal tragedy to mourn before it was all over.

Parsons pulled out his data-padd and went through the list, one by one. "The good news is that we've managed to pull every safeguard we could find in the system that might inhibit the modifications to the core."

"Are you sure you got all of them?" Michael asked.

Parsons nodded. "According to system diagnostics, the only way to be sure is to attempt to detonate the core and see if it goes. We've only got one shot here, sir and ma'am. Once the safeguards are down, the core will go critical. Around thirty seconds later... Well, we'll have ourselves a big *boom*." Parsons then showed them the readout on the screen above the control board. "I hope it's enough."

Kate nodded. "Where's the detonator?"

"I used the link to the *Alexa* and programmed the go frequency into her weapons system. You can detonate from there. Push the button, and safeguards and shielding fails. Thirty seconds later, the reactor goes critical, and you've got your neutron surge. This one will make the one out by Neptune look like little more than a sneeze by comparison, so make sure you and any other friendlies are nowhere in the blast radius when the thing blows."

"And you're sure this will all function as you described?" Kate asked.

Parsons smiled, forcing his gray mustache and beard to push out from his face. "I've been an engineer on Earth as well as in space. I was in charge of a number of atomic power plants in those thirty or so years, but until today, no one has ever asked me to create a disaster I've spent all my life training to prevent. Will it work, you ask? There are 100 things that could go wrong, but I would say yes, it should. I haven't told you the bad news yet."

Kate and Michael turned to the chief and wondered what was going to go wrong now.

"All the ships were able to pack in a little more than 60 percent of the population," Parsons finally said. "There are still more than 35,000 people left in the city."

"Thank you, Chief," Kate said as she took his hands in hers. "The best of luck to you. Please evacuate with the rest of the staff. There's a ship waiting for you."

Parsons shook his head. "I was hoping to go with you and the rest of the team in the *Alexa*."

"Too dangerous, Chief Parsons. You have your orders."

The chief smiled and saluted. "Good luck to you as well, Captain."

Kate nodded, then watched as Parsons went out the door to his waiting transport. "Where's Morrison?" she asked Michael.

"He's already prepping the *Alexa* for launch. He thought you might be a little impatient to get off this planet."

Kate smiled and pulled out her comm. "*Dakota*, this is Dante. Do you read?"

"Captain Dante, this is Williams on the *Dakota*. The Jek'Tan got here a little sooner than we projected. The fleet is engaging."

"Captain, try to withdraw. You are carrying a civilian population. The Jek'Tan need to advance the rest of the way to New Earth City on Mars. Where's my father?"

"Understood, Captain. We will withdraw when able. The admiral is coordinating the counterattack," he said as the sound of static started to override the transmission. "He's trying to use heavy cruisers to cover the retreat of the ships carrying the evacuees. It's not going very well. What is your status?"

"We're about to leave. Everything is secure."

"Great," Williams replied.

Kate and Michael could here explosions in the background, even louder than the static.

"Now all we need is the *Bonaventure*, because we're taking quite a pounding, and—"

Without another word from Williams, the transmission dropped.

Kate and Michael made it to the *Alexa* and found Morrison already in the pilot seat, prepping for launch.

Kate jumped into the tactical seat and grabbed a headset. "Morrison, get us out of here!"

Michael shut the hatch and jumped into the co-pilot seat next to Morrison as the ship started to rise into the dense Martian air.

Kate adjusted the communications frequency until she found the *Bonaventure*. "Captain Brady, Kristin, where the hell are you?"

"This is Brady. We're ten seconds from engaging. Stand by."

They would have listened for more had static not wiped out the rest of the transmission.

"Probably interference from the core," Michael told her.

"Where to now, Kate?" Morrison asked.

Kate knew they needed altitude to get above the interference the unshielded plant below them was creating. She wished there was something they could do to make a difference in the battle, but she wasn't sure what. After all, a fleet of Alliance cruisers commanded by her father hadn't even accomplished much. She was desperate to be of more help than holding her finger on the nuclear trigger. Suddenly, it came back to her: There was someplace she could make a difference. Parsons had told them there were still 35,000 people left in the city below, and someone had to warn them to get as far away from the blast front as they could, preferably indoors and under an insulated covering. "Head to the city!" Kate finally ordered.

Michael turned in his seat and stared at her. "What?! You really are insane after all. The Jek'Tan will be here in a few minutes."

"Mike, we need to save those people if we can," Kate argued. "We can't leave them behind again. Cole, do it."

"Yes, ma'am," he said. "Changing course."

"It'll only take us a few seconds to get to the landing bay. We'll get to the PA and send out an alert message, and then we're out of here, okay?"

Michael nodded. "Fine, but remember that the success or failure of this whole plan hangs on us. We can't lose a whole star system for 35,000."

"Michael, would you feel differently if Kristin or I were down there?"

Michael didn't answer; he only turned his chair in silence and looked to the sky.

Chapter 30

Brady pushed the *Bonaventure* for all she was worth, as if their participation in the battle would turn the tide. Kristin sat at ops, pushing the engines knowing that the battle had already begun. Sensors showed that three of the Alliance heavy cruisers were engaged, firing everything they had at the five alien ships, with little to no effect. It was like rain on a summer day as the Jek'Tan ships turned back missiles and plasma beams as if they were nothing. They were covering the other ships in the fleet, those that held the city evacuees. Despite their efforts, the powerful Jek'Tan weapons were removing those ships from space one by one.

The enemy continued to fire at the three ships. Kristin could see that one of them was the *Dakota,* her father's flagship. Whatever weapons they possessed, they cut into the ships as if they were made of paper. Sensors showed secondary explosions in each as they tried to maneuver for better firing angles, as well as the need to protect damaged sections that were already open to space.

"Kristin," Brady snapped, "stand-by on all weapons. As soon as we're in range, I want you to fire."

They were closing quickly, but they could see that the *USS Berlin* was already in flames. She didn't know if they could make it in time to save them. "What about the *Berlin*?" she asked.

"Tactical," Brady snapped, "report!"

Simpson scanned the cruiser, but the results weren't encouraging as he posted them to the view screen. "Damage to all systems, sir. Life support is fading. Shields are gone."

Before he could say another word, two Jek'Tan ships fired simultaneously at the *Berlin.* The ship split in two before exploding in a bright flare of energy and debris.

"No!" Kristin screamed at the screen. "We're in range and firing." She then cut loose with everything the *Bonaventure* had left to offer.

"We're getting hits on both ships!" an excited Simpson called out. "Explosions registering on the hulls, and they are scattering."

Cheers from the bridge crew added fuel to Kristin's rage as she continued to fire. This time, the Jek'Tan were prepared, and the energy from the plasma cannons was easily turned aside. The return fire from the alien ship washed over the *Bonaventure* defensive shields, nearly throwing them all from their seats.

"Damage control reporting," Kristin said. "Hull breach in Section Forty-Two, emergency bulkheads closing to seal off the section. Shields down to 43 percent."

"Casualties?" Brady asked.

"We lost eight, sir," Kristin sadly reported. "Twenty-two injured."

"Excuse me, sir," Lieutenant Cranston interrupted from communications. "Message coming in from the *Dakota*. It's Admiral Dante."

"Put in on the screen," Brady ordered.

The tactical view on the forward screen faded and was replaced with the *Dakota* bridge. Smoking wreckage and fires were everywhere. Kristin gasped when she saw her father sitting in the command seat, his face covered in blood as someone held a bandage to the cut across his forehead.

"Admiral Dante," Brady asked, "is everything okay there, sir?"

"No, Captain," Dante said, pushing the medic away. "You need to break off your attack and protect those other ships that are full of evacuees."

"But, sir, we can do this," Brady countered. "Let us help you with the fight."

Kristin watched silently as her father coughed, then pulled away a blood-filled hand. "Dad, please let us help," she pleaded.

Somehow, even through all that stress and pain, Dante managed to look down at his daughter and smiled. "No, honey," he said, feeling a tear forming in the corner of his eyes. "You and the *Bonaventure* need to keep those people safe. You're ship already has a hull breach. I'm sorry, but I won't lose it...or you."

"Dad, I'm so sorry," Kristin said sadly through her own tears, "for everything."

"Kristin, you have nothing to be sorry for," Dante assured her as he straightened his uniform, "I must be a mess. I am so proud of you, Michael, and Kate. Take care of each other, and remember that I love you."

"Bye, Dad," she said softly as she watched the image fade from view.

Brady gave Kristin the few seconds she needed to compose herself before he spoke again. "Commander, break off the attack and head for the retreating ships, ahead full."

"Altering course." Kristin peeled away from the Jek'Tan ships and put as much distance as she could between the *Bonaventure* and the aliens as she set a course for what had become an evacuation fleet.

They watched as Mars and the Jek'Tan ships shrank in the distance. With their ship no longer an active threat, the Jek'Tan advanced on the *Dakota* and the *Independence*, the two cruisers still engaged in the battle.

"Simpson, scan the two cruisers," Kristin ordered, her tone low as she tried to retain control of her emotions. "Status?"

"Propulsion and weapons are dead on the *Independence*. Life support is fading. Not many life signs," Simpson said weakly as he switched to the admiral's cruiser. "The *Dakota* still has some, but I'm reading multiple hull breaches. Life support is barely registering. I'm sorry, Commander."

They all watched as the lead Jek'Tan ship fired on the *Independence* twice more; the first shot pierced her engine core, causing a breach in her fusion reactor. Unchecked, the overload would have destroyed the ship in a matter of minutes. The second shot quickened the process, reducing the cruiser to a cloud of debris

Nicholas Dante looked around the bridge of the *Dakota* at both the living and the dead. He didn't want to take command of the cruiser, but her captain and first officer were dead, and the crew needed someone to take charge. His ship was full of holes and dying, with too many hull breaches to count and too many systems in the red. The only thing he had in short supply was enough healthy crew remaining to fix the issues.

Life support and weapons were gone. Remarkably, the only major system still online was the FTL drive. It was a shame that the air would run out long before they actually reached anyone who could help. He looked at the tactical display and noticed that the incoming Jek'Tan ship was quickly closing. It appeared that they wouldn't have to worry about suffocating slowly. In another minute or so, they would be blown to bits, just like the *Berlin* and the *Independence*.

He sat back in his command chair and felt his head hurting again. *At least,* he thought, *it won't be this damn cancer that kills me.* He was content though, and he was thrilled that he'd been able to speak to Kristin and let her know how proud he was of her. His only regret was not saying goodbye to Kate and Michael. Being a details man, though, of course the admiral had made sure to leave something for them to remember him by.

Dante looked at each of his remaining bridge crew and thanked them for their service. They told him it was *their* honor to have served with him. He asked for the damage report one last time. After reading it, he turned to his bridge crew and said there was one last thing they could do that would make a difference. He asked if they trusted him, and without a word, they saluted and turned back to their stations.

"Mr. Okawa," he said to the helmsman, "please bring the FTL drive online."

"Yes, sir," the young ensign replied strongly.

"Course, sir?" the navigator asked.

Dante pointed to the cracked forward view screen. "Aft view please." The screen image changed to the two alien ships closing on them, preparing to fire. "Your choice, Mr. O'Keefe. Pick one."

"Yes, sir," O'Keefe said as he locked the course into his nav board.

Dante stood one last time; he had decided long ago that he would die on his feet, and not in a bed with tubes running in and out of him. "You have all been like family to me, even if we only had today. Now, let's kill that bastard. Whenever you're ready, Mr. Okawa."

Dante closed his eyes and felt the *hum* of the FTL drive spooling up. In his mind, he thought of happier times, of three children and a wife he loved with all his heart and soul. He hoped when he saw her that she would welcome him into her heart again, for the rest of eternity.

There was a brief moment of forward motion, a very bright light, and then...

"Look!" Simpson yelled, pointing at the view screen.

Everyone turned to see the brilliant flash of light, followed by another, even larger flash in the darkness as the *Dakota* and the two alien ships vanished in the expanding ball of light, likely brighter than the fires of creation.

"What was that?" Brady asked as the sun-like brilliance slowly faded away.

Kristin looked at the screen and smiled. "That was my father, doing what he does best."

Simpson ran the sensor scans again and discovered that the *Dakota* had activated her FTL drive seconds before the explosions. "That was the *Dakota*. They activated their FTL and rammed them.

The admiral took out two of the Jek'Tan ships." Simpson couldn't help squirming in his seat a bit; he finally had something to be excited about.

"Kristin, are you okay?" Brady asked, concerned.

For an answer, Kristin did something no one would have expected: She laughed out loud.

"What are you laughing about?"

Kristin turned to her captain and smothered her chuckle just a little. "Excuse me, sir. No disrespect to the admiral, but it just occurred to me that the way he went out… With a bang? What a show-off!"

Brady allowed himself a brief moment of joy before reality set it. "There are still three alien ships heading to New Earth City, Commander. Any word from Kate or Michael? It's up to them now."

"On it, Captain." Kristin scanned for frequencies that she could still push a signal through, but had no luck. "There's too much interference from the reactor core on the planet. The only way we can find out is to go check."

Brady shook his head. "No, Commander. I intend to follow the last order Admiral Dante passed on to me. We will just have to find out when the rest of the system does."

"Yes, sir!" Kristin acknowledged, just a little too strongly, she realized in afterthought. She would have preferred to go to the surface and check it out for herself, but she now she had to stay and just hope the legends of her sister were right. The last thing she wanted was to lose someone else from her family. "C'mon, Kate," she whispered to herself. "You and Michael can do this…for Dad."

Chapter 31

Kate directed Morrison to the dock she'd escaped from just a few days earlier. Never in her wildest dreams would she ever have imagined being back in it, but here she was. Crowds had gathered there and at all the other docking facilities that ringed the city. It was the area where most of the population had been picked up, so they thought it was best to converge there. They had no idea it was the worst place in the city they possibly could have chosen. Once they landed, she unbuckled her belt and made her way to the door.

"Kate, this isn't wise."

Kate looked at him and nodded. "It might not be wise, but it's the right thing to do. Keep an eye on things."

"Crap," Michael said as he watched the scanner.

"She's right, man," Morrison said.

"I hope you still think so tomorrow."

Kate made her way to the security shack. With Rosten gone, she was sure the rest if his goon squad had either departed with him or simply deserted during the evacuation. The shack held a city-wide public address system. She would make the quick announcement, then head back to her ship.

Her office was exactly the way she left it, with the exception of the mess on the floor. She sat at her console and keyed in the comm system. "Attention, all residents of New Earth City. You need to move away from the eastern side of the dome. We are going to detonate the reactor, as a defense against the oncoming invasion, and you must be clear of those areas and in an insulated structure toward the center or western edge of the city. You don't have much time, so please hurry. This will be your only warning." She then shut down the comm and glanced up at her office door to see Morrison standing in it.

"Well? Was it worth it?"

Kate thought about it and nodded. "It's what makes some of us human. We'd better go now. By the way, what are you doing here?"

"Michael sent me. He punched through the interference and got to the *Bonaventure*. The aliens are already settling over the city."

"In that case, let's go now!"

They both headed for the door and took the steps two at a time. Kate looked around and was happy to see that her warning had done some good. They ran headfirst into a crowd of people heading away from the eastern docks.

Morrison stopped and signaled for Kate to as well. "Do you hear that?"

Kate stopped and listened closely to a clicking sound, like rain pelting a tin roof. She tried to focus on the sound as she looked up at the dome. "Shit," she said to herself as the clear dome began to darken to black, covered by N'Torr dropped from the alien ships.

"Really?" was all Morrison had to say.

They increased their pace to a sprint until they reached the dock where they'd left the *Alexa*. The N'Torr were already entering through the ventilation system and had reached the landing bay and her ship. They watched from the glass-enclosed office of the dockmaster as the N'Torr filled the bay. If they had found the ventilation ducts, there was no doubt that they were in the city as well.

"Michael," Kate said into her radio, "we're trapped in the dockmaster's office. The bay is filling with N'Torr. We're never going to make it to the ship."

"I won't tell you I told you so," the static-filled response from Michael said.

Kate tried to figure out a way through the moving carpet of alien parasites and couldn't conceive of an alternative to what she was thinking at the moment. "Michael, you're going to have to detonate. You need to do it now, before the N'Torr swarm the entire city."

"Kate, I can't. You're too close. The radiation will kill you and Morrison," Michael pleaded. "Can you head back to the center of town and get back to the security shack? You might be able to ride out most of the radiation surge there."

Morrison shook his head. "Too late to leave."

The same noise they'd heard in the bay was now right outside the exit door of the office.

"No, Michael, we're trapped in here. There's no more time, baby brother. Do it! That's an order."

Michael sat back in his seat and felt the pain of the decision she was forcing him to make. He knew she was right, and there really was no other choice. He sighed heavily and said, "Detonating in five…four…three…two…one…" Michael flipped the switch Parsons had left for them and waited. Parsons had said it would take thirty seconds for the core to melt down, but it was already at forty-five.

"Michael, what's going on? Why the delay?" Kate asked. "You need to detonate." She grasped her comm tightly and waited for Michael to answer.

"I did!" he answered. "Something's wrong."

Morrison sat in the dockmaster's chair and laughed. "You want to know why?"

Kate nodded.

"Because all the N'Torr on the dome. They've been absorbing the signal. The *Alexa* needs to transmit outside the city, out in the open."

"Michael, transmit outside the city," Kate said. "Morrison said the N'Torr are absorbing the signal."

"I'm not leaving you," Michael stated firmly, "and screw your orders. There has to be a way to get you back here."

"Michael, please!" Kate pleaded. "Go!"

"Wait! I'm thinking." Several seconds later, he was back, a lot more excited than before. "Hang on, sis. I have an idea. Get ready to make a run for it."

"Michael—"

"Kate, we seem to have no choice," Morrison said with a shrug. "Get ready."

"All right. I'm gonna force a diagnostic of the *Alexa* core onto the central computer and vent the core gases real quick," Michael said slowly. "This is still the original core Dad installed when it was his ship. Some of the waste materials will be neutrons. It may have a brief effect on the N'Torr, and it may not, but it's worth a try. Get ready."

Kate put the comm back on her belt and waited for Michael. She was amazed that he remembered the specs of her ship's core, and it was their good luck that the Alliance hadn't modified it, at least to the best of her knowledge.

They watched as the rear exhaust port slid open and a hazy mist of radioactive gases slowly spewed out. The N'Torr seemed to slow their advance for a moment, then stopped moving completely.

"Now!" Kate snapped to Morrison as they made a run for the *Alexa*.

The door opened, and they dived inside as the first N'Torr shook off the effects of the radiation and barely missed Morrison as the door closed behind them.

Kate dashed for the pilot seat and brought the engines online. She rotated the scout on her axis until they were nose to the doors. "Hang on!" she snapped as she opened up with the twin plasma cannons and blew the doors off and into the Martian day. Pushing the *Alexa* to full thrust, and with N'Torr hanging from it, they shot into the sky.

"Kate," Morrison yelled, "watch out for the Jek'Tan ships!"

The three remaining Jek'Tan vessels were still belching out N'Torr onto the city, but it was their sheer size and low altitude that made her alter her collision course with them.

"Shields up!" Kate said as she headed east, toward the reactor.

At that moment, the rear of the ship was hit by weapons fire from one of the alien vessels, blowing already repaired circuitry and dropping engine power at an alarming rate.

"We're losing altitude. Now, Cole! Detonate."

Morrison tried the switch again. This time, he had the return code from the reactor; the breach had begun. Kate poured all available power to the engines in an effort to escape the radioactive blast wave. The damage to the engine had reduced their climbing speed by half, with the thirty-second clock ticking their lives away. Even worse, the blast took down her aft defensive shields.

"We're not gonna make it, are we?" Michael asked. "Aft shields are down."

Kate smiled at her bother and squeezed his hand with hers. "I don't think we have enough power to reach escape velocity. You should have gone when I told you to."

"Twenty seconds," Morrison counted. "Wait! There's a ship incoming!"

"Identify!" Kate could see something appearing above them, but it was still too far away.

"It's the *Bonaventure*!" Morrison yelled excitedly.

"Hang on, guys," Kristin said over the comm. "We're coming for you."

"Kristin, pull up! There's no time." Kate replied.

"Shut the hell up already," Kristin argued. "You can be a real pain in the ass sometimes, but it's my turn now. Hang on!"

The *Bonaventure* quickly swooped in and took a position directly over the smaller ship as it opened its lower cargo door. Kate saw what her sister was planning and angled for the opening in the hull as magnetic beams from inside attempted to increase the scout's climb.

"Ten," Morrison countered.

Kate every bit of power her crippled ship had left into one last burst of speed. The thrust sent them crashing against the side of the entrance before momentum and the magnetic tractor beams carried them inside. Kate tossed her headset to the console and closed her eyes as the cargo doors closed.

On the bridge of the *Bonaventure*, Kristin's board told her the doors had shut and the area was pressurizing.

"Get us the hell out of here!" Brady called out. "I don't know how you talked me into this. Give me a rear angle on the viewer."

Kristin threw the engines on full as they climbed out of the Martian atmosphere and into space.

"Zero," Simpson said quietly, as the image of the Martian surface on the rear view screen exploded in bright white light.

The bridge crew watched as the core exploded, but just as Parsons had planned, most of the shockwave dissipated upward and toward the east, away from the city. The neutron radiation was another thing; it that was directed up and west, toward New Earth City. Eventually, the force of the blast reached the *Bonaventure*, buffeting them a bit as the rear shields glowed from absorbing a minimal exposure of the neutron force that followed.

"Give me sensors on those three Jek'Tan ships," Brady ordered as Kate, Michael, and Morrison stumbled breathlessly onto the bridge.

"Well? Did it work?" Kate asked as she stopped to catch her breath.

"We're trying to ascertain that now, Captain," Brady said as the data started to arrive.

"You guys okay?" Kristin asked, swiveling her chair and smiling at her brother and sister and Morrison.

Kate walked down to Kristin at her ops panel and knelt in front of her. "That was the most reckless stunt I've ever seen in my life," she said sternly, but that expression soon morphed into a broad smile. "However, it was also the most amazing flying I have ever seen. Since when did my by-the-book little sister become such a risk-taker and a daredevil?"

Kristin stood up and gave Kate a hug. "Since I found out that things like that run in the family. Oh, and you're welcome."

Michael, smiling as well, mostly because he was alive, walked over and joined his two sisters in their hug.

Brady cleared his throat and gestured to the screen. "If I can possibly break up this Dante moment, something's happening down there."

The view screen was on full magnification, offering a top-down view of New Earth City and the three hovering Jek'Tan vessels. Indeed, something was happening.

"Look at the dome," Kate said in wonder as the layers and layers of N'Torr began to peel away and just blow off like dust. As each layer fell away, it exposed another and another, until the dome was clear again.

"The dome?" Michael responded quickly. "Look at the ships!"

Everyone turned their attention to the three Jek'Tan ships. One minute earlier, they'd been dropping N'Torr onto the city, but now they were wobbling like drunks on New Year's Eve. The ships began to veer into each other as explosions, both on the inside and the outside, took a toll on the enormous five-mile long vessels. They quickly lost altitude, and the ground soon claimed one of them, throwing red Martian dust and rocks into the air as it cut a groove in the surface. The other two vessels staggered into one another, one penetrating the other like a stake through some evil vampire's heart. They stayed locked together in a weird mechanical dance of death for almost ten miles before they made impact on a very red Martian mountainside. The force of the explosion decapitated the mountaintop, raining debris on surface below.

Silence filled the command center of the *Bonaventure* as everyone accepted the scene before them in their own way. Finally, cheers rang out from the entire staff, led by Captain Brady, of all people. The impossible battle had ended, albeit not without significant losses.

"Sir, I'm getting a signal from the *Churchill*," the communications officer reported. "It's Captain Summers. As the only surviving cruiser, he has taken command of what's left of the fleet."

"Put him on," Brady said slowly. "We've got quite the report for him."

As Brady filled Captain Summers in, Kate pulled both Michael and Kristin to the side. "Where's the *Dakota*?" she asked.

Kristin explained to her brother and sister how heroically their father and the crew of the *Dakota* had met their end, taking out not one but two of the Jek'Tan ships. She was surprised that neither one of her siblings seemed overly distressed to hear it. They both just nodded and smiled before Michael gave each of his sisters a kiss on the head, then headed back down to the cargo bay to check on the *Alexa*.

"What's up with you two?" Kristin finally asked. "I would have expected more grief out of both of you, especially that one. He was always Dad's favorite."

Kate laughed. She and Michael had decided not to tell Kristin about the admiral's condition unless it became necessary. Now, there was no reason to tell anyone. He died a hero, and that was enough. "I'm grieving his loss, Kris," she finally said to her sister, "but can you imagine a more appropriate way for him to go? What a show-off."

"Hey! I said that same thing. Out in a blaze of glory."

Kristin was about to say something else when Kate gave her a tight hug. "Love you, little sister. You take care." Kate then gave her sister a kiss on the cheek and turned toward the bridge exit.

There, sitting at the chief engineer's station was Cole Morrison. There was no way any of them would be alive without his help. She thought back to her early years at the Academy, when he was crazy in love with her. Back then, she couldn't understand why. Now, she understood it completely.

"Hey," she said to him with a smile.

"Hey," he replied. "I guess that's one for the home team."

"Certainly looks that way," she said with a nod.

"Listen, I'm sorry about the admiral. Jakes and I loved him too. He was like a father to us, something we never had." Morrison stood and offered Kate his seat.

"No thanks. My father died and made sure he left a legacy for everyone, just like your brother did. We wouldn't be here now if not for both of them."

Morrison tried to smile and succeeded to a certain extent. "They both died doing what they loved the most, saving family."

"Cole, how about a drink in the officers' club?"

Morrison thought about it for a moment and finally offered a smile that wasn't so forced. "Okay, but only if it's in their honor."

Kate returned the smile and grabbed his hand. "Can't think of a better reason."

Kristin happily watched them leave the bridge hand in hand. She remembered hearing stories about the two of them at the Academy. She knew they must have been something pretty serious at the time if the admiral had stepped in to break it up. Kate might have been a legend in the intelligence game, but she was far from a legend in her relationships—not that her little sister's had fared any better.

Thinking of Morrison made her miss Jakes all the more. She had no idea that they were brothers or that all their lives were so intertwined, with her own father as the common denominator. She wasn't blind; there had always been an undeniable attraction between them. He told her he wanted to keep her safe, and right to the end, that's what Jakes did.

Brady finished filling Captain Summers in on the Jek'Tan and the N'Torr, and now he had received new orders. When the radiation levels allowed a landing, medical and engineering teams from the fleet were to go down to New Earth City with decontamination equipment and medical supplies to treat the wounded and the sick. Some were suffering from radiation poisoning, and others were victims of the N'Torr, just as those on the *Bonaventure* had been. Additional ships were on their way from Earth and Lunar One to assist in evacuating the remainder from the city. Considering the radiation hazard, the lack of power, and the mess left behind, it would take time to complete such a huge undertaking.

Kristin looked around the bridge and realized they had quite a mess of their own to clean up. They had left Earth with a brand new ship and would return with damage requiring months of repair in an orbital dry dock. The captain had informed them all that once their relief arrived from Earth, they would head there. The entire crew would also be on medical leave until the Alliance could be reassured that there were no lasting effects from the N'Torr possession.

She and Simpson were the only members of the crew cleared for thirty days of shore leave. Normally, she abhorred time away from her duties. Her father had told her that it dulled her edge. This time, though, she knew it would be all right. There was family business to tend to, because if there was one last important thing she'd learned from her father, it was that there was nothing in the universe more important than family.

Epilogue

*Three weeks later: Shagwong Point,
Long Island, New York*

The memorial service for Admiral Nicholas Dante was held on the beach outside the home he thought of as his retreat from a world of excess. Out of respect and admiration, the Alliance government agreed to compensate the family for Striker's attack on the beach house and had it fully repaired, right down to the wind chimes over the front door, as well as updates for the more secretive below-ground areas that were damaged in attack.

The ceremony was short, and anyone who knew the admiral understood that that would have been his preference. Despite the length of the proceedings, there had never been such a gathering in the history of the Alliance. Representatives from every branch of the civilian and military government were in attendance, including presidents, politicians, military leaders, and the captains of industry, all there to pay their respects. Of course, the only people who truly cared were those who remained in the house after it was over.

They had all dressed appropriately for the service, each in their dress uniforms, complete with black armbands in a show of solidarity and respect for their father. Kristin's uniform reflected her recent promotion to the rank of captain, as did Michael's. Kate noted that her promotion would take a little longer. Even though she'd been proven innocent of any of the crimes she'd been accused of while she was working undercover, there were still a few at Fleet Command who were a little leery of her relationship with Rosten. In the end, she didn't care who believed her and who didn't, nor did she care about the promotion, one way or the other. What mattered was that her father knew the truth and believed in her till the very end. She was happy for her brother and sister and thought their promotions were deserved and hard earned. Kate, on the other hand, was happier to be in the background; it helped to push forward that legend everyone seemed to tell her she was.

It was cold and windy on the beach, with a stiff breeze coming off the water. Kate had made certain that her eulogy was long and boring, with just enough pauses to let everyone feel the cold, wet air all the way down to their bones. She knew watching so many of the Alliance VIPs shivering in their dress blues would have made Nicholas Dante very happy. She could picture him staring down at them, at the ridiculousness of the service, and enjoying a hearty laugh at their expense. *Enjoy this, Dad*, she thought. *This is for you.*

Kate finished just as the winds started to pick up. Michael, Kristin, and Morrison headed for the house as the VIPs shook hands and said their goodbyes to each other. Within minutes, Kate found herself alone, staring at the rough surf as storm clouds appeared on the horizon. The wind intensified, and she decided it was time to head inside and join the others.

She stopped when she thought she heard a voice in the wind. There was no one else left on the beach, so the only explanation was that overactive imagination of hers; the alternative was too fantastic to contemplate. Shivering, Kate made her way to the warmth of the house. She tried to make sense of what she thought she'd heard, that voice broken and scattered in the wind, but she wasn't sure if it was a message, a threat, a warning, or nothing at all.

"Death is coming." What could that possibly mean? She wondered if her untrusting subconscious had been at it again. *Could some of the Jek'Tan on Earth have survived?* Either way, she'd find the answer; that was what legends did. *Just not today.*

Once inside the house, Kate found Michael, Kristin, and Cole sitting around a table in the second-floor command center, with four glasses of champagne and a large padded envelope on a table between them.

'Do any of you know what's in that thing? Kate, you must know something," Kristin said.

"Nope," Kate answered as she took a seat at the table. "It was delivered by a military attorney, with orders that we were not to open it until we were all together."

"Great," Morrison said, reaching for the envelope. "So let's open it."

Kate smacked his hand and put the glass of champagne in it, then handed one to Michael and Kristin.

"Before we do anything, we toast the admiral. Michael, would you do the honors?"

They all raised their glasses in the air.

"We never knew you for the loving father you were until the end. You were a legend in war and now at home. We will miss you, Dad."

"Cheers!" they all said as they clinked their glasses together.

"Kristin, what ever happened to the people from New Earth City? Did they ever find a home?"

Kristin nodded. "The Alliance Council quarantined the city and everything around it, including the wrecked Jek'Tan ship, until they figure out what the hell to do with it. They claim the radiation levels are too high, and they still fear contamination from the remaining N'Torr inside the wreckage."

"They want the ship. They just aren't sure how to approach it," Kate reasoned. "There are secrets in there that the Alliance—and possibly people like Rosten—would kill for. How about the people? Did they find anyplace for the survivors, Kris."

"Funny you would mention them," she said with a laugh. "Most decided to settle on either side of the East River, some in Brooklyn, and some are actually starting to rebuild the homes and businesses along the tour route on the southern tip of Manhattan."

"Outstanding!" Kate applauded. "I like Brooklyn.

"You are so lucky we recovered the Cobra."

"Thanks for helping me with that, Cole. Dad would have killed me," Kate said, thinking of the car that was now stashed in the underground hangar with the *Alexa*, safe and sound. "Oh, I forgot.

We have something else to drink to. I heard through the grapevine that I am looking at the newly promoted captain of the *Bonaventure*."

"Here, here!" Michael said as they all raised their glasses once again.

"Thank you all. The official announcement is still a week or so away, but when Captain Brady was promoted to admiral and given command of the new fleet under construction, he considered me the best choice to take his ship. I could use your help, if you'd like to join me. Think of all the fun we can have out there."

Michael looked at Morrison and Kate and said what they were all thinking. "Kris, you don't need us around to help you be the commanding officer you already know you are."

"No more training wheels, kiddo. We'll be there if you need us or even when you think you may not. That's what family is all about," Kate added with a smile. "Now, before I get too drunk, will someone open that damn envelope?"

Michael leaned forward and picked it up, then weighed it in his hand before pulling on the release tab. "Not very heavy," he said. He reached in and pulled out a smaller envelope and a portable computer drive. "What's this?" he asked, examining it. The IO connection matched the input slot on the terminal at the main control console. He opened the smaller envelope and pulled out a written piece of paper, read it, then handed it to Kate.

"What does it say, Kate?" Kristin asked.

"It says, uh… 'Insert into second-floor control room terminal and run program.' It's signed, 'Dad.'"

Michael examined the drive before plugging it into the port on the console. The screen on the wall came alive with one word: "Run?"

"Yes," Michael typed, then pressed the enter key.

In front of the console formed the figure of the holographic Dante, this time dressed in an admiral's uniform.

"Dad?" Kristin asked in surprise.

Kate walked up to it and smiled. "Hey! If it isn't good ol' Holo-Dad. Michael, I thought you already had the program. How did it end up in Dad's envelope?"

Before Michael could answer, the hologram spoke. "It's really easy to understand, Kate. I am not the original primitive hologram I left here for you. In fact, I'm not really a hologram at all."

"Dad, what did you do?"

"When I found out I was going to die—"

"Die?" Kristin snapped. "How did you know you were going to die on that ship?"

Dante smiled at Kristin and continued, "When I discovered I was going to die, I updated the hologram programming with a more recent memory and personality matrix. I am interfacing with the computers in the house, and I can see everything that happened. Thank you all for the touching memorial. You really didn't have to do that."

Michael smiled and jumped in. "We didn't do it for you. We did it for everyone who respected you, for the people who wanted to say goodbye."

"Scanning the guest list," Dante said, "I really can't say I liked too many of them."

"God," Kristin snapped. "You *are* him. You were such a pain!"

"I may have been a pain, but it landed you a seat in a captain's chair, did it not?"

"Dad, Kris earned that promotion and seat. It had nothing to do with you."

Kate laughed and wondered why Michael found it necessary to jump in. It was funny; considering everything they had gone through, everyone who had died to protect Earth, and the distance she had run to get away from her father while he was still breathing, she found herself home. Now, if only they all could survive this reunion.

"Come on, Cole," Kate said, kissing him on the lips. "If the past is any indication, this could go on for a while. You're going to take me to dinner, and I know the perfect vehicle to carry us there."

Morrison took Kate's hand and kissed her again as they headed for the elevator and the hangar where the Cobra was parked. As the door closed, the two of them could hear the admiral's voice calling out to them.

"Don't you dare touch that car, Katherine! I thought I told you to stay away from my daughter, Morrison!"

Kate threw Cole the keys and opened the garage door before getting into the passenger seat.

"Ready?" he asked as he turned the key and revved the ancient V-8 to life.

Kate closed her eyes and listened to the throaty roar of the engine and felt the leather of the seat under her. "Ain't family grand?" she said with a smile. "I'm hungry. Did I forget to mention that dinner is on you?"

The Mustang pulled out of the hangar and into the cool late evening air. Kate looked up at the stars and, for the first time in years, felt at peace with herself and the world around her. Whatever fate had in store for her, she was ready, and God help whoever or whatever stood in her way.

About the Author

A fan of sci-fi, fantasy, and horror, C.J. Daniels has three novels, and a short story in the Lost Planets anthology alongside legendary authors including Ray Bradbury, Philip K .Dick, Edgar Allan Poe. Born in Brooklyn, but living in New Hampshire, C.J. is a comicbook, video game, and crazed techno nerd, with a passion for the classics, as well as everything Star Trek and Star Wars.

Originally a marketing guru and now a double threat - pushing the boundaries in genre literature has always been the excitement of writing fiction. With *The DarkLight,* and first two books of T*he Coming* trilogy already available, *Evolution's End* pushes the boundaries even further with the beginning of the *Dark Frontier* series. Two hundred years from now, the Dante family is helping the Earth Alliance push the boundaries of man's expansion into the Solar System and beyond? But what happens when the dangers of space push back.

Stay tuned for more from the creative mind of C.J. Daniels, as we'll be giving closure to *The Coming,* as well as pushing beyond the System with *Dark Frontier 2.*

For news and information on C.J., follow him on Facebook and Twitter, or go to the website at www.thecjdaniels.com.

www.ingramcontent.com/pod-product-compliance
Lightning Source LLC
Chambersburg PA
CBHW070754280626
47162CB00016B/291